ALPENA COUNTY LIBRARY

W9-CLJ-693

ALPENA COUNTY LIBRARY
211 N. First St.
Alpena, Mich. 49707

DEMCO

Touched by the Gods

OTHER BOOKS BY LAWRENCE WATT-EVANS

The Chromosomal Code
Crosstime Traffic
Denner's Wreck
Newer York (editor)
The Nightmare People
Nightside City
The Rebirth of Wonder
Shining Steel
Split Heirs (with Esther M. Friesner)

LEGENDS OF ETHSHAR

The Misenchanted Sword
With a Single Spell
The Unwilling Warlord
The Blood of a Dragon
Taking Flight
The Spell of the Black Dagger

THE LORDS OF DUS

The Lure of the Basilisk
The Seven Altars of Dusarra
The Sword of Bheleu
The Book of Silence

THREE WORLDS TRILOGY

Out of This World
In the Empire of Shadow
The Reign of the Brown Magician

WAR SURPLUS

The Cyborg and the Sorcerers
The Wizard and the War Machine

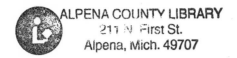
ALPENA COUNTY LIBRARY
211 N. First St.
Alpena, Mich. 49707

TOUCHED BY THE GODS

LAWRENCE WATT-EVANS

WATT
J

TOR®

A TOM DOHERTY ASSOCIATES BOOK

NEW YORK

This is a work of fiction. All the characters and events portrayed
in this novel are either fictitious or are used fictitiously.

TOUCHED BY THE GODS

Copyright © 1997 by Lawrence Watt-Evans

All rights reserved, including the right to reproduce this book,
or portions thereof, in any form.

This book is printed on acid-free paper.

A Tor Book
Published by Tom Doherty Associates, Inc.
175 Fifth Avenue
New York, NY 10010

Tor Books on the World Wide Web:
http://www.tor.com

Tor® is a registered trademark of Tom Doherty Associates, Inc.

Design by Ann Gold

Library of Congress Cataloging-in-Publication Data

Watt-Evans, Lawrence
    Touched by the Gods / Lawrence Watt-Evans.
        p.   cm.
    "A Tom Doherty Associates book."
    ISBN 0-312-86060-9
    PS3573.A859T68   1997
    813'.54—dc21   97-15569
                                          CIP

First Edition: November 1997

Printed in the United States of America

0 9 8 7 6 5 4 3 2 1

DEDICATED TO MY DAUGHTER,
KYRITH AMANDA EVANS

29495 d3 86-5-1

TOUCHED BY THE GODS

PROLOGUE

The priest walked neither fast nor slow, but at a steady, relentless pace that drew the eye of the handful of other travelers he passed along the Yildau road. Dust stained the hem of his white robe a golden brown, but he paid no attention; he looked straight ahead and marched on, arms swinging with each stride. Behind him he left the scent of sweat and sandalwood.

He was plainly a man with a purpose, and those he encountered along the road stared after him and wondered aloud what that purpose might be. Lone priests were rarely seen outside their shrines and temples—especially not in the summer triads, since priestly robes were heavy and hot. The annual graveyard rites and other such errands were usually performed in cooler weather.

Some of the older observers speculated that the oracles had sent this fellow on some unusual errand for the gods, but the younger and more cynical generally dismissed that with a laugh and a crude jest, suggesting that the priest more likely sought to ease some more worldly ill—such as a lover's itch.

The priest paid no attention to any of this; he walked on, as he had been directed. The fierce heat of Midsummer's Day, the second day of Ba'el's Triad, when the war god stoked the sun's furnace, covered his face with a sheen of sweat but otherwise did not seem to bother him. He did not glance up at either the sun or the several moons faintly visible here and there.

The very largest of the moons, named Ba'el after the god who dwelt there, had partially eclipsed the sun earlier that day—but with so many moons in the sky that was hardly worthy of note, and besides, it had passed on by the time he reached Grozerodz. Only an astrologer would concern himself with the possible significance of the war god's moon eclipsing the sun during that same god's turn at the fires.

In the center of the village the priest hesitated momentarily, looking about, then turned from the high road and made his way across the square and down the lane, past the graveyard with its flower-bound iron gate to the blacksmith's shop. He did not stop at the forge, but pushed on to the tidy little house beyond, where a small crowd of villagers had gathered. They were fanning themselves with their hands and chatting cheerfully among themselves, but quickly fell silent when they saw the priest approaching.

The priest stopped at last at the door and waited.

The big, bare-chested man blocking the entrance had been watching events within the house; now he turned and stared at the white-robed stranger.

"May I enter?" the priest asked.

The big man hesitated, and glanced back in.

"I don't know," he said uneasily. "Who are you?"

"I am Mezizar, from the temple at Biekedau."

That meant nothing to the guardian. "There's women's business here," he said. "No call for a priest."

"A child has been born?" the priest asked, a note of eagerness in his voice. "A boy?"

The big man blinked. "Now, how'd you know that?" he asked warily.

"Must've asked an oracle," someone called.

"Why would he ask about *that*?" someone else demanded.

The priest did not answer; instead, he repeated, "May I enter?"

The big man shrugged and called, "Ho, Dara! There's a sweaty fellow here in a priest's robe, says he wants to come in!"

That caused a flurry of activity within, and a moment later a plump woman with her hair bound back beneath a kerchief emerged to confront the stranger. Her hands, held out before her, were wet, as if she had just washed them.

She looked the stranger up and down, pursing her lips as she considered him.

"Don't see many priests here," she said. "With no shrine or temple in Grozerodz, we don't usually get anyone but some stuttering novice stopping by once every winter to pray over the graveyard."

That was stating the obvious, and the priest ignored it. "You are the midwife?" he asked.

"That's right," the kerchiefed woman replied. She gestured toward the big man. "And this fellow here is Sparrak, the babe's uncle, and I've asked him to keep strangers out. This is a private business, not some temple spectacle."

"I must see the child and his parents," the priest said. "I assure you that I will not harm him, or them, nor am I unacquainted with the mysteries of birth— I have presided at our temple's deliveries. I underwent a ritual cleansing before I departed to come here; I carry no disease, nor need I touch the child." He wiped the sweat from his face with his right sleeve, and showed her that the resulting stain was relatively free of dirt—he had clearly bathed no more than a day ago.

"Got all your answers ready, I see," the midwife remarked. "Ought to carry a cloth, though, not use your sleeve. Who sent you, then? One of the gods?"

"Not directly," the priest replied. "I haven't spoken to any of the oracles myself. Dolkout, the high priest at Biekedau, sent me; I believe *he* spoke with an oracle. At least one oracle."

"I can't say that I ever heard the name Dolkout," Dara remarked.

That started a discussion among the gathered villagers; after some debate, it was generally agreed that yes, the high priest at Biekedau was named Dolkout, or at least he might be. The priest waited silently for the conversation to die down again.

When it had, the midwife eyed him carefully, then shrugged. "Well, it's not my house," she said, stepping aside, "and I doubt Hmar is going to object to anything just at the moment. Come on in, but wipe your feet."

The priest conscientiously obeyed, and a moment later he was ushered past half a dozen grinning women into a bedroom that smelled of blood and sweat and other animal scents.

There a woman lay in bed, her husband at her right hand, and five young girls of varying ages, the youngest not much more than a baby herself, clustered about as the woman held her newborn son to her breast. Two large basins and several bloody cloths were scattered on a nearby chest of drawers, and the midwife, following the priest into the room, hurried over to them to finish her tidying up.

The new mother looked up, startled, as the priest entered; the five girls stepped back and stared in surprise, the youngest letting out a sort of cooing yelp. The husband, a man even larger than Sparrak, had been grinning broadly at the arrival of his son; now his grin vanished as he watched the priest warily, as if he thought that this white-robed stranger had come to snatch the boy away.

"May I see the child's face?" the priest asked gently.

Puzzled but obliging, the woman shifted, turning the infant without removing his mouth from her nipple. A red birthmark cut diagonally across his face, from the left temple to the right side of his jaw, like a shallow bleeding wound.

"That'll fade," the midwife said as she dried her hands. "He'll be pretty as any baby in a dozen triads."

"That long?" the priest said. "I hurried, to be sure of seeing it."

The midwife shrugged and left without replying, carrying one of the basins out of the room.

The mother looked up at the priest questioningly.

"My lady," the priest said, "your son has been touched by the gods. Their mark is on his face, and though it will fade, as that good woman says, he will always, so long as he lives, be their chosen champion, to be called upon when the need arises." He reached his right hand into his left sleeve and drew out a polished ivory case, a gleaming white cylinder roughly eight inches long and three inches in diameter; he handed it to the man standing by the bed.

"Sir," he said, "this is for your son, when he is ready."

The big man accepted it silently, too surprised to speak.

The priest bowed, and turned to go. Everyone watched in silent astonishment as he hurried out of the smith's house without further ado.

The midwife, reentering the bedroom, was the first to regain her voice.

"Well, whatever was *that* about?" she asked no one in particular.

"A lot of religious nonsense," Hmar the smith rumbled. "Our son the divine champion? Ha!" He looked down at the ivory case, then shrugged and set it carefully on the shelf above the bed. He smiled down at his exhausted wife and newborn son.

"It'll make a good story for the boy, though," he said.

CHAPTER I

It was a slow day at the forge, and Hmar was making nails. There was no call for anything more elaborate just now, and it was good business to keep a stock of nails on hand.

Malledd wasn't interested in nails. Oh, they were useful, and the glow of the iron was as fascinating as always, the clang of hammer on metal was as musical and exciting as ever, but in his ten years of life he'd seen his father make thousands of nails, and on a day like this, when the sun was warm and the flowers blooming, Malledd was just not interested in standing by the forge, motionless and sweaty, watching his father make yet more of them.

If he were allowed to swing the hammer . . . but no, Hmar insisted that despite being exceptionally big for his age the boy didn't yet have arms big enough to wield the hammer on hot metal. Malledd might be Hmar's only son, but he was also an apprentice, and Hmar wasn't about to indulge him by letting him use the hammer before he was ready; it would be bad for discipline.

On the other hand, the boy was obviously not going to pay attention to the nail making, so at last Hmar sent him out to play.

Reveling in his freedom and enjoying the gentle breeze, Malledd hopped a few times across the muddy little moat that served as a firebreak around the forge, practicing his jumping—he was proud of how far he could leap. Tiring quickly of that pastime, and particularly of the rather rank smell that rose from the inch or two of stagnant water in the trench, he turned aside, jogged back toward the family's house, where he wandered slowly through the kitchen yard, past where his mother was washing out linens. Then he looped back past the smithy and onto the lane that led to the center of the village; his lazy amble turned to a trot.

He stayed to the left side of the road, keeping well clear of the graveyard gate, with its chain of fresh daisies looped through the iron bars; his sister Seguna had been telling him scary stories about nightwalkers again, and while Malledd didn't really believe most of what she said, he still felt a bit safer if he didn't get too close to the graveyard fence.

There weren't any nightwalkers anymore, he reminded himself; everyone agreed on that. Besides, fresh flowers and cold iron were both supposed to keep the dead from rising. Malledd had helped weave new blossoms into the ironwork often enough without ever being frightened before, and if there were still any nightwalkers around they would hardly come out in the sunlight in any case—

but even so, he hurried past the gates without stopping, far enough away that he couldn't smell the flowers. He trotted on to the tiny square by the high road.

Grozerodz was just a village, and not a particularly large one; Hmar was the only smith of any kind there, the first ever to work in Grozerodz, and had had to apprentice up in Yildau to learn his trade. The little town's one inn also served as a bakery and meeting hall. There was no temple, nor even a roadside shrine—some of the villagers complained about that occasionally, but no one wanted to go to the trouble and expense of building one and getting it sanctified. Anyone who wanted a proper wedding, or to petition the gods, or to consult an oracle, had to walk ten miles down the highway to Biekedau. Anyone who wanted to keep a patron deity happy with an annual obeisance—as Hmar did—had to make it a pilgrimage to Biekedau. For that matter, anyone in Grozerodz who wanted any number of things had to hike the ten miles to Biekedau, or wait for a trader to pass through.

Malledd didn't mind; he'd never lived anywhere else, and while he enjoyed his annual visit to Biekedau with his father, and loved to listen to the stories he heard about the rest of the world beyond the horizon, he was satisfied with Grozerodz.

In fact, as he wandered into the center of town, he was quite pleased with it. The hundreds of assorted flowers in the square were bright and fragrant, much prettier than the graveyard daisies, and their perfume mingled interestingly with the fresh sawdust smell from Uderga's carpentry shop. Two horses were tied up in front of the inn, which meant travelers—no one in Grozerodz owned a horse, and for that matter, neither did most of the travelers who passed through; horses were expensive. Those travelers who *did* have horses usually had them hitched to carts or wagons, hauling goods from Yildau or Biekedau; these two carried nothing but saddles, as if their riders were noblemen of some sort. Malledd could hear insects humming, and voices drifting from the open windows of the inn; the travelers were undoubtedly talking.

That was interesting, and tempting—but Malledd also heard the laughter of children from behind old Daiwish's house mingled with the adult chatter from the inn, and the children were obviously having a wonderful time with their games. He hesitated.

The children behind Daiwish's herb garden would be the younger ones, the boys and girls who were too young to be expected to work; he had been there often enough himself in previous years.

But he wasn't a baby anymore. He was ten years old now, as of a triad ago—almost a man, and big for his age. He was too old to play with the little kids.

And a chance to see noblemen didn't come along every triad—this stretch of hill country had no lord of its own, answering directly to the Empress instead, through her representative in Biekedau.

Malledd headed for the inn.

He knew the travelers would be drinking ale or wine, and that any villagers who knew there were travelers in town and who could spare the time would be there buying them drinks in exchange for the latest news and gossip from afar. He also knew that Bardetta, the innkeeper, wouldn't sell him ale or wine, even if he had a coin, which he didn't—she didn't believe children should be permitted strong drink.

But he could still sit and listen, couldn't he?

The door of the inn was standing open, and Malledd slipped in unobtrusively.

It took a moment for his eyes to adjust to the cool dimness inside after the bright outdoor sun, but when he could see clearly he saw two men in bright clothing sitting at one of Bardetta's tables, gulping cold ale and talking and smiling between gulps. Despite their travels they were cleaner than ordinary people, their hair polished and shining; their clothes were very fine, and the broad-brimmed hats hung on the backs of their chairs were trimmed with long, curling feathers, an affectation Malledd had heard of but never before seen.

Eight or nine villagers in their ordinary homespun were clustered about, none being so audacious as to actually sit at the same table as the strangers. The listeners were carefully leaving space for Bardetta to get in and out with trays of cakes and ale.

"It's happened everywhere, they say," announced one of the travelers. "The temple magicians report it's the same every place beneath the Hundred Moons. It's not just Seidabar, or Biekedau, but everywhere—the whole empire, the entire world, from sunrise to sunset and sea to sea." He spoke with a charming accent not quite like anything Malledd had heard before. "*All* the oracles, of *every* god. The other magicians are still as good as ever, but the oracles won't have another word to say."

"Well, that's an appalling thing, if it's true," a villager said—Malledd recognized him as Nedduel, one of the wealthier farmers in the vicinity. "How are we supposed to manage our affairs without oracles?"

The other traveler laughed and jabbed his companion's shoulder. "Didn't I tell you they'd say that?" he said. He, too, had that odd, lilting accent.

"Yes, you did," the first agreed. He turned to Nedduel. "According to the oracles, my friend, that is exactly why the gods have put an end to oracles."

Nedduel frowned angrily, his face reddening to match the cloth he wore around his neck.

"I don't understand," said a woman's voice from a shadowy corner, and Malledd realized that it was his own eldest sister, Vlaia, who had spoken. He hadn't known she was there.

"What my friend means," said the second traveler, "is that the gods allegedly feel the time has come for the people of the Domdur Empire to stand on our own feet and make our own destiny, without the direct intervention of our gods. The priest who told us the news took pains to explain that this doesn't mean that the gods have abandoned us—quite the contrary, he said. He compared it to teaching a child—a time comes when you must stop telling the child what to do every step of the way, and let him make his own mistakes. So it is with the gods and *their* child, which is to say, the Empire—after a thousand years in which the oracles guided us, we have grown enough that the time has come to let us make our own mistakes and find our own solutions."

"And if you give a child answers too easily," the first traveler broke in, "the child will come to depend upon them too much, and will never amount to anything on his own. It's *because* we've come to depend on the oracles—like our friend here in the red neckerchief—that the gods will no longer provide answers to our questions."

"That's all very well for the Empress and all those courtiers in Seidabar," Nedduel said, jabbing an angry finger at the air, "but for a plain farmer there are questions no one but the gods can answer. Who but the gods can predict the weather, and tell us when to plant, or what to do to save our crops from hail or blight?"

"You'll just have to take your chances, I suppose," said the second traveler, glancing at his companion with a smile.

"The gods would let us *starve?*" Nedduel demanded.

The traveler shrugged, turning serious. "Hardly. They'll still send the rains and still fire the sun, and the earth will still be as fertile as Vedal wishes it to be—isn't that enough?"

"No!" Nedduel insisted.

"We're not children, Nedduel," someone else said. "We'll get by."

"But it can't be true," Nedduel insisted. "Why would the gods desert us?" He turned away from the strangers to confront his fellow villagers. "I say it's a lie—either these two are teasing us with their stories, or the priests are lying for some purpose of their own."

"Why would the priests lie?"

Two or three angry voices began speaking at once, and the noise level in the room rose abruptly. Malledd decided maybe he didn't want to be in here with the adults after all, and ducked back out the door.

The fresh air felt good; he hadn't consciously noticed the stuffy air and smell of old wood and stale wine in the inn, but now that he was outside again he noticed their absence.

Before going anywhere he paused to study the travelers' horses—his father wouldn't mind if Malledd came home with a couple of paying customers, and besides, Malledd liked horses.

The harness all looked sound and new enough, but even so, the animals might need new shoes. Malledd didn't have the nerve to lift a hoof and see, but he watched the two beasts carefully for any sign of sore feet. One of them might lift a foot just on a whim, or to chase away a bothersome insect.

As he looked, he could still hear men shouting in the tavern, and he thought over what had been said.

The gods would no longer speak through their oracles? Is that what the travelers had said?

He glanced up at the sky. The sun was high overhead, and the sky was blue streaked with white cloud, but Malledd thought he could see the faint crescents of three or four of the larger moons.

None were particularly near the sun, which was bright and hot—Ba'el had only recently yielded his turn powering the sun, and Vedal, who currently stoked the fires, was very nearly as powerful.

Malledd's mother had told him that when they weren't fueling the sun or doing their work here and there in the world below, the gods lived on the moons—each of the Hundred Moons belonged to one particular god or goddess. The priests, she said, knew the names of all the gods and all the moons, and which god lived on which moon; they had scholars called astrologers who studied the movements of the moons to learn more about the gods. She had pointed out and named the largest moons for him—Ba'el, the red one, largest of all, where the god of war lived; Sheshar, the blue one, home to the sea goddess; greenish-gold Vedal, the earth mother's domain; and so on. She knew a score of them, at least—but not all of them, of course.

Once when Malledd was little, he had asked whether the stars belonged to *little* gods, and his mother had laughed and said that was probably exactly right, but she didn't know. He still wondered about that.

Malledd had liked the idea that the gods were up there, watching over everyone, running the world for the benefit of the Domdur Empire. He had imagined them leaning over the edges of the moons, chattering among themselves about all the silly things people did down here in the world, sending storms and lightning to punish the wicked, steering rain clouds where the farmers needed them, and so on.

And when someone's prayers asked a question that the gods thought was important, the gods would send a message down to one of the temple oracles with the answer—whichever god's concern it was, that god would hear the question from up on his moon, and would tell his oracle what to say. If no particular god was invoked, then Samardas, god of wisdom, busybody of the heavens and speaker to the most oracles, would handle it. If no questions were asked but the gods wanted something done, they told the oracles, and the oracles let everyone know what the gods had said. It had all been very comforting.

But now, according to the travelers, the gods weren't going to send any more messages or tell the oracles anything.

That wasn't comforting.

Were those moons a little higher than before, a little farther away? Were the gods getting bored with the world? Malledd wondered—might they all just sail away someday, sail the moons off to somewhere else?

Was there anywhere else for them to sail to?

Were the stars perhaps moons that were not smaller, but farther away, moons that were homes to gods who had gotten bored and left long ago? Perhaps they were the homes of the gods of the lands the Domdur had conquered, in the long-ago times when the world was divided and the different peoples fought one another instead of living in harmony under the Empire's rule. Perhaps those gods had fled. Perhaps their departure was what had allowed the Empire to defeat the people who had worshiped them.

Or perhaps he was just making up stories. His father had sometimes chastised Malledd for letting his imagination run away with him, and here he was doing it again.

But what *did* it mean, if the oracles had fallen silent? How would anyone know what the gods wanted done?

And would people still do what the gods wanted, if the gods didn't tell them to?

Just then one of the horses snorted and stamped a hoof, and Malledd looked down in time to see a good new shoe—the traveler who rode that particular animal must have had her shod just before he started his journey. There was no work to be had for his father here.

Malledd hesitated, unsure what to do next, but before he could reach a decision the door of the tavern swung wide and the two travelers stepped out.

Malledd decided he didn't want to bother them. He turned and headed across the square and down the lane, past the graveyard to the forge, eager to tell his parents the news, that these travelers said the oracles would no longer answer questions.

Three of his sisters were playing a game of tag around the circumference of the moat, dodging and laughing on the grassy brink, braids and skirts flying. One misplaced foot might send them tumbling into the malodorous muck at the bottom of the ditch, but none of them seemed to care.

"Ho, Malledd!" Vorda called, pausing in her wild pursuit of Deleva. "Father let you out?"

Deleva turned and sneered at her brother. "Well, *really*, Vorda," she said, "a mere *smith* wouldn't dare try to order around the favorite of the gods!"

Deyonis giggled. She was twelve, closest to Malledd's own age; Vorda was fourteen, Deleva fifteen.

Malledd didn't bother to answer Deleva's gibe, or ask why the girls weren't helping their mother; he hurried on between the two ends of the moat, and on into the forge.

Hmar was working the bellows, getting the fire hot, when Malledd burst in. Hmar looked up through air that rippled with heat.

"Father," Malledd called, "there were travelers at the inn, and they said that the oracles are no longer going to speak to us!"

Hmar grunted. "I never spoke to an oracle in my life," he said, heaving on the bellows cord.

"I mean, they aren't going to talk to *anybody*," Malledd explained. "The gods have decided not to use them to help people anymore."

"Probably just some silly trick of the priests," Hmar replied, pumping the bellows again and looking at the glow of the coals. He obviously wasn't interested.

Disappointed, Malledd turned away.

Then, as he stepped back out of the smithy, he brightened again. He could still tell his mother; *she* cared about the gods, even if his father didn't.

Then he noticed Vorda and Deyonis standing one on either side of the door, giggling. Deleva was already running toward the house, and Malledd realized that she'd overheard his news and was running to tell their mother first.

He couldn't outrun her; not only did she have a head start, but at fifteen she had her full height, almost four inches taller than he was, and it was all in her legs. And that was assuming Vorda and Deyonis didn't trip him up.

Well, he could at least confirm the story, and maybe think of some details Deleva wouldn't know. He sighed, and started walking.

Vorda and Deyonis promptly jumped him from behind and knocked him to the ground; he tasted dirt, and a blade of grass went up his nose, tickling him horribly. He had been caught completely off guard, the wind knocked out of him by the fall, and he was unable to resist as Vorda rolled him into the firebreak ditch.

He tumbled in faceup, and landed with a splash in the stinking mud at the bottom. He lay there for a second or two, utterly astonished.

Then he sat up, dripping and covered with mud, and gazed up at his sisters.

"What did you do *that* for?" he asked.

"Deleva told us to," Deyonis said proudly.

Malledd blinked up at her, and brushed a muddy forelock away from his eyes. "Do you do everything she asks you?"

"No," Vorda said, "but you deserved it."

"Why?" Malledd wailed. "What did *I* do?"

Vorda shrugged.

"You wanted to tell Father and Mother before you told *us*," Deyonis said.

Malledd looked down at his soaked, mud-covered shirt and breeches, and fought back tears. He had deserved *this*?

There wasn't any point in arguing. His sisters hated him—three of them, anyway. The oldest two just ignored him, for the most part, when Seguna wasn't trying to scare him to death with her stories about monsters and black magic.

Deleva was the worst, but all the younger three hated him. They always had, for as long as he could remember—but he didn't know why.

He'd never really thought much about it before; he'd just accepted it as the way things were, that anytime he tried to do any least little thing to draw attention to himself his sisters would gang up on him and ruin it. He'd just accepted it.

But there had to be a reason, didn't there? They wouldn't just throw him in the ditch without a *reason*, not when their parents had ordered them all to stay out of it.

If he argued about it they'd just go on teasing and harassing him, and he was determined not to give them the satisfaction this time. Without another word, he got up out of the muck and clambered carefully out of the ditch, on the outside, away from Vorda and Deyonis.

Deyonis promptly jumped across the moat, landing a yard away from him; Vorda went around by the gap.

Malledd ignored them. He simply walked homeward without so much as glancing at his sisters. He could hear them whispering to each other, debating whether to follow him, but he didn't say a word. He forced himself to walk; his mouth trembled with the effort of not running, not crying.

Halfway to the house the girls stopped and watched as he marched soggily up to the door. He tried the latch—he intended to go inside and get himself into clean, dry clothes before his parents saw him like this.

The door wouldn't budge. Someone had locked it.

That meant he couldn't get inside unseen unless he climbed through a window, and that would leave a big muddy stain on the wall and sill—assuming he found an open window. Most of them were shuttered today, to keep the house cool.

He stood for a moment, fighting the temptation to break down in tears and yelling, collecting himself. If he had to let his mother see him after all, well then, he would. With an unsteady sigh he trudged around to the kitchen yard.

His mother wasn't there.

He frowned and looked around, unsure whether that was good or bad. He might yet manage to change his clothes undetected—but where was she? He didn't like to admit that he wanted his mother to comfort him, but he couldn't help feeling a bit abandoned. He stepped up to the back door, lifted the latch, and pushed.

The door didn't move.

That was ridiculous. His parents *never* locked both doors. He wasn't even sure the back door *had* a lock.

He pushed again, and thought he felt the door yield slightly, then push back into place. He put his ear to the wood, and thought he heard a half-smothered giggle from the other side.

Then he knew what was happening. Deleva was holding the door closed. His soggy misery faded, replaced by anger.

"Deleva, let me in!" he called.

She didn't answer, but he was sure she was there.

Malledd fought down his anger and tried to consider the situation logically, the way his father always said he should. Deleva knew he was out here, dripping wet and covered in mud—she'd arranged it. Their mother, though—where was she?

She must be inside the house, Malledd decided. Deleva would have talked to her in the house. But Deleva wouldn't dare bar the door like this if their mother was in sight, so she wasn't in the back room. . . .

Malledd went to a bedroom window and knocked on the shutter. "Mother?" he called.

"Malledd?" The shutter rattled, then swung open, and his mother's face appeared in the window.

"Deleva won't let me in," he said, "and I need to get cleaned up." He gestured at his clothes.

"Oh, by all the gods," his mother muttered. She turned away from the window. "Deleva!" she called angrily.

A moment later Malledd was inside, stripping his clothes off while his mother warmed a bucket of clean water on the stove for a sponge bath. Only the two of them were there; Deleva had been banished from the house for the remainder of the day.

Malledd hadn't explained how he had gotten muddy; he didn't want to make his sisters even angrier at him. He knew his parents could guess, though. He sighed bitterly as he climbed into the tin tub.

CHAPTER 2

That night, when Hmar returned home from the forge, each of the three guilty sisters got a swat from his cane; Deleva, as the ringleader, got three more. Seguna and Vlaia watched, clearly enjoying the superiority of their own innocence in this particular misbehavior.

Malledd did not look; he kept his eyes on his mother as she set out the supper dishes. He wasn't sure whether any of the blame for the prank would fall on him or not, nor whether he deserved any of it, and in any case he took no pleasure in his sisters' suffering.

When Hmar was done with his daughters he turned away, disgusted, leaving the children to their own devices; Malledd was not addressed.

At least, not by his father. Deleva, gently rubbing her injured backside, brushed against Malledd and then stuck her tongue out at him when he looked up. "It was worth it," she whispered to him.

He didn't answer. He didn't even smile.

Malledd did not say a word as he ate; he was deep in thought. He sat staring at his plate, trying to decide what he should do. Deleva ate standing up, but seemed far less troubled than her brother.

After supper Malledd stood at the back door and beckoned to Deleva until at last her curiosity overcame her. When she finally stomped over to him he led her out to the kitchen yard, where they could speak privately.

The sun was below the horizon but the western sky was still richly golden, and the light of several bright moons shone down as well, painting the hard-packed dirt and the drab wall of the house in pastels. Insects buzzed in the garden nearby, and the scent of cooking fires lingered in the air.

"What do *you* want?" Deleva demanded, glaring down at her brother.

"I just wanted to ask you something," he said quietly, standing motionless, his hands behind his back.

"What is it?" she growled. "And if this is a trick, I'll beat your head in."

"It's not a trick," Malledd said, struggling to keep his voice steady. "When was the last time I played a trick on you, Deleva?"

"Not long enough ago," Deleva replied.

"It's been years, Deleva," Malledd said. "For *years* I've been trying my best to stay out of your way or be nice to you, and you still hate me." He almost trembled as he asked, "*Why* do you hate me?"

She stared silently at him for a moment before replying. "Because you think you're so *special*," she said angrily. "Because you're the only boy, so you get to be Father's apprentice because he says women aren't strong enough to be smiths. And you're the youngest, so Mother treats you nicer than she treats the rest of us. You get your own clothes made new, no hand-me-downs. You're so big for your age the other kids all treat you almost as if you were a grown-up! You don't act like the other boys—you never get tired or whiny, as if you're too *good* for that. And that silly priest came when you were born and said you were some sort of gift from the gods, so whenever we talk to anyone in the village they always ask us, 'Oh, how's that brother of yours, how's little Malledd, isn't he *wonderful?'* And I've been hearing that as long as I can remember, and I'm *sick* of it, you little weasel!"

"That isn't anything *I* did!" Malledd protested. "*I* can't help being a boy, or being big, or being the youngest!"

"So what?" Deleva demanded. "I'm still not going to let you get away with it."

"Get away with *what?*" he asked, baffled. More of her complaints were sinking in, but he didn't understand them—she was upset because he didn't tire easily or get ill-tempered? Those were the very things other girls professed to despise in their younger siblings!

"With thinking you're special!" she shouted. "You're not anyone special, you're just my obnoxious little brother who deserves to get dumped in the mud sometimes!"

"I don't think I'm special," Malledd protested.

"No? If you don't, you're the only one in Grozerodz who doesn't! Nobody *else* had a priest show up when she was born!" Deleva's voice cracked and she blinked as if something was bothering her eyes.

"I don't *want* to be special!" Malledd insisted.

"Are you finished?" Deleva demanded. "Because if you don't have anything else to say, I'm going back inside; it's getting chilly out here."

"Go ahead," Malledd said—though it wasn't chilly at all; summer was still strong, and the gentle breeze from the east was warm.

He watched as Deleva went into the house and slammed the door; then he stood there in the kitchen yard and looked up, past the drying linens, up at the darkening sky.

A dozen moons were overhead, a large reddish one he thought was Ba'el and several little ones in various colors—the homes of the gods.

"Why'd you have your stupid priest pick *me?*" he shouted up at them. "I didn't ask to be picked!"

No one answered, and he remembered suddenly that according to those travelers, the gods were no longer answering *anyone's* questions. He blinked, startled.

He had known, for as long as he could remember, that the day he was born a priest had walked into Grozerodz and come into their house and told his parents that he, Malledd, had been touched by the gods, that the long-vanished birthmark on his face meant that he was the divine champion, the gods' chosen defender of the Domdur Empire—assuming the Empire still needed a champion.

He didn't even remember *having* a birthmark, but everyone agreed it had been there when he was a baby.

His father dismissed the whole thing as nonsense, and had on several occasions suggested that priests probably went around to any number of places telling people they'd been marked by the gods somehow. He said the Empire didn't need any champions anymore, so there *weren't* any, and if there were they'd be princes or nobles, the same as they had always been before, and not the infant son of an ordinary smith, and it was all absurd.

Malledd's mother had never said anything about whether it was nonsense or not, but she had told Malledd some stories about the ancient champions who had helped build the Domdur Empire—how Rubrekir the Destroyer had broken the siege of Rishna Gabidéll, how Prince Greldar of the Domdur had hunted down the Red Traitors, and so on. Malledd liked her stories much better than Seguna's scary ones.

He noticed that some of the champions his mother talked about weren't born princes at all, but were given titles *after* their adventures. No one ever mentioned that detail to Hmar, though; Malledd's father was not a man anyone cared to argue with.

Malledd thought there might be something genuinely unusual about him, since he *was* so much bigger than the others his age, and since he did not begin to tire until long after other boys were exhausted—but was that a gift of the gods, or just a bit of ordinary good fortune?

Malledd's mother had explained once that when Malledd was grown-up, if he wanted to find out more about his birthmark or the priest's visit, he could always go to the temple in Biekedau and ask the priests there.

Except now, Malledd thought, with the oracles silenced, the priests might not *know* anything.

That was bad. He didn't like that thought at all. If he was going to be hated by his sisters, and maybe by others as well, for being the chosen of the gods, he at least wanted to know more about *why* he was hated.

Frowning, he lowered his gaze from the moons to the back door of his home, and hurried inside, through the little back room into the main living area.

Vlaia was sitting by the hearth, talking quietly to Hmar, who stood poking the ashes in the fireplace—Malledd guessed they were probably discussing potential husbands. The other four girls were all giggling in their shared bedroom—the house had two real bedrooms, both large and airy, parents in one and daughters in the other, and also a small, poorly ventilated loft where Malledd slept.

It occurred to Malledd that all the time he had envied his sisters their closed little community in that shared room, Deleva had probably considered his own tiny, stuffy space to be a special privilege. He thought it was lonely, but she probably thought of it as private.

Anything that marked him as different would anger Deleva, he realized.

Malledd's mother Madeya was sitting silently in one corner of the main room, cross-legged on the wide, low stool she preferred, sewing; her needle dipped and rose, dipped and rose, ducking in and out of a mass of golden-brown cloth. Malledd stood by her side and watched for a moment before speaking.

"Mother?" he asked.

She looked up at him, and the needle paused.

"The priest who came to see you and Father when I was born," Malledd asked. "What exactly did he say?"

Madeya pulled the thread tight and put her sewing down on the carved wooden box that held her needles and threads. "I don't remember *exactly*," she said, unfolding her legs.

"You didn't write it down, or anything?"

"No, I didn't write anything down, but the priest did leave a note for you."

"He *did*?" Malledd was astonished. If anyone had ever mentioned this to him before, he'd forgotten it.

"Yes, he did, in a fancy ivory case." She got to her feet. "Let me see if I can find it—you're old enough to read it for yourself now."

"Have *you* read it?"

"Oh, of course," she said as she led him into the master bedroom. "Your father and I read it almost as soon as the priest had left."

"And you never told me?" He couldn't help sounding hurt.

"It's really not all that exciting, Malledd. You already know just about everything in it. You'll see." She opened a drawer and rummaged through it, pushing aside iron combs and ragged handkerchiefs, then pulled out an ivory case, somewhat yellowed by age. She flicked open a brass hook and flipped up one end, then handed it to Malledd.

He peered inside and found a rolled-up parchment; he drew it out and unrolled it carefully.

He knew how to read; his parents had insisted that all their children learn to read, on general principles. Hmar had justified it to them by saying, "You never know when it may come in handy. If you ever get a job order in writing, for example, it's helpful to be able to read it yourself, instead of hunting up a priest or scholar. And it's not as if it were *hard* to learn."

So Malledd had learned. He hadn't had much practice, though; they didn't own any books. Even though the writing was unusually clear, it took him several minutes to puzzle out everything in the note.

"To the son of the smith of Grozerodz, greetings," it said. "By the time you read this you will undoubtedly have heard tales of the champions of old, who were given great gifts by the gods so that they might help the Domdur, Chosen of the Gods, to attain mastery over all that lies beneath the Hundred Moons. These tales, though sometimes exaggerated, are substantially true. In the distant past the gods saw that it was not good that the world should be divided, and that nations should war one against another, for not only did these wars cause much suffering and kill many of those who worshiped the gods, but they often divided the gods against themselves.

"Accordingly, the gods debated among themselves, and at last resolved that one people, ruled by one house, should alone be given the favor of the gods, that that people, and that house, might unite all of humanity in peace and prosperity. Though some among the gods were not pleased, yet was a great magic made that prevented forever after any of the gods from aiding any people other than the Domdur.

"That proved not in itself enough to bring about our present happy state. Many of the other nations, though abandoned by the gods, yet fought valiantly against us, and there were likewise powers in the earth that defied us, strange dark powers that hated us. At times the resolution of the Domdur weakened.

"Those among the gods who had resisted the decision to grant the Domdur dominion over all lands prevented the other gods from interfering too directly in human affairs, but it came about that an agreement was reached whereby the Domdur would at any given time have one champion, gifted by the gods with supernatural endurance and vitality, who would serve to rally the people of the Domdur Empire, who would fight always for the good of the Empire and the power of the Domdur. These champions, each in his turn, led us in battle against our foes, and cast down enemy warlords and the creatures of dark magic.

"Now, of course, we have no need of a champion, for the Domdur Empire holds sway over all, yet the gods' magic still holds its course, and there is always a chosen champion.

"The last champion who was actually called upon to serve the gods was Faial the Redeemer, in the year 854 of the gods' favor. Upon his death the duty passed to a man named Dunnon, of whom no service was ever required; nor did the gods ask anything of his successor, Mannabi.

"As I write this, on the morning of your birth, Mannabi has been dead for three days, having perished on the second day of Sheshar's Triad. Three of our oracles, speaking for Samardas, Ba'el, and Vevanis, have informed me that you, the still-unborn and nameless child of the only smith in Grozerodz, are to be the next champion. We know nothing of you, save that you will be born on this second day of Ba'el's Triad with the red mark of the war god's claw across your face, and that this mark is the sign of the chosen champion who is charged with the defense of the Domdur Empire, and gifted by the gods with supernatural endurance. It seems likely that, like Dunnon and Mannabi, you will live out your life without ever being called upon; still, we feel it appropriate to warn you that should the Empire ever be endangered, it shall be your duty to defend and preserve it.

"Since it is likely your services will never be required, we see no need to reveal your identity widely. I have informed Bonvas, the Archpriest of the Great Temple at Seidabar, and all in all some eight of us here in Biekedau know of your existence, but no one else has been told as of this writing. I suppose the delivery of this letter will spread the news to the village of Grozerodz, but that should be the end of it; I do not expect you to be besieged by petitioners seeking your aid.

"Should you have any questions or concerns about your duties, every priest in the Empire, including most particularly the oracles, is required to render you whatever aid you might need.

"May all the gods bless you.

"Signed, Dolkout, High Priest at Biekedau, on Midsummer's Day, the second day of Ba'el's Triad, in the year of the gods' favor 1082."

Malledd read this through carefully, then went back to the beginning and read it through again.

"Me?" he said.

"You," his mother said. "But as your father has surely told you, you mustn't take it too seriously. Hmar thinks this is some sort of priestly trick—that the priests give these out to one boy in every village, to make them more loyal to the Empire. It says right there that they haven't even told the *Empress*, after all, and does that seem reasonable? Besides, even if every word of it is true, who ever heard of this Dunnon, or Mannabi? So don't go thinking you've got some great destiny waiting if you run away to Seidabar, Malledd—you're a smith's apprentice, and you'll be a fine smith, and probably no more than that."

"Oh, I know, Mother," he said, carefully rolling up the parchment and stuffing it back into the ivory case. Then he stared at the case for a long moment, thinking.

He didn't particularly want to be a hero like Greldar or Rubrekir or even Faial—those stories were exciting, but all that fighting and killing and dying sounded nasty, and besides, the Empire had been at peace for two hundred years. Nobody needed heroes now.

Being chosen as the champion of the Empire wasn't exactly a great honor anymore. It wasn't as though he'd done anything to earn it; the gods had apparently chosen him before he was even born, if the birthmark really meant what the parchment said it did.

It didn't do him any good to be chosen. In fact, so far, all that silly parchment had done for him was get his sisters angry—and if the oracles had stopped giving answers, that was probably all it ever would get him.

The best thing he could do, he decided, was to forget it—and to make sure everyone else did, too. He handed the case back to his mother and turned away as she tucked it back into the drawer.

The more he thought about it, the more certain he was that he would be better off if he could convince the rest of the village to forget all about it.

For the next several years he tried his best to do just that.

CHAPTER 3

Ale," Malledd said, a trifle nervously, as he sat down. He was several days past his sixteenth birthday, and Bardetta had made a point of serving him ale to celebrate his coming of age, but he still wasn't entirely used to the idea.

"Coming right up," Zenisha, Bardetta's new serving girl, said. She turned with a swirl of skirts and headed for the taps.

Malledd settled back in his chair and looked around the tavern. It was a rainy afternoon, driving the farmers in from the fields, so the room was fairly crowded, and the air was heavy with the moisture brought in on wet clothes. There was no fire on the hearth, not this time of year, but the place still seemed to be steaming.

Malledd could have been working, since the forge had a sound roof, but he had decided he could afford a break—especially since Anva was likely to be here with her father.

His heart quickened and his hand trembled slightly at the thought of her. Anva was, in Malledd's opinion, the most beautiful creature to ever walk beneath the Hundred Moons—tall for a woman, and shapely, with great dark eyes and smooth clear skin. And she spoke, when she spoke at all, calmly and well, not at all like the giggling nonsense of most girls Malledd knew. The mere sight of her took his breath away.

She wasn't here yet. Her father Drugen was, though, so Malledd was still optimistic. If Drugen stayed for any length of time his wife would almost certainly send Anva to fetch him home, and when that happened Malledd could lend a supporting arm. He could at least say a few words to Anva as they helped her father home, and Drugen would probably be too drunk to notice if Malledd stole a kiss or two from Drugen's daughter.

Drugen was at the big table in the center of the room, with several of his friends about him, all laughing at some jest Malledd hadn't heard; Malledd watched, then glanced at the door, to see if Anva might be arriving.

Sure enough, just then the door opened, admitting a swirl of warm rain, but it wasn't Anva who stepped in; it was Gremayan the merchant.

A dozen voices greeted Gremayan, who waved to everyone with one hand while shaking the rain from his hat with the other. He glanced at the unlit hearth, then threw his soaking-wet cape across one chair and fell heavily into another. The hat landed on the table before him.

"Bardetta," he called, "brandy!"

Bardetta was not present, but Zenisha quickly thumped Malledd's mug of ale down and hurried to fetch the brandy Gremayan demanded.

"Back from Biekedau, are you?" Drugen bellowed drunkenly at Gremayan.

"Just as you see me," Gremayan called back. "And believe me, a ten-mile ride in this rain is something I'd not wish on anyone!"

"Better the ten miles from Biekedau than the twenty from Duvrenarodz!" Drugen replied. He looked around as if expecting a laugh, but got none. He subsided and gulped beer.

Zenisha reappeared and handed Gremayan his brandy.

"Thank you, lass," the merchant said, pushing his hat aside to make room for the brass cup. "And would you have a little water to go with that? You'd think I'd have had enough of water, I suppose, but it was all on the outside, and my inside is dry as dust."

Zenisha nodded and hurried away again as Gremayan called after her, "And could someone see to my ox?"

Malledd cautiously sipped ale, watching Gremayan, and watching the door.

"So what's the news in Biekedau?" someone asked as Gremayan tossed the brandy down his throat.

"Oh, they're all abuzz there, they are," Gremayan said, wiping his mouth on his sleeve. "They've just heard the latest, relayed from Seidabar by the temple magicians—it seems that someone out in the eastern lands somewhere, in Govya or some other godsforsaken place like that, has discovered a new sort of magic."

The farmers turned to stare at him, and several voices muttered.

"A new kind of magic?" someone asked. "How can that be?"

Gremayan shrugged. "I have no idea, but they say it's true."

"Oh, really?" A young farmer named Onnell glanced around the room and noticed Malledd. "Did the gods tell you anything about that, O Chosen One?"

Malledd, who had been sitting calmly minding his own business, went suddenly cold with anger. His eyes narrowed as he focused on Onnell's face, and the room suddenly fell silent.

"Shut up, Onnell," Malledd said.

Onnell was sufficiently drunk to protest, "I was just . . ."

Malledd stood up without bothering to move his chair, and sent the table and his mug of ale crashing to the floor. His fists were clenched.

"I said *shut up*, Onnell," he growled.

Onnell's face went white. His friends tried to slide away from him without being seen to do so. Gremayan's hand fell toward his boot, where the pommel of a dagger showed.

Onnell was not a small or timid man; he was, in fact, a great drunken brawling lout, Malledd's second cousin and six years Malledd's senior. For years he had been the largest man in the village, if not quite a match for Hmar in strength.

Those years had ended not so very long ago when Malledd had come into his full growth.

Malledd had long since made it known that no one was to speak of the curious incident at his birth, and had enforced this by any means available. In recent months this had included soundly thrashing several grown men, sometimes two or three at a time.

Onnell got slowly to his feet, and for a moment the two men sized each other up in deadly silence.

Onnell stood a few inches over six feet, muscled like an ox; Malledd, still growing, was already an inch or so taller, and even broader, with the massive strength that came from hours of beating iron into shape. Onnell had been drinking for hours; Malledd hadn't finished his first ale.

And Onnell had nothing against Malledd, no long-held grudges or general dislike. Malledd had done him no wrong. Malledd was, except for this one quirk, a very pleasant, if rather quiet, fellow.

"It was meant as a harmless jest, Malledd," he said. "I'm sorry."

"Jest all you like when I'm not here, Onnell," Malledd said, "but every man, woman, and child in Grozerodz knows I will not tolerate any mention of that damned priest and his stupid stories in my presence!"

"I know, I know," Onnell said, "I'm sorry. Drink got the better of me."

Malledd hesitated. His fit of temper was passing, and he knew that Onnell was genuinely contrite. The best thing to do might have been to storm out, but he wanted to hear what Gremayan had to say.

And he wanted to be there when Anva came.

"All right, then," he said. He bent down, tipped the table back into position, and picked up his now-empty mug. He beckoned to Zenisha, then turned to Gremayan and said, "You were saying?"

Someone laughed nervously.

"I was saying," Gremayan said, a bit warily, his hand still close to his boot, "that a new sort of magic is reported, somewhere in the east."

One of the farmers snorted. "As if it mattered! Unless they've found a way to make the oracles speak again, who *cares* what the priests can do?"

"Ah," Gremayan said, straightening as he warmed once again to his tale, "but that's what makes this interesting. According to the stories, this new magic can be used by people who are *not* priests! Naturally, all the high priests and temple magicians are upset about that, but I don't know if there's much they can do."

That started several people speaking at once, but after a moment they sorted themselves out, and Nedduel was chosen to ask, "So what does this new magic *do*? Can it foretell the future, as the oracles could?"

Gremayan shook his head. "No, no, nothing like that," he said. "At least, I don't think so. The stories say these new magicians can fly like birds, and heal wounds, and make stones glow, and a dozen other things, but they can't see the future even as well as the astrologers."

"Fly?"

"Like the gods?"

"Blasphemy!"

"Madness!"

Again, a dozen voices spoke at once.

Malledd's was not among them; he was content to listen.

He noticed that the older men, Nedduel in particular, seemed to be upset by the news, while the younger seemed, like himself, merely intrigued. He supposed that was because the older men were more set in their ways. Change of any sort would upset them.

He remembered how they had ranted and raved when word came that the oracles had fallen silent, how Nedduel had, once the harvest was safely in, taken a deputation to the temple in Biekedau to protest.

It hadn't done any good, of course; the priests had wearily confirmed that the gods had stopped answering questions, had repeated the explanation that the gods thought it was time humanity became less dependent on divine guidance, and had called the temple guards when the farmers raised their voices.

Apparently there had been several incidents of violence when the news broke. Some people had been completely unreasonable; one group had proposed seizing the shrine in Duvrenarodz, which Malledd thought was totally absurd, since there had never been an oracle there in the first place. Others had suggested marching on Seidabar, which made somewhat more sense—but Seidabar was a hundred miles away, at least, and there were already reports of riots there, riots that were forcibly put down by the Imperial Guard.

Nothing had come of it, and life had gone on much as before; there had been no great unforeseen disasters, despite the lack of oracular advice. The Empire endured, with the aid of its soldiers and the magic the priests still had.

There was a widespread suspicion, though, that the silence of the oracles meant that the Empire's best days were past.

Malledd could see being upset at the silence of the oracles; that was undeniably bad news. This new magic, though, sounded as if it might be very useful, and still the older men of the village were upset.

Malledd supposed it was the mere fact of change that upset them. After all, there were so few changes in the world these days. The Empress Beretris had been on the throne since before most of them were born—since before his father Hmar was born. The Domdur had ruled all the world for generations; no one remembered a time when they had not. The gods reigned undisputed, the Hundred Moons followed their complex paths through the skies, and all was at peace, and had been for as long as anyone present had lived.

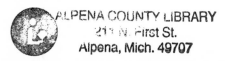
ALPENA COUNTY LIBRARY
211 N. First St.
Alpena, Mich. 49707

They weren't accustomed to change.

It wasn't like the bad old days in the stories, when the Empire was surrounded by enemies and constantly at war, when the gods themselves had demanded that the Empire expand and expand regardless of what its people might want, demanded that mortal men and women die for the Empire.

A new kind of magic that could be learned by laypeople—that was an interesting thought, and nothing to be afraid of. Malledd wondered what it would be like to fly like a bird.

Then he shook his head and took a gulp of ale.

He wasn't going to go off to the mountains of Govya, a thousand miles or more to the east, to learn magic. He had a perfectly good life planned out right where he was. He was his father's junior partner in the smithy now, and when Hmar grew old and retired Malledd would be the only smith in Grozerodz. He would marry Anva, if he could possibly convince her and her parents to have him, or one of the other pretty girls in town if he could not, and he would build himself a house on the other side of the forge from his parents' house, and raise a dozen children there. He would go to the temple in Biekedau once a year to make his ritual obeisance to Dremeger, god of metalworkers, and maybe someday he would visit Seidabar to get a look at the Empress, or perhaps someday, the farther in the future the better, to see one of her three children crowned as her successor.

But he wasn't going to go a thousand miles to Govya, or anywhere else in the east.

Gremayan was explaining for the third time that he didn't know how the new magic worked when Anva arrived, looking for Drugen. Malledd gulped down the rest of his ale, almost choking on it, and hurried to her side.

She smiled at the sight of him, but said only, "I'm looking for my father."

Malledd wordlessly pointed out Drugen and his cronies; he was too stricken by Anva's presence to speak.

It was another hour or so before they managed to get Drugen out the door, with Anva on one side and Malledd on the other; when their hands touched against Drugen's back Malledd started as if he had been poked with a needle. Anva's hand was warm and small and smooth, and he wished he could clasp it in his own without worrying about old Drugen, but he couldn't. Together, they escorted Anva's father out of Bardetta's little tavern.

The sun was down and the rain had become a torrent by the time they got Drugen safely home to his wife, soaking them both to the skin. Anva's mother took one look at Malledd and invited him in to dry off.

He was only too glad to accept.

They sat side by side before the fire, with Drugen slumped in the chimney corner, drying out. Anva's hair hung in dripping ropes—and even so, Malledd thought she was beautiful. He stared at her, at the curve of her chin and the drop of water hanging from the tip of her nose.

She glanced over and saw him staring, and blushed—but for the first time, neither of them looked away.

Ten days later the engagement was announced, and Malledd had forgotten his interest in any magic but that special magic the gods give young lovers. He sat beside Anva in the tavern, his arm around her shoulders, as their friends cheered the news.

"May Baranmel dance at your wedding!" Onnell called—he and Malledd had fully made up their differences.

The crowd echoed the traditional blessing.

Malledd smiled and hugged Anva, but somewhere in the back of his mind he wondered whether Baranmel *would* dance at their wedding. It was a sign of the gods' favor and a promise of good fortune if the god of festivities came to a marriage celebration—and wasn't Malledd supposed to be favored by the gods? Wasn't that what Dolkout's letter promised?

But in these days when the oracles no longer heard the gods, it might be that Baranmel, the god of celebration, no longer attended human weddings.

Whether Baranmel and the other gods smiled on him or not didn't matter, Malledd told himself. So long as he had Anva, that was all the good fortune he needed.

CHAPTER 4

Bardetta's nameless inn, where Malledd and Anva sat among their friends, stood in the center of Grozerodz, facing south onto the village square. The "square" itself was an irregular open space, only vaguely rectangular, surrounded by a dozen separate houses and shops, with patches of garden between them. Three lanes meandered away from this center; two rambled out past various shops and farmsteads, while one ran past the graveyard and down to the smithy and a nearby stream.

In addition to the lanes the square was bisected by a genuine highway. This road ran through roughly fifty miles of gently rolling hills, from the river port of Biekedau at its northeast end to the hilltop town of Yildau, founded a thousand years before as a border fortress but now a center for mining and manufacture, at the southwest; along the way it passed through the villages of Grozerodz, Duvrenarodz, and Uamor. The road had no universally agreed upon name; the people of Biekedau called it the Yildau road, while the folk of Yildau naturally referred to it as the Biekedau road. For the most part, the villagers in between called it simply "the road."

Biekedau itself stood on the southern banks of the Vren River, just below the lower falls that marked the limit of navigation. Since the reign of Suogai III people had spoken of building a canal and locks around the falls, but so far the merchants of Biekedau had prevented the construction of such a thing, for fear it would threaten their profits. The wisdom of this policy had been debated for some three centuries.

The hill country ended at Biekedau; once across the Vren, a traveler heading east would find the land utterly flat and largely featureless for well over a hundred miles. The rich soil of this plain fed the troops of the Domdur Empire from the earliest days of its expansion.

Almost two hundred miles east of the lower falls of the Vren the plain was broken again by the broad, shallow valley of a wide river. For centuries, as the Domdur spread their power and influence largely by sea, before the gods demanded further expansion overland, the Grebiguata River served as the eastern boundary of the Empire.

Beyond the Grebiguata the plain continued, extending hundreds of miles farther before it almost imperceptibly began to fade into the rolling foothills of the Govya Mountains. All this open land fell in a single long campaign in the reign of Gogror II as the Domdur marched relentlessly eastward, driving the disorganized natives before them.

The mountains, however, proved as great a barrier as anything the Domdur had ever encountered, and where a few brief years saw the entire plain captured, a century was not enough to take the Govya Mountains. Pockets of resistance held out in isolated valleys for generation after generation, long after the Domdur had swept through the passes and over the peaks into the lands beyond.

There were tales that not all the resistance was entirely natural. Stories of black magic, and of *things* lurking in or under the mountains, persisted.

Beyond the mountains the ancient, wealthy lands of Matua and Greya were conquered in short order, requiring about a decade apiece to be absorbed into the Empire. The northern wastes of Shibir put up no resistance, and needed merely to be occupied.

To the south, though, the nomads of the deserts of Olnami struggled fiercely against their fate. Under the leadership of the Nazakri clan the Olnami fought a guerrilla war against the Domdur for a hundred and fifty years before at last, in the year of the gods' favor 788, the Domdur general and divine champion Ruamel captured Basari, the leader of the Nazakri, together with his six sons, and forced a surrender.

Basari Nazakri swore then that he would never again take up arms against

the Domdur, and that neither would his sons nor his grandsons; each of his sons
swore, as well. An oath is a sacred thing among the Olnami, and that ended all
organized resistance; the desert became the province of Olnamia, and the Nazakri disappeared from the Domdur histories.

They did not, however, disappear from beneath the Hundred Moons, or from
their own histories.

Basari Nazakri died in 791, poisoned by a member of the rival Chisari clan
who had declared him a traitor for his surrender. His sons avenged him, though
two of the six died in the process—the Chisari were not Domdur, and not
protected by Basari's oath. By 802 the Chisari clan was no more—but the Nazakri were broken as well, all but forgotten by the rest of the Olnami.

Basari's four surviving sons lived out their natural spans—though for Asanli,
the youngest, that was brief, as the gods sent a fever that claimed him in the
spring of 809. They raised their own sons, and taught them the history of the
Olnami, of the Nazakri, and of Basari's oath.

And they, in turn, raised and taught *their* sons, the grandsons of Basari's sons.

And it was with the generation after that that the Nazakri were free of their
oaths—but by then the other Olnami had lost any interest in fighting the Domdur. The old nomads were scattered, their way of life lost; more Olnami lived
in Domdur fortress towns than in their traditional tents. The Domdur had pre-
vailed over the entire continent, from the Forsten Peninsula in the farthest west
to the Greyan coasts in the east, and under their rule the land was peaceful and
prosperous; the oracles guided the Domdur in governing wisely and generously.

Some of the Nazakri despaired; some shrugged and went on with their lives;
but a handful nursed their ancient hatred of the Domdur and waited, waited for
some opportunity, searched for some means, any means, to avenge Basari's
defeat and the destruction of the old Olnami nation.

One such was Rebiri Nazakri.

Of Basari's six sons, the eldest had sired no children before dying in the
vendetta against the Chisari, and the second sired only daughters. The third,
Dayeri, had four sons, of whom the eldest, born in the year 798, was named
Shaoni.

Rebiri could trace his ancestry through nine generations, eldest son of eldest
son, to Shaoni Nazakri; he was the rightful lord of the Nazakri, leader of the
clan, and therefore warlord of all Olnami. By rights, he believed, he should be
clad in the richest silks and living in a fine pavilion, eating sweetmeats from
golden platters.

And on the summer night when Malledd the smith's son announced his
betrothal in Grozerodz, Rebiri Nazakri sat hunched over a small cooking fire in
a cave in the eastern foothills of the Govya Mountains, wearing goatskin breeches
and a tattered woolen cloak, listening to his stomach growl.

He looked up at the mouth of the cave and in his native tongue elaborately cursed the gods of the Domdur who had reduced him to this, and the gods of the Olnami, lost or dead, who had permitted it.

His ancestors had left the deserts of Olnami more than a century ago. Inspired by the old stories of supernatural resistance, they had in time come to these mountains searching for some weapon they might use against the Domdur. While they had found many strange things in Govya, they had found no power that could defy the Domdur gods. Rebiri was reduced to shaking a fist at those gods and shouting his spite.

Sometimes he almost thought he could feel someone, or some*thing*, listening to him—but usually there was only empty silence. On this particular occasion his curses seemed no more than useless, meaningless words.

Then a shadow fell across the opening, blocking out what little daylight remained. Rebiri squinted through the cookfire's smoke.

"Father?" a boy's voice called, in the Olnami speech.

"Aldassi?" Rebiri replied, recognizing his eldest son. "Come in here where I can see you. What have you brought?" He thought he could smell the scent of something freshly dead—their supper, he hoped.

"Duck, Father—I caught a duck!"

Rebiri smiled. "Excellent!" he said. "Bring it here."

The boy obeyed quickly, handing his father a plump dead fowl; the man began efficiently stripping it of its feathers.

"I got carrots, too," Aldassi said, kneeling at his father's side. "I ran some errands in the market at Dolya Korien to earn them."

"Good, good," Rebiri said, concentrating on plucking the duck. "And was there any news in the market? Has Beretris dropped dead, perhaps, and started a war of succession?"

His tone was sarcastic, but Aldassi knew his father's moods, knew that he hoped for exactly that. No succession to the Domdur throne had ever been openly disputed, in all of recorded history, but everyone agreed that the oracles were no longer telling the imperial family what the line of inheritance should be. Beretris had twin sons, and an elder daughter who, it was rumored, did not see why her sex should remove her from serious consideration as her mother's heir; the potential for disagreement was greater than ever before.

What good a disputed succession would do the Nazakri was not really clear. Aldassi knew that his father thought a civil war would provide opportunities for a resurgence of the Nazakri and the restoration of Olnami independence, but he had serious doubts about the likelihood of such opportunities. Mostly, Aldassi knew, his father simply wished ill to befall the Domdur, even if it did the Olnami no good.

There had been no word in Dolya Korien that Beretris was in anything but the best of health, and as far as Aldassi knew all her children were on the best of terms with one another.

"Nothing like that," Aldassi said. "But there's a rumor going around that some people just the other side of the mountains have found some new way of making magic, one that doesn't need Domdur priests."

The boy had intended the remark as idle chatter, but Rebiri's hands suddenly stopped their rapid motion. He looked up, staring at his son's face.

His grandfather had come to these mountains seeking black magic to use against the Domdur; he had found traces of it, deep in the earth, but had been unable to use them. Rebiri's father had spent his life struggling to control the dark energies beneath the mountains, and had never managed it. In fact, his sudden and mysterious death might have been caused by those forces.

Rebiri himself had followed in his father's footsteps to some extent. He had been seeking useful magic other than the mind tricks of the Domdur priests for most of his life, but had abandoned the quest at last, and had sworn not to pass it on to Aldassi. There was no point in wasting another generation in such a fruitless pursuit.

But perhaps it didn't have to be fruitless. Had someone else succeeded where the Nazakri had always failed?

"A new magic?" he said. "What sort of magic?"

"I don't know," Aldassi said, startled by his father's intensity. "The stories say the man who first learned it used it to fly like a bird. What else it might do, I couldn't say."

"Fly?" Rebiri's gaze became less focused, more thoughtful. "That might have its uses. This man—who is he? Is he Domdur? Olnami?"

Aldassi shook his head. "Neither, Father; he's from one of the mountain tribes, the Diknoi or Megani or one of those. He's supposed to be starting a school to teach his arts. And the priests in Ai Varach are said to have sent one of their magical messages to Seidabar to ask if this skill should be banned, or brought to the capital."

"He's in Ai Varach?"

"Near there."

"We need to see this man." He got to his feet, the duck forgotten.

"Father," Aldassi protested, "the sun's below the mountains, and I'm hungry!"

Rebiri hesitated, then looked down at the duck and the cookfire. Reluctantly, he seated himself again.

"Tomorrow," he said. "Tomorrow morning, by dawn, we shall be on the trail to Ai Varach."

CHAPTER 5

It was forty days later, half a season, that Rebiri and Aldassi finally reached the little Diknoi village of Fadari Tu, a cluster of a dozen clean, well-made houses built on a broad, grassy ledge below the mouth of a cave, some fifty miles north of the major Domdur outpost in the area, Ai Varach.

Aldassi seemed to have grown visibly during the journey; he had begun it a boy, but now, though he was still only in his fifteenth year, he looked almost a man. Rebiri was proud of the lad's progress.

They had reached the stone-walled citadel of Ai Varach ten days before, and had asked everyone they encountered there about the stories of a new kind of magic. The result was a tangle of contradictory reports. Some of the people they questioned had told the two ragged Olnami wanderers that the magician was a fraud, and the priests from the temple at Ai Varach had proven it. Others had said that he was genuine, and the Empress had ordered him slain, and that soldiers from the garrison at Ai Varach had carried out those orders. Still others had said the orders had been given and the soldiers sent, but the magician had escaped.

And a few had said that soldiers had been sent north, all right, but that they had gone to invite the magician to appear before the Empress in Seidabar—not to harm him, but to reward him.

Everyone had agreed that priests and soldiers had gone north to Fadari Tu, and had returned, but that was all that they agreed upon.

The two Nazakri had gone on from Ai Varach to Fadari Tu, hoping that the magician was still there and alive—but Aldassi, at least, had not been optimistic. Rebiri did not choose to state an opinion.

Deep in his heart, though, Rebiri could feel, with a certainty he could not explain, that whether the magician was there or not something great would come of this journey. He sensed a dark power in the world around him, a power that he somehow knew favored him in his desire to destroy the Domdur Empire.

He had never before known such a sensation, but he believed in fate, and he believed that this power he felt was his destiny, coming to him at last.

He said nothing of this to his son; Aldassi had quite enough to concern him with just his share of keeping the two of them alive and getting them safely to their destination.

When he and Aldassi finally stumbled up the road into the tiny community of Fadari Tu, half a dozen of the pale, brown-haired villagers came out to greet them, and one of them almost immediately asked, in the Domdur tongue rather than their own incomprehensible tribal dialect, "Are you here to learn the New Magic?"

Rebiri looked at the speaker warily; he could feel nothing of that looming destiny in her, and he did not trust these strange-looking foreigners, with their washed-out coloring. They didn't smell right, either, though he didn't care to think about why. He asked cautiously, "New Magic?"

The villagers made little effort to hide their amusement. The Diknoi were well known to be a direct people, not given to subtleties in their speech or manner—though they were reputed to be very subtle indeed in their arguments and philosophies.

"Do you expect us to believe you had some *other* reason to come to Fadari Tu?" another woman asked. "You're no mountain-born Govyan, that's certain, and you don't look much like a Domdur scholar or tax collector; you look Olnami or Matuan, by your skin and hair. What *else* would bring an easterner up to this part of the world?"

She spoke Domdur fluently—better than Rebiri did. He supposed that was not surprising; anyone who dealt with travelers or any part of the imperial government would need to use Domdur, and the Diknoi, despite their isolation, had always been interested in the outside world. They were, in fact, notorious for their inquisitiveness—"curious as a Diknoi" was a common expression in Govya.

"Could I not be a Matuan scholar, come to study your folkways?" Rebiri asked.

"Are you?"

Rebiri smiled at the blunt question, the sort of thing a child might say. "No," he said. "I am Olnami." Despite his sorry condition he still felt a surge of pride in stating that simple fact.

"And in all their history, the Olnami have never studied anything for its own sake," the woman declared. "You desert folk never had time to spare for such pursuits. So you're here to see whether the stories of the New Magic are true, and maybe to join the school."

"And if I am?" Rebiri asked. "Is this inventor, this teacher, still here?"

"No," an older man said. "Vrai Burrai, who discovered the secret, is on his way to Seidabar for an audience with the Empress. But the school he founded remains."

"And who teaches in this school, if the magician is gone?" Aldassi asked.

"*I* do," said a new voice, and both Rebiri and Aldassi looked about for its source.

Then they saw the villagers looking up, as if at the various moons in the sky, and the two Olnami looked up as well, to find a young man hanging in the air above their heads. He held a peculiar short staff before him in both hands; at either end of the staff was something that glittered so brightly in the sun the Nazakri could not see it clearly.

Aldassi's mouth fell open with surprise; Rebiri's eyes widened slightly, but no more than that.

This man was a key to his destiny; Rebiri *knew* that, without knowing how he knew. Nothing in the workings of that destiny could truly astonish him.

"I am Tebas Tudan," the flying man said, "foremost among Vrai Burrai's pupils."

As the Nazakri and the villagers watched Tebas Tudan settled gently to the ground, descending slowly until he stood on his own two feet before the strangers. Once down, he lowered his staff and bowed.

"Welcome to Fadari Tu," he said. "What would you like to learn of our New Magic?"

"Everything there is to know," Rebiri replied.

"And can you pay for this knowledge?"

"No," Rebiri admitted, "but I will swear that if I am satisfied, I shall find a way to pay you generously for your teaching." He nodded toward the woman who had spoken earlier. "Your friend here knows something of the Olnami," he said. "She will tell you that if I swear an oath, I will keep it."

"I know that much of the Olnami myself," Tebas Tudan retorted.

"Then will you teach me? And my son?" Rebiri's eyes were alight with anticipation. Here was the moment when his fate would begin to unfold, and the doom of the Domdur would be sealed.

Tebas Tudan considered, then smiled and held out a hand for Rebiri to grip after the Diknoi fashion. "Why not?" he said.

And Rebiri felt that mysterious power in the world around him exult.

The next triad—the Diknoi had adopted the Domdur custom of dividing the year into three-day periods rather than using the less exact Olnami use of seasons and fractions thereof—was spent settling in; Rebiri and his son found lodging in an unused storage loft, and learned their way around the village. Then, when their instructor was ready, their training began.

The first lessons were the hardest; Tebas Tudan admitted that this was deliberate.

"Why should I waste any longer than necessary on a student who will not work hard enough to learn what he needs to learn?" he asked when one of the students questioned the need to cram so much into each class.

At least, Rebiri thought, they had not had to learn the Diknoi language, with its precise shades of meaning and multilayered compound words; the lectures were given in Domdur.

The classes were held in a chamber of the cave above the village, well up inside the mountain, where a magical crystal provided plentiful light and kept away any evil things that might have lurked in the surrounding stone. Besides Rebiri and Aldassi there were six other students—four of the Diknoi villagers, a Domdur trader whose ancestors might have been Megani, and a tall, dark-skinned Sautalan who wore the red uniform of the Imperial Army, but without insignia—either a veteran or a deserter, and none of the others dared inquire which. A fifth villager had given up during the first lesson, justifying Tebas Tudan's decision to start off with the hard part.

The eight of them persevered, however, as Tebas Tudan explained how Vrai Burrai had discovered a method of forming crystalline structures that trapped and magnified the sun's light, and that could then be linked to a person's spirit and used to perform various wonders.

How he had stumbled upon this Tebas Tudan could not explain; Vrai Burrai himself had said that one day the idea was there in his head, and he didn't know how or why.

Rebiri and Aldassi studied hard, but there was much to learn. Vrai Burrai had been a glassblower, a skilled artisan, before stumbling upon his magic, and Tebas Tudan had been a gemcutter, while the two Nazakri had never been called upon to perform any task more delicate than threading a needle; the fine handi-work did not come easily.

Likewise, the mathematical methods that the Diknoi used to determine the best shapes for their constructs were unfamiliar, and the meditation techniques needed to attune the crystals to the user's spirit so that the trapped energy might actually be used required a calm and a concentration unlike anything Rebiri had ever attempted.

When he meditated, though, Rebiri could sense the dark power of his destiny all around him, eager to be unleashed.

At last, some twenty-five triads, almost a season, after their arrival, when the cold winds of approaching winter were howling outside the cave and sending occasional spirals of bitterly cold air around the students' feet, Aldassi lifted with both hands an ugly, intricate crystal construction roughly the size of his own head.

"I think it's done," he said.

"Let us see about that," Tebas Tudan said. "Anyone else?"

The Sautalan, Wasyanei, lifted his own device—smaller and sleeker than Al-dassi's, but just as complex.

"Anyone else?" The teacher looked around.

A Diknoi girl studied hers critically. "Almost," she said.

The other five said nothing. Rebiri's own still needed several days more work.

"Well, let us test these two, at any rate." Tebas Tudan led the way down toward the cave mouth.

Aldassi and Wasyanei came immediately; Rebiri hesitated, looking at his own unfinished crystal, then followed, as did all the other students but the Diknoi girl.

The day outside the cave was cold, the wind hard and carrying the scent of coming snow, but the sky was clear and intensely blue. A dozen moons gleamed pale and faint, like reflections on blue ice, and the sun blazed yellow-white in the western sky.

Rebiri shivered at the chill; the air felt sharp in his nose and throat as he breathed, and each breath was plainly visible. He did not hesitate, though, and he was close on Tebas Tudan's heels as the party arrived at a stony, more or less level area.

Here the Diknoi magician stopped and waited for the others to gather. Then he beckoned to the younger Olnami. At Tebas Tudan's direction, Aldassi raised his crystal above his head to trap the sun's light.

The day seemed to dim perceptibly for an instant, and then there were two glittering lights—the sun, and Aldassi's crystal. Everyone present could hear the glass humming, and Aldassi gasped as he felt the power surging through his spirit.

"Lift, as I taught you," Tebas Tudan said.

Rebiri watched with fierce satisfaction as his son rose unsteadily into the air, like a flag being hoisted.

A battle flag, he told himself—a Nazakri battle flag, raised in defiance of the Domdur! That unseen power seethed around him; Rebiri felt it.

Wasyanei's crystal proved to have a flaw; it whistled piercingly, and would not hold steady. He was unable to maintain his flight for more than three or four seconds.

Aldassi watched from fifty feet up as Wasyanei's attempt failed; then he settled gently to the ground.

After that excitement none of the students could concentrate on the delicate work of crystal construction, but Tebas Tudan was not willing to waste that excitement by letting them go for the day. Instead, when everyone was back in the cave workshop, he took questions, on anything and everything related to Vrai Burrai's magic.

"What limits the amount of sunlight you can absorb?" asked Vedrur, the Domdur trader.

"The strength of the crystal's substance," Tebas Tudan answered. "Too much energy, and it will explode. Messy. Vrai Burrai and I had that happen twice; I still have the scar from the second one." He held up his left hand and displayed the fading red marks on either side where, Rebiri realized, a small fragment had gone *through* the teacher's hand.

"Fortunately, the purity of the light apparently prevents the wound from becoming infected," Tebas Tudan remarked. "Every wound we ever experienced from a shattered crystal healed quickly and cleanly."

The Olnami frowned. Something was nagging at him, a question he needed to ask, as if his destiny were prompting him. He said, "Can other sources of energy be used, rather than sunlight?"

Tebas Tudan shook his head. "We have not found any other light strong and pure enough to be useful."

"What about darkness, then?" Rebiri asked.

That, he knew, was the right question, another key to his destiny.

Tebas Tudan frowned.

"I haven't tried it," he said, "but I can't see how that would work; after all, what is darkness but the absence of light?"

Rebiri said no more, but inside he almost laughed at the simple ignorance of this Diknoi teacher.

An ordinary darkness might be merely the absence of light, but Rebiri knew there were other, deeper darknesses. There were things in the night and in the depths of the earth, things that shunned the sun and the Hundred Moons and all the gods of the Domdur, things that had their own power. Rebiri and Rebiri's ancestors had struggled to control them for decades, to find some way to turn them against the Empire, but always, that dark power had slipped through their fingers. The darknesses in the earth had no language that anyone could understand; they could not be bargained with, could not be controlled.

But perhaps, with these power traps, they could be *caught*.

And *used*.

Somewhere, somehow, Rebiri Nazakri felt sure something much greater than himself approved of the idea.

CHAPTER 6

The torchlight painted the stone walls in shifting patterns of black and gold, light and shadow, as Rebiri Nazakri made his way deeper into the cave.

This was not the gentle, tamed cave of the Diknoi magicians, high on the western slopes; this was instead the wild cave at the base of the eastern cliffs where Rebiri's father Tolani had brought him, long ago, so that Rebiri might see for himself that there were powers in the earth that did not answer to the Domdur priests.

Rebiri had come here not for any clear, carefully thought out reason, but because it felt right; he had felt his destiny calling him back to this place, and he had come.

The floor was rough, broken stone, not even remotely level, smoothed in spots by patches of mud that had somehow found their way down into this strange realm; gravel crunched and slid under Rebiri's feet, and before him, here and there in the muddy spots, he could see the footprints that he and his father had left more than thirty years before, undisturbed by the passage of time.

The cave smelled of damp stone, a lifeless, unappetizing odor; Rebiri ignored it. The only sound was the soft padding of his sandaled feet; no wind, no other movement disturbed the eerie silence. Still, Rebiri thought he could sense another presence, something that was not physically there but was nonetheless real.

Save for that feeling of some supernatural presence, he was alone down here; Aldassi had remained aboveground. Aldassi still possessed his magical crystal, that first crystal he had made seasons ago as a student back in Fadari Tu; he had become adept in its use, drawing power from the sun, from the gods who powered the sun. For the sake of his intended experiment Rebiri could not allow that crystal down here, nor did he want Aldassi to leave it unattended.

The experiment would be dangerous; he knew that, and he saw no need to risk his son's life as well as his own. Aldassi was the last in the direct line of the Olnami warlords; if both Rebiri and Aldassi perished, the hereditary title and responsibility would fall upon their cousin Seloti.

Seloti was a merchant in the Domdur fortress town of Kubezhin, back in what was now the province of Olnamia. Despite living in the heart of his ancestral homeland, Seloti had abandoned the old ways and embraced the new; he barely remembered the Olnami language, and had never so much as held a sword. If Seloti became warlord, all hope for vengeance was lost. Aldassi's life could not be risked.

And besides, Rebiri liked the boy, perhaps even loved him. Aldassi was a good lad.

It was better he not risk entering the cave, and no one else could be trusted. Rebiri had come alone.

The Olnami warlord had to move carefully, watching his footing; he had no hands free to catch himself if he stumbled. His right held the torch; his left clutched a thick bundle of black cloth.

Inside the bundle was the short staff of black wood he had prepared back in Fadari Tu, a staff like the one Tebas Tudan carried, with one of the Diknoi power crystals at either end.

These two were the largest crystals Rebiri could make, each almost as large as his own head, considerably larger than the ones on his teacher's staff. It had taken him the better part of a year to get them made to his satisfaction.

These crystals were not charged with magic, though; indeed, the Nazakri had taken every precaution to ensure that they would not be exposed to sunlight prematurely. He had made two, despite the extra time and effort that required, entirely in case one did somehow trap a little of the gods' power. He had completed them by the light of a single candle, working as much by touch as by sight, then immediately shrouded them in heavy cloth and sealed them in a box. Unlike Aldassi, Rebiri had destroyed his first crystal, which had been used in sunlight, lest it somehow contaminate these others. He had wanted them to remain utterly virgin until he reached his destination.

Now that destination was just a few yards ahead. He paused, considering.

He had come here at the urgings of fate—or of *something*, at any rate. Now, though, the time had come to think out what he should do next.

Ahead the cave sloped down into a pit, a pit so totally black that the torch's light seemed unable to penetrate its darkness. Rebiri remembered when he had seen that pit before; *no* light had been able to pierce it. It swallowed whatever light touched it, and almost seemed to reach out for more.

That was the darkness he wanted to capture in one of the crystals of the New Magic. He intended to trap the dark powers of the earth as the others had trapped the bright light of the sun.

Now, though, he faced the moment when he must decide how best to attempt his task. Need he douse the torch to lure the darkness out? Must he plunge the crystals into the pit itself?

If he put out the torch he might never find his way out. Besides, he remembered that when he had come here all those years ago the lanterns they had carried had not kept the dark things from approaching.

There was no point in risking too much. He wedged the torch securely between two rocks, then knelt and carefully unwrapped his staff.

The crystals glittered brilliantly in the torchlight and sent golden flickers across the stalactites overhead as Rebiri picked the staff up in both hands.

The flickers were like eyes watching him. Certainly he felt *something* watching him.

Perhaps, he thought, the old gods of the Olnami were not all dead after all. The shamans had said that the lesser gods of blood and clan had deserted the Olnami, had vanished from the world forever. They said that the greater gods of sky and desert had been the same the Domdur had worshiped all along, under different names, and those gods had long ago abandoned the Olnami in favor of the Domdur. But perhaps, Rebiri thought, some divine power had come to see that the cause of the Nazakri was just and right after all, and was guiding him, watching over him.

Leaving the torch and the heavy cloth there on the stone, he stepped forward cautiously, down the slope toward the pit's darkness.

The cool, still air of the cave seemed suddenly alive, crawling across the exposed skin of his arms and face like insects, like fluttering spiderwebs. He blinked, and when his eyes opened again the gloom of the pit seemed to be rising toward him. The torch's light was faint and far away, and the stone walls that had been golden an instant before were suddenly gray and dim. His own shadow stretched out before him, merging with the darkness of the pit and spilling up the far wall.

The comforting guiding presence was gone. He was alone in a cave with those *things*, those black, evil powers. . . .

He stepped back involuntarily, and lost his footing as a stone went out from under his sandal; he fell, his arms flying up, taking the staff with them.

He landed hard on rough stone, flat on his back, the wind knocked out of him, his right hand still clutching the staff and holding it up above his chest. One crystal was mere inches from the torch.

The darkness was still oozing up from the pit; he could see it crawling across the cave walls, dimming and erasing the torchlight, washing everything it touched in impenetrable shadow.

He lay motionless, dazed, trying to think what he should do.

A tendril of darkness climbed the stalagmite by his right shoulder, reaching for the staff.

That was what he had come for, of course, but at that moment he panicked, thinking only of how precious the crystals were, how long and hard he had worked on them. He swung the staff farther away from the stalagmite.

And one crystal plunged into the flame rising from the torch.

That should have been harmless, meaningless; back in Fadari Tu the students and Tebas Tudan had performed any number of experiments, trying to use light other than sunlight. None of them had worked; to any sort of flame or glow other than the direct rays of the sun, the magical crystals were nothing but ordinary glass.

But here, in the cave where the old dark powers lurked, something leaped from the stone and merged with the flame, and with a flash and a rush of air the crystal absorbed the torch's fire.

The torch went out instantly, reduced to a smoking stump, but the light did not completely vanish; instead the crystal now glowed a smoky red, as if it were a coal from some gigantic forge.

The Nazakri stared at it for a moment, trying to understand. Then he slowly sat up, still holding the staff, still staring at the glowing crystal.

The world around him was red and black now, a world of jagged crimson shapes and crowding darkness, and he could feel the power through the staff. He didn't know just what this power could do, but he knew it could do *some-thing*; he felt it straining at its bonds, dark and hungry.

Keeping the staff in his right hand, he grasped the tip of a stalagmite with his left and pulled himself to his feet. He stared at the glowing crystal a moment longer, noticing that smoke seemed to be seething in the air around it, not rising and dissipating as smoke ought to, but appearing, swirling, and vanishing in an unnatural vortex.

This was what he had come for. It was not, perhaps, quite what he had expected—he had not planned on using the torch's flame—but it was what he had, and he thought it would serve.

It was time, then, to leave. He looked down at the floor of the cave, trying to find his path.

Thin fingers of blackness were inching across the red-lit stone toward his feet.

"No!" he shouted, stepping back.

The darkness followed him.

He looked desperately at his staff. He couldn't use the glowing crystal; that was the same stuff that was after him, and besides, if he used it here he would have no more light, no way to find his way out.

He turned the dark, unused crystal downward and jabbed it at the nearest of the approaching tendrils.

Something screamed soundlessly; Rebiri sensed it, thought he felt the air vibrate with it. As he watched, the crystal sucked the darkness in, leaving the stone bare and unshadowed.

"Oh," the Nazakri said.

He could no longer see the dark crystal; where it had been was a blackness his gaze could not penetrate, a blackness exactly like that darkness in the pit.

He could feel something moving in the staff, something cold and hostile; the black wood seemed suddenly slick and icy in his hand.

That was enough. That was *more* than enough. The time had come to get *out* of this place. He had what he had come for, and more than he had reckoned on. Staggering in the smoky red light, he made his way upward as quickly as he could, up toward where Aldassi waited.

As he climbed, he felt his destiny gathering about him once again.

CHAPTER 7

Asari Asakari picked up his begging bowl and rattled it, then grimaced ruefully. He wasn't trying to attract donations, as the courtyard was deserted; he made the gesture from habit.

The clinking of the coins was unsatisfying. The day's take had been poor, which was why he had stayed at his post so late, but there was no point in staying any longer. The streets were empty, the windows on all sides dark. He would have to fast a little, that was all.

He fished a rag from his pocket and spat on it, then began wiping away the makeup that provided his "skin disease" and drew the pity of the city's wealthy.

Maybe he hadn't put it on well today, he thought. Maybe he'd looked too healthy. If . . . no, *when* Bekra ever came back, he'd have her help him with his appearance, and he'd do the same for her.

He was just removing the last of the paint when he heard footsteps.

"Oh, the gods do like their little tricks!" he said in his native Olnami as he looked down at the rag he held. If he had waited just another few minutes he might have collected enough for a meal—or he might not; there was no knowing whose footsteps he had heard.

The Matuans of Hao Tan were not likely to be out at this hour, for fear of footpads and assassins, but the Domdur were fearless, especially when drunk, and were often generous, as well; if the steps he heard were those of a Domdur officer, Asari might well have collected a handful of silver in his bowl had he kept his makeup on.

On the other hand, Asari was unsure just how groundless the Matuans' fears were. If the footsteps were those of a footpad or assassin . . .

Asari peered into the gloom of the street. The sky was cloudy, the light of the Hundred Moons obscured, and most of the town's lights had been doused hours ago, so visibility was very poor.

He thought he could see something, though—a red glow was moving closer.

It was *very* red—no torch or candle would make such a light. Perhaps a coal lantern might, or hot iron, though Asari could not imagine why anyone would be carrying a hot iron about the streets an hour after midnight.

Old tales began to stir in the back of his mind. Would an assassin have a use for hot iron?

Perhaps, Asari thought, the essence of wisdom would be invisibility. He retreated toward the mouth of an alley, trying to move as silently as he could; he scooped the pitiful few coins from the bowl and tucked them in a pocket, where they wouldn't rattle.

"Olnami!" called a voice from the direction of the light.

Asari froze.

Whoever was there must have heard him speak a moment before, and must have recognized the language; no one could have known his nationality otherwise. His rags were scarcely his people's traditional robes; they had largely been collected from Matuan sources.

Was there, perhaps, some other Olnami about? Or was this mysterious stranger simply exclaiming about something else, rather than calling to someone?

"Olnami, come here! I would speak with you!"

Asari hesitated. The words were in Olnami, rather than Domdur or Matuan.

The footsteps were coming closer—two sets of them, he realized—and the red glow was growing brighter, lighting the tiled walls in a hideously distorted parody of their true colors. A scent of something burning, something unpleasant, reached him.

Asari could still not see the source of the glow. "Who calls?" he asked, in Olnami.

A figure appeared, a black outline at the center of the red glow, but Asari could make out little of it; it seemed to be swathed in black smoke.

Another figure, behind the first, was clearer—it was definitely a man, though Asari could not see his face.

"I am Rebiri Nazakri, rightful hereditary warlord of the Olnami," the first figure said. "Who are you?"

Asari blinked.

As a child he had heard stories about the old days, about how the Nazakri had led the Olnami in the war against the Domdur conquerors—but weren't the Nazakri all long since dead? The Olnami had no warlords anymore. The Olnami were herdsmen or craftsmen or merchants or laborers, or beggars like himself, not warriors. For the most part the Imperial Army would not have them. They were not even welcome among the local guards.

"My name is Asari Asakari," he said warily. He peered at the mysterious arrival who called himself Rebiri Nazakri, and thought he could make out a man in a black robe, holding a staff—the red glow seemed to come from one end of the staff.

But there *was* smoke, or something like it, swirling about him—swirling, and not dissipating.

"The Asakari keep cattle in the southwestern hills," the apparition said. "What are you doing in *this* place?"

"Begging," Asari said, holding up his bowl. "I came here seeking a better life, and did not find it."

"The Domdur denied you?" the Nazakri asked.

It had been the Matuans, more than the Domdur, but the more Asari saw of this stranger the less natural he looked, and Asari did not care to argue with him. "Yes," he said.

"Would you avenge yourself upon them?"

It was obvious what answer the apparition wanted, and while Asari had no particular grudge against the Domdur, he had no objection to giving the desired response. Beggars learned to be agreeable—either that, or they starved.

"Yes," he said, "if I could."

"Join me, then. I have sworn to destroy the Domdur, in vengeance for all the wrongs they have done to our people, and I believe I have found the means to do so."

"What do you mean?" Asari asked uneasily.

The red glow suddenly faded, and darkness seemed to pour from the shadowy figure.

"I have found a way to use the powers of black magic," the Nazakri said. "Our own gods deserted us, and the Domdur gods cast us down in defeat, but there are other powers than those gods. There is a destiny guiding me. There are dark powers beneath the earth, and I have mastered them!"

The darkness seemed to wrap about Asari, an unnatural darkness that was thicker and more tangible than mere night, and he was suddenly cold, colder than he had ever been before in his life; then the darkness sucked the air from his lungs, and he was suffocating. Panic surged through him, and he suddenly knew that he was doomed, he would never see Bekra again, he would die here, alone and unloved. He dropped his bowl, and the sound of it striking the cobbles seemed to come from a great distance, as if echoing down a long tube. . . .

And then the unnatural darkness was gone, and only the ordinary gloom of the late-night streets remained.

Asari gasped, trying to recover himself.

When he could think clearly again, he saw that he was facing two men—the pair had approached while he was dazed.

One was a young man in traditional Olnami garb somewhat the worse for wear, a man of medium height, strongly built, carrying a large sack.

The other was an old man in a ragged black robe, carrying a staff with things at either end that Asari could not see clearly. One end glowed a dark red—that was what had lit the street moments before. The other end seethed with darkness, a blackness deeper than any night; Asari shuddered as he looked at it.

"What do you want of me?" Asari asked.

"I have spent my life in exile," the old man replied, "and know little of the modern world. I do not even know the name of this place. I need your knowledge of this city, and the others like it."

"This city?"

"Yes. What is it called?"

"This is Hao Tan," Asari said.

"Not Pai Shin?"

"No." Asari shook his head. "Pai Shin is the provincial capital of Matua, and much larger than this. This is just a market town."

"Ah. You know the way to Pai Shin, though?"

"I know Pai Shin," Asari agreed. "I lived there for a season." Had he been speaking Domdur he would have said "a few dozen triads," but in Olnami the older term came more naturally. He had not held so long a conversation as this in his mother tongue since he had left his parents' home, long ago.

"You could guide me there? And this Hao Tan—who rules it? Who represents the Domdur here? And where can he be found—and killed?"

Asari blinked, and then smiled.

This wizard clearly knew *nothing* of Matua. But he had real, powerful magic, and obviously intended to use it to assassinate the local prefect.

Black magic. A wizard with black magic. An Olnami wizard out to destroy the Domdur, a wizard who knew nothing *but* magic.

And he wanted Asari to help him.

If he couldn't find some way to make himself money off this, Asari told himself, he *deserved* to be a beggar!

W̲ai Ko looked at the angle of the sun's light on the painted wall and frowned. The Domdur prefect had never been *this* late for the day's business before!

"Perhaps he's ill," he said to the waiting aide. "Has he eaten yet today?"

"No, sir," the aide replied. "The servants say he has neither come to the refectory nor called for a tray."

That settled it. "Come, then," Wai Ko said. "We must check on him."

"Yes, sir," the aide said.

Together, the two men walked down the passageway, wooden soles tapping sharply on the polished wooden floor.

Wai Ko rapped on the gilded door and called, "Prefect? Are you well?"

When no reply came he opened the door and peered in.

Wai Ko gasped. "Gods, behold!" he said in his native Matuan. He flung the door wide, and the aide, too, gasped.

The light was too bright; oddly, that was the first thing that they noticed. Sunlight was pouring in through a gaping hole in the roof.

The red and gold walls of the prefect's bedchamber were spattered with a darker red-brown; scraps of the richly embroidered coverlet were strewn about on all sides, but the tapestries that had hung on the walls were gone.

The great golden statues that had stood on either side of the immense bed were gone, as well, along with the lacquer cabinets that had held the prefect's private stocks of gold and drugs.

The prefect and his concubine lay still in the great bed amid the scattered cushions and the tattered remains on the coverlet. Both of them were naked— and both of them were torn open from throat to crotch, gutted like fish.

The aide fainted, and fell heavily to the floor of the passage.

Wai Ko remained conscious and upright, and even managed to retain his breakfast, though it took a struggle.

When he had recovered from his initial shock, he exclaimed, "Who did this? How? Where were the guards? Why was nothing heard?"

He repeated these questions at length throughout the day, demanding answers from everyone in the prefect's palace.

The most important question, however, was never spoken aloud: What would the Domdur do about it?

The wagon arrived in Fadari Tu while Tebas Tudan was in the cave with his latest group of students, and the villagers argued cheerfully with the wagon's drivers about whether someone should be sent to fetch the magician out, or whether the wagoneers should go up into the cave themselves, or whether they should simply wait until Tebas Tudan appeared on his own.

Eventually a messenger was sent, and not long after Tebas Tudan came out to see what was going on. He brought his short staff, just in case, and upon emerging into sunlight began charging the crystals on either end.

"You're Tebas Tudan?" one of the wagonmen demanded.

"I am," the magician said.

"Then everything in the wagon is yours," the head driver said. "Where do you want it?"

Tebas Tudan looked curiously at the several large boxes and bundles in the wagon. "What *is* it?" he asked.

The driver shrugged. He reached down and fished around by his feet for a moment, then came up with a rolled parchment. "Here," he said.

Tebas Tudan accepted the parchment, unrolled it, and read, "Our payment, as promised. Our oath is fulfilled. Rebiri Nazakri and Aldassi Nazakri."

The words were in Domdur. The handwriting was terrible.

Tebas Tudan frowned, and clambered up into the wagon, where he partially unwrapped one of the bundles and found a fine Matuan tapestry. Another bundle contained a fortune in gold and silver. The two largest were golden statues, such as the Matuans used as spiritual guardians for the homes of the wealthy and powerful.

Tebas Tudan stared at those for a moment, then climbed down.

He was not sure just how he would deal with this, but he couldn't keep the teamsters waiting indefinitely while he thought it out. "In here," he said, leading the wagonmen to his house.

He stood by and watched as the wagon was unloaded, his frown deepening steadily.

He knew that the two Olnami could not have come by these things by honest means so quickly, not even with the magic he had taught them. They had stolen all this, almost certainly—and probably by using the New Magic.

The magic that he had taught them.

He should have realized this would happen, he told himself. Now he was partially responsible for whatever crimes the two committed. He would have to go to Ai Varach and explain to the garrison commander there just what had happened.

He would also probably have to return these things to their rightful owners—once he knew who those owners were. And assuming, of course, that the owners were still alive—which, he had to admit, seemed unlikely.

And this would have to be the end of his school here; he could not go on teaching the New Magic after seeing how easily it could be misused.

He sighed.

An hour later the now-empty wagon was on its way back down the mountain, each of the two drivers richer by a dozen pieces of silver from the stolen trove. It wasn't until the next morning that Tebas Tudan took his staff in both hands and lifted himself into the air, heading for Ai Varach.

CHAPTER 8

Lord Gornir leaned forward and frowned at the note in his hand.

"I don't like this," he said. "What under the Hundred Moons are those confounded Matuans doing?"

Lord Shoule, who had been slumped half dozing in his chair, looked up, startled. "What Matuans?" he asked.

The two men were seated in an antechamber near the base of the central tower of the Imperial Palace, in the middle of the Inner City of Seidabar—the heart of the Domdur Empire, the core of Domdur power over all the world. They were awaiting an audience with Prince Granzer, President of the Imperial Council, who was in the midst of a discussion with his mother-in-law, the Empress Beretris.

The Prince had said the discussion would take perhaps a quarter of an hour; the two noblemen, both members of the Imperial Council themselves, had now been cooling their heels for something more than two hours, and had long since studied every detail of the rich carpet, the brocade curtains, the rather faded tapestry on the north wall, and the view from the broad windows to the east. Neither was in a mood to speak to the other; they worked together well enough, but neither would call the other a friend, nor did either care to speculate aloud about what might be responsible for the delay.

As a result, they had resorted to simply sitting, waiting for the Prince to appear.

The boredom had been interrupted a few minutes before by the arrival of a temple messenger bearing a brief letter for Lord Gornir, Minister of the Provinces—a letter that had been marked "Urgent," and that Gornir was now holding.

"What Matuans?" Shoule repeated.

"The Matuans in Hao Tan," Gornir replied. "In Matua."

"Oh," Lord Shoule said, losing interest. "Never been there."

"Neither have I," Gornir said. "It's a town of no particular distinction, so far as I know; by all accounts it's just another collection of merchants and bureaucrats. Matua's full of places like it. But someone's murdered their prefect."

Shoule, who had meant not merely that he had never heard of the particular town but that he had never been to Matua, sat up.

"Murdered?" he said.

"So they claim. Murdered in his bed."

"Wait a moment, Gornir," Shoule said, gripping the arms of his chair, "was this a *Domdur* prefect, or a Matuan?"

"A Domdur," Gornir said. "Not Matuan, anyway—his name looks Karamador to me."

"Whatever." He waved the detail of the name away. Shoule, like most people, considered any government official not a native of the area governed to be a Domdur, regardless of actual ancestry; the gods had long made clear their disapproval of excessive concern with pure bloodlines, and even with the oracles silent the word "Domdur" still meant much more than a specific ethnic group. "A *Domdur* official was murdered in his bed? Not in a drunken brawl, or by a cutpurse in the street, but in his own home?"

"So it seems."

"He had no guards?"

"He had guards. There's been no trouble in Matua in years, but he had guards. The killer came in through the roof."

"The audacity!" Shoule sat back, shocked. "In the old days, no one would *dare* harm a Domdur official!"

Gornir did not need to ask what Shoule was talking about, and in fact there was some degree of truth in what he said—once upon a time they could simply have asked an oracle for the name and whereabouts of the assassin, and gotten it. Very few people were stupid or desperate enough to attack their rulers under such circumstances.

That had all ended more than seven years ago, though, when the oracles fell silent, once and for all.

Gornir felt a pang of envy for his predecessors—this post, Minister of the Provinces, must have been so much easier in his father's day. Almost *everything* of importance must have been easier in his father's day. Or most of his father's day, anyway; the last two years before the old man's death had reportedly been very bad indeed, simply by the contrast with what had gone before.

Of course, if the oracles had still been speaking five years before, Gornir thought, he himself might not even *be* Minister of the Provinces—the gods had chosen heirs on the basis of divinely determined merit, not just primogeniture. They might have stuck his younger brother, or one of his sisters, or a cousin, or even some total stranger, with the job.

All that was long gone, though, and now the Domdur had to muddle through as best they could without any supernatural guidance. Gornir continued silently rereading the note, making no further comment as Shoule continued to grumble aloud.

Gornir didn't like what he read. Matua had never seriously chafed under Domdur rule, and this prefect—Anoka Kahi by name—had never come to Gornir's attention before. There were supposed to be spies keeping track of any misbehavior by Domdur officials, or anything else that might stir up trouble, and the sort of aggravating actions that could have spurred someone to murder should have been reported.

Of course, the spies' report, if one existed, might not have made it all the way to Gornir; he could scarcely be expected to keep track of every single prefect, viceroy, or governor in the entire Empire, and one of his underlings might have decided that particular item wasn't worth passing along. Gornir told himself he would have to check on that.

The letter included a brief verbatim statement from one of the prefect's Matuan aides, however, and there was no hint there that Anoka had been disliked by his subordinates, or that anyone might have seen this coming.

"I tell you, there's trouble brewing," Shoule said, getting to his feet. "Now that we don't have direct daily contact with the gods, there are people out there who don't believe we still have divine favor. They're beginning to think they can do as they please, and treat the Domdur as if we were just ordinary people."

"We *are* just ordinary people now," Gornir muttered, not really listening.

The letter mentioned a concubine who had been killed as well—could that be the cause of this mess? Had she had a jealous lover, or a berserk father or brother who disapproved of how Anoka treated her?

The traditional method for disposing of rivals in Matua was poison, not breaking in the roof and cutting them apart while they slept, but perhaps the concubine's family was not traditional.

And then there was a mention of gold and other precious things that had been taken, though the letter was appallingly vague about the quantity and value of these items—had the killer snatched a few things as mementos, or had this simply been the work of a spectacularly bold gang of thieves? Matua certainly had its share of thieves—not as many as Olnamia, where theft was considered an art, but certainly more than, say, Sautala, or Daona. . . .

"We are the chosen of the gods!" Shoule shouted, startling Gornir.

"We used to be," Gornir said, looking up from the note. "Now we're just the people running things, and I wish they'd run more smoothly. . . ."

The sound of a door latch interrupted him; he glanced over and saw that Prince Granzer was at last joining them. Quickly he folded the letter and tucked it out of sight in his blouse.

"Your Highness," Gornir said, rising.

"My lords," Granzer said, nodding an acknowledgment.

"And how is Her Imperial Majesty faring today?" Gornir inquired politely.

"Her Imperial Majesty is an arthritic, dyspeptic old woman who can't abide her children's squabbles, but she's otherwise well enough," Granzer replied dourly. "At least she kept her breakfast down today."

Gornir frowned, not at Granzer's disrespect—he was accustomed to that, and after all, the Prince's position entitled him to a certain familiarity—but at the reminder of the chronic digestive difficulties the Empress had developed in the past year or so. Her health was important; the Empire was not prepared should anything happen to Beretris. She had been on the throne for almost half a century, and the mechanisms for the installation of a new sovereign were rusty—or gone altogether, since the oracles were no longer capable of warning of an impending death, or affirming the choice of an heir.

"And what brings the two of you to see me?" Granzer asked, rubbing wearily at his temple.

"Famine, Your Highness," Gornir said quickly, before Shoule could speak. "Crops have failed on the outer archipelago of the Veruet Isles, a plague has wiped out thousands of sheep, and the fishing has been poor. Food reserves were low to begin with. . . ."

Granzer sighed. "*Why* were reserves low?" he interrupted. "Haven't we warned them often enough that we can't predict the weather anymore?"

Gornir shrugged apologetically. "Grain prices in the Isles were high last year, and the farmers sold their grain. Fish and mutton don't keep."

"If they made so much money selling grain, can't they buy it back?" Granzer asked.

"Prices are even higher this year," Gornir explained.

"So they've called on the Empire to save them from their misfortune, and of course we shall." Granzer nodded. "But why is this *my* concern, rather than something to be handled at a lower level?"

"Because I don't have the resources to supply the shortfall on my own," Gornir replied. "With Lord Dabos's assistance, I have collected the food the islanders need—in fact, it's waiting on the docks at Forsten and Rishna Gabidéll.

But I must call on others to transport it, and neither Lady Mirashan nor Lord Orbalir is willing to commit to doing so. I assume you would prefer not to ravage the Imperial Treasury by simply purchasing space on privately owned vessels."

Granzer considered that. "Mirashan . . . how would she do it?" he asked. "She doesn't have anything that could make the trip to Veruet."

Gornir had the explanation ready; Lady Mirashan was Minister of Trade, but that gave her control of the ports, not the ships themselves. The fat little flat-bottomed harbor craft under her jurisdiction could hardly be expected to cross the stormy Northern Seas. "She could, as a docking fee, require every merchant ship bound for Veruet to transport grain as ballast, and to deliver it to the governor at Mabor for distribution," he said.

Granzer nodded. "Whereas Orbalir could simply send the fleet," he said. Lord Orbalir was Commissioner of the Imperial Fleet, responsible for every warship afloat.

"Exactly, Your Highness."

"And how severe *is* this famine?"

Lord Gornir launched into a recitation of facts and figures.

Half an hour later the matter was settled—due to the severity of the shortage the islanders might prove unruly, and for that matter merchants might balk at hauling freight unpaid; therefore Lord Orbalir's fleet was called for, so that the navy's trained warriors could maintain order while the grain was distributed.

"Was there anything else, my lord?" Granzer asked.

Gornir hesitated; one hand touched his blouse where the letter from the temple's magicians, bearing word of the situation in Matua, waited.

A simple murder, however unexpected, hardly called for the personal attention of the President of the Imperial Council. And the Prince looked exhausted.

"Not today, Your Highness," Gornir said with a bow.

"Good," Granzer said. He turned to Lord Shoule. "You've been very patient, my lord," he said. "What can I do for you?"

Lord Shoule launched into another of his diatribes about the need to radically restructure the government, removing the Great Temple and its priests from authority and rearranging the Imperial Council to better suit present-day realities.

Lord Gornir did not stay to listen; he slipped away, anxious to relay the Prince's orders to Lord Orbalir, and then to go to the Great Temple to send a message back to Pai Shin, authorizing the governor of Matua to appoint a new prefect. Another message would go directly to Hao Tan, exhorting the surviving officials there to make every effort to apprehend the murderer and ensure that there was no repetition of the crime.

It wasn't really an important matter, but it had to be dealt with.

CHAPTER 9

The confounded iron did not want to bend properly. Bardetta wanted a perfect circle for her new chandelier, and Malledd could not get the curve right. He glowered at the uncooperative metal he held in the heavy tongs, then glanced at the banked fires of the forge. Did he need to soften the iron more, perhaps?

No, he couldn't see how that would matter. He suspected there was some simple trick to this that he was missing, something his father could explain in a few moments, but Hmar wasn't around to ask; he'd gone up to the minehead at Yildau to haggle for a better price on the ores they used, and wouldn't be back for at least another two days.

If Bardetta had wanted it smaller Malledd could have shaped it around a cartwheel, but she wanted a great huge thing, big as a millwheel. . . .

A millwheel. Was there any way he could get a millwheel? Malledd glanced up through the open side of the smithy in the direction of Biekedau; there were grist mills there, two or three of them. One might have an old stone, though transportation would be . . .

Then he blinked in surprise, leaving the thought unfinished. Someone was coming down the lane from the square—someone wearing a white robe.

At first he thought it might be Onnell, dressed up as a joke, but he dismissed the notion quickly—this was a stranger, his walk very different from Onnell's familiar swagger.

No one in Grozerodz ordinarily dressed like that, and while Malledd thought that he and Hmar were widely known to be proficient at their trade, nobody from Biekedau or Duvrenarodz would bother coming to Grozerodz for smithing work; they had their own smiths.

Travelers did turn up at the forge occasionally, with a thrown horseshoe or a broken axle fitting or the like, but what sort of traveler would wear something as utterly impractical as an ankle-length white robe?

As the stranger drew nearer Malledd answered his own unspoken question. There was only one answer, the obvious one. "A priest," he said aloud. *That* was who would go traveling in a white robe.

"Ho there!" the priest called when he saw Malledd looking at him. He waved a greeting.

Malledd put down his hammer and tongs, leaving the unfinished metal band draped across the anvil, and wiped his hands on his leather apron. He peered out of the smoke-blackened gloom of the smithy into the sunlight.

The priest looked harmless enough; he was an old man, older than Hmar, his hair and beard streaked with gray, but still broad in the shoulders and standing straight and tall—as tall as Malledd's own shoulder, perhaps. He appeared unarmed, but Malledd thought almost anything might be hidden in those ridiculous oversized sleeves.

The priest was strolling along briskly, paying no attention to the iron-fenced graveyard or the fading, grassy meadows, or the bright colors of the autumn leaves. He passed the firebreak without hesitation, and Malledd met him at the door of the smithy.

He had never really spoken to a priest. He had seen them many times, of course—officiating at festivals, or conducting the annual graveyard ceremony that was supposed to assure the souls of the dead safe passage to the afterlife and guard their bodies against defilement. And the priests at the temple in Biekedau had conducted the wedding ceremony when Malledd had married Anva, a ceremony where Baranmel's nonappearance had been the subject of some uneasy jests among the villagers of Grozerodz. Priests also oversaw the shrine of Dremeger when Malledd made his annual pilgrimage there, and one could hardly reach the shrine without seeing half a dozen assorted priests scattered around the temple.

But Malledd had never had any reason to talk to a priest outside the temple, or discuss anything other than ritual with one. Furthermore, after having his childhood ruined by the pronouncement of a priest, Malledd was not particularly eager to have anything further to do with them. The wedding and the annual pilgrimage were necessities, and Malledd had never hesitated where necessities were involved, but he had no desire to go beyond necessities in his dealings with priests.

"Can I help you?" he asked, looking down—though not so far as usual—at the priest.

The priest smiled up at him. "Perhaps you can, my friend. Now, would you be the same smith who was here twenty years ago? You look too young."

Malledd's eyes narrowed. "Would you be the same priest who was here twenty years ago?"

The priest's smile widened to a grin, but he shook his head. "No, no," he said cheerfully. "That was Mezizar. I know him, but my name is Vadeviya. You know about Mezizar's visit, though?"

"The whole *village* knows about that visit!" Malledd growled.

The anger in his voice penetrated, and the priest's smile vanished. "You don't sound pleased about it," he said, cocking his head curiously to one side.

"What do you want here, priest?" Malledd asked wearily. Half a dozen sentences had been exchanged, and already he was tired of the man.

"I'm looking for the child who was born that day, the one Mezizar found," Vadeviya replied. The lighthearted tone was gone; he spoke quite seriously.

"Why?" Malledd demanded.

"I wish to talk to him."

That seemed obvious. Malledd considered his options. He doubted the priest would give up if he said he was not the right man, and anyone in town would direct the priest back here, so he might as well get it over with.

"You *are* talking to him," Malledd said.

"Ah," the priest said. He studied Malledd's face silently and intently.

Probably looking for the long-vanished birthmark, Malledd realized angrily. "You said talk, not stare. What did you want to talk to me about?" he demanded.

Vadeviya didn't answer directly; instead he asked, "Could we sit down? I've walked a long way."

Malledd frowned again, but he stepped aside, allowing the priest into the smithy, and gestured to an iron bench against one wall, a bench that Hmar had made years ago as a showpiece. The priest settled onto it with a grateful sigh, but Malledd remained standing.

Some smithies, he had heard, served as gathering places for the locals, at least in winter—even with the shutters open, the forge was too hot for comfort in the summer. The smithy Malledd and Hmar shared, however, did not welcome visitors; Malledd and his father preferred to keep their business and their social lives separate. As a result of this attitude there were no good seats other than the ornate bench and the well-worn stool by the bellows, and most visitors hesitated to use either of those.

Vadeviya did not hesitate. When the priest was comfortable he ran a hand along the bench's elaborate scrollwork, then looked up. "Lovely work—yours?"

"My father's," Malledd replied. "But you didn't come here to talk about ironmongery."

"No, I didn't," Vadeviya agreed. "You've read Dolkout's letter?"

Malledd resisted the temptation to ask which letter the priest meant. He nodded.

"Then you know that you are the gods' chosen champion, the defender of the Domdur Empire."

"I know that someone signing himself Dolkout said so," Malledd replied.

"Oh, it was Dolkout, all right," Vadeviya said cheerfully. "I happened to be the messenger the oracles sent to fetch the high priest, and I remember it well. A chance to notify the new champion comes no more than once in a lifetime, after all, and even then to only a single temple in all the world, so it was quite an event for those of us who knew about it. Dolkout didn't announce it widely, either, so we were a select few. He kept the privilege of writing that note entirely to himself, wrote it with his own hand—his two secretaries were furious, as they knew it meant something important was happening, and they were excluded.

And all the rest of us who had heard the news were envious of Mezizar, since he would be the first to see you."

"I doubt I looked like anything very special; one newborn is much like another, they say." Malledd watched the priest suspiciously. This talk of how extraordinary an event his birth had been made him nervous. He had not spoken openly of his supposed divine selection for years.

"Most don't have Ba'el's clawmark across their faces," the priest said.

Malledd decided not to pursue that; instead he asked, "So Dolkout really was the high priest?"

"Oh, yes, of course he was!" Vadeviya looked shocked. "A fine man. Dead for seven . . . no, eight years now."

"And you claim that everything he wrote in that letter was true?"

Vadeviya blinked at him in surprise. "Did you doubt it?"

"I still do, priest."

"But don't!" The old man's expression was suddenly intent. "You *are* the one and only divinely appointed defender of the Empire."

"And no other temple sent out similar notices?" Malledd asked. "There isn't some fine strong lad in High Karamador or the Veruet Isles who was told the same thing?"

"Certainly not!" Vadeviya folded his arms across his chest and jerked his bearded chin up. "It was a great honor that the gods should choose someone within my temple's jurisdiction; we few who knew about it were all surprised and pleased."

"Ah, yes, a great honor," Malledd said, nodding. "And yet, in almost twenty years no one from the Biekedau temple ever before bothered to come take a look at me." He made no attempt to conceal his bitterness. "The letter said that every priest in the Empire is required to render me whatever aid I might need, but none of those priests ever came to see whether I might have some request to make. I don't suppose that that could possibly be why *you* are here?"

"Not exactly," Vadeviya admitted, unfolding his arms, "though in fact, since you remind me of my duty, I hereby place myself at your service." He bowed his head.

"The letter also mentioned that the oracles in particular are to help me," Malledd growled.

"And there *are* no oracles now," Vadeviya said. "Yes, I know. You have no idea of the consternation the oracles' silence has caused my order."

Malledd snorted. "I'd suppose it probably cut the temple's income considerably," he said. The high fees oracles had charged for consultations were still legendary.

Vadeviya shrugged. "Some," he said, "but we aren't suffering from *that*. It's not knowing whether we're really doing the gods' will that hampers us. Before we could simply *ask* if there was any doubt, but now there's constant bickering about every least little detail—and about major issues, as well. There are some people who maintain that if the gods no longer need oracles, they no longer need any priests at all—and we can't prove that's wrong. I wouldn't ordinarily talk of such things to an outsider, but you, sir—you haven't told me your name—are a very special case."

"My name is Malledd."

Vadeviya nodded. "A good name. It will look well in the records. Faial, Dunnon, Mannabi, Malledd."

"And outside Grozerodz and the temple at Biekedau, no one will ever hear of me any more than they've heard of Dunnon or Mannabi," Malledd said.

"Perhaps," Vadeviya said, sitting back and folding his arms again. "If the peace continues. Or if you wish it. And that, Malledd, brings me to why I have come."

"And about time," Malledd growled. "Get on with it."

"There are rumors," Vadeviya said, leaning forward, elbows on his knees. He seemed to be incapable of sitting still. "From the east, from Govya and Olnamia and so on. For more than a year now we've had reports of murders, banditry, assassinations—bureaucrats found strangled or dismembered in their beds, shrines desecrated, and so on. Do you know anything about any of that?" He looked up hopefully.

Malledd glowered. He picked up his hammer and hefted it. "I'm a blacksmith," he said. "How would I know anything about what's happening in Govya or Olnamia?"

"You are also the chosen of the gods," Vadeviya replied calmly. "We'd thought that perhaps they had seen fit to inform you of these events."

"Well, they haven't," Malledd said bitterly. "Nobody's sent any oracles here. No god has spoken from the bellows or written me messages in the coals or sent visions down from the moons. Baranmel did not dance at our wedding, let alone tell me any secrets there. Maybe *you* think I've been touched by the gods, but *I* haven't seen any sign of it."

"No odd dreams, perhaps? Prince Greldar used to say he had prophetic dreams."

"Prince Greldar?" Malledd shouted. "In the name of the gods, Greldar was a *prince*, not a smith! And he's been dead for hundreds of years!"

"And you have his old job," Vadeviya retorted, shouting back.

"Well, I haven't got his dreams! I don't know anything about Govya or Olnamia; I probably couldn't even find them on a map. Is *that* what you came to ask me?"

Vadeviya shook his head. "Not really," he said.

"What, then?"

"These rumors from the east have some of us very concerned," Vadeviya explained. "Strange things have been happening during your lifetime, Malledd, things that have us wondering what the gods are up to. The oracles have fallen silent, and the New Magic has been discovered—and now, from almost the same part of the world as Vrai Burrai and the first New Magicians, there are these stories of unrest. There are reports of black magic involved in some of these troubles, Malledd. Some people say it's the New Magic, fallen into the wrong hands, or that the New Magic has unleashed forces we don't understand—and the Empress has established the Imperial College of the New Magic right in Seidabar."

Malledd frowned.

"We don't know if the stories of black magic are true," Vadeviya continued, rising to his feet and beginning to pace hither and yon. "And even if they are we don't know whether there's a connection to the New Magic, but whether there is or not, the stories are worrisome. So far, it's only rumors and a few dead or frightened officials and merchants, but if it should become more than that, if there's really something mysterious that could strike even in Seidabar, then it might threaten the Empire itself." He stopped pacing and pointed a finger at Malledd's face. "If it should come to that, Malledd of Grozerodz, will you fight for the Empire?"

Malledd stared down at the priest silently for a long moment, frowning. He wanted to reply, "Of course not! It's not my problem. I'm no champion, I'm a blacksmith." Then, instead, he thought he might answer, "Of course; I'm a loyal subject and of Domdur blood." After all, even if this talk of being the gods' champion was nonsense, he had a duty to his people, didn't he?

But he was a blacksmith, not a soldier. He had a home and a family. He almost shuddered at the thought of leaving Anva and Neyil—he hadn't spent a night anywhere but his own bed, with Anva beside him, since their wedding, and he never wanted to. And he had plenty of other friends and family in Grozerodz and the surrounding area—his parents, his uncle Sparrak, his sisters and their husbands, Onnell and Bousian and the other men he drank with at Bardetta's sometimes.

But he was no coward, and there were things a man had to be ready to do for his people and his gods.

Torn between those two extremes, he almost said, "I don't know." He didn't say it aloud, though; he wasn't satisfied with that. The priest might have accepted it, but Malledd wouldn't accept it of himself.

What he did finally say was, "That would depend."

Vadeviya lowered his finger and stared up at Malledd. He nodded thoughtfully. "On what?" he asked.

"On the nature of the threat. On what was expected of me. On what it would mean for Anva and little Neyil."

"Who are they?"

Malledd was irrationally angry at the priest for not already knowing. "My wife and son," he said. "And there might be another child coming, too—we aren't sure yet. I'm not going to go running off to Govya to see if some nasty rumor is true, not when my family needs me."

"But if the enemy is real?"

"It would still depend. The Empire has armies and a navy, it has all you priests and your magic, it has the Imperial College of the New Magic that you just spoke of—what would it need with a blacksmith?"

"You are the gods' champion," Vadeviya pointed out.

"So you say," Malledd growled.

"It's true."

Malledd turned away and tossed the hammer on a handy shelf. "Well, even if it is, maybe the Domdur don't *need* a champion anymore."

"And maybe they will again someday," Vadeviya said. "If that day comes, and all that stands between a deadly foe and the gates of Seidabar is your strong right arm, will you be there?"

Malledd didn't look at the priest as he said, "If I see the need—if *I* see the need, not some priest or general—then I'll do my best."

"And do you think you'll know when you're needed? Do you not trust, say, the Archpriest to call upon you only when necessary? Or the Empress?"

Malledd hesitated, knowing he was about to say something that the priest would probably not want to hear, something that a good many people would find offensive.

It was the truth, though. "No, I don't trust them," he said. "What do I know of your Archpriest, or even of the Empress, if it comes to that? The gods chose Beretris to rule the world, but I don't know *why* they did, any more than I know why they chose me, and I won't trust her to know what's right for me." He turned back to face Vadeviya. "But if an army is at Seidabar's gates, I think the news would reach me even here in Grozerodz, would it not?"

"It should, certainly," the priest admitted.

"That's good enough, then. If I'm needed, the gods can find a way to let me know, I'm sure. I don't want a bunch of courtiers and imperial bureaucrats calling on me because some bandit's killed a magistrate somewhere; better they never know that the gods still choose champions. Assuming, of course, that the gods truly still do."

"The gods chose you," Vadeviya said, "but the courtiers in Seidabar don't know you exist. Only a handful of priests know—four of us who yet live in

Biekedau, and perhaps the current Archpriest, I'm not sure. But no one else was told. Not even our present high priest knows."

"*Good*," Malledd said emphatically. "Don't tell him." He jabbed a finger at Vadeviya. "Don't tell *anyone*—and you can tell your fellow priests that, too. I don't want anyone who doesn't already know I'm supposed to be the champion to find out. Bad enough that everyone in Grozerodz knows, without all the world finding out. If I'm needed and I don't find out for myself, one of you four priests can come tell me about it."

"Then if we learn that an enemy seriously threatens the Empire itself, you'll come?"

"Of course," Malledd said. "But it won't come to that. All's been peace beneath the Hundred Moons since before my grandfather's grandfather was born."

Vadeviya nodded again, and slapped Malledd on the shoulder. "Well, let's hope you're right, lad!" He turned away. "I'll be going, then," he said. "If you ever wish to talk to someone about your duties as the champion, you come see me in Biekedau—just ask for me at the temple. Vadeviya. My best to your wife and son, and my blessing upon you."

Malledd blinked in surprise. "You're leaving?" he asked.

Vadeviya nodded. "I have my answer," he said.

"But . . . you walked ten miles to ask me that?"

"And to get a look at you. You're a good, strong young man, Malledd. The oracles said you would be more than that, if the need arose, and I believe them, but I wanted to see you, and hear your words. I've done that, and it's a long walk home if I want to be back at the temple by nightfall."

He was already shuffling out the doorway by the time he finished this speech.

Malledd hesitated, but then simply stood and watched the priest go.

He didn't like it.

The priest said he really was the gods' chosen champion, and that there were no others. And he might be needed as the defender of the Empire.

Nonsense, he told himself. He was a blacksmith with a wife and a baby and another baby on the way. Surely the gods could fight their own battles. They didn't need an ordinary smith blundering about.

He watched the priest walk up the lane, past the graveyard with its flower-locked gate. Then, when the priest was out of sight, Malledd turned back to the forge and picked up the hammer and tongs.

CHAPTER 10

Asari blanched as Rebiri Nazakri growled. He backed against the rough brick of the alleyway wall, away from his master's anger.

"It uses too much energy fighting through all these guards, or blasting in through the roof," the wizard said. "I spend all my time rushing to and from the caves! Is there no other way to get at these stinking Domdur bureaucrats?"

"None that I know of, Master," Asari said.

"I have only just returned from the mountains, and if I have to blast my way through the soldiers I'll need to return there tomorrow!"

Asari stammered, unsure what he was trying to say.

He was terrified of the old man. The black magic of that double-ended staff was foul, dangerous stuff; Asari had seen it in action, and just being near it was uncomfortable. How Rebiri could hold it and use it was beyond Asari's comprehension.

"Is there no other way to restore the staff's power?" Asari asked. "Your son's staff . . ."

"My son's staff uses sunlight," Rebiri said, interrupting, "and is weak and ineffectual in consequence. I draw on the dark powers of the earth, and those can be found only in the deep caves."

"Are you sure there are no caves nearer than Govya that might serve? What of the crypts beneath the governor's palace?"

"And how am I to enter those crypts?"

Asari had no ready answer for that. He turned and peered around the corner at the plaza outside the city's government offices.

At least a dozen heavily armed, heavily armored soldiers were patrolling the plaza. The Domdur had not been so cautious when Asari Asakari had first led Rebiri Nazakri and his son to Pai Shin, three years before, only to find the governor of Matua too well guarded to kill. They had returned here to Pai Shin half a dozen times since, each time with plans to deal with the Domdur defenses—and each time they had found the defenses strengthened, and had gone elsewhere.

For three years they had roamed across Matua and Olnami and back and forth to and through the Govya Mountains, three years of murders, sabotage, and general harassment of the Domdur and their puppets among the Matuans and other subject peoples.

Never Olnami, though. The Nazakri did not harm Olnami, not even those who worked willingly in the Domdur provincial governments. Instead, Rebiri and Aldassi tried to recruit any Olnami they encountered.

So far, only a few had joined the Nazakri campaign of terror—a campaign that had been frequently interrupted by the need to return to the mountains to restore the wizard's dark magic. Those interruptions had made it hard to build any sort of ongoing structure or develop any real momentum in their rebellion.

"This is not enough," Rebiri said. "These assassinations are nothing more than pinpricks to the Domdur Empire. We haven't done any real damage. We haven't struck high enough. I need an *army*."

"You have threescore men," Asari reminded him. "If Aldassi led them here, even with the new walls and the increased patrols we could force our way in without depleting your staff's power."

"We might reach the governor, yes—but threescore men against the entire world, Asari? What could threescore men do against a city—any city, let alone a fortress like Seidabar? I want to destroy Beretris and all her kind!" He shook his head, and the red-glowing end of his staff crackled. "I need more, more men, more power . . ."

"Could you train others to use black magic, perhaps?"

"Perhaps—but could I trust them, if I did?"

"You could trust *me*," Asari said. "You could trust Aldassi."

"I could trust Aldassi, yes—but he's used too much of the bright magic; the dark powers won't obey him. As for you—*could* I trust you?" He stared penetratingly at Asari.

Asari hesitated. To anyone else he would have said something reassuring, whether it was true or not, but to Rebiri . . .

He respected and feared Rebiri, and he knew that Rebiri would prefer the truth to a lie—especially on a question of trust. "I don't know," Asari admitted. Eager to change the subject, he looked back at the plaza, and as he did an idea struck him.

"Suppose," he said, "you were to kill one of those guards—just one. And then we'd leave. And tomorrow night we'd come back and kill another, and the next night another, and so on, no matter how many men they posted. In time, the soldiers would grow frightened and rebel against their masters, and then you'd *have* your army!"

Rebiri considered that, stroking his beard thoughtfully. Asari had seen him do that often. The wizard had once said that he was not so much thinking when he did this as trying to feel whether or not a proposed course of action suited his destiny.

The Nazakri spoke often of this supposed destiny, this fate that guided him; Asari suspected that it was one thing that kept potential recruits from joining.

Everyone knew that destiny favored the Domdur, and only madmen thought otherwise. For most people the ten years of oracular silence had not yet changed this belief.

"No," Rebiri said at last, "I would not have *my* army. I'd have an unleashed mob that I could not control. And it would take longer than I like. But it's an interesting notion, very interesting."

"You could make it clear that it's something horrible happening," Asari suggested. "Then it wouldn't take as long. For example, what if you made the dead soldier walk out into the middle of the plaza and then collapse at his comrades' feet?"

Rebiri glanced out at the plaza, and something seemed to stir in him. "*Very* interesting," he replied. He looked up at the sky, where a large red moon shone directly down on him, then back out at the plaza. For a moment he gazed at the guards, thinking; then he apparently reached his conclusion, satisfied with whatever he had discerned about his destiny. "Come on!" he said.

Asari knew better than to ask where they were going; instead he followed silently as the old man led the way through the maze of alleys. Flickers of lamplight from half-shuttered windows drew yellow daggers across the brown bricks and black wood of the city, and smoke curled lazily across the score of multicolored moons overhead; the smells of incense and ordure twined about them as they skulked and scurried.

For someone who had lived most of his life as a lone exile in the mountains, Rebiri Nazakri had done an amazingly good job of learning his way through the back streets of Pai Shin. It was mere moments later that Rebiri and Asari were climbing over the blackened stone wall that blocked the end of the alley the plaza guards used as their latrine. That was, Asari realized, about the only place they could catch one of the guards alone.

They stopped at the top of the wall and perched there in the dark. A broad overhanging roof cut off most of the moonlight, and no windows opened here—that was presumably one reason the guards were permitted to use it as they did; no one would see or smell the result.

Rebiri Nazakri wrapped the skirt of his robe around the red end of his staff, hiding its glow. All they had to do now was wait.

Sure enough, perhaps twenty minutes later, as they crouched uncomfortably atop the wall, the heavy footsteps of an armored soldier approached. Asari tried to hold himself motionless, to silence his breath and heartbeat.

The Nazakri did not bother with such precautions; instead he pulled out his staff, letting the red glow spill down. The soldier looked up, startled, just as the darkness surged forth from the black end of the staff.

The blackness was like a physical thing. It wrapped itself around the approaching guardsman, yanking him forward.

"Kill him," Rebiri hissed from the side of his mouth.

Asari hesitated, then glanced at the old man's face, lit by the red glow of the staff. When he saw the wizard's expression his hesitation vanished; he leaped down from the wall, ignoring the splash when he landed and the latrine stench, and ran forward, drawing his knife.

The darkness had formed a sort of cocoon around the soldier; he was struggling, but unable to move more than a few inches. It was a simple matter for Asari to reach up with his dagger, slip the blade between breastplate and backplate, and ram it home. He sawed the knife back and forth as blood spilled out, running down across the armor and the dagger's hilt, black against black in the unnatural crimson light from the staff.

Asari felt the man convulse, then go limp, as the dagger found his heart.

Asari yanked the blade out, wiped it off with a rag from his pocket, and stepped back as the darkness released the dead soldier and let him slump to the ground.

By the time Asari had sheathed his blade Rebiri had descended from the wall to stand beside him, looking down at the corpse.

"Make him walk, you said," the wizard said.

"Yes," Asari said. "Can you do that?"

"I don't know," Rebiri admitted, "but I'll find out." He hefted his staff, looked at the two ends, then pressed the black end to the dead man's chest.

The corpse stirred, as if startled. Rebiri lifted the staff.

Asari had expected the dead man to go limp again when the staff was removed, but he did not; instead, he sat up, as if he were still alive.

That clearly surprised Rebiri, as well; he swung his staff away and stared at the corpse.

"At last!" the dead man said, in harsh Matuan.

The two Olnami both stepped back involuntarily. Asari could feel the hairs on the back of his neck standing on end at the sight of this hideously unnatural phenomenon. He had been living with black magic off and on for three years now, but *this* was new—and terrifying.

Rebiri lifted his staff as he backed away, holding the red end foremost—the red end that held mystical fire commingled with darkness, the destroying end.

"Who speaks?" Rebiri demanded.

The dead man turned his head to look at them, revealing dead eyes that seemed to gleam a dull red. "I have no name," the corpse said.

"You aren't the man we just slew?" Asari asked.

"No," the thing said, speaking slowly and thoughtfully. "I have his form and his memories, but I know I am not he."

"Nor are you anything I intended my magic to do," Rebiri said. "What *are* you?"

"I am the darkness beneath the earth, the darkness that is not the mere absence of light, but its opposite," the corpse replied. "I am a creature of ancient legend, the scourge of the night and the sworn enemy of the Domdur gods. The Domdur of old called my kind nightwalkers."

Asari and Rebiri looked at one another; both of them had heard the old stories of nightwalkers, undead beings that defied the gods and roamed the countryside doing evil.

"But there are no more nightwalkers," Asari said uncertainly.

"The gods cast us down into the earth," the corpse agreed, speaking as much to itself as to the two Olnami. "We were trapped there for centuries, bound in the stone and clay one with another, our identities lost in the darkness, all of us unable to think, or to move with any purpose."

"How do you come here, then?" Rebiri asked.

"You brought me," the nightwalker answered, turning to stare into his face with those dead eyes. "You sucked me from the depths of the earth into that crystal you carry and brought me to this place, where you sent me into this body."

Rebiri stared at the black end of his staff. "Did I? Do I have other nightwalker spirits here, then?"

The nightwalker laughed horribly. "That is *all* you have, old man. All that darkness you draw upon is my people's essence."

Rebiri looked at the nightwalker, then back at his black crystal. He raised the staff angrily, and Asari wondered if he intended to blast the nightwalker, or to smash the crystal against the pavement and shatter it. "All I have done I have done with your kind? This darkness has minds and voices in it? Then why, in the years I have wielded it, has it never spoken to me before?"

"Because our consciousness was destroyed, long ago," the nightwalker replied. "We were torn from ourselves and made to forget, and we have all existed in endless dreams . . . until you put me in this body, and the lingering memories, the heart and brain, reminded me what life was and restored me to myself. Never before have you let one of us touch a corpse."

For a moment the three of them remained silent, the two Olnami standing, the nightwalker sitting, each contemplating the others. Asari struggled to absorb what the dead man had said; he glanced at Rebiri's face to see how the old man was taking it, and didn't like what he saw there. The old man's face was alight with the obsessed look he wore whenever he felt his supposed destiny most strongly.

Then the nightwalker began to get to its feet.

"Now what?" Asari asked, backing away. "Are you going to kill us?"

"Should I?" the nightwalker asked calmly. "Do you mean me harm?"

"No," Rebiri said quickly, stepping forward. "No, not at all. In fact—would you be interested in a bargain, dark spirit?"

Asari cringed. Nothing good could come of bargaining with a thing like this.

"What sort of bargain?" the nightwalker asked.

"You say the gods cast you down, the gods of the Domdur," Rebiri said, and his voice had the crazed quality that Asari had heard several times before—each time before Rebiri's destiny led him to do something reckless or simply insane in his perpetual war against the Domdur.

"Would you have vengeance, nightwalker?" Rebiri shouted. "And you say I have your compatriots trapped—would you have them freed? Would you have the others still confined in the earth brought out and given form?"

The nightwalker studied the wizard with interest; Asari stared at him in shock. One of these horrors was unsettling enough; was Rebiri really planning to unleash more?

"All this would please me," the nightwalker said.

"Swear to serve me, and you shall have it!" the Nazakri cried.

"Serve you? Forever? I think not. . . ." The nightwalker took a step forward.

"Not forever, then!" Rebiri shouted. "Only until Seidabar falls!"

"Master," Asari said, "think what you're doing. . . ."

"I *am* thinking, Asari," Rebiri replied. "I am giving myself an army! Fate is with us! Can even the Domdur defeat an army of the undead? Each of their soldiers who falls will join my army, as this one has—we'll be unbeatable!"

"But can you *trust* them?"

"Until Seidabar falls," the nightwalker said. "I will swear to that, and I will keep such an oath."

Asari glanced uneasily at the undead creature, but the words had to be said. "But, Master, nightwalkers are evil. . . ."

"Do you think I care?" Rebiri demanded, and the nightwalker smiled in response.

"They cannot move by day, the legends say. . . ."

Rebiri glanced at the animated corpse.

"The legends are correct," the nightwalker admitted. "The gods' sunlight forces us down into mindlessness."

Rebiri frowned, but quickly devised a solution. "We will raise an army to guard them by day," he said. "When the rest of the Olnami and the other conquered people see what we have fighting for us, they'll flock to our banners—we have something more to offer now than vague promises! And until we are ready to march on Seidabar, these nightwalkers will serve as our assassins—no more will I need to blast my way in. The guards will flee in terror!"

"And if they do not," the nightwalker said calmly, "we will kill them."

Asari looked from nightwalker to wizard, wizard to nightwalker, and knew he would not be able to prevent this horror from happening.

Worse, he realized, was that he was inextricably caught up in this unholy agreement. He looked from Rebiri to the reanimated soldier, and could not tell which of the two looked less human.

CHAPTER II

Lord Duzon flicked an invisible bit of dust from his velvet sleeve, then settled into an elegant and comfortable slouch as he watched the proceedings from his place at the back of the council chamber. His left hand held his broad-brimmed black hat artfully draped on one hip, the plume curling suggestively around his thigh.

A little Matuan stood nervously before the Imperial Council at the center of the half ring of the Council's table, fumbling with his own ugly dyed-straw hat and throwing frequent glances at his patron, Lord Gornir, rather than meeting the gaze of Prince Granzer, the President of the Council. Duzon smiled ironically to himself; the Matuan was probably uncomfortably aware that Granzer was not only President, but also, not coincidentally, husband and consort to Princess Darisei, eldest child of Her Imperial Majesty Beretris.

Prince Granzer's seat was in full sunlight, while most of the Council sat in shadow; that added to the impression that he was something more than a mere mortal. Duzon supposed that the council chamber's designers had done that intentionally, trying to emphasize the President's importance. Duzon still suspected that Granzer's family connections were at least as much the cause of the Matuan's nervousness as facing the Council. Most people, Matuan or Domdur or otherwise, seemed to be superstitious about the imperial family and terrified of dealing with its members, as if any one of them might use their supposed divine favor to call the wrath of the gods down on those presumptuous enough to address their betters.

That was foolish, though; it was the sixteen members of the Imperial Council who really ruled the Empire, and the gods hadn't visibly favored the Empress or her family since the oracles fell silent. Duzon knew that, even if this poor stranger didn't. The Council's authority was why Duzon had wangled an invitation to watch the Council in session. He had even, to the astonishment of his friends, passed up a possible tryst with the beauteous Lady Vozua to be here.

And it wasn't that he didn't enjoy Lady Vozua's company, either; ordinarily, he'd be delighted to spend some time with her, and the more privately the better.

He remembered the green velvet gown she had worn when last he had seen her, and the way she had smiled at him. . . .

But an observer's place at a council session might well be harder to come by than a night with Seidabar's loveliest, and Duzon had made his choice. He was here, beneath the famous gold-coffered dome with its sixteen clerestory windows, and Lady Vozua would have to survive the evening without him.

Most of his contemporaries wouldn't have made that choice. Most of them didn't care about council sessions; they weren't concerned with matters of state, preferring to leave that to those anointed by the gods or the Empress.

Duzon, however, was determined not to be just another handsome young courtier, whiling away the years with intrigue and gossip in hopes of finding a tolerable bride higher in the imperial hierarchy than himself. He wanted to *do* something, to make something of his life. He wanted to be useful, to serve the Empire, to somehow improve the lot of the people beneath the Hundred Moons. He didn't have the temperament to be a priest, and advancement was slow in the army these days, but there had to be *some* way he could become more than he was. He'd hoped that he might find some way to serve the Council, something special he could do, and so he'd arranged to be one of the handful of observers allowed into the council chamber.

He hadn't known just what the session would be like, though, and hadn't expected to see Lord Gornir, the Minister of the Provinces, present a Matuan official in full ceremonial garb and foot-long waxed mustache. Duzon was fascinated by the easterner; he thought some of the Councillors were, too. He noticed that Lady Dalbisha, that formidable old harridan seated half in shadow and half in sun at the Prince's left, had even put the ancient carved cane she carried everywhere down on the table, rather than continuing to fiddle with it as she usually did.

Duzon thought he could smell the Matuan's mustache wax—though perhaps that was just the lingering scent of the varnish on the painted wooden walls.

He wished that Granzer would get on with it, and put an end to this pitiful fellow's agony of suspense—not to mention his own curiosity about why this man was here. The formal introductions had been made, the herald had returned to his station by the door, and it was time to get down to business.

As if on cue, Prince Granzer spoke without rising. "All right," he said wearily, "tell us whatever it is you came to tell us."

The Matuan dropped his hat, snatched it up again, glanced down as if afraid he had scratched the finish on the hardwood floor, then looked at Lord Gornir with outright terror. "I thought . . . I mean, I am here at the Council's invitation, Your Highness," he said.

"You are here at Lord Gornir's insistence," the Prince corrected him. "I assume he wanted you to tell us something."

Duzon saw Lady Dalbisha frown and reach for her cane.

The Matuan glanced at Lord Gornir. His mouth came open, but no sound emerged.

And at last Lord Gornir came to his rescue. He let the front legs of his chair fall to the ground with a thump, then leaned forward across the table.

"If it please the Council," he announced, "I have brought this man, whose name I cannot pronounce correctly but it's something like Shin Tsai, here to confirm the reports from Govya and Olnamia that most of you have refused to take seriously—for which I do not greatly fault you, since I, myself, failed until recently to appreciate their serious nature. You all know that there have been disturbances in the east for the past three years, that after decades of peace Matua, Govya, and Olnamia have been plagued by assassinations, vandalism, and random terror; most of you seem to think this is normal unrest, perhaps brought about by the silence of the oracles, and will pass. I have finally become convinced that it's more than that, and have brought this man here in hopes of convincing the rest of you. Shin Tsai, by virtue of his office as a magistrate and criminal investigator for the province of Matua, is an eyewitness to some of the atrocities committed by these Olnamian rebels; he'll answer whatever questions you put to him about them."

Prince Granzer waved a hand. "Does anyone have questions for our guest?"

"You call them rebels, Lord Gornir?" Lord Kadan, the Commissioner of the Army, immediately asked.

"I do," Gornir replied.

"And you, whatever your name is," Kadan demanded, rising and turning to face the easterner, "do *you* call them rebels? Do you think they're seriously defying the Empire, or are they just bandits and hooligans?"

"My name is Hsin Tsa'i, my lord," the Matuan said. "And yes, they are rebels. Their leaders are Olnami"—Duzon noticed that he pronounced it as the Olnami themselves did, with the accent on the first syllable, rather than using the Domdur "Olnamian," accented on the second syllable—"and they have sworn to drive the Domdur from Olnami forever. They have boasted that they will destroy Seidabar itself, and free all the world of Domdur dominion."

Lord Kadan smiled crookedly, leaning forward across the table. The gold clasp on his robe caught a ray of sunlight from the clerestory windows and gleamed brilliantly as he spoke. "You've seen Seidabar, and they haven't," he said, his tone almost conspiratorial. "Think they can destroy it?"

Hsin Tsa'i spread his hands. "I merely report their boast, my lord." Duzon noticed that he seemed to have gained considerable confidence now that he was actually speaking, rather than waiting.

And of course, it was Lord Kadan who was questioning him, not Prince Granzer, and while Lord Kadan might command all the armies beneath the

Hundred Moons, he was no kin to the Domdur Empress. Duzon's smile twisted. For himself, he'd much prefer to face Prince Granzer than some of the other Councillors.

"And I merely ask your opinion, Magistrate," Kadan said, with only a hint of sarcasm discernible. He straightened, taking that clasp out of the direct sun, and it seemed as if he were fading back into the shadows. "Do you think this rabble could destroy Seidabar?"

The Matuan magistrate hesitated, and Duzon sympathized; no one wanted to tell a superior an unpleasant truth, and the peoples of Matua and Greya were notoriously polite, but the man obviously didn't want to lie.

Duzon thought the hesitation itself should have been answer enough for Lord Kadan, but the Commissioner of the Army continued to glare at the Matuan, awaiting an answer, and at last the little magistrate said, "I do not know, my lord. Surely, a fortress such as this can withstand any attack by ordinary men, but the rebels use black magic. Their leader, the Olnami warlord Rebiri Nazakri, is said to be the mightiest black magician of our age, perhaps of all time. How am I to know what this sorcerer is capable of?"

Lord Kadan sat back down in his chair and threw a glance at the Archpriest Apiris, then looked back at the Matuan. "You believe in black magic?" he said.

"I have *seen* black magic, my lord," the Matuan replied. He'd definitely found his nerve, Duzon thought. Duzon found himself liking the little easterner.

"The gods, so we are told, forbade black magic centuries ago," Kadan pointed out.

"The gods, my lord, can change their minds. Did not the gods forbid magic to any save their priests? Yet Vrai Burrai and his disciples are here in this very city, teaching their discoveries at the Imperial College of the New Magic. And did not the gods give us oracles, to direct us when we were in doubt? Yet the oracles no longer speak in any voices save their own human tongues."

Kadan frowned. "What is this black magic you have seen, then?"

The Matuan shuddered and cast a glance behind him, at the securely closed council-chamber door and the half-dozen observers the Council had allowed in this session, Duzon among them.

"I have seen a dead man walk and fight, my lord," he said. "An assassin sent to slay the chief secretary to the governor of Matua was caught in the act and trapped in his victim's office. I was summoned, and arrived as the office door gave way beneath the assassin's battering. I was there when the assassin marched out laughing, covered in the secretary's blood, and I saw him continue to walk away as the guards ran their blades through his chest, as they chopped at his arms and legs. I saw them cut away his right hand, and no blood flowed. I still have that hand, my lord, in a sealed box—I brought it with me to Seidabar, and have it in my chambers even now. Our finest doctors, and the priests of the temple at Qui Yan, agree that the hand was that of a corpse already dead a triad when the assassin struck—and yet, even after I retrieved and studied it, that hand will sometimes move."

Duzon shuddered at this description, and even Lord Kadan's sardonic expression had vanished. Lady Dalbisha's hand was clutching her cane so tightly her knuckles were turning white, but she didn't seem to be aware of it; she was staring at Hsin Tsa'i.

Duzon supposed that all of them recognized the resemblance between the Matuan's description and the old legends people still used to frighten children—but this man was no child, and the stories were alleged to be true. Duzon leaned forward intently; this might not be as pleasant as a chat with Lady Vozua, but it was fully as interesting, in its way.

"Anything else?" Kadan demanded.

The Matuan nodded. "I have seen a cloud of red flame move through the city streets at night, and cast forth lines of fire, so that whatever they struck burst into flames as well. As the cloud moved, a voice spoke from it, proclaiming death to the Domdur and all their allies." He hesitated. "The voice did not speak well, and I dared not stand too near; I cannot quote the exact words, though I am sure of the sense of it."

For a moment no one spoke. Then Kadan regained his composure enough to ask, "A walking corpse and a cloud of fire—do you think that would be enough to threaten Seidabar?"

The Matuan shrugged. "How do I know that Rebiri Nazakri has no other, greater magic?"

"It seems to me," Lord Orbalir interjected, before Kadan could find anything else to say, "that this is irrelevant. Surely, we don't need black magicians sacking our homes before we recognize a matter that must be dealt with. What have your soldiers been doing, Lord Kadan, while this menace ravages Matua?"

"My soldiers," Kadan replied coldly, "have been guarding temples and government offices throughout Matua, Greya, Govya, Olnamia, and even Shibir—I've drawn men from garrisons as far away as the Veruet Isles to provide the necessary manpower, as you'd know if you kept track of your own vessels, Orbalir. Even now General Balinus, the commander at Ai Varach and one of the best men I know, is under orders to assemble a force that can find and destroy this so-called Nazakri."

Duzon smiled to himself. There was no love lost between those two, certainly. The Commissioner of the Army and the Commissioner of the Fleet were supposed to be allies and equals, but Kadan and Orbalir had never seen it that way.

"And is it working?" Lady Mirashan asked.

Kadan turned red, and the Matuan magistrate replied, "No, my lady."

"We've had problems with desertion," Kadan admitted. "Whoever's committing these crimes has done a good job of frightening our more superstitious troops."

"It's more than that," Lord Gornir said. "Shin Tsai can tell you it is. It's black magic! I'm not faulting Lord Kadan—he did send his men, and gave General Balinus the authority to do whatever needed to be done, but it hasn't been enough. It's as Shin Tsai said—it's black magic, and mere soldiers aren't enough against it."

That created something of a stir among the Councillors—and among the observers.

Lord Duzon found himself wishing he could go to Govya or Matua or Olnamia and see for himself what was happening, rather than relying on these secondhand reports. Maybe there was something he could do to stop this abomination.

But what?

As if echoing Duzon's thoughts, Lord Dabos asked, "What would you have us do, then?"

"What else *can* we do?" Lord Niniam said.

"Plenty," Lady Dalbisha muttered—Duzon could hear her clearly, despite the intervening distance.

"You say you've had desertions, Kadan," Lord Shoule said. "Have they simply deserted, or have they gone over to the enemy? Were these local troops you relied upon? This may not be black magic so much as treason."

Lord Kadan turned redder.

"That's absurd," Lord Passeil replied. "Why would any of our soldiers betray us? What would he have to gain? Besides, you heard the magistrate's report— treason won't make corpses walk."

Mirashan said, "I don't think there's any great question of incompetence or disloyalty here. We're facing rebels armed with black magic—Lord Gornir's friend here says so, and that agrees with my own reports from the east. I have no reason to doubt a word of what this fine man says. Lord Kadan has taken the proper steps, and those have not been enough, but we have not been willing to go further. We preferred to ignore the whole thing—I admit it, I did, too. Well, now Lord Gornir has made it impossible for us to ignore it. We need to do *something*."

"What?" Niniam asked.

"We might try negotiating with this Olnamian," Lord Sulibai suggested. "Surely, we can find some way to appease him. What is it that he wants?"

"Revenge," Lord Gornir said.

"The destruction of the Domdur," Hsin Tsa'i added.

"I'll not be a party to yielding to this rebel," Lord Kadan said angrily. "We'll find a way to defeat him—if not with my soldiers, then with something more."

"If soldiers aren't enough, we'll have to fight magic with magic," Gornir suggested. He turned to look at Archpriest Apiris.

Apiris threw up his hands in a gesture of hopelessness, and began, "The temple magicians are hardly—"

"In the old days," Lord Graush interrupted, "we'd have sent the gods' champion to find this Olnamian troublemaker and rip his head off."

Lady Dalbisha nodded agreement.

"In the old days the *gods* would have sent the champion to fight for us," Orbalir said, looking significantly at Apiris. "Or at any rate, they'd have advised us what we should do."

"I'm sure they would have," Apiris agreed. "Alas, the oracles are silent, and there's nothing we can do about it. If a divine champion has been chosen, I am not aware of it. My predecessors, in their reliance on the oracles, did not bother to keep written records on such matters. If there is some magic that can counter what this messenger has described, I suspect it's more likely to come from the Imperial College of the New Magic than my temple crypts—our magicks are the magicks of knowledge and communication, of light and growth, not of war or destruction."

At the mention of the New Magic attention fell upon Prince Granzer—Duzon knew that the Prince was nominally in charge of Vrai Burrai's rowdy gang of magicians, though Lady Luzla seemed to handle most of the actual administration of the Imperial College.

Apiris seemed to have successfully distracted everyone's attention away from himself; Duzon wondered why. Wasn't this an opportunity for him to gather power by using his magicians effectively? Even if the magicians couldn't actually do anything, putting them into action, no matter how pointless it might prove to be, was clearly the right move politically.

But it apparently wasn't a move the Archpriest cared to make. From all reports, Apiris seemed determined to have his priests do as little as possible—not just in this matter, or as a Councillor, but in everything that lay at all outside the area of traditional religious practice. The entire priesthood seemed paralyzed with indecision.

That puzzled Duzon. Quite aside from the old stories about warrior priests and magician adventurers, Duzon thought he remembered the temple priests being much more active when he was a boy; part of that might be the glow of childhood, but part of it he believed to be a genuine change in priestly behavior. He supposed that was because of the silence of the oracles; perhaps, with the passage of time, they'd get over it.

It had already been a dozen years, though.

If he'd been Archpriest, Duzon thought, he'd have had his magicians hard at work, looking for ways to destroy this rebel leader and his black magic.

"Perhaps we could send a couple of New Magicians out to advise General Balinus," Prince Granzer said. He glanced at Kadan.

"Glad to have them," the Commissioner of the Army said. "Glad to have anything that might help. If you find out who the divine champion is, we'd certainly be glad to have *him*!"

"That's all very well, but what about the *old* magic?" Lord Shoule demanded.

"We have already instructed the magicians of all the eastern temples to serve General Balinus however possible," Apiris admitted reluctantly. Duzon shook his head at this display of political ineptitude—Apiris should have been proclaiming proudly that he had already moved against the foe, not trying to hide the fact.

"And what about the champion, then?" Lord Graush shouted. "He should be out there!"

"We don't know who he is," Apiris pointed out. "It might be that General Balinus *is* the divine champion, my lord. Or perhaps this Vrai Burrai is, or someone else. The champion could be right here in this room, for all we know. We have no way of telling who it might be, without the gods' guidance." He gestured, a wide, sweeping gesture that was meant to take in the entire chamber.

It seemed to Duzon, though, that when the gesture ended, Apiris's hand was pointed straight at him, Duzon of Snauvalia.

He blinked. Odd thoughts began to bubble through his head, vague and half-formed.

The divine champion could be *anybody*, Apiris said.

It could be *him*.

The gods were no longer saying who the champion was; perhaps mortals could decide for themselves.

Perhaps *that* was why Duzon had always been filled with ambition and no idea how to use it. Perhaps he really was meant to be the champion.

Perhaps the gods had intended him to be the champion. Perhaps it was divine inspiration that had brought him to be in this chamber, hearing what was said, seeing the Archpriest's gesture.

"I say we should find out," Lord Graush proclaimed. "You, Archpriest, you ask your magicians and priests, find out if any of them might have any clues. And, Kadan, you ask your soldiers. The old stories say the champion's supposed to be an unbeatable warrior, a man who never tires—you ask if anyone fits that description."

Apiris glanced at Granzer.

"That sounds like an excellent idea," Granzer said.

"Very well," Apiris sighed.

The remainder of the session was mundane and dull, and Duzon barely listened. He was lost in his own thoughts, thoughts of potential glory.

The divine champion, defender of the Domdur—*he*, Lord Duzon of Snau-valia, might be the man!

He left the chamber at a brisk walk, with his head high and his eyes bright. His cloak swirled about him dramatically and the plume in his hat bobbed handsomely, as always, but more from habit than any conscious attempt to maintain his usual style. He was too busy thinking about how he might present himself to claim the role he was surely meant to play to worry about his appearance.

Behind him, Apiris waited until the chamber had emptied before gathering himself up for the walk back to the Great Temple.

He hadn't argued with them; he tried not to, nowadays. The whole thing was absurd, though. Find the divine champion? Nonsense! There was no more divine champion. How could there be a champion when there were no oracles to guide him?

But he had said he would make inquiries, so he would make inquiries.

CHAPTER 12

Danugai, high priest of Biekedau, knelt on the cold stone floor before the ornate blue-and-gold shrine of Samardas, god of wisdom, and prayed for the restoration of the oracles. He had been at this task for several minutes when he heard the discreet cough.

He sighed, raised his head, and asked, "Yes?"

The young priestess wearing the red armband of a temple messenger stepped forward and silently held out a folded piece of paper. Danugai accepted it and rose, brushing off his knees as he did. He looked inquiringly at the messenger.

"From the Great Temple in Seidabar," she said. "Demishin received this, just a few minutes ago."

Demishin was one of the temple magicians, one of those who kept the Bie-kedau temple in instantaneous contact with every other temple beneath the Hundred Moons. Danugai looked at the note and saw the symbols for "urgent," "private," and "highest level possible" on it.

He frowned. "Go," he said, waving the messenger away.

She bowed, then turned and hurried away through swirls of incense, back to her post in the crypts.

Danugai unfolded the paper and read the message. It was in Demishin's handwriting, of course, but signed, "For Apiris, Archpriest, by his command, on the last day of Orini's Triad in the year of the gods' favor 1104."

The gist of it was simple enough, and easily satisfied; Danugai crossed the sanctuary, beckoning to his waiting secretary, and a moment later both men were seated in the high priest's office while Danugai dictated a notice to be posted in the temple refectory.

That evening Vadeviya and Mezizar read the notice.

"Apiris, Archpriest of the Great Temple at Seidabar, Spokesman of the Gods and Speaker to the Gods, Councillor to Her Imperial Majesty Beretris Queen of the Domdur and Empress of the Domdur Domains, has requested that any priest or other person possessing information regarding the identity or whereabouts of the divine champion immediately forward that information to the Imperial Council at Seidabar."

Vadeviya frowned, and glanced questioningly at Mezizar. No words were needed to convey his query.

Mezizar thought for a moment, then shrugged. "I leave it to you," he said. "You spoke with him; I only saw him as a baby, more than twenty years ago."

"He told me not to tell anyone," Vadeviya replied. "He was quite definite."

"And the Archpriest asks you to tell the Council," Mezizar replied. "Who will you obey?"

Vadeviya considered that for a moment.

"Danugai requests," he pointed out, "while Malledd *told* me, very definitely."

"That's a point," Mezizar agreed. "But did he have the authority to tell you what to do? And you know as well as I do that a request from the high priest, especially one made on behalf of the Archpriest, while not an order, is not to be taken lightly."

"Malledd was selected by the gods themselves, before the oracles fell silent," Vadeviya said. "That does give Malledd authority. The Archpriest was chosen by means unknown to me, perhaps oracular, perhaps not; he is nonetheless the ultimate religious authority in the Empire. So the question becomes, which is the *higher* authority?"

He stood silently, considering this for so long that Mezizar grew impatient. "And?" he demanded.

"And judging by the old tales, taking everything into consideration, I would choose the divine champion over the Archpriest," Vadeviya said, "but it's not an easy choice. I'll want to think about it some more."

"And what shall I tell Dirwan and Talas when they read this notice?" Mezizar asked, naming the other two surviving priests who knew that the gods had in fact chosen their champion twenty-two years before.

"Tell them to leave it to me," Vadeviya said. "I accept full responsibility. They're to say nothing until I've had a chance to think it over."

Mezizar stared at his companion for a moment, then nodded.

"As you say," he said. "Think carefully." He lifted his plate and headed for the table where the temple cooks waited with the evening meal.

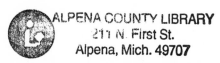
ALPENA COUNTY LIBRARY
211 N. First St.
Alpena, Mich. 49707

Vadeviya thought carefully. He thought as he ate his supper, and later in his chamber. He thought about it the following morning, and the day after.

But with each passing day, he thought about it less and less.

Two triads had passed without incident, and without word of the champion, when Danugai, overcome by curiosity, made his way down into the dim stillness of the crypts seeking Demishin.

The magicians generally worked in tiny dark rooms with thick stone walls, where nothing would distract them; messengers brought them food and drink, as well as carrying messages and instructions in and out. Demishin's room was virtually indistinguishable from the rest; Danugai found it barren and uncomfortable, but Demishin seemed perfectly at home there.

"What word from Seidabar?" Danugai asked when Demishin had shaken off the last effects of his trance.

"Nothing much," Demishin replied. "Reports of continuing trouble in the east. The Empress's health remains poor, but has not worsened. No one speaks openly of the succession, though Princess Daunla reportedly made a tactless remark about poor Prince Maurezoi at a recent wedding." Princess Daunla was the wife of Prince Zolous, the younger of the Empress's twin sons, and mother of all six of Beretris's surviving grandchildren; Prince Maurezoi, the sickly only child of the older twin, had died a few years before at the age of nine.

Danugai took no interest in palace politics. "Has the chosen of the gods been located?" he asked.

"Not that I've heard," Demishin said. "If anyone knows where he is, they aren't telling us magicians."

Danugai frowned.

"There may not *be* a divine champion anymore," Demishin pointed out.

Danugai admitted that that might be the case, then turned to go. He stroked his beard thoughtfully as he made his way back up the stairs.

That evening he called together a dozen of the senior priests in the lesser sanctuary. Each of them stacked three or four of the red velvet prayer cushions to make an improvised chair, and settled comfortably in a group around the altar of Samardas. The sun was down, but a hundred candles burned behind the altar, providing plenty of light and warming the incense-scented air.

Danugai took his place directly before the altar, sitting cross-legged on his cushions. He reviewed the situation quickly, then said, "I have been thinking that perhaps we should post a notice out on the plaza—perhaps some layperson knows something."

"How would a layperson know anything about the divine champion?" a middle-aged priestess named Medei asked.

"That *does* seem to be something only an oracle would know," Talas agreed with a glance at Vadeviya. Talas had himself once been an oracle of Vevanis, one of the three oracles who had described where the new champion could be found, twenty-two years before.

"Perhaps someone *asked* an oracle, just out of curiosity, who would be the next divine champion," suggested one of Danugai's secretaries from the left side of the altar.

"Oh, yes, of course," Vadeviya said, his voice dripping sarcasm. "We usually charged three vierts for a private talk with an oracle—more, of course, if there were several questions or the conversation ran more than a few minutes. I'm sure there were *dozens* of people in Biekedau who handed over *three vierts* to ask, just out of curiosity, who would be the Empire's chosen defender twelve years later. And of *course* none of them ever mentioned the incident, and obviously the oracles who answered all these questions are among the dead or departed, not those who remain among us."

The secretary looked uncomfortable, and Danugai sighed.

"As I understand it, the Archpriest merely requested that anyone in the temple who had such information pass it on," Mezizar said. "He didn't order you to make a great search."

"True enough," Danugai said, "but great things are not accomplished by doing no more than necessary. Yes, it's probably futile, I know that, but it's such a small effort—is there any reason *not* to post a notice in the plaza?"

Mezizar hesitated; he and Talas glanced at Vadeviya.

Vadeviya cleared his throat. "Well, actually, sir," he said, "I believe there *are* reasons not to."

Danugai looked at him, annoyed. "Oh?"

"Yes. Please think about it. If you post such a notice, then word will spread from here to Yildau in a matter of days; everyone will know that we are seeking the divine champion. And they will surely wonder *why* we are looking for the defender of the Empire. They will assume that we, in fact, know something we aren't telling them. They will quite reasonably conclude that we are looking for the defender of the Empire because the Empire needs defending, that for the first time in two hundred years the Domdur are facing a menace we cannot handle without divine assistance. Furthermore, sir, they will remember that we can no longer rely on divine assistance—for twelve years, after all, we have been utterly without divine guidance."

Danugai looked thoughtful.

"Do you really want to remind everyone that the gods have apparently abandoned us? That the temples no longer provide them with the aid their ancestors enjoyed?"

"You have a point," Danugai conceded.

"I'd think that if the Imperial Council wants us to do more than we have, they'd *tell* us to," Talas said.

"That, too, is sound," Danugai admitted. He thought for a moment as the others waited.

"Very well, then," the high priest said at last. "You've convinced me. We have done as we were asked, and need do no more." He clapped his hands together. "Then we're done here, and let us all go about our business. My thanks to you all." He rose.

As the priests made their way out of the sanctuary Dirwan stepped up beside Vadeviya. "I thought you were still considering," she said.

"I am," Vadeviya said. "But I know a bad idea when I hear one, and posting a notice in the plaza is a bad idea."

"And it's not just that you don't want word to reach Grozerodz?"

"Not entirely," Vadeviya said with a grimace. "The reasons I gave are sound enough; our friends in Grozerodz are one more I chose not to mention."

Dirwan smiled at him. "And if you reach a final decision, you'll tell us?"

"Of course," Vadeviya said, smiling back.

And for the next few days he would sometimes find Mezizar or Talas or Dirwan looking at him inquiringly; on occasion one or another of them even ventured to ask if he had made up his mind yet.

And thus, while Vadeviya continued to think the matter over, no word of the search for the divine champion escaped the temple at Biekedau. A few hints perhaps seeped out into the streets of the city, but not even the vaguest rumors reached Grozerodz.

CHAPTER 13

The guest house smelled of pine and woodsmoke, and perhaps there was a lingering trace of blood. It was an odor the Nazakri did not care for—but it was better than the stench of nightwalkers. He had been living with the reek of death for the last two seasons. The arrival of winter had lessened the stink, but not eliminated it.

And he was about to return to it; he took a deep breath of the cool air of the guest house, then pulled his fur cloak more tightly about him and stepped out onto the verandah.

A light snow had fallen sometime during the day, covering the rows of corpses with a thin layer of white, concealing their bloated, rotting flesh. The snow would doubtless remain undisturbed until the sun vanished completely below the mountains and the light faded from the western sky; the nightwalkers could not move in sunlight, and their flesh was as cold as that of any other cadaver.

The snow hid their differences, making one dead body indistinguishable from the next; Rebiri could not tell which were the nightwalkers he had brought with him from Matua, and which were the people the nightwalkers had slaughtered when they captured the guest house the night before.

They were all nightwalkers now, of course. The nightwalkers Rebiri had brought up the road from Matua had marched in, knives drawn, an hour or so before dawn, and had butchered everyone in the place. The Nazakri and his living followers had followed them in, and Rebiri had walked through the place, the black end of his staff held out before him, reanimating each of the dead in turn with one of the dark spirits he had captured in the Govyan caves.

He had wanted to be sure he got them all before the sun rose, so he had hurried inside while the killings were still going on. As he stood on the verandah he could still remember the sounds he had heard as he began the resurrections— the distant screams, the cold laughter of the nightwalkers, and even the sharp, sickening crunch of the knives punching through flesh and bone.

There had been twenty-three people in the guest house, in all. Those twenty-three—dead now, or at least undead—lay in rows on the hillside below the verandah, side by side with their killers.

Rebiri Nazakri looked down at them with satisfaction.

His army was growing. He had over two hundred nightwalkers now, and despite desertions and other problems he had more than ninety living men, as well. About a third of those men were standing guard over the corpses; the nightwalkers were vulnerable when paralyzed by sunlight, and the wizard did not care to lose any to whoever might happen along.

He wasn't about to let them lie in the guest house, though—the smell would be too much.

And of course, it was unlikely that anyone who happened along would know the secret of destroying a nightwalker. The old horror stories were surprisingly and pleasantly vague about it. Rebiri had learned it from the nightwalkers themselves, not from the legends—so long as a nightwalker's brain and heart remained attached to each other, no matter how badly mutilated the brain and heart and body might become, the nightwalker would survive. Break the last link between heart and brain, though, and the black essence would escape and revert to its mindless, harmless state, while the physical remains would be just so much dead flesh.

It seemed odd that the old stories never explained this. Oh, one might describe how a hero lopped the head off a nightwalker, another how a nightwalker's heart was cut out, but the general rule was never given.

But then, until Rebiri Nazakri had discovered how to use the New Magic to create them, nightwalkers were rare. Even before the gods taught the Domdur how to protect the dead and keep the black spirits deep below ground, it had been an unusual happenstance for one of the wandering spirits to stumble across a suitable host body. Without a body, they were incapable of any coherent thought, unaware of their own identity. Nightwalkers had *happened* occasionally; no one had ever *made* them.

Until now.

The last sliver of sun had vanished, and the red sky behind the mountains was beginning to fade. As Rebiri watched, a shadowed lump of ground jerked suddenly, and a hand thrust up, flinging aside the snow that covered it.

Then the hand fell lifelessly back as the lingering daylight touched it.

Rebiri was unconcerned; in a moment, as night drew on, that nightwalker, and all the others, would rise, ready to do as he, Rebiri Nazakri, warlord of Olnami, commanded.

And what he would command was simple—the nightwalkers were to march up the mountain to the next stop on the road west, killing anyone they encountered who refused to join Rebiri's growing rebel army. Each Domdur sympathizer thus killed would be raised as a nightwalker and added to their growing army.

They would continue in this fashion, adding to their numbers, until the Nazakri controlled an unbeatable force, a force that could march across the central plains to Seidabar and destroy the Domdur capital, throw down the walls of their vaunted citadel and slaughter their abominable Empress and all her kin. Rebiri estimated ten thousand nightwalkers would be sufficient.

He had had his fill of the little pinpricks he had inflicted on the Domdur here in the lands east of the Govya Mountains. Killing a few officials, terrorizing Matuans—what good was any of that, in the long run? The Domdur could endure a century of such trivial attacks; they could simply outlive Rebiri, and Aldassi, his spirit contaminated by his feeble sun magic, could not control the nightwalkers or make more of them once Rebiri was gone.

No, if he was to avenge Basari's defeat and free the Olnami from Domdur oppression, he had to strike at the Empire's heart, at Seidabar.

It was his destiny to destroy Seidabar; he knew it.

A god had told him.

He had not known it was a god at first; he was not even aware that anything had been addressing him. He had known things, known that fate had chosen him for greatness, but he had not known how he knew until that first nightwalker, the one he had created in the alleys of Pai Shin, had told him.

"A god speaks to you," the nightwalker said.

At first Rebiri thought the undead thing was speaking metaphorically in referring to the sense of destiny the Olnami warlord felt, but eventually he realized that the creature meant it literally.

"Then the gods favor me?" he asked it.

"I know only that one god speaks to you," the nightwalker said. "I can sense it, one of my ancient foes, at times."

"One of your foes? One of the Domdur gods? Which is it?"

"I don't know," the nightwalker said. "It is a god, and it speaks to you. That's all I know."

That was hardly a satisfying explanation, but in time Rebiri realized that it was enough.

A god spoke to him. The sense of destiny he felt was the words of a god.

The gods *favored* him, then. The gods wanted him to carry out his plan. They wanted him to destroy Seidabar and throw down the Domdur.

The rumors were surely true, then; the Domdur had fallen from divine favor. The oracles had fallen silent not because the gods thought the Domdur ready to rule the world without divine guidance, but because the gods had abandoned the Domdur. The gods wanted an end to their domination of everything beneath the Hundred Moons.

That was surely it—but the nightwalker would not confirm it, nor did the god who spoke to him manifest in any more obvious manner. There were times when he *knew* things, when he was certain of the rightness of an action, when he could sense that his eventual triumph was inevitable.

But that was all. No oracles spoke to him, no visions came to him in his dreams.

Still, it was enough.

The gods favored him. He would make his ten thousand nightwalkers, and he would destroy the Domdur.

Of course, making ten thousand nightwalkers would take *time;* the black crystal on his staff could only contain enough darkness to create perhaps forty or fifty before it required renewal.

But he *had* time. The fire in his staff's other crystal made him strong, gave him the power to defend himself from whatever might threaten him. He was old, but still far from death. He could build his forces up steadily, moving about the slopes of the mountains, letting the nightwalkers guide him to the caves and hollows where the darkness could be found. In time, he would have his army, enough to destroy Seidabar.

Already, he thought, he might have enough to take the Domdur fortress at Ai Varach. If the Empire ever stirred itself enough to send an army to hunt him down, he would do that, make Ai Varach his base, and build his forces there until they were ready to make the long march across the open plain.

But he doubted he would ever need to. So far the Empire had done almost nothing to oppose him. Guards had been increased, warnings issued, but no armies had marched out against him.

Three centuries earlier Domdur armies had swept through Olnami like swarms of locusts, thousands upon thousands of soldiers, overwhelming everything with their numbers. But now the garrison at Ai Varach was a few hundred men, the city guards in Pai Shin the same. The Domdur had grown weak. Their time was over.

He would march unopposed across the plain, and would smash the gates of Seidabar. It was inevitable.

And the Domdur would not, could not, stop him.

He smiled as the snow began to erupt, and corpses to stir and sit upright. Even the stink was not enough to ruin his mood.

P̲rince Granzer looked at the report Lord Gornir had handed him and frowned. He settled farther back in his chair, then looked up across the table at Gornir.

"You're sure of the accuracy of this?" he asked.

"As sure as I can be," Gornir replied. His chair at the Council's table was empty; he stood at the center of the half ring to address his fellows. "The rebels have switched their tactics, from scattered assassinations and terrorism to systematic slaughter. Furthermore, their numbers are growing steadily."

"But how is that possible?" Lady Mirashan asked. "I don't doubt it, my own sources report the same, but I *still* have no reports of serious discontent with anything but our failure to destroy the insurgents. Where are they recruiting these new members?"

"They are apparently transforming the dead into nightwalkers, my lady," Gornir said. "I don't know how, or even why, but they seem to be doing it."

"That's insane," Lord Kadan protested.

"That does not mean it isn't true," Lord Sulibai remarked from the far end of the table.

"It doesn't mean it *is* true, either," Kadan retorted.

"Lord Kadan," Prince Granzer said, his voice deep and commanding. "Why have your soldiers not yet hunted down these troublemakers and dealt with them?"

Kadan's jaw worked, and his face reddened.

"I'm not the divine champion," he said. "I don't have any oracles telling me what to do."

"We know that," Lady Dalbisha snapped. "But you *do* have the Imperial Army. So why haven't you used it?"

"Because I don't have the numbers I need to do it," he said. "I don't have the resources."

"Why not?" Granzer asked.

"Because I haven't *needed* them," Kadan replied. "We've been at peace for centuries; who wants to pay a lot of soldiers to sit in a barracks, eating and drinking with tax money? We keep enough men in the cities and garrisons to deal with any ordinary trouble; we never expected anything like *this*."

"Expected or not, it appears to be happening," Granzer pointed out. "Had we acted immediately when this black wizard first appeared, perhaps we could have prevented it, but we did not, and it's happening. Now, what can we *do* about it?"

"If the champion were known . . ." Lord Orbalir began.

"He's not," Lord Graush snapped. "We've been looking for him, believe me. We've got a dozen people claiming to be him. What we don't have is *him*."

"Well, champion or no champion, give me the men and the money and the other resources, and I'll take care of it," Kadan said angrily.

"You guarantee that?" Gornir asked.

Kadan's face grew even redder.

"No, I don't guarantee it," he said. "We're up against hundreds of night-walkers, according to these reports, and a black magician who might be capable of *anything*. The earth could open and swallow us all at any moment. But if these creatures can be stopped by any natural means, and if you give me what I need, yes, I can stop it."

"Good enough," Granzer said, slamming a fist down on the table. "Then you'll have what you need, whatever it is."

CHAPTER 14

Malledd smiled as Hmar showed him the trick. It was a simple little twist that did it, that locked the two pieces of iron solidly together.

It was good to know that there were still things the old man could teach him. And it was always satisfying to learn something useful. He picked up the device and studied it.

"That'll stay sealed tight," Hmar told him. "Unless you know the trick to opening it."

"You can't just untwist it?" Malledd asked. Then he saw that no, you couldn't, once the iron tongue had snapped into place.

"Not just like that. You have to press *here*, you see. . . ."

"Father! Grandfather!"

The two men looked up, startled, to see Neyil running down the sunlit lane toward the smithy, his little boots splashing heedlessly through the puddles left by the morning's rain. Malledd put the locking device down on the workbench and went to the door to meet the boy.

Neyil stopped, panting, with one hand on the door frame; Malledd knelt down to talk on the boy's own level, and waited for him to catch his breath.

It worried him, sometimes, that Neyil seemed to be winded so easily. When Malledd had been six—or for that matter, any other age—he had been able to run all day without tiring. He'd mentioned it to Anva, and to Hmar, and to his mother and his sisters and his uncle Sparrak, but none of them seemed at all concerned.

"*You* were the odd one, boy," Uncle Sparrak had told him. "Neyil's just not as sturdy as you were—and neither is anyone else."

"What is it, Neyil?" Malledd asked as he knelt.

"Soldiers!" Neyil said excitedly. "In the square! Coats red as blood, with swords and helmets!"

Malledd glanced up uneasily at Hmar, then turned back to the boy.

"What do they want here, did they say? Are they just passing through?"

Neyil shook his head. "They're recruiting," he said. "They said so. And they've got the tax collector with them, with the tax rolls."

Malledd looked up at his father. "Do you think we should go see?" he asked.

"As smiths, we're probably exempt from whatever demands they're making," Hmar said, chewing thoughtfully on his beard, "but yes, I think it would be a good idea to find out what's going on."

Malledd nodded.

This wasn't really a surprise. The rumors Malledd had first heard from Vadeviya almost five years before had become commonplace not long after the priest's visit, and within a year or so stories had begun to trickle in of open insurrection in Olnamia and Matua, and atrocities committed in the other eastern provinces.

And as if that weren't bad enough, there had been tales of darker things than simple rebellion. The Olnamian rebels were reportedly using black magic of some sort, magic that could blast through fortress walls, magic that could make the dead walk, could make corpses fight against the Domdur like the night-walkers in the old legends.

Black magic of the kind in the ancient stories didn't sound likely—but in these days of silent oracles and the New Magic, who could be sure? The older folk said that the gods wouldn't allow such things, but the gods didn't seem to be paying as much attention to the Domdur Empire as they once had. As Malledd stepped out of the smithy he glanced up at the shining sky and saw a score of tiny moons gleaming overhead, scattered among the wisps of cloud.

As a child he had imagined the gods sitting up there on their moons, looking down benevolently at their human subjects; now he wondered if perhaps they weren't too busy with their own mysterious concerns to remember that a world lay below them.

Certainly it was hard to understand how the gods could allow the eastern lands to erupt in rebellion. The unrest had spread from Olnamia to Matua and Greya and Govya, and the gods had done nothing. And the priests had simply shrugged when they were questioned about it. "The oracles are still silent," they said.

Malledd had heard the stories of Domdur outposts burned, Domdur governors horribly murdered, and had wondered with the rest why the gods did nothing—but he had also wondered, as no one else in Grozerodz dared do openly, whether *he* should be doing something.

Was he really the gods' champion? Should he be in Olnamia, fighting the rebels?

And what could he do that another man couldn't? What did it mean to be the champion? The letter from Dolkout spoke of supernatural endurance and vitality, but as far as Malledd knew, that just meant he was big and strong and didn't tire easily. What difference could one man, however strong, make?

Those questions never went away entirely; anytime any mention was made of the turmoil in the east, they assailed him anew. As he and Hmar and Neyil marched up to the town square they were back again, stronger than ever. The beautiful spring weather did nothing to assuage his doubts; if anything, seeing how lovely the world could be made them worse. The last traces of the recent winter—which had been mild, in any case—had vanished, and the trees were green, the untilled fields thick with wildflowers.

It seemed, by the time they reached the square, that the entire population of Grozerodz was there. Malledd saw his sisters and their husbands, saw Onnell and all his other friends, all his regular customers, gathered around the front of Bardetta's tavern.

Even tall as he was, Malledd couldn't see much at first over that throng; he could see sunlight glinting from polished metal helmets and a bright flash of red that might be a soldier's tunic, but no more than that.

But then someone lifted one of the helmeted men up on something—Malledd guessed that Bardetta had rolled out a barrel for the purpose.

Sure enough, the man was a soldier, wearing the red and gold of the Domdur dress uniform. Malledd had glimpsed soldiers sometimes on his visits to Biekedau; he had never seen one in Grozerodz before. It was a disquieting sight, a sign of the troubled times.

The soldier raised his hands for silence, and the crowd quieted.

"People of Grozerodz!" he called. "I am Lieutenant Grudar, and my companions and I have come here today looking for volunteers!"

That was just as Neyil had said. Malledd's lips tightened.

"As some of you may have heard," Grudar said, "there is unrest in the eastern continental provinces. A wizard calling himself Nazakri and claiming to be the

King of Olnamia has rebelled against our beloved Empress. He has used his black arts to raise an army, an army that is even now crossing the Govya Mountains intent on the destruction of the entire Domdur Empire! The Empress and the Imperial Council have authorized the army to issue a call for volunteers—and here I am. I'm passing through on my way to Yildau; when I return this way, in three or four days, I will be glad to escort any men from this village who are willing to fight for the Empire to Seidabar, where they may join the Imperial Army."

He paused to catch his breath, and murmurs ran through the crowd.

"I would remind you," Grudar continued, "that it is the Empire that feeds and shelters us, the Empire that the gods chose as the rightful government of everything beneath the Hundred Moons. To serve the Empire is an honor and a privilege!" Then he reached down and caught the hand of another man, and raised it up. "I would also remind you that the Empire has the ancient right to claim the services of one man from each household in lieu of taxes, and that soldiers and veterans are exempt from all taxation. Vanuir here is the tax collector responsible for Grozerodz and Duvrenarodz and Uamor, and has brought a copy of the records with him—the names and families of any volunteer will be recorded, and when that volunteer passes muster in Seidabar, his family will be struck from the tax rolls."

"Are you pressing men?" someone called.

Grudar shook his head. "It will be a sad and sorry day, my friend, when the Domdur Empire must once again resort to the right of conscription, as we did centuries ago! No, we are calling for *volunteers*—but if we do not have enough, and someday we find a foe at the gates of Seidabar . . . well, the Empire does have that right."

"I'll go," a man called.

A chorus of shouts burst out—a few men volunteering, while others cheered them on or called back that they were fools.

Grudar held up his hands for silence.

"We're not taking anyone with us *now*," he said, "but when we come back this way with the recruits from Yildau, Uamor, and Duvrenarodz in a triad or so, anyone who wishes to join us will be welcome. You have at least two days, probably four, in which to make up your minds and pack up whatever possessions you feel you must bring—including one day's food and water, please. Since we don't know how many we'll have, we weren't able to bring provisions. We'll take care of that in Biekedau before we make the march to Seidabar, but please bring enough for the first day." He looked out over the crowd, then spread his arms wide. "That's all, I think—and I trust Grozerodz will do the full measure of its duty to the Empire. If anyone has a question, my companions and I will remain here for another hour or so to answer you. Thank you!" He bowed, then climbed down from the barrel.

The crowd began to shrink then, as some crowded in more closely and others drifted away. Malledd stood where he was, observing.

Hmar put a hand on his shoulder. "Come on, son," he said. "We have a lockbox to finish."

"You go on," Malledd said, not moving. "I need to think."

Hmar glanced uneasily from his son to the recruiters and back. "You aren't seriously thinking of *volunteering*, are you?" he asked.

"I don't know," Malledd said. "Why not? I'm a healthy man in the prime of life, and of Domdur blood." He didn't mention the priest's letter, but he didn't have to.

"Are you, Dad?" Neyil asked, excited. "Are you going to be a soldier?"

Malledd smiled down at him, but didn't answer. They had never told Neyil about the priest, and thanks to Malledd's adolescent suppression of the subject no one else in the village had yet mentioned it to the boy. Neyil didn't know his father was allegedly some sort of divine champion; he just thought Malledd was the greatest man in the world.

"You're a *smith*, not a soldier," Hmar said. "You have a wife and children. And it's not as if the enemy were besieging Seidabar—you heard the man, they're still in the Govya Mountains!"

Malledd didn't answer. He was thinking about Anva, her soft hair and dark eyes, wondering whether he could bear to leave her to go fight. The idea was almost painful. If he were just an ordinary blacksmith he would never even think of leaving her side—but he had been told all his life that he was something more.

"Listen," Hmar said, abandoning any pretense that he didn't understand why Malledd hesitated, "if you were needed, wouldn't the priests have summoned you? In the old stories there's almost always a priest or an imperial messenger who brings word to the champion that he's needed, isn't there?"

"Usually," Malledd admitted, "not always. But this isn't a story."

Hmar glowered. "Look, Malledd," he said, "is there anything you want to ask those men?"

Malledd hesitated, glanced at the recruiter, then shook his head. "No," he said. "If they have a message for me, they can find me the way the priest did." He turned away at last, and together the two smiths ambled back down the lane, while Neyil ran wildly back and forth, dodging the puddles and swinging an imaginary sword at the flowers by the roadside.

CHAPTER 15

About a dozen men from Grozerodz announced that they would be volunteering; that was more than Malledd had expected. Each afternoon the would-be soldiers gathered in Bardetta's tavern and drank and roistered while they waited for Lieutenant Grudar to return.

Onnell was one of them. Malledd was not really surprised; Onnell had seemed to be looking for something new to do with himself lately, and had never lacked for courage. He had had several brief romances but had never married; his parents were dead, and his surviving family was not particularly close. There was little to hold him in Grozerodz.

If Onnell went, though, Malledd realized he would miss him. The two had been friends ever since that incident in the tavern, years ago, when Malledd had threatened to beat Onnell and Onnell had backed down—the two of them had sought each other out to apologize the following day, and matters had progressed to the point that Onnell had been the loudest celebrant at Malledd's wedding to Anva, and the most frequent visitor to their home ever since.

But he had been restless for years, dissatisfied with farming; a term in the army would give him a chance to get away from the village and see more of the world. Malledd could scarcely object to that.

Other friends—sardonic Bousian and little Timuan—had also announced their intention to sign up, but Malledd found himself much less concerned with those two than with Onnell.

Malledd's own uncle Sparrak was another matter, though; he was family, and not a young man. Despite his age he was wavering, genuinely considering enlistment. Hmar was doing his best to talk his brother out of it, telling him he was too old for any such nonsense.

Malledd left that to Hmar, and half seriously tried to convince that miserable old grouch Nedduel to go. It kept his mind off his own doubts about both Onnell for going and himself for staying.

On the first day of Rabib's Triad, which was the second day after Grudar's first visit, the volunteers were all laughing and joking as they gathered at Bardetta's. Some had brought their belongings in old sacks or bundles; others had nothing but what they wore.

"Let the Empress buy my clothes from now on!" one man called, to general laughter and applause.

Malledd, his mood sour just at the moment, remarked quietly, "The soldier said to bring a day's food and drink."

"I'll worry about that when he shows his face again," a volunteer replied. "I wouldn't want the beer to go flat before we leave."

Malledd smiled thinly, and said no more.

On the third day, the second of Rabib's Triad, the mood was somewhat more somber. No one had expected Grudar to return on the second day, not if he was actually going all the way to Yildau, but now, if he had hurried, he might actually show up at any time. The reality was beginning to sink in. The men who went with him would be leaving their homes and families for days, for triads, many triads, maybe for a season or more. Oh, it would be a grand adventure, certainly, going all the way to Seidabar and seeing the famous city walls, the Great Temple, the Imperial Palace, and all the rest, and the fighting in the east would probably be long over before they could march all the way out to Govya . . . but still, they would be away from home, away from everyone and everything they knew. The joking and laughter had not ceased entirely, but it was far more subdued.

Malledd sat at a table in the back, apart from the others—after all, *he* wasn't going anywhere. He sat silently, drinking ale and minding his own business.

Or rather, not minding his business, since he was here at the tavern instead of down at the forge where he belonged, but keeping his own counsel, listening to the volunteers without saying anything.

"Onnell," said Timuan, staring into his empty mug after refusing a round of ale, "you and I, we'll stay together, right? I mean, if the lot of us get sent to different places or something, you and I, we'll stay together?"

Onnell shrugged. "We'll do as we're told, lad," he said mildly—Timuan wasn't much more than a boy, and Onnell had no desire to frighten him. "That's a soldier's job."

"I'd always heard that they try to keep the men of a given village together," Malledd offered, trying to cheer the lad past his nervousness.

Onnell turned and smiled crookedly at the smith. "Aha, the corpse in the corner speaks! Perhaps some spark of life still lingers after all!"

Malledd ignored this and smiled encouragingly at Timuan.

"Ho, Malledd," said Bousian. He was a slender man, a landless younger son who'd been working as a laborer since falling out with his older brother. "Why aren't *you* volunteering? Or is that why you're here? You're coming with us, maybe, but keeping it quiet so Anva won't find out?" He turned his chair to face the smith, carefully holding his mug well out from his body as he did—he was wearing the green velvet vest that was his most prized possession and didn't want to risk spilling anything on it.

"Ha!" Malledd put down his own ale. "You think I'd leave Anva's bed to go sleep in a tent in the mud somewhere with the lot of *you*? Assuming I'd even get a tent? Do I look as big a fool as that?"

"You certainly look *big*," Zenisha called loudly from the kitchen door.

The men laughed at her sally as she vanished through the doorway. When she had gone, Bousian added, "I don't know about Anva's bed, but I, for one, wouldn't blame you for wanting to escape her tongue. She just about made my ears bleed the other day when I let Neyil help me plow Nedduel's upper field."

"Oh, is *that* how Neyil got so dirty?" Malledd asked, smiling. The smile was a bit forced.

Bousian didn't realize how close Malledd had come to actually volunteering, or that his own words had just now convinced Malledd not to. None of the recruits had children; only two had wives, and both were well known to be less than delighted with their marriages.

Malledd had Anva, and he couldn't imagine a better woman; he knew that the neighbors thought she had a sharp tongue, but *he* had never been its target. She was warmth and comfort to him, the center of his life.

Malledd had Neyil and Poria and little Arshui, too, and he loved them all. Neyil could find a thousand ways to get dirty—helping Bousian plow was nothing. Poria was always eager to help her mother with everything, and determined to take care of Arshui. And Arshui was perhaps the most beautiful little boy Malledd had ever seen, no more than a baby, not yet speaking in complete sentences. To even *think* of leaving them for a soldier's life was madness.

So what was he doing, he asked himself, sitting here watching these fools instead of staying home with his family?

Wasting time, clearly, he answered. He gulped the rest of his ale and made a hasty departure, slapping Onnell heartily on the back as he found his way to the tavern's door.

On the fourth day, the last of Rabib's Triad, Malledd did not go to the tavern, but Neyil told him at supper that there had been a fight, and one of the men had decided not to be a soldier after all.

And on the fifth day, first of Mivai's Triad, around midafternoon, Lieutenant Grudar and his two companions came slogging back through pouring rain, leading a company of forty or fifty well-soaked recruits into town just as the clouds finally broke and the sun reappeared. None of them were in uniform yet; instead they wore ordinary clothing, mostly under an assortment of dripping cloaks and jackets—blouses and breeches for the most part, and ranging from finery such as no one in Grozerodz could boast to outfits that were little more than rags. A few men carried old swords, heirlooms passed down from long-dead ancestors, hung on their belts or slung over their shoulders.

Thanks in part to the weather the company wasn't marching so much as trudging when it arrived. That was hardly a surprise; it was a long way from Yildau through Uamor and Duvrenarodz, and the recruits were undoubtedly tired.

Word spread quickly, carried largely by the village children. Virtually the entire town turned out to see their local heroes depart; Malledd, Anva, and their children were all in the crowd that collected in the square. Hmar had been busy with something at the forge and had not wanted to leave it for fear of losing the metal's temper, but Malledd's mother, Madeya, was there, and so were Uncle Sparrak and his wife and daughter. Vlaia and her man stood together at one side of the square, and Malledd was sure his other sisters were present, as well. He glimpsed one or another of them occasionally as everyone milled about, chattering excitedly.

Sparrak had made his final decision the night before, and chosen not to go; in fact, none of the men who had been wavering had decided to go. Of the original dozen volunteers, only nine actually showed up with their supplies when Grudar called for them.

Onnell was one of them; Malledd had hoped he might change his mind at the last moment, but he was there, a knapsack in his hand. Bousian and Timuan were there as well, and the twin brothers Orzin and Ozerga from down the hill, and Nesalas, Vorif, Gaur, and Delazin.

Nedduel was not going, nor three or four others who had said they would.

The lieutenant seemed satisfied with nine, though—as well he might be, Malledd thought. If the army took nine or ten men from every village in the world they would add up very quickly to an inconceivable number. Just looking at the horde of recruits from Yildau and the other villages was mind-boggling; Malledd thought that the gathering in the square might include more strangers than Grozerodz ordinarily saw in half a year.

An army so huge as the one the Empire seemed to be raising surely didn't need him, Malledd told himself. That was a relief; he breathed more freely than he had since Lieutenant Grudar's first appearance.

The company took a rest in the village square, sitting down wherever space permitted, before moving on; this gave the Grozerodz contingent time to gather up their belongings and say good-bye, and let the men from Yildau and Uamor and Duvrenarodz take a break in their march and get something to eat.

Most had presumably brought a day's provisions, as Grudar had instructed them, but Bardetta wasn't one to miss such a business opportunity, and most of the recruits were not eager to eat what they had brought; when she called out that the inn would be serving, a cheer went up.

Bardetta didn't try to fit Grudar's entire company in her tiny inn; instead she and Zenisha brought trays of bread, cheese, and ale out into the square and carried them around to the would-be soldiers. Most of the men were honest enough to toss a coin or two on the tray, but some simply snatched the food and drink, and neither Bardetta nor Zenisha pressed the issue.

Malledd supposed some of them might not *have* any coins; certainly, plenty of the local farmers never had cash money. Bardetta let such farmers have credit, and pay off in whatever goods they could spare—but these people would not be staying around to pay their bills.

Still, it was Bardetta's problem, not his—and it probably wasn't much of a problem, as both women had to go back to dump the money and refill the trays, and as they did Malledd could see that there were coins aplenty, at least two, probably three vierts in all—maybe even more. It was a good thing the weather had turned sunny and bright; continued rain would have watered the ale and soaked the bread and made people less eager to dig hands into purses.

Grudar seemed in no great hurry to move on; instead he sat on the doorstep of Daiwish's house chewing on a stick of dried spiced meat, watching as his men ate and drank, and as the newest recruits said their farewells to friends and family. Vanuir the tax collector, and the other soldier whose name Malledd had never heard, were mingling with the townspeople, but Grudar remained somewhat apart.

Malledd noticed him there. The children were busily running back and forth through the mud puddles with Anva keeping a watchful eye on them, leaving Malledd on his own for a moment, and he took the opportunity to slip past the crowd to approach the soldier.

"Ho, there," he said, "might I join you for a moment?"

Grudar looked up. "Certainly, sir," he said, moving over to make room.

"I am Malledd," Malledd said as he settled onto the step. "I'm a smith."

Grudar nodded an acknowledgment. "Lieutenant Grudar," he said.

Malledd sat politely silent for a moment, then asked, "This war in the east—is it serious? Have many been killed?"

"So they tell me," Grudar said.

"You have not seen it for yourself?"

Grudar turned a hand in a negative gesture. "No," he said. "Zorha and I are from the garrison at Biekedau. We get our reports through the priests, the same as everyone else. I suppose the army in Govya can't spare anyone to act as messengers, let alone recruiters—or they can't spare the time for anyone to come this far. It's a long, long road to Govya; why send a messenger when the priests can tell us overnight?"

Malledd nodded. "You said you'd be taking these men to Seidabar?" he asked.

"That's right. We've been reassigned, along with a dozen others who are out recruiting. Raising an army at the capital is more important than keeping the Biekedau garrison at full strength."

"Will you be going east, then?"

"If it comes to that. I'm a soldier, sir; I go where I'm told."

Malledd nodded. "Let me buy you an ale," he said, beckoning to Zenisha.

Grudar hesitated, then looked up at the sun. Malledd glanced up, as well; he thought he could see two small moons in front of the sun, but it was still hot and bright. Steam was rising from the rooftops across the square as the sun dried the wet thatch.

"I'm not really supposed to drink anything stronger than fruit juice when I'm on duty, but it's still ten miles to Biekedau, and I'll undoubtedly sweat it off," Grudar said. "Thank you, sir."

He accepted a mug; Malledd took one as well, and tossed a small coin on Zenisha's tray.

A moment later Grudar's ale was gone, though Malledd's was hardly begun, and the lieutenant stood up and shouted, "Soldiers of the Empire! Finish up, please—and it's on to Biekedau, and Seidabar!"

A murmur ran through the crowd, and Malledd imagined he could hear a score of throats gulping ale. He rose and began looking for his wife.

It was actually a good quarter hour before the newly enlarged company of recruits marched on out of Grozerodz, bound for Biekedau. Once he and Anva had said a brief farewell to Onnell and Bousian, Malledd stood by the tavern door and watched them go with a sort of uncertain relief, while Anva collected Poria and Neyil. Arshui had fallen asleep curled up at Malledd's feet, oblivious to the noise and excitement.

When the last of the recruits was out of sight around the bend in the Biekedau road at the foot of the village, Malledd let out a sigh and turned away.

It was over; Grozerodz had done its duty for the Empire. The war in the east would surely not last long, or do any serious harm. When the mad wizard Nazakri saw the Imperial Army he would surely have to surrender or flee.

And Malledd was not involved. No one had called on him. He could go home with his wife and children and stay there, in peace.

The champion, if that was what he really was, was not needed.

He put an arm around Anva's shoulders and embraced her as they walked.

CHAPTER 16

Lord Duzon stood looking about the quietly busy hall with his hat dangling gracefully from one hand, and wondered if he were really needed here. This was not what he had had in mind three years before, when he had offered Lord Graush his assistance in identifying the divine champion.

He had been thinking more of trial by combat—contests between the various claimants to the title, open to all comers, with the winner declared champion. He had intended to enter the competition himself, and had been guardedly optimistic that he would win.

He hadn't realized that gruff old Lord Graush, that man of action and direct speech, put such faith in scholarship.

Graush had turned the great hall of his own palace over to the task of finding the champion. The couches and tables had been pushed aside and were gathering dust along the walls, and now Duzon looked over three rows of desks and work-tables where some two dozen priests and scholars were studying. Several of them were bent over ancient, crumbling documents—letters, chronicles, legends, reports, anything that described the previous champions, from Urzuan the Great right up to Faial the Redeemer—looking for clues, for similarities or differences between past champions that might prove useful in knowing what to look for.

Others were reviewing the histories and descriptions of candidates—people who had presented themselves as perhaps being the champion, and people who had been suggested by others.

The whole room smelled of dust and parchment, and Duzon found it depressing. For two years they had been poring over the records, comparing notes . . . while Rebiri Nazakri gathered an army and began fighting his way westward across Govya.

A roomful of scholars to stop a mad wizard's undead army—it hardly seemed a fair match.

At least, he thought sardonically, the scholars were making some progress. A few dozen claimants had already been eliminated—at least tentatively. The scholars had reported that every prior champion had been male, over five and a half feet in height, and a native speaker of the Domdur tongue—though some were not of the pure Domdur blood. Every woman, every man under five and a half feet, and every person whose milk tongue was something other than Domdur had been asked to go away. Most of them had obeyed.

Vrai Burrai, the eccentric inventor of the New Magic and master of the Imperial College, had been a popular candidate until it was pointed out that Burrai's native language was Diknoi. He spoke Domdur so fluently that people tended to forget his origins. He didn't go away; he argued that since the Domdur Empire was now the same thing as the world that all languages were now Domdur tongues. Lord Graush didn't accept this, nor did Duzon, but there was no point in arguing it beyond a certain point.

Duzon had thought he had found a way to eliminate Burrai, though. The old stories all agreed that the champions had great stamina, especially in battle; Duzon had suggested testing that, at least for those who were actually in Seidabar, with a run around the city walls, and had succeeded in eliminating several candidates who could not cover the entire distance without collapsing.

Vrai Burrai was not one of them. Duzon suspected that he had only managed to complete the run by using his infernal New Magic, but he couldn't prove it, nor could he prove that such a use would disqualify the Diknoi.

Quite aside from Vrai Burrai, about three dozen contenders remained.

Duzon himself was one of them. Naturally, he was a full-blooded Domdur and had spoken the true tongue from his cradle, though he'd picked up a smattering of other languages as well; he stood fully six feet in height, and any number of young noblewomen, including the infamous Lady Vozua and even one member of the Imperial Council, would attest to his masculinity. As for the run around the walls, he'd always prided himself on his strength; when some of his contemporaries made much of a languid, weary style, Duzon had refused to join in. He was willing to drape himself gracefully and fashionably on couches or against pillars, but he had never made any attempt to disguise his own robust health. He'd scarcely been breathing hard when he completed the circuit.

Prince Bagar, the Empress's youngest grandson and Duzon's own first cousin once removed, was another contender. The scholars had pointed out that never before had a descendant of a reigning monarch been chosen as champion, but this was not considered conclusive. After all, Prince Greldar had been a reigning Emperor's half brother. Bagar had joined in the run, and had successfully completed it, though he had been exhausted by the time he staggered across the finish line.

Lord Kadan had been suggested as a candidate, and though Kadan himself had said that was foolish, he hadn't been ruled out. No one had tried to make *him* run anywhere or prove anything, though.

General Balinus, who was currently leading the Domdur armies in holding off the rebel forces until the volunteers of the new Imperial Army could be assembled, had also been suggested and had not been ruled out. In fact, Duzon rather liked the idea.

He liked the idea of himself as the champion even better, though.

The rest of the would-be champions were a motley crew of younger sons of minor nobles, village strongmen, and wild-eyed dreamers. Duzon knew that technically, he, too, was a younger son of a relatively minor noble—it had been three generations since his family had held a seat on the Council, their hereditary post as lords of Snauvalia was virtually meaningless under the current regime, and his father's post as imperial representative in Rishna Gabidéll, while lucrative, didn't impress anyone. True, a cousin on his mother's side had managed to marry Prince Zolous and bear the Empress six grandchildren—including Bagar—but Daunla had done nothing to elevate the rest of the family. They remained minor nobility.

Duzon didn't class himself with the others, though. He had felt all his life that he had a destiny, that some great purpose awaited him. He had been at the council meeting when Lord Graush had said the champion should be found, and he was certain that this was the workings of fate, or the gods, or both—the question of whether there was any fate other than the whims of the gods he left to the priests.

And he wanted to get on with it, to confront his fate, not to sit here in Seidabar, stagnating while Graush and his scholars deliberated, and while Lord Kadan, nudged into action at last, gathered, prepared, and launched an immense army to confront Rebiri Nazakri and his Olnamian rebels.

The standing army that had served the Empire well for so long was not enough, and could not be spared from its regular duties at garrisons all over the world. The call had gone out, just a few triads ago, for volunteers to form the largest army since Faial put down the last resistance against Domdur rule, back in 854.

And when that Imperial Army was gathered there should be a champion to lead it. Kadan had stalled the collection of his forces for some time, apparently in hopes Lord Graush would provide one, but now the army was being assembled, and it would not be long before the vanguard of that army headed east to join General Balinus's regulars and confront the foe.

Maybe, Duzon thought, he should just head east himself—but without the official title of the Empire's defender, what would he be able to do? General Balinus would surely not take his word about being the divine champion, and past champions, as he knew, had succeeded not so much through their own personal prowess as by inspiring and leading the ordinary Domdur soldiers.

Those soldiers wouldn't follow his lead just because he looked dashing in his scarlet cloak and could run the city wall in good time; they'd want someone to confirm that Duzon was, indeed, the chosen of the gods. Past champions had had the priests and oracles to confirm their claims, and the priests nowadays would confirm nothing but their own uncertainty.

Lord Graush had taken it upon himself to replace the priests in identifying the champion, and until his scholars reached a conclusion, Lord Graush would not say that Duzon or anyone else was the champion.

But perhaps another authority could be found. Lord Kadan was eager to have someone who could rally his soldiers—General Balinus was doing his best, but he was not a young man, and Duzon had the impression that he did not capture the imagination of the common soldiers. Perhaps if Lord Kadan were approached properly . . .

It was, Duzon decided, worth a try, and in any case he was sick of staying here, in Graush's hall, watching scholars' pens scratching. He turned and marched out through the foyer and onto the street, his cloak flapping.

There he paused, blinking in the bright sunlight. He glanced up; at least two dozen moons were overhead, barely discernible in the blue of the sky. Three human shapes were more plainly visible—New Magicians, flying about over the city.

Why weren't *they* in the east, he asked himself, fighting Rebiri Nazakri and his walking dead?

He lowered his head and answered his own question—they were presumably still here for much the same reasons that he, Duzon, was still here. They hadn't been sent yet.

He clapped his hat on his head, the broad brim hiding the moons and magicians, and strode onward.

The streets were mobbed; men and women were hurrying everywhere, hauling bundles. Duzon saw the livery of a dozen great houses, as well as the red-and-gold uniforms of the Imperial Army, scattered in the crowds. Two officers were directing a troop of poorly dressed young men in a trot down the avenue, while women and children scurried out of their path—new recruits, not yet in uniform, Duzon supposed.

The Palace of the Army was even busier than the streets; Duzon had to shoulder his way past crowds of men just to get in the door, past men in rags, men in finery, men in the uniforms of common soldiers and senior generals, coming and going or waiting in various lines. The scuffle of so many boots on the marble floors was like distant thunder or rolling surf, and the dirt from all those boots had covered the fine inlays in a thick layer of brown grit; the wall hangings seemed to have been dulled and dimmed simply by being breathed on too much.

Duzon had never spent very much time in the place, but he knew his way around it. It had always been one of the quieter and cleaner government buildings; it was rather a shock to see it like this. He hadn't had a chance to stop in lately; his time had been devoted to Lord Graush's studies, or to maintaining his social connections. One couldn't neglect the ladies, after all, especially when one happened to catch the beauteous eye of a Councillor like Lady Vamia, and a rushed seduction was hardly satisfying.

He was rushing now, though. He hurried through the halls and antechambers, past lines waiting everywhere.

One of the longest lines was waiting to talk to Lord Kadan's scheduling secretary, to make appointments. Duzon frowned. He'd been waiting long enough, waiting on Lord Graush; he didn't want to wait through that line for Lord Kadan.

That was easy enough to avoid, he decided; he simply didn't wait. Instead he walked to the door of the secretary's office, pushed past the man there with a matter-of-fact "Pardon me," then announced to the secretary, "I've just come from Lord Graush. I must speak with Lord Kadan at once about the identity of the divine champion."

The secretary looked up from his appointment book. "Just a moment," he said.

Another man was bent over the desk and appointment book; he looked up as well. Duzon thought the fellow looked vaguely familiar, but he couldn't place him.

The secretary and the other man returned to the book and conferred quietly for a moment; then the secretary wrote something on a page, returned his pen to the inkwell, and put the book aside.

"Thank you," the secretary said. He rose, and announced to the waiting crowd, "I will be back in a quarter of an hour." Then he marched across the room and joined Duzon at the doorway. "This way," he said.

Duzon followed the secretary down a passage and up a stair, along a curving corridor and past a pair of guards to a door. There the secretary knocked.

"Come in," Lord Kadan's voice called.

The secretary opened the door and gestured for Duzon to enter. When Duzon obeyed, the secretary called over his shoulder, "A young man from Lord Graush to see you, my lord."

Then he closed the door, leaving Duzon in the room with Lord Kadan.

The room was a spacious office, paneled in dark wood, with fine many-paned windows on two sides and bookshelves on the other two. Much of the space was taken up by a huge wooden object midway between desk and table in design, and two people were bent over several large maps that were spread out on this table.

One of them was Lord Kadan, Commissioner of the Imperial Army and Councillor to Her Imperial Majesty. The other wore the white robe of a priestess; Duzon didn't recognize her. Kadan looked up from the maps.

"Duzon, isn't it?" he said. "Graush sent you?"

Duzon snatched off his hat and bowed slightly. "To be honest, my lord," he said, "Lord Graush did *not* send me—though I confess I allowed your secretary that impression. I said I came from Lord Graush, and that's true, but he did not send me."

Kadan glanced at the priestess, who kept her expression carefully blank. Both of them straightened up and faced the interloper.

"Graush would have you beaten and thrown in the gutter for that," Kadan remarked. "For using his name to get in here under false pretenses, I mean."

"Indeed he would, my lord," Duzon agreed solemnly, "and you might well do the same, but I hope you'll at least give me a chance to justify my deception first."

"Go ahead."

Duzon bowed again—not so much out of genuine respect, but to give himself another second to phrase his thoughts. When he rose, he spoke.

"My lord," he said, "Lord Graush and all his scholars have been unable to find a way to identify the divine champion. Apiris and his priests—and priestesses, lady—swear they have no way of identifying the gods' own choice, since the gods will no longer deign to address us directly. Yet a champion would be of great value to us; a champion could rally troops disheartened by the foe's black magic, a champion would be a rallying point, a sign that while the gods no longer instruct and command us, yet do they still favor the Domdur over all nations, as a father will favor a grown son."

He paused, to judge Kadan's reaction, but could not read the older man's face.

"Go on," Kadan said.

Duzon nodded. "Notice, though," he said, "that I say *a* champion, I do not say the *one true* champion. For if the gods will not tell us who the true champion is, then neither will they tell us if we have chosen wrongly. Let us then simply *choose* a champion! You, sir, as master of the Imperial Army—were you to pronounce yourself satisfied that some individual is indeed the champion, and were Graush and Apiris to neither deny nor confirm your claim, what then? Would not the people believe you? Or if you could bring an endorsement from someone even higher than yourself perhaps—Prince Granzer, or . . . well, I'd not be so bold."

"I doubt the Empress is going to get involved in this," Kadan said dryly.

"Of course," Duzon agreed quickly. "But your own word would surely be enough in any case, my lord! Think of the boost for morale if a champion were to be paraded before our troops in the east, if that champion were to lead them into battle against the vile foe!"

"And if that so-called champion were to get himself killed?" Kadan suggested. "*That* would be worse than if we never found him. If you think people are worried *now* about being abandoned by the gods, imagine if we proclaimed our champion and some grinning nightwalker ripped his head off. We'd have a full-scale panic and a rout."

"Ah," Duzon said, caught off guard. He hadn't thought of that. The rest of his speech, half-formed in his head, shriveled and vanished.

"I take it, Duzon, you were nominating yourself for the role of champion," Kadan said.

Duzon bowed, sweeping his hat dramatically. "Immodest though it may be, my lord—yes, I was."

Kadan nodded, eyeing him with interest.

"You see, though, why I can't proclaim you to be him."

"Regretfully, my lord, I do. I would gladly swear to do my best not to get killed, but I can scarcely bend the whims of fate."

"I take it, though, you're certain that neither Graush nor Apiris would attest that you're *not* the champion?"

Duzon hesitated, then bowed to the priestess. "My lord," he said, "I cannot speak for Apiris, but perhaps, when I have had my say, this young lady will do so. As for Lord Graush, I have been three years in his service, in the quest to locate and identify the gods' chosen, and I have kept myself fully apprised of the results of his research. Those results, my lord, are minimal. Lord Graush knows little more about the divine champion than the lowliest hedge-wife telling tales to her brats; in fact, much of what he's done is to *un*-learn what little he thought he knew. For a thousand years the gods have chosen their champions, and in all that time there's been no discernible pattern, no visible logic to the choices whatsoever. The astrologers have found no signs in the moons or stars at the times of the various births, the geomancers see no connection in the places, the genealogists can make no links of blood or heritage. Some champions have been marked out at an early age, others not until adulthood; some bore physical signs of their distinction, while others could blend into any crowd unnoticed. My lord, the gods' choices seem to have been the merest whim; whatever criteria they employed, we cannot begin to discover. Lord Graush knows this, yet he has his scholars searching for something we've missed. At present, he would hesitate to deny that the Empress herself might be the champion!"

Kadan stroked his beard, then glanced at the priestess.

She caught the look. "My lord," she said, "we priests make no claim to special knowledge, now that the oracles have fallen silent. There may be some mention, somewhere in some temple's records, of who the champion is to be; other than that, we know less than Lord Graush."

"So if I *did* declare someone to be the champion, and he performed up to expectations, no one would argue with me?" Kadan asked.

"It's the performance to expectations that's difficult," Duzon suggested. "When I came here I hadn't thought that a problem, but I must confess, were my head removed, I expect I would die, and that would not be suitable. While champions are human and susceptible to injury, dying in the line of duty without first slaying the Olnamian wizard would, I believe, be an unfortunate violation of precedent."

"Have no champions ever been killed, then?"

"Oh, on the contrary," Duzon replied. "At least three appear to have died in battle—but in each case only after the battle was won and the foe destroyed."

"Hmph." Lord Kadan stroked his beard, then demanded, "How many viable candidates have you and Lord Graush got?"

"Ah . . . about three dozen, perhaps two score," Duzon replied, startled.

"Suppose I sent *all* of you east," Kadan said. "Suppose I said that Ba'el had come to me in a dream and said that the champion was among this group, but that the god had refused to name him."

Duzon cocked his head to the side as he considered the idea, and he smiled.

"You'd have three dozen good fighters," he said, "and at least some of the boost for morale. And any of us who might perish prematurely, you'd but say, 'Well, he wasn't the one, was he?' "

"And one of you might actually *be* the champion, complete with divine gifts," Kadan agreed. "I'd think that in time it would show."

"I think it might," Duzon agreed. "If by nothing else, the last of us left alive must needs be the champion, no? And since you'll surely put us in the thickest of the battle, it might well come to that." He glanced down at his hat. "Need I fear that beating, and the gutter, then?"

Kadan smiled.

"I think not," he said. "I've got a better penalty for your impertinence, Duzon."

"Oh?"

"Certainly. Thirty-six men, if that's the number, make a fair company; someone's going to have to be the captain of this company of champions, and that's not a job I'd ordinarily wish on anyone, dealing with a bunch of braggarts and lunatics—but I'm wishing it on *you*, sir. Congratulations!"

Duzon considered that for a moment, nodded, and bowed deeply.

"I am honored, my lord," he said.

CHAPTER 17

In the triads after the volunteers left for Biekedau news of the war in the east trickled in steadily, relayed by the temple magicians. Most of it was then carried to Grozerodz by villagers who had gone to the temple and asked for word of their friends, sons, or brothers among the nine volunteers. The war quickly became the dominant topic of all conversation in Grozerodz, supplanting the weather, the crops, and the gods.

And most of the news was unsatisfactory, in Malledd's opinion. He never said so, but as he sat in Bardetta's tavern, listening to the gossip and taking an entire evening to drink a pint of beer, he became more and more convinced of its inadequacies.

There were reports of how the mightiest army the world had seen in several centuries was forming at Seidabar, being trained and equipped at the Empire's expense. There were reports of how the Imperial College of the New Magic was sending its finest students out to slow the enemy's advance until the army could arrive, and how priests throughout the world were studying old, almost-forgotten military magic, as well. There were reports of skirmishes—and always, in these reports, the Imperial forces were victorious.

But always, it was reluctantly admitted, the enemy continued to advance, west through the Govya Mountains and out onto the central plain.

And there was never any word about individuals; the priests, Malledd was told, were far too busy to relay personal messages for all the hundreds of anxious relatives back home. The recruits from Grozerodz were all now part of the Third Company of the Biekedau Regiment, but that was all the word anyone in the village had of them.

A call for more volunteers went out about half a dozen triads after the recruits had left—a less-urgent call, as no recruiters came through and no speeches were made. It was simply announced by the priests in Biekedau that the Empire would welcome anyone who wished to join the war effort.

And not just eager young soldiers, this time—the army wanted tailors and seamstresses to make uniforms and tents, cobblers to make boots, cooks and scribes and administrators. They wanted glassblowers and artisans, though no one seemed to know why.

And they wanted smiths, to train as armorers, to equip the Empire's fighting men.

When Malledd heard that, he felt his stomach sink within him; his lips tightened. The Empire had not called for the gods' champion, the champion he might or might not be, but the call had come for smiths, and he was very definitely a smith.

But then he glanced across the table at Anva, who had accompanied him on the evening that particular announcement arrived in Grozerodz, and he saw the stricken expression on her face. He could see the fear that he would leave her, and he could not bear to see it realized. He closed his hand reassuringly over hers. The Empire would have to find their smiths elsewhere, he resolved grimly—at least for now.

Perhaps if the priests admitted the Empire's losses, he thought, he would go, but as long as they continued to give only these cheerful reports of small victories and the glorious gathering of an unbeatable army, why should he bother? The world was full of smiths.

Still, a certain nagging uneasiness remained, and grew over the next few triads.

It was the first of Vedal's Triad, about fifteen triads after the volunteers had left and just two days after Malledd's twenty-sixth birthday, when word arrived that the Biekedau Regiment had finally left Seidabar.

It was evening, the sun an hour gone. Malledd was sitting in front of his house, leaning against the wall and looking up at the moons—there were at least forty in the sky, several of them in a cluster in the southwest, over where Malledd imagined Yildau to be, gleaming in a dozen shades from bone-white to breadcrust brown. Anva was inside the house, feeding little Arshui; Neyil and Poria were already in bed.

If Malledd lowered his gaze, he would be able to see his parents' house on the left, the smithy on the right, both plainly visible in the light of so many moons, but his attention was on the sky—until he heard footsteps.

Even then, he didn't lower his gaze until he heard his uncle Sparrak's voice call, "Ho, Malledd!"

Sparrak was standing near the smithy, just outside the firebreak ditch—Malledd no longer liked to think of it as a moat. "Moat" was a military term.

"Ho, uncle," Malledd called back.

Sparrak waved and approached; Malledd got to his feet.

"There's news from Seidabar," Sparrak said. "I thought you'd want to know."

"What is it?"

"The Biekedau Regiment has left the city and is marching east on the Gogror Highway. Helsia just brought the news from Biekedau."

Helsia was Bousian's sister. "Is Bousian with them?" Malledd asked.

Sparrak shrugged. "I don't know."

"What about Onnell? Or Timuan?"

Sparrak shook his head. "The priest wouldn't say. You know how they are, Malledd."

Malledd knew, all right—and he had had quite enough of it. It was time to get some straight answers about what was *really* happening in the east, and whether they *really* needed smiths in Seidabar.

"Thank you, uncle," he said. "Good night." He turned and lifted the front-door latch.

"You're going in?" Sparrak asked, startled by his nephew's rudeness—he had obviously expected to sit and discuss the news for a while.

Malledd nodded and opened the door, carefully doing and saying nothing that could be interpreted as an invitation. Sparrak stared after him for a moment, then shrugged and turned away, toward his brother's house.

The boy had always been moody, a bit strange—but after all, Sparrak reminded himself, he was the chosen of the gods. He probably knew and saw things others did not. Undoubtedly there were reasons for his recent morose silence.

Sparrak frowned. The connotations of that particular thought were not pleasant.

He stepped up the pace, trying not to think about what Malledd's behavior might mean. By the time he rapped on Hmar's door he had convinced himself the lad was just tired.

In the main room of the younger smith's little house Anva was seated in her iron-framed rocker—Malledd's handiwork—with Arshui asleep in her arms. She was humming quietly to herself, not rocking; she stopped and looked up as Malledd entered.

She saw his expression and asked, "What is it?"

He hesitated, then said, "I'm going to Biekedau tomorrow." Until the words left his mouth, he himself had not been certain of his intentions.

She blinked up at him in unhappy surprise. "But it's summer! The feast of Dremeger isn't for triads—for almost half a *year!*"

"This isn't for Dremeger," he said. "I have business at the temple, all right, but it's personal, not anything to do with the forge. I need to see a priest there."

Anva glanced up at the loft where Neyil slept, and Poria's little room at the back. Her expression was worried. "Why?" she asked. "What priest?"

"A man named Vadeviya," Malledd replied, answering only her second question.

"Who?" she asked. Confusion added to her worry. Malledd had never told her about the priest's visit years before. He hated himself when he saw her face growing pale. She had never liked surprises, never cared for anything that disrupted the calm routine of their lives.

"Vadeviya," he repeated.

Anva hesitated, then asked, "Is that the one who came here when you were born?"

She had never before mentioned the notorious incident to him, not in all the years they had been married, or the years before. She knew he didn't want it mentioned, and she had obliged—until now. But she had grown up in Grozerodz, and she had heard the story, of course, and she naturally couldn't help wondering if it had some connection with this sudden mysterious errand in Biekedau. She had been following the war reports as well, and had never heard of anyone named Vadeviya in connection with them.

"No, that was Mezizar," he said, "or so I'm told. Vadeviya came to talk to me a few years ago, when trouble first started in the east."

"Talk to you about *what?*" she demanded unhappily.

Malledd struggled, but couldn't think of any way to avoid saying it.

"About being the gods' champion," he told her.

Anva stared at him for a moment, then looked down at Arshui, still asleep in her arms. "I need to put the baby to bed," she said. Carefully, so as not to disturb the sleeping child, she arose and walked into the big bedroom she and Malledd shared, and where Arshui still slept in a cradle in the corner.

Pretty soon, Malledd thought, it would be time for Arshui to move up to the loft with Neyil, or perhaps to take Poria's room—Poria had slept in the loft for a few triads, but the constant squabbling that had resulted had driven Malledd to add the back room. But the children were older now, and might do better.

He stood waiting by the front door, and a moment later Anva emerged from the bedroom and closed the door quietly behind her. Then she turned to him and said, "Malledd, I know you don't like to talk about it, but we must. Do you really think you're some kind of favorite of the gods?"

"No," he said. "Not a favorite. The greatest blessing I have is *you*, and I don't think the gods sent you to me. But the priests at Biekedau say I'm the chosen defender of the Empire, like Urzuan or Rubrekir or Faial."

"But you don't believe it?"

Malledd turned a hand. "I'm just a man," he said. "A smith. If I were more than that, wouldn't Baranmel have danced at our wedding feast? *I* didn't see him there." He smiled. "But then, I didn't see anyone but you that day."

"Then why . . ." Anva began, her voice suddenly loud and unsteady. She realized she was almost shouting, and started again, more quietly. "Then why are you going to see this Vadeviya, if you don't believe it?"

"To find out what's really happening in the east," Malledd explained. "To get some news of our townsmen. I think they've been lying to us, Anva— shouldn't the war be *over* by now?"

"I don't know," Anva said sharply, "and neither do you. Neither of us knows anything about wars."

"Well, I want to find out what's going on," Malledd insisted.

"And why should the priests tell you any more than they've told Helsia or Komorrin or any of the others?"

"Because I have a letter from the high priest Dolkout *ordering* them to."

Anva stared at him, her face white. This was new. This was the first she had heard of any solid physical evidence that the priests of Biekedau genuinely thought her husband to be something more than an ordinary man. "You do?" she asked.

Malledd nodded. "One my mother gave me. The one Mezizar brought."

"You never told me that," she said accusingly.

"I never had any reason to."

"You shouldn't keep secrets from me, Malledd," Anva said. The words were chiding, but her face and the tone of her voice were utterly woebegone.

"I didn't keep it secret," Malledd protested, his throat tightening at the sight of his beloved's hurt. "It simply never came up."

"This letter really says the priests must answer your questions?"

Malledd nodded. "It says . . ." He frowned, trying to remember the exact words. "It says, 'Every priest in the Empire, including most particularly the oracles, is required to render you whatever aid you might need.'"

"But there aren't any more oracles," Anva pointed out, puzzled.

"I know that! But there are still all the others. It says *every* priest."

Anva struggled to understand. "And you think because of that letter, the priests in Biekedau will tell you whatever you want to know?"

"I think it's worth a trip to Biekedau to find out."

"*Just* to Biekedau?"

Malledd hesitated. "What do you mean?" he asked.

"You aren't going to go on to Seidabar, or to wherever it is they're fighting?"

"Just to Biekedau."

"You're *sure*?"

Malledd couldn't lie to her. "I think so," he said. "I'm not sure."

Anva frowned, and her hands, which had been held in front of her, below her breasts, dropped to her hips. A trace of color returned to her face as her temper flared. "And suppose they tell you what's happening in Olnamia, or wherever it is, and suppose it's *bad*, Malledd. Suppose they need every smith they can get, to forge their weapons and armor. I heard the call, just as you did, and I thought you might go then, and when you didn't I thought that was the end of it. I *prayed* that was the end of it!"

"It probably was," Malledd said. "There are plenty of smiths in the world."

"But suppose they tell you the divine champion is needed. Is that still the end of it? I don't want you to leave me, Malledd; I don't want you to go. I'm sure you intend to go no farther than Biekedau, but suppose they *beg* you to go save the Empire. Will you just say, 'Oh, I'm sorry,' and come back home to me?"

"I don't know," Malledd admitted miserably. "It depends."

"You think you might really *be* the gods' champion?"

"I . . ." He stopped.

"If you love me, Malledd, tell me the truth."

"I always do!"

"Then tell me—do you think you're the divine champion?"

Malledd stood silently for a long moment, then said, "I don't know. I don't think I am, really—but I don't *know* I'm not. Who understands the gods?"

"Not *you*, that's certain!" She crossed her arms over her chest and turned away, skirts swirling; Malledd thought he glimpsed a tear in her eye as she did.

He came up behind her and put his arms around her, almost resting his chin on the top of her head.

"Anva, I love you," he said. "I'm just going to Biekedau to find out what's happening, that's all. Please don't be angry with me."

To his surprise, she didn't yell at him; instead she sniffled, as if fighting back more tears.

"Don't worry," she said, "I'm not going to ruin what might be our last night together, ever."

That shocked him. For a moment he was silent. Then he said, "It won't be. I'll come back. You'll see. Even if the gods appear in the temple and order me to go, I'll come back to you in time."

She sniffled again, then turned around and flung herself against him. His arms closed tight, pressing her to him, and he kissed her forehead as she began sobbing.

"You might die," she managed to say, minutes later. "*Then* you won't come back."

"I won't die," he told her reassuringly. "The champions have *always* lived to come home, haven't they? And surely none of them ever had anyone like you to come home to."

She pressed herself against him. He picked her up, kissed her, and carried her to the bedroom.

CHAPTER 18

Malledd slept late the next morning, and by the time he had packed a few things and stepped out the door the sun was halfway up the sky, brushing between a thinly crescent Ba'el and two small, dark moons Malledd couldn't name.

Someday, he thought as he looked up, he ought to learn the names of all the gods, and all the moons, and which went with which. He knew there weren't really exactly a hundred, there were more than that, but he wasn't sure of the exact number, and he didn't know all the names, by any means.

Ba'el's moon, though, was unmistakable, even when faded by daylight—it was the largest of the moons by a narrow margin, and by far the reddest, with distinctive markings. He wondered if its presence overhead on this particular occasion was an omen of some sort.

He certainly hoped not. Ba'el might be the most powerful of the gods, but as god of war and conflict he was hardly the best loved or most propitious.

He turned back in the doorway and gave an unsmiling but dry-eyed Anva a final embrace and kiss. Then he hoisted his pack onto his shoulder, waved a final farewell to Anva and the children, and headed out.

He had no concerns about the route; he had been to Biekedau often enough that the road was familiar, and besides, the road did not fork or branch anywhere. The only possible turns were a few grassy farm roads, and no one could mistake any of those for the highway. That allowed him to not worry about where he was headed, but simply to enjoy the day, and to think his own thoughts as he walked.

By the time he'd covered half the distance he almost wished he'd gotten an earlier start, so as to have reached Biekedau before the full heat of the day—but that would have meant missing sleep, or else missing his last hours with Anva, and he didn't think he'd have cared to have given up either of those. Walking in the dry heat of midsummer was the price he paid, and it was worth it.

The fields on either side of the highway were green with grain and other crops—not the rich, lush green of the spring shoots, but a paler shade that would soon be turning to yellow, ready to harvest. This road would be far busier then, Malledd thought—farmers would be bringing their crops to market, and merchants would be roaming back and forth, Yildau to Biekedau and back, trading with the farmers.

Not yet, though; the road was empty save for Malledd and an occasional snake sunning itself on the hard-packed earth, or a bird foraging along the verge. He could hear insects buzzing in the fields, and he hoped that he mostly heard bees and the like, rather than anything that would eat the crops. Occasionally he would hear a voice calling in the distance or someone whistling as the farmers worked their land, but he could never make out any words or see more than a distant glimpse of a bent back or a broad-brimmed summer-straw hat. There were no faces in the doors or windows of the houses he passed; it was almost as if he had the entire world to himself, as if the gods had swept away everyone else.

The gods . . . Malledd wondered about the gods.

He knew any number of old stories about the gods, tales his mother had told him when he was a child—stories about how the gods had tried to choose a king to rule the heavens, how the various major deities had tried to attain the position and had failed; stories about how the gods of old had meddled in human affairs, pitting human kings against one another for the amusement of their divine patrons, playing tricks upon men and women, striking down any mortal who happened to offend them. He knew the tales of how the gods had arranged the world beneath the Hundred Moons so that people could live upon it, and how they had worked together to create humanity, each of the gods helping for his or her own reasons. He knew that the gods had created the sun to light the world and give it life, and had fueled it with their own glorious essence, and that they took turns maintaining it, each for a three-day shift, creating the triads by which the Domdur measured time. He knew that when the greater gods were on duty, in the summer, the sun burned hot and fierce, while under the ministrations of the lesser gods it grew cold and weak and winter came.

Dremeger, the god of smithcraft and therefore Malledd's own patron, took his turn stoking the solar furnace in late autumn, which pretty clearly showed his place in the hierarchy.

It had been Ba'el, mightiest of all, who had been fueling it on Midsummer's Day, when Malledd was born, but his turn for this year had just passed. Vedal, goddess of the earth, who fed the crops by the road and made them grow, was on duty right now, as Malledd recalled—and the sun was hot and fierce indeed. She was clearly not a deity to be trifled with.

On the other hand, Malledd remembered that she had failed in her bid to become the queen of the heavens because she was so softhearted that she had fed her own enemies and let them grow strong enough to overthrow her.

And that brought him to the point of thinking about the gods as he walked. The Domdur Empire had been appointed by the gods in their councils to rule all the world beneath the Hundred Moons. They had decreed it to be so to put an end to the useless fighting between the various nations, and also, some of the stories said, to stop themselves from using mortal tools in their own squabbles.

Malledd was not sure he believed that particular detail—even if gods could be sufficiently petty to fight among themselves, would they really have used mere men and women as their weapons? And if they had, how did the storytellers know it?

But that was irrelevant. The point was that the gods had chosen the Domdur to rule the world, and had made certain that the Domdur eventually *did* rule the world. For eight hundred years the Domdur armies had marched out to conquer because the gods had *told* them to, in no uncertain terms. Often entire nations had fallen to the Domdur without a fight simply because they saw no point in opposing those the gods favored; their defeat was predestined, irresistible, and to struggle against it would only delay the inevitable at the cost of many lives and great suffering. The Domdur Empire was divinely ordained.

But then, how could this black wizard in the east dare to defy the Empire? Why did the gods not strike him dead for his effrontery?

Had all the gods become as foolishly softhearted as Vedal? Were mortal men to fight and die to pay for the gods' unwillingness to intervene?

Or were they more like Samardas, god of wisdom, who had failed to become king because he became so involved in his own thoughts that he did not notice the others plotting against him? Were the gods simply not paying attention?

The withdrawal of the oracles seemed to fit this second theory better than the first. It was as if the gods had cut themselves off from humanity. Their voices were no longer heard, their advice no longer given—and now their command that all the world should obey the Empress was being defied, and they did nothing.

But the sun still shone, and the crops still grew, and the moons still drifted across the skies—the gods were still *there*, still keeping the world running.

Maybe they had withdrawn themselves not from everything beneath the moons, but only from humanity. Maybe they had finally had enough of human folly, but still took an interest in the natural world.

And if they had—what, then, of their chosen champion? *Was* there still a champion?

And if there was, was it he?

Malledd had mulled these questions over many times through the years, as he lay in bed waiting for sleep or hammered at a piece of iron. He had never reached any conclusions—or at least none that survived the dawn, or the completion of whatever he was making. He simply didn't have enough information to know for certain the will of the gods.

His musings on the road to Biekedau were no different. As he came in sight of the dome of the Biekedau temple he had still not come up with any new insights—only more questions.

CHAPTER 19

The Company of Champions, Lord Duzon thought as he looked out under the dripping brim of his hat—ha! *That* was a sorry joke. Of all the ill-disciplined, mismatched, egotistical, thumb-fingered troublemakers beneath the Hundred Moons, this bunch had to be the cream of the crop. If the gods really *had* chosen anyone from this crowd to defend the Empire—anyone other than himself, at any rate—then the gods were quite mad. Of the forty-one men nominally under his command, Duzon considered all but a handful to be useless.

Half of them couldn't even ride a horse.

Vrai Burrai, of course, didn't *need* to ride a horse—he flew everywhere with that confounded gadget of his. He was up there now, flashing through the clouds like heat lightning and making the horses nervous.

Most of the others, though, were splashing through the mud on foot, leading their mounts, or bouncing in their saddles like a bunch of children. Jolting about like that tired the horses—not to mention how sore and stiff the riders would be when they stopped.

Some of them could ride, of course—the second sons and petty nobles were doing fine, and Prince Bagar almost seemed more at home on horseback than on foot—but the village strongmen and the assorted poets and madmen were simply a disaster waiting to happen.

Lord Kadan had suggested that the company might serve as light cavalry—General Balinus had been complaining about a severe shortage of cavalry—but Duzon was not about to send some of these fools into battle on horseback unless Ba'el himself came down from his moon and gave the order.

Duzon took off his hat and shook it to dry it, then glanced up. The rain seemed to have stopped—just a summer shower, as he had expected. They were common enough. The sun would probably be out in a moment, and that would brighten everyone's mood, including his own. The mud would dry—it wasn't deep, just a thin slick where the rain had mixed with the dust; the hard-packed earth of the road itself was still solid underfoot.

He scanned the horizon. Wheat fields, pastures, farmhouses, stretched away forever to the north and south; before and behind them lay the Gogror Highway, which was little more than a strip of bare earth between the farmers' fencelines. There were allegedly towns and inns along the highway, but none were in sight at present. In the west Seidabar could be seen only as a thin line of smoke rising and blending with the clouds; the city walls and towers were finally out of sight. Ahead . . .

Duzon squinted, then wiped the rain from his eyes with his sleeve and looked again.

There were people on the road ahead—still a few miles away, Duzon judged; he couldn't make out much beyond faint shapes. A trading caravan, perhaps?

Or had they caught up to the vanguard of new recruits that Kadan had sent out to reinforce General Balinus? Duzon hadn't really expected to see those troops until they reached the staging camp near Drievabor, on the Grebiguata, where Balinus was supposed to take command.

Duzon wondered how far they were from the Grebiguata.

He turned and looked over his men again.

They were a sorry-looking crew—in fact, Duzon judged they looked far worse in company than they would as individuals. Most of them were big men, accustomed to standing out in a crowd simply by virtue of their bulk, and in this company, where everyone was at least good-sized, they seemed sadly diminished. They weren't all in uniform—some had been eager to don the Imperial scarlet and gold, as it was far better garb than they had to begin with, but others had argued that the divine champion would scarcely wear the tunic and breeches of a common soldier.

A few had argued that Lord Kadan should dress them as generals, or at least officers, but Kadan had stood fast—commissions and commands in the Imperial Army were *earned*, he insisted, not given out as favors. If one of them proved himself to be the true champion he could wear any uniform he pleased, but until then they would dress as ordinary troopers, or they would provide their own clothes.

Lord Duzon glanced down at his own uniform. He had accepted a captain's commission, and dressed the part—but he had kept his own red cloak and his plumed hat, as well. Fortunately, the two shades of red of tunic and cloak went well together, and the black hat and white plume looked good with anything.

He didn't honestly think he'd earned a captain's commission, but he'd had more sense than to say so in front of Lord Kadan, or in front of anyone else, for that matter. Commissions in the army *were* handed out as political favors, of course—everyone who mattered knew as much—but it was scarcely a practice Duzon, or anyone with any sense, cared to encourage. If Kadan wanted to say otherwise, and to keep his patronage to a minimum, that suited Duzon very well indeed.

For centuries it hadn't really mattered much if half the officers were incompetents, commissioned to placate their fathers or patrons. It hadn't mattered if they had no cavalry, either. The army hadn't needed to do anything but hunt down a few bandits and suppress an occasional riot. If the army was actually going to fight battles, though, Duzon, for one, wanted officers who would win, and who would lose as few men as possible doing it, rather than officers with the right ancestors and friends.

He liked to think he'd be here in any case, but he had to admit that he had yet to actually prove himself.

And with the motley group that was following him across the plains right now, he wondered whether he'd ever manage to prove anything.

"All right, men," he called, "mount up, those of you who've been resting your horses! There's a company of men ahead of us, and whoever it is, I want to give them a good show! I want us to ride past looking as if we were *all* champions!"

"But we're all muddy!" someone called. Duzon noticed another man eyeing his horse with obvious distrust, clearly not eager to return to the animal's back.

"So are they!" Duzon shouted. "Listen, I want the men in uniform in the fore, those in their own clothes to the rear—let's see if we can't look a little more like a company, and not a bunch of wanderers thrown together by chance!"

Almost as soon as the words were out, Duzon realized he'd probably just made a mistake. The competent riders were mostly in their own clothes—those were the petty nobles who had resisted accepting uniforms. It would make a better show to put them in the lead, the others trailing behind.

A leader couldn't be constantly changing his mind, though; he'd made his decision and he'd best stick with it.

The company stopped moving while the men slowly sorted themselves out.

"Come on, come on!" Duzon shouted. He glanced up the road at the party ahead; they were now drawing farther away, almost out of sight, while the Company of Champions rearranged itself. A fat lot of good it would do to get the company into decent order if they couldn't catch up with whoever that was without coming all disarrayed again.

The temptation to shout and swear like a drill sergeant was strong, but Duzon resisted it; a good officer led his men, he didn't bully them. And the champion should inspire by sheer example.

Duzon straightened his own cloak and hat. He glanced down the road. Was that an Imperial banner he saw on the horizon? It looked like one from this distance.

It still might be just a merchant's flag, of course.

The men had sorted into two groups now, uniformed and otherwise, and Duzon urged his mount forward.

"Form up in rows of four," he said. "Any more than that and we'll be bumping fences or trampling someone's crops. You, you, you, and you, take the lead, and you, you . . ."

Overhead, Vrai Burrai glanced down—he didn't want to get too far ahead of his nominal companions. They weren't directly below him, though. He swooped around and spotted them half a mile back, stopped for some reason; they seemed to be moving horses about.

Vrai Burrai was mountain-born, and didn't think much of horses. He'd never been on one until this journey, and he never wanted to be on one again. They were such finicky creatures. There were all these mysterious and complicated things you had to do with horses, not like good machinery or New Magic at all. This rearranging was probably yet another silly ritual to keep the infernal beasts from running amok or breaking legs or something.

At least that Lord Duzon hadn't insisted that Vrai stay mounted. His supplies were all bundled on his assigned mount, and his assistant, that Veruet woman Bouditza, was leading the animal along.

Vrai wasn't sure he'd have stayed on the horse even if Duzon *had* insisted, but it was a relief not to have to find out.

Duzon seemed like a sensible boy, really; it was almost a shame he seemed determined to play all the traditional military and aristocratic status games. He might have made a good New Magician.

He'd rather be the Domdur champion, of course. Vrai Burrai snorted. As if there *were* a Domdur champion anymore! It stood to reason that if the gods were no longer directing the Domdur government, then they'd no longer be providing it with its chief enforcer.

If the Empress and her Council wanted someone to intimidate the peasants, Vrai Burrai thought, they really ought to accept his own offer to take the job. Not that he particularly favored the Domdur, or had anything against the peoples they'd conquered, but he saw the sense in a single world state, and the one the Domdur ran wasn't unpleasant. They let most people do as they pleased, and they kept people from killing each other, and that was about all the Diknoi had ever asked of any government.

That was more than they'd had before the Domdur conquered Govya; they'd had to fight constantly against their neighbors. Vrai Burrai had heard the stories. It was all nasty and messy and inefficient, and that history had made Vrai a supporter of the Domdur cause—at least until something better came along.

This Rebiri Nazakri, with his campaign of terror and revenge, did not sound like something better. In fact, he'd killed a few New Magicians, and Vrai took that as a personal affront.

Which was why Vrai Burrai was up here, watching Lord Duzon sort out horses and riders, instead of back in Seidabar teaching the New Magic. He wanted to see for himself what the Nazakri was up to. He wanted to see if this black magic was related to the New Magic, and if so, how the Nazakri had managed it—Vrai certainly couldn't turn corpses into warriors. He could make them walk; he'd discovered that much in secret experiments that the doddering old Empress would almost certainly not have allowed, had she known about them. But he could only move them puppet fashion, one step at a time, and with great effort, and from the reports it was quite clear that that was not what this Nazakri was doing.

And he wanted to stop Rebiri Nazakri and his army from breaking up the Domdur Empire, unless they had something better to replace it with, which they apparently did not.

So Vrai Burrai had proclaimed himself the gods' chosen defender of the Empire. Claiming to be the divine champion was as good an excuse as any to get himself sent back east into the fight. He could have simply left, but this way the Imperial Council didn't object.

Vrai decided against flying back down to rejoin the others; they'd probably set him to tightening girths or something. Instead, with a twist of his staff, he turned eastward again, and looked down the road that way.

There ahead of him was a large body of men—several hundred, he judged, perhaps even a couple of thousand, and all wearing red, from what he could see. Imperial troops, he supposed; hadn't he heard something about a vanguard being sent out from Seidabar to reinforce General Balinus? He hadn't paid much attention.

Whoever they were, they were marching down the Gogror Highway in a great red river between the green fields on either side. Toward the head of the column he could see banners flying, red and gold with runes on them, though he couldn't read them from this distance.

He decided to take a closer look. He swooped eastward and lower.

The banners bore the names of regiments. This particular group included the Biekedau Regiment, the Nuzedy Regiment, the Daudenor Regiment, the Second Agabdal Regiment, and the Second and Third Seidabar Regiments, according to their standards.

Vrai Burrai smiled derisively. Banners and uniforms and marching—what foolishness! The Diknoi had never bothered with any of that when they fought; they had relied on traps and deceptions.

Then the smile vanished. The Domdur had defeated them anyway, despite the gaudy costumes and bright banners. The Domdur might seem foolish, but they had still won.

Vrai hoped the present-day Domdur were as fortunate as their ancestors. He hovered for a moment, watching the standard-bearers.

Carrying the regimental banner was an honor, of course, but Onnell of Grozerodz, the man carrying the banner of the Biekedau Regiment, thought it was an honor he'd gladly have forgone. The confounded thing got heavy after twenty minutes, and each standard-bearer served an hour's duty.

Onnell had fallen back behind the other standard-bearers. As long as he stayed ahead of the main body of troops no one cared if he dropped back a little, and the walking was easier if he let others trample the mud first.

He didn't quite see the point of displaying the colors out here anyway. Who were they trying to impress? No enemy was in sight; no one would see them but the local farmers, and who cared what *they* thought?

He shifted the banner's shaft slightly, and admitted to himself, *he* cared what the locals thought, actually—he was proud of Biekedau and of Grozerodz and he wanted the regiment to look good. But he didn't think the banners were going to impress anyone.

"Ho, Onnell," said the man next to him—Bousian, one of his friends from Grozerodz. The seven of them who had made it through training together tended to stick together, and the others had come forward, ahead of the main body, to accompany him as he bore the regimental standard.

Two of the nine volunteers from Grozerodz were not among the marching soldiers, however; Vorif had broken a leg during training and would be sent home once he could walk again, while Gaur had deserted, vanishing into the labyrinthine streets of Seidabar's Outer City.

"Look up there," Bousian said.

Puzzled, Onnell turned and looked where Bousian pointed, not knowing what to expect; was there an odd conjunction of moons showing through the clouds, perhaps?

Then he saw the man with the glowing staff, hanging in the air above them, and he almost dropped the regimental banner.

He caught himself in time and kept walking, with the easy amble they'd been taught that let everyone keep up and didn't tire a man out. He shouldn't have been so shocked; after all, he'd seen New Magicians back in Seidabar, during his training.

He hadn't expected to see any out here in the middle of nowhere, though—not until they reached Drievabor, where the Gogror Highway crossed the Grebiguata River, and where they would join General Balinus at his camp outside the city. He was supposed to still have a couple of New Magicians with him, despite rumors that the rebels had killed a few and others had deserted.

But surely they weren't anywhere near the Grebiguata yet; who was this, then? Was the Imperial College sending out more magicians to help in the coming battle?

"Who's *that*?" asked Timuan, the youngest of the Grozerodz contingent.

"I don't know," Onnell answered.

A nearby soldier wearing the insignia of the Third Seidabar Regiment overheard and replied, "It looks like old Vrai Burrai himself to me."

Someone laughed, but another man shushed him. "Seriously," he said, "it *does* look like Vrai Burrai!"

A moment later the figure swooped down out of the sky and landed somewhere up ahead, out of sight beyond the other standard-bearers and their friends.

"We'll know soon enough," Onnell told Timuan.

They had both been in the army for a good many triads now, and had learned how fast and efficiently news spread. The flying man, whoever he was, had presumably landed to talk to the officers at the very head of the column, ahead of the standard-bearers. It was absolutely inevitable that everything said would be overheard by the sharp ears of nearby soldiers, and the news would be passed back along the column within minutes.

Sure enough, the report arrived even before the New Magician was well off the ground again.

"It *was* Vrai Burrai," Onnell told Timuan and Bousian and a dozen others. "He's with an entire company of men who claim to be the divine champion— Lord Kadan's sent them all forward with us, to give them a chance to prove themselves."

Timuan blinked and looked puzzled. "But Malledd the smith is the gods' champion," he said. "Everyone knows that."

"Everyone in Grozerodz," Onnell said. "Nobody around *here* knows it."

"Well, but . . . shouldn't we tell them?"

Onnell shrugged, and the regimental banner wobbled dangerously. "Malledd doesn't want anyone talking about it," he said. "I'm going to keep *my* mouth shut. Besides, how do we know that old priest wasn't lying, all those years ago?"

"Well, but . . ." Timuan persisted.

"Forget it, lad," Bousian said. "If the gods want their champion here, Malledd will be here. And until then, let these other folks make fools of themselves if they want."

"They'll be riding past us anytime now, supposedly," Onnell said. "We can get a look at them, anyway."

In fact, it was almost an hour and a half later, and Onnell had long since turned the banner over to a former carpenter from Duvrenarodz, when the foot soldiers crowded over to one side to let the horsemen pass.

The seven from Grozerodz watched in silence.

When the last horse had ambled by, the men turned eastward and resumed walking.

"Watch where you step," Bousian remarked.

"I hope we won't be seeing too many more horsemen," grumbled Orzin, for whom Bousian's warning had come a second too late.

"I wouldn't think so," Onnell said, "not if that lot is the best the Empire can do! Half of them could hardly stay in the saddle, from the look of them. And why were half of them in uniform and half of them not?"

"I liked the one in front, with the plumed hat," Timuan said.

"He was all right," Onnell grudgingly admitted. "He could ride, anyway, and had some meat on his bones."

"Watch where you step," Bousian repeated.

CHAPTER 20

The temple porch was cool and pleasant, shaded by its high roof of heavy slate over ancient oak but open to the slightest breeze. Malledd lowered his pack to the marble floor and stood for a moment, just enjoying the sensation of being out of the sun.

All around him, the priests and people of Biekedau were going about their business. White-robed men and women stood by each of the three doors and by several of the immense pillars, answering questions and directing visitors, or simply watching; the visitors, dressed in a wide variety of colors and styles, came and went, or milled about, talking among themselves. Whenever a group seemed uncertain, or began to impede traffic, a priest would approach and ask if he could help.

Malledd watched this bustle for a moment, then looked out over the town. The temple stood atop Biekedau's highest hill—but Biekedau had no really high hills. The land here was flatter than around Grozerodz, the buildings taller, so Malledd's view was somewhat limited.

A dozen white marble steps led down from the temple porch to a plaza paved in gray and red stone; half a dozen streets radiated from that plaza, lined mostly with two- and three-story buildings built of yellow brick or gray stone, many of them replete with gargoyles and other fancywork, all of them far grander than the humble structures of Grozerodz. By looking down the streets between the buildings, Malledd could see, in the distance beyond the town, red and blue sails moving on the Vren River; by standing on his toes, he could even glimpse the glitter of sunlight on water.

Before he returned home, he promised himself, he would go down to the river and follow the river road half a mile upstream, to the lower falls—he hadn't seen them in the summer, free of ice, since he was a young boy. From town, one couldn't see the lower falls, or hear their rush at all; the river wound its way around too many hills, and any sound that might have carried so far was lost in the hum of voices and footsteps and cartwheels.

And maybe someday, he thought, he might even follow the river to the upper falls, sixty miles upstream. Or perhaps he could go the other way, to the Illazi Sea, hundreds of miles downstream. He had never seen the sea, and couldn't quite imagine a body of water so large the far side couldn't be seen.

But any such journeys wouldn't be made anytime soon. Today he was here to speak to Vadeviya, and then to head home to Anva and the children.

He turned away from the plaza, picked up his pack, and marched up to the central door.

"May I help you, sir?" asked a priestess, looking up at him.

"I need to talk to the priest Vadeviya," Malledd said.

Startled, the priestess glanced at her fellow doorkeeper. The young priest hesitated, then said, "I'm not sure whether Vadeviya is available at present."

"If he's not, I'll wait," Malledd said.

"Could I ask what this is about?"

Malledd frowned.

Most people, of course, didn't come to the temple's front door looking for a specific priest; they came seeking a particular sort of magic, or the shrine of a particular god, or a counselor, or a priest to officiate at a function of some sort. Malledd knew that—but surely *some* people must arrive here looking for specific priests! Relatives, old friends, lovers . . .

Well, perhaps such people came to some other entrance to the temple complex. Or perhaps Vadeviya was notoriously unsocial. At any rate, Malledd didn't care to spend his time arguing about it. He had an obvious way to end any disputes, and he would not have come at all if he were not willing to use it.

"Just a moment," he said, lowering his pack. He loosened the drawstring, reached inside, and found the ivory letter-case.

"Here," he said, opening the case and handing over the letter. "Read this. Then find me Vadeviya."

The priest accepted the letter and read it carefully. At first his expression was puzzled; then, as he neared the end, it transformed to astonishment. His hand began to tremble.

When he had finished he looked up.

"You are the son of the smith of Grozerodz?" he asked. "The one in the letter? It's true? The divine champion, here in Biekedau?"

Malledd frowned, and wondered whether he might have been too hasty in displaying the letter. "I am Malledd, son of Hmar," he said, "and that message was left with me when I was an infant." He held out his hand for the scroll.

The priest handed it back and said as he bowed, "I am honored, sir! Come with me; we'll find Vadeviya." He turned and led Malledd into the temple, leaving the priestess gaping in surprise.

Malledd tucked the letter back into its case, then with the letter-case in one hand and his pack in the other he followed the priest into the cool dimness of the temple's central sanctuary, an immense circular hall beneath the great dome. The exterior of that dome, above the slate of the surrounding roof, was gleaming white marble, but the inside was gray from centuries of incense and candle smoke, and the air in the sanctuary was even now sweet and thick with smoke. The shrines on every side, each with its kneeling worshipers, were indistinct in the haze, as if seen in a dream rather than in hard reality, but Malledd could see that they shone with gold and jewels. Candles flickered behind colored glass, and plumes of incense spiraled lazily upward in intricate patterns, streaked with sunlight from the ring of windows far above.

Malledd had seen this chamber before, of course, but he only remembered actually entering it once, almost ten years earlier, when he and Anva had come to pledge themselves at the marriage altar—Dremeger's shrine, where he made his annual obeisance, was in one of the side galleries, not even the lesser sanctuary at the rear. This central hall, dedicated to some of the most important deities, was far more impressive than the other rooms, and Malledd looked about with interest.

The priest paid no attention to any of their surroundings, but led the way directly across the sanctuary to a small door to the right of the marriage altar, just beyond the statue of Vevanis. As the priest fumbled with the latch, Malledd looked up at the image of the god of love and duty. What, he wondered, did Vevanis want a man to do when love and duty were in conflict? Malledd loved Anva, but didn't he have a duty to the Empire? The call had gone out for smiths; was he right to ignore it?

The left-hand statue was that of Vevanis's wife and sister Orini, and there was no question what she would prefer—as goddess of passion she would want Malledd to stay home with Anva, where he belonged. . . .

Or would she? Hadn't she, along with the other gods, chosen him to fight for the Empire?

Then the door opened, interrupting Malledd's thoughts, and the two men stepped through into a cool stone corridor. The priest led the way down the passage, past closed doors on the right and windows overlooking a sunny courtyard herb garden on the left, to a side passage. At the end of this he knocked on the right-hand door and waited.

"Come in."

The young priest swung the door open, hesitated, then stepped aside and let Malledd enter.

Vadeviya was sprawled comfortably on a window seat; Malledd knew him instantly, though his hair and beard were now entirely gray. The old priest turned his attention from the outside world to the doorway and saw Malledd.

For a moment his expression was blank; then recognition dawned, and he smiled.

"Malledd!" he said. "Come in, come in! What can I do for you?"

"You can answer a few questions, I hope," Malledd replied, stepping into the room. The sun through the great many-paned window had warmed it; where the sanctuary and the corridors had been cool, this little room was almost hot.

"I hope so, too," Vadeviya said. He glanced past Malledd at the young priest in the doorway. "Malledd, do you want Helizar here, or should he return to his duties?"

"Doesn't matter to me," Malledd said.

"You can go, Helizar," Vadeviya said with a gesture of dismissal. He glanced at Malledd. "Does he know who you are?"

"He read Dolkout's letter."

"Ah. Helizar, be so kind as to close the door on your way out, and to close your mouth, as well. Tell no one of my guest, neither his presence nor his identity."

Helizar bowed and departed, and Vadeviya smiled. "I can't resist the temptation to keep you all to myself, you see," he told Malledd. "It'll make Mezizar and Helizar and Talas and Dirwan so *very* jealous."

Malledd snorted. "If they're fool enough to be jealous of a conversation with a smith, they're fools indeed. Anyone who wants to could walk the ten miles to Grozerodz and visit me at the forge." He dropped his pack to the floor.

"Ah, but they don't know that," Vadeviya said. "And besides, priests do not leave the temple grounds without the high priest's permission."

"You had permission, six years ago?"

"Oh, certainly. I have Danugai's full support for my studies. Of course, I didn't mention why I wanted to go to Grozerodz, merely that I wished to go."

For a moment, then, the two men were silent; Malledd was trying to think of some graceful way to bring the conversation around to the questions he wanted to ask, and nothing was coming to mind. He hated to seem like an ignorant peasant—after all, he could read and write, he knew a skilled trade. But he knew he was out of his depth here; a glance around the room made that obvious. There were shelves on three sides, stacked with scrolls and codices; there was a large writing table holding an inkwell, a rack of quills, and several sheets of parchment. Vadeviya was obviously a scholar.

"You wanted to ask me something?" Vadeviya said, breaking the silence.

"Yes," Malledd said. "About the war in the east."

"I thought that might be it." Vadeviya turned and lowered his feet to the floor. "What would you like to know?"

"I would like to know what is actually happening," Malledd said. "The reports that have reached Grozerodz are obviously either lies or incomplete. We are told that a single wizard, using black magic, has raised an army—and after a full season of open warfare, this black magician has not been defeated, and the Imperial Army is marching east to fight him!"

Vadeviya nodded, then stood up. "That's essentially correct, yes."

"*One man?* The Imperial Army to fight one man?"

"Rebiri Nazakri is no ordinary man, Malledd—any more than you are. And he's not alone in his insurrection. There are always malcontents, and he's gathered them from all the eastern part of the continent—Olnamia, Govya, Matua, everywhere."

"But still, aren't there garrisons? Aren't there magician priests?"

"Certainly—but Rebiri Nazakri's magic is powerful and strange. It's not like our traditional magic at all; it seems somewhat like the New Magic in some regards, but in others it's completely unfamiliar, and it's far more powerful than anything Vrai Burrai or the others at the Imperial College can do."

Malledd frowned. "What can this wizard do, then, that's so formidable?"

Vadeviya sighed, then turned to look out the window again.

"You understand that we have been asked, by the Imperial Council, not to reveal this to anyone outside the government and the priesthood?" he said. "That I've already said more than I should by admitting the Nazakri's magic is unknown to us?"

"I suspected as much."

"But you want me to tell you more anyway?"

Malledd hesitated, then said, "Yes, I do. Dolkout's letter requires you to, if I ask you."

"I know," Vadeviya said. He sighed.

"Well?"

"Nightwalkers," the priest said.

Malledd blinked. "What?"

The old priest turned to face him again.

"Nightwalkers, I said. Rebiri Nazakri has learned how to create nightwalkers, how to make corpses walk and fight under his direction."

Malledd felt suddenly cold, even in the overheated little study. He had heard the rumors, but he hadn't believed them. He hadn't *wanted* to believe them.

"Nightwalkers are a myth," he said, "a story to frighten children."

Vadeviya turned down a hand. "I wish they were," he said.

"There haven't been any nightwalkers for centuries!" Malledd insisted.

"So far as we know, you're right, there hadn't been," Vadeviya agreed. "Not until this Nazakri found a way to make them."

"The gods *destroyed* the nightwalkers! My mother told me the story." He didn't mention that she had done so because his sister had terrified him with tale after tale of nightwalker horrors.

Vadeviya nodded again. "That was my understanding, as well. You see why we do not want this news spread, Malledd? Look at how you've reacted, and imagine the panic if everyone were to learn that an ancient childhood terror had been brought to life. But these are not the same nightwalkers that fought Zobil and the rest eight hundred years ago, Malledd—they're *new* nightwalkers, men and women Rebiri Nazakri raised from the dead with his dark magic."

"And the gods permitted it?"

Vadeviya sighed, and settled back on the window seat.

"Malledd," he said, "we don't know *what* the gods permitted. We don't know *anything* about the gods anymore, not since the oracles fell silent." He gestured at the surrounding shelves. "You see all these books, Malledd? Do you know what these are? Do you know what I do all day?"

"No."

"These are temple records, dating back centuries. This temple has stood for close to nine hundred years; it's one of the oldest in the Empire. Oh, the original portion of the Great Temple at Seidabar has almost two hundred years on us, and some of the shrines in Agabdal and Rishna Gabidéll are so much older than that that no one even *pretends* to know their age, but still, this is an old temple, older than a dozen lifetimes. And in all that time, until sixteen years ago, no one had ever bothered to collect and codify the temple records. No one had written down much of what the oracles said, or what the priests did. There was no reason to. If anyone had an important question, he just asked an oracle. We never worried very much about what the gods wanted us to do, or whether we were doing it properly—if there was any doubt, we could always ask. If a famine was coming, the oracle of Vedal would warn us, and we'd stockpile food. If a storm was due, Sheshar would tell us, and the merchant ships would stay in port until it had passed. If we were ever unsure who to ask, we consulted Samardas. It was an easy life; we had no doubts about the gods' favor, no questions about what they wanted of us. For a thousand years, the Domdur were guided by the oracles." He sighed. "And then the oracles stopped talking to us—or rather the gods stopped telling the oracles what to say. And suddenly, we had to *guess.*"

Malledd grunted. This was hardly news—though it was interesting to hear a priest admit just how easy the priests had had it, in the old days. Ordinary villagers hadn't been able to consult oracles at whim.

"We don't *like* guessing, Malledd," Vadeviya said. "So we're trying to find other ways of knowing what the gods want, and what they have planned for us. We're trying everything we can think of to learn more about the divine wills. *My* job, here, is to go through every single written record in the temple, and to note down everything anyone ever said about any of the gods, and to sort it all out and try to make sense of it."

"Oh, is *that* what this is?" Malledd said, waving at the loaded shelves.

Vadeviya nodded. "Exactly," he said. "And, Malledd, look around you—this is *all*, after almost nine hundred years, that anyone ever bothered to write down. It all fits in a single small room. When I started my codification, I worked with two other priests, Mezizar and Lasridir—but after a year or so there wasn't enough work for all of us, and they were reassigned to recording whatever the oldest priests could remember from their youth. Now I go through *that*, through the notes Mezizar and Lasridir take, and sort *that* out—and they've worked their way down to the priests who were still novices when the oracles fell silent, to memories of hearing about memories."

"Oh," Malledd said, impressed by the thoroughness of such a project.

"And we scholars are not the only project," Vadeviya continued. "The astrologers have been studying the moons far more carefully than ever before. We used to want to know when two moons were to pass very close to one another, since that always meant some sort of interaction between the gods who occupy those moons, but it wasn't really important—we could always ask the oracles." He sighed. "Well, *now* it's important! Every mathematician, every priest with good eyesight, has been put to work charting the movements of the moons, looking for patterns and predictions. And there are geomancers studying traces left in the earth, and oneiromancers recording dreams in hopes of finding that some are divinely inspired. . . . Malledd, for centuries we priests were the gods' servants and messengers, running their errands and telling everyone what they wanted, and relaying everyone's prayers as if we were errand boys bringing orders to a firm of merchants. Well, the merchants have sailed off and left us with no way of knowing what's to be on the next ship, or even what's in the warehouse.

"We don't know what the gods want.

"And it scares us. It scares us very badly."

CHAPTER 21

Tso Hat chewed on his crust of bread and looked uneasily about. The sun was setting, far off across that infinite plain that they were supposed to cross, and the nightwalkers were starting to awaken. It wasn't anything obvious, it wasn't any specific movement he could point to; he could simply tell, somehow, that the rows of stacked corpses laid out on the mud weren't quite as dead as they had been a moment before.

They still smelled just as bad, though; the stench made it hard for Tso Hat to eat. Not that he really wanted to eat this stuff anyway.

He chewed determinedly, not looking at the bodies. He glanced at the men to either side of him, chewing on their own meager supper, and carefully did not look at the bodies. In half an hour or so, when the sun was entirely below the horizon and the sky darkening, those bodies would begin to stir, to sit up, to look around and get ready for the night's advance.

Tso Hat and the other living people under Rebiri Nazakri's command would prepare, as well, and would follow the nightwalkers westward, toward Seidabar. And when the sun rose the next morning, and the nightwalkers slowed and stopped and dropped to the ground, the living would make camp, and settle in to sleep—unless the Domdur attacked again, in which case they would fight, defending the nightwalkers. Tso Hat shifted, and felt his sword, stolen from a dead magistrate, shift with him. If the Domdur came at night, the nightwalkers fought and the living stood back out of harm's way, but by day the nightwalkers were just corpses, and it was the duty of the living to defend them until the next sunset.

It was a life of hard work and constant exhaustion and endless confusion caused by sleeping half of each day, in shifts, and walking by night and perpetually struggling to avoid the Nazakri's wrath. It was not a *good* life.

This was not how Tso Hat had pictured it when he had joined the rebels. He had imagined quick, victorious battles in the city streets of Matua, the Domdur overlords ground underfoot as the people cheered for their liberators; instead he had fought and struggled through the freezing, rocky mountains of Govya, and now faced weeks of trudging westward toward the legendary fortress city of Seidabar that supposedly stood somewhere beyond this unbelievably huge, flat plain. What's more, he expected a long, slow siege if and when they ever got there; somehow he doubted that the people of Seidabar would look on a horde of walking corpses and their allies as liberators. Certainly most Matuans hadn't.

He looked down at the bread he was chewing, and dropped the rest of it in his bowl; even *that* wasn't right. He should be eating rice, like a civilized man, but there was no rice to be had here on the dry western side of the Govya Mountains. They were forced to steal wheat from the farms they trampled across and the villages they marched through, to grind and bake it into this chewy, gritty stuff.

Beside him he could hear the other men eating and complaining quietly to one another. They didn't dare complain aloud; Rebiri Nazakri had spies everywhere, and couldn't trouble himself to distinguish between discontent and treason. Tso Hat ignored the complaints; they'd do no good.

One of the corpses twitched in the gathering twilight; Tso Hat glanced up, then looked away.

Some of the nightwalkers weren't bad. They were all pale and dead-looking, of course, and the smell of death was everywhere around them, but if you didn't look at their lifeless black eyes and didn't take any deep breaths, some of them could pass for living, albeit unhealthy, people.

Others weren't so pleasant—especially the ones who'd been fighting. Their wounds gaped open, bones and organs showing through; flies buzzed around them, and the torn flesh rotted, blackened, and stank. No one would ever mistake *those* for anything but corpses. Tso Hat dreamed of the day when he would no longer have to stay anywhere near them.

For one thing, quite aside from the smell and the ugliness, it was demeaning, serving as a guard for a bunch of reanimated corpses. Tso Hat had seen himself as a revolutionary, planning strategy, leading the peasants in uprisings, and someday taking his place in the new government of a free Matua; he had not expected to be a mere guard for an unburied graveyard.

Someone had to guard the nightwalkers, certainly—they were utterly defenseless during the day—but *he* didn't want to be the one to do it.

Not that he had much of a choice. Anyone who served Rebiri Nazakri served as a guard for the nightwalkers. Anyone who refused to serve died. And anyone who died became one of the nightwalkers. Far better, Tso Hat thought, to guard them than to *be* one.

If he had realized the situation, Tso Hat thought, he would never have joined the rebellion. He had thought that the Nazakri was a revolutionary determined to free the east from the Domdur and re-create the old nations; he hadn't realized that Rebiri was a madman bent only on revenge. He had expected the rebellion to overthrow the Domdur puppets and set up new, better governments that would either fight the Domdur or negotiate with them—perhaps, Tso Hat and his friends had theorized, now that the oracles were no longer ordering the Empire around, the Domdur wouldn't bother trying to reconquer Olnami and Matua and Greya. Tso Hat had heard Domdur grumble sometimes about being ordered about by their gods, had heard it claimed that their ancestors would have preferred to have stayed home and minded their own business. If the conquered nations refused to stay conquered, the Domdur might well have accepted it.

But the Nazakri hadn't been interested in new, native governments. He certainly hadn't been interested in negotiations.

Tso Hat sighed and picked up the chunk of bread again. He should have known better than to expect sense from an Olnami. All Rebiri Nazakri wanted was revenge. He didn't care about governments or freedom or justice; he just wanted to kill all the Domdur.

He wanted to destroy Seidabar and everyone in it. People had pointed out to him that this would throw the world into chaos; he didn't care. Most of the people who had pointed it out were now nightwalkers, and the nightwalkers *never* argued with the Nazakri.

Nightwalkers generally didn't exactly *argue* with anyone. The ones whose mouths and throats were intact could speak, and often did, but they didn't argue. If someone got in a nightwalker's way, the nightwalker would just kill him.

Unless the someone was the Nazakri, of course, or someone the nightwalkers knew the Nazakri didn't want harmed. If a nightwalker said or did something that Rebiri Nazakri didn't like, the nightwalker was just a corpse again, its dark essence sucked back into the wizard's staff. Nightwalkers didn't feel pain, and didn't care about much, but they did *not* want to be reabsorbed into that staff.

The last bit of bread was just too hard, too disgusting; Tso Hat tossed it aside and got to his feet, brushing off crumbs.

Just then thunder rumbled.

Startled, he looked up; the sky was still mostly clear, a few scattered clouds scudding between the moons. Sheshar was a thick crescent almost directly overhead, light blue against the darkening blue of the sky. There couldn't possibly be a storm brewing—at least, not a natural storm.

Tso Hat shuddered and looked across the field of now-twitching corpses at the great black tent that served as Rebiri Nazakri's home and headquarters.

The Olnami could have used the farmhouse that stood nearby, but he had refused, preferring his traditional pavilion, and had left the house to some of his officers. Tso Hat thought that was typical of the crazy old man.

The Nazakri hadn't always had the pavilion; he had had it made in Ai Varach, when the rebels had captured the fortress and holed up there over the winter. He claimed that a true Olnami warlord would always prefer a tent to the confining walls of a house—but Tso Hat had noticed that he had stayed in the garrison commander's quarters until they left Ai Varach.

On the plain, though, he stayed in the black tent, no matter what better accommodations might be available.

Tso Hat peered at the tent. Sure enough, he could see an unnatural red glow flickering below the sides and through the seams of the pavilion as another peal of thunder sounded; the Nazakri was working magic.

Then the tent flaps flew open, flinging themselves back flat to either side, and the Nazakri stepped out.

He was a man well past his prime and never truly formidable, Tso Hat knew that, but now, as he stood there in the twilight, Rebiri Nazakri looked anything but harmless. He stood with his feet braced apart and his arms raised, holding his staff over his head; red flame danced eerily around one end of the staff, while the other seemed to seethe with black smoke that never dissipated, but clung tenaciously. The red glow of the flame ran down the wizard's arms like water down stone, outlining him in fire.

Perhaps he was not a tall man, or a young one, or a strong one, but standing

there, a monstrous figure of fire and shadow, Rebiri Nazakri was utterly terrifying. Tso Hat froze and stared.

The normal sounds of the camp, the rustlings and low voices, vanished; even
the eternal wind that swept the great plain seemed to have stilled. Only the
nightwalkers still moved, as the gathering darkness restored them to their sem-
blance of life.

"There will be no march tonight!" the Nazakri bellowed.

Even the nightwalkers stopped moving then, and listened.

"Tonight we will stay here," the Olnami warlord proclaimed. "The dead shall
dig a pit, down to the mother darkness beneath the earth, while the living shall
stand watch, to ensure that the vile Balinus and his lackeys shall not trouble us!"

Tso Hat blinked, puzzled. Dig a pit? Well, at least the nightwalkers would be
doing the work, and not him.

But what did the Olnami wizard want with a pit?

He glanced around and spotted a fellow Matuan nearby—most of the living
soldiers who had made it this far were Olnami or members of the various Govyan
tribes, but there were a few Matuans and Greyans scattered throughout.

"H'ai ko cha'i mashi," he called—what's going on here?

The Matuan looked up and shrugged.

At least he spoke Matuan, Tso Hat thought, or he wouldn't have responded
even that much. There were some Matuans who didn't even speak their own
tongue anymore. It was perhaps evidence of how successful the Domdur conquest had been that the Nazakri himself had made his announcement in Domdur, rather than Olnami; *everyone* understood Domdur.

The nightwalkers were getting to their feet now, slowly and awkwardly—the
western sky was still warm with color. When full night had fallen the nightwalkers would be as strong and fast and graceful as any living man. Rebiri Nazakri and his aides were directing the dead to find tools and start digging.

He didn't seem to be paying any attention to his living followers; Tso Hat
tucked his dinner bowl in his sleeve, brushed the last few crumbs from his
mustache, and strolled over to the other Matuan.

"U sin Tso Hat huru chi," he said, using the formal form of introduction.

"Hachi," the other replied. "Don't you speak Domdur?"

"Of course I speak Domdur," Tso Hat replied, nettled. "I thought perhaps
we might want a little privacy."

The other glanced meaningfully at the wizard just as a ripple of fire rose
crackling from the staff. "I don't think so," he said. "Domdur is good enough
for me."

"All right," Tso Hat said. "Whatever language you want, then. Do you know
what's going on? Why does he want a pit?"

The Matuan shook his head, but a nearby man Tso Hat took for a Diknoi spoke up.

"He's restoring his magic," he said.

"What?" The two Matuans turned to the Diknoi.

"His power. His magic. He stores it in that staff of his, but it comes from underground, from the deep darknesses. Back in Govya he took it from caves, and in the cities he could tap into it in the deepest dungeons and crypts, but out here on the plain he has to dig for it."

"You mean it doesn't just come to him?" Tso Hat asked. He had known that the Nazakri slipped away on private errands fairly often, but he had never known the nature of these secretive expeditions.

The Diknoi shook his head. "If black magic were easy, there'd be wizards everywhere. The Domdur say the gods sealed all the dark powers away in the earth thousands of years ago; I don't know about that, but I do know you can't find it anywhere the sun has ever shone. So not only does he need to dig, but he needs to do it at night; once sunlight shines into his pit it'll be useless to him."

"How do you know this?" the other Matuan asked as Tso Hat looked at the wizard and considered.

The Diknoi shrugged. "You know how it is. I picked up a little here, a little there."

Tso Hat smiled to himself. Just like a Diknoi, obsessed with learning and explaining.

"So if he did not dig this pit, he might run out of magic?"

The Diknoi snorted. "Not anytime soon," he said. "I mean, just look at him. He's probably just being careful. Or maybe he's running low on the spirits he uses to make nightwalkers."

Tso Hat blinked at that one. "You mean they really *are* demons, and not the dead brought back?"

"I don't know if they're demons, but they're *something* that isn't human, that lives deep in the earth—it's just like the Domdur always said, with all their worries about sealing graveyards with cold iron and flowers, there are things in the earth that want bodies to live in and will take our dead if they can."

"If the Domdur think that, then why do they bury their dead?" interrupted a Loghar woman who had overheard. "Why don't they burn them, like sensible people?"

The Matuans, whose tradition was to entomb the dead, resisted the temptation to argue as the Diknoi replied, "Because their goddess Vedal requires them to bury the dead, as sacrifices to ensure fertility."

"She requires this, even though it makes them susceptible to becoming nightwalkers?" the Loghara asked.

Tso Hat turned away as the Diknoi tried to explain some of the fine points of Domdur theology and funerary customs to her; he wasn't interested in that.

What he was interested in was the fact that Rebiri Nazakri was at the low ebb of his power, and was going to be busy for some time renewing it with this pit of his. And the army wasn't going to be marching westward. When the army was on the move, anyone heading any other direction would stand out.

If he were to say he was scouting for Domdur raiders he could go a half mile or so from the camp. And if he were then to make a run for it, who would stop him? The nightwalkers would be digging their pit, the wizard would be overseeing the digging, and the living . . . well, why would they care?

Of course, when roll call was taken at dawn, his cohort's officer, Hirini Abaradi, would report Tso Hat missing, but by then surely he would be far enough away to be safe.

If they did come after him they would expect him to head due east, back toward civilization. Therefore he would head south, and sooner or later he would come to either the southeastern spur of the Govya Mountains or to the highlands of Kashbaan. *Then* he could turn east, and make his way through Olnami back to Matua.

It was a good plan, he thought. He could beg food and water from the farmers on the plain; they would have no way of knowing he had ever rebelled against the Domdur. He could claim to be a refugee displaced by the rebel army's advance. There were certainly plenty of those.

Of course, most of them weren't Matuan, but he thought he could talk his way around that detail.

He began sidling away from the group that had gathered around the Diknoi, listening to his explanations. He worked his way gradually around to the south side of the camp, always looking busy as he moved.

Around him watchfires were being lit, supplies collected and distributed, orders relayed among the living. At the camp's center a ring of dirt had piled up to about shoulder height as the nightwalkers dug with shovels, axes, swords, and their bare hands. Rebiri Nazakri hovered in the air above the hole, shouting orders; his aides—his son Aldassi and a handful of others he trusted—milled about outside the growing mound.

Tso Hat reached the southern perimeter without incident, and stood there, looking alert as he stared out into the night, for a few moments. Then he waved to the nearest officer—an Olnami, of course, almost all the officers were Olnami, standing by a watchfire. Tso Hat did not recognize this particular one.

"I thought I saw something move," he called. "It could have been one of Balinus's scouts. Out there. Want me to go see if I can spot him?"

"Go ahead," the officer called.

Tso Hat waved an acknowledgment and marched forward, into the darkness and the green wheat, brushing between the stalks, trying not to trample them. Trampled crops would leave a trail the nightwalkers could follow. He made his way slowly through the rows, glancing back every so often to see if the officer was paying attention.

When he had looked back three times without seeing the officer's eyes he thought he was safe; he dropped down to his knees and began crawling between the rows.

He worked his way southward in zigs and zags, staying down out of sight as much as he could, avoiding the paths and farmhouses. The darkness made it difficult; he was constantly putting hands or knees on sharp bits of stubble or other obstacles. The thick wheat kept most of the moonslight from penetrating.

He used the light of the watchfires to guide him; he steered always into the deeper night.

Sheshar moved eastward, waxing as it moved farther from the sun, its color deepening as it neared the horizon; no other major moons rose, and the darkness thickened with each passing hour.

Tso Hat lost track of time; it began to seem as if he had been crawling through the wheat fields forever. The night around him was silent and empty.

And then he heard a rustling. He stopped and listened.

Yes, something was definitely rustling the wheat—and it seemed to be behind him and coming closer.

Surely, he thought, surely they couldn't have come after him!

Cautiously, he turned around and got his toes under him; then he gradually shifted his weight backward, off his knees, and raised his head.

Someone was coming through the wheat—and unlike Tso Hat, whoever this was was making no attempt at subtlety or concealment. In the dim light of the scattering of small moons overhead, Tso Hat could see the newcomer only as a dark shape; he couldn't tell whether it was man or woman—or something else.

Then he saw a raised arm, and the glitter of moonslight on the blade of a sword, and a low moan escaped him. It could be one of General Balinus's scouts, he tried to tell himself. It could be a farmer, wanting to know who was creeping about in his fields.

But Tso Hat didn't really believe either of those possibilities, and he drew his own sword and stood.

If it was only a single man, or even a single nightwalker, he might have a chance. He was no swordsman, not really, but neither were most of the others, and he might get lucky.

Then he got a good look at the approaching figure, and he almost dropped the weapon.

It was a nightwalker. A big chunk was missing from one side; exposed hipbone gleamed golden in the dim moonslight. No living man could walk around with such a wound.

Nightwalkers could be slain, he reminded himself. Some of Balinus's men had managed it, in their various skirmishes. If he could separate the heart from the brain, the nightwalker would die.

The nightwalker spotted him, and spoke, its voice harsh and slurred—its throat must be partly decayed, Tso Hat thought.

"They told me that if you surrender, I'm to bring you back alive," it said. "They'll let you live."

"Give me a minute to think about it," Tso Hat replied, trembling.

The nightwalker smiled horribly, and now Tso Hat could see that part of its upper lip had been cut open.

"They didn't tell me to do that," it said, and it swung its sword.

Tso Hat stumbled and fell backward into the wheat; he clutched his sword in both hands and held it up as if its mere presence would somehow protect him.

The nightwalker advanced, grinning.

Tso Hat jabbed with his sword, but the nightwalker swung its own weapon and knocked Tso Hat's aside. Tso Hat's head fell back as the sword fell from his hands.

Far above, in the sky, something was moving—something the wrong shape for a moon, something that didn't move in a straight line as the moons did.

A god, perhaps? Was one of the old gods of Matua coming to guide his soul to its place in the heavens?

"*Ka'i!*" he called—help!

Then the nightwalker's sword plunged down into Tso Hat's chest.

It didn't mutilate the corpse, or make the wound any larger than necessary; after all, one of its fellows would soon be animating the body that had been Tso Hat's. Instead, once the nightwalker was sure the man was dead, it withdrew its sword, wiped it on the dead man's tunic, and sheathed it. Then it bent down and picked the body up, heaved it up onto its shoulders and turned to head back to camp.

And found itself facing a glowing figure that stood in midair a foot above the wheat, a glittering white crystal in its hands, two smaller glowing crystals mounted on either end of a staff slung across the figure's shoulders.

For a moment the two beings faced each other, nightwalker and New Magician, scarcely two yards apart. Then the magician held out his large crystal, pushing it practically into the nightwalker's face. Two rippling streams of golden force spilled from the lesser crystals into the greater one; then a flash of white fire burst from the large crystal and instantly consumed the nightwalker and its grisly burden, reducing them both to fine ash.

Tebas Tudan settled to the ground and kicked at the little pile of hot ash, scattering it among the trampled wheat.

What a waste, he thought. If he had been just a few minutes sooner, a little closer, he might have saved the deserter's life—but magical fire could not be projected more than a couple of yards, and he had not been able to get near enough in time.

The man might have been useful; General Balinus wanted to know everything he could about how the Nazakri operated. This deserter might even have known why the rebels weren't marching tonight, why they were digging a pit instead. Tebas suspected it had something to do with Rebiri's magic, with whatever power source he had found for his crystals.

It infuriated Tebas Tudan to know that it was the New Magic that had been perverted to this, to the creation of nightwalkers and this idiotic vengeance march. It infuriated him even more that he, Vrai Burrai's own pupil and sup-posedly one of the true experts in the New Magic, could not figure out how Rebiri Nazakri had done it.

Well, he would have to return to Balinus and report the incident—and after using so much of his stored sunlight in the fiery burst that had destroyed the nightwalker, he would have to walk at least part of the way.

Whatever the Nazakri used for power was far less exhaustible than sunlight—yet another cause for annoyance. The Olnami wizard just seemed to keep on going and going and going, raising corpses as nightwalkers and burning down anything in his path . . .

How did he do it?

With an annoyed grimace, Tebas Tudan turned and began walking back to-ward the Domdur camp.

CHAPTER 22

Malledd pushed aside a parchment, set his ivory case down, and sat on the writing table. It was clear that he was going to be here for a while.

"Tell me about these nightwalkers," he said.

Vadeviya shrugged. "You know the old stories," he said. "A nightwalker is a corpse that lives again, sleeping by day and active at night. Having died once, they're hard to kill—the old stories vary on how to destroy them, but the reports from Govya indicate that the only thing that seems to work is to separate the heart from the brain. The easiest way to do that—not that it's easy—is to cut off their heads; our soldiers have experimented with captives, sticking them as full of swords and spears as a pomegranate is full of seeds, lopping off arms and legs, and so on, and as long as the brain and heart had any connection, even if it's merely a thread, the nightwalkers still lived. They're utterly fearless, and stronger than living men—perhaps because they're unafraid of hurting themselves. Some of them give every appearance of being ordinary people, so that spies were a concern during the fighting in Govya, while others have decayed into foul-smelling monstrosities."

"And flowers . . ."

"Flowers do nothing. Perhaps these things are not truly what our ancestors called nightwalkers, but we have no better name for them."

"They sleep during the day, though—can't they be beheaded while they're asleep?"

Vadeviya sighed. "I am a scholar, Malledd, I'm not a strategist, nor am I one of the messenger magicians relaying everything; I don't know all the details. They tell me some of what they learn in hopes I'll be able to find something helpful in the old records—which I have not been able to do. As I understand it, the nightwalkers do indeed sleep during the day, after a fashion—or perhaps they return to death—but they're guarded by mortal men, soldiers recruited by Rebiri Nazakri. Their guards need only keep our men away until sunset each day. And the Nazakri can always create more nightwalkers if we destroy them."

"So the stories of victories are true, then? Not lies?"

Vadeviya nodded. "They are true," he said, "but partial truths. The New Magic can be very effective against the nightwalkers, and our garrison troops have fought bravely. We *have* destroyed companies of nightwalkers, and slaughtered Olnamian rebels, but there are always more, and our own losses have been heavy, heavier than we are willing to admit. We need to destroy Rebiri Nazakri, and we have not even come close to that."

"But the army will?"

"The theory is," Vadeviya said, "that the Imperial Army now preparing at Seidabar will be so overwhelming that it will sweep right through the nightwalkers and the rebels, and even Rebiri Nazakri's magic will be unable to stop it. The New Magicians and a cadre of priests are expected to defeat the sorcerer himself, and put an end to the menace."

"You don't sound convinced."

Vadeviya sighed. "I'm not, Malledd," he admitted. "We don't know what the Nazakri's magic *is*; how can we know enough to be sure we can defeat it? Twenty years ago we'd have asked the gods what to do; now we can't. There are some who believe that this war is a test the gods have set us, to see if the Domdur still deserve to rule—and maybe they're right. Maybe the gods have turned against us, and this Nazakri is their new champion. It's all guesswork."

"Who *is* this Nazakri, anyway? Why has he defied the Empire?"

"Do you know, it took us almost five years to learn even that much? That's yet another reason I am not optimistic."

"But you *did* learn it—who is he?"

"An Olnamian, a descendant of the last of the old Olnamian warlords; apparently his family, the Nazakri, swore vengeance against the Domdur when they were defeated three hundred years ago, but it's only the discovery of his black magic that has actually given this Rebiri the power to attempt anything."

"But . . . but three hundred years?" Malledd stared. He tried to imagine how a family could hold a grudge for so long. His own family did not even know their ancestry that far back, let alone which side they had fought on in any of the old wars.

"Some people have long memories," Vadeviya said. "Not all the world is like the central provinces."

"I know that!" Malledd snapped—but in fact, he had never really thought about it much. He had always known that all those faraway places and foreign lands had been different *once*, but weren't they all Domdur now?

Apparently not.

"Malledd," Vadeviya said, "why did you come here today?"

"To ask you about the war, of course."

Vadeviya smiled gently. "Of course. But why did you want to ask? Because you think you might be needed, that the gods want you to save the Empire from this evil wizard?"

Malledd flushed. "Maybe," he said. "Or maybe I just want to know what's become of Onnell and Timuan and Bousian and the rest, and when we can expect them to come home—if they ever do. Their families miss them, priest, but they expect them to come marching home covered in glory in a few more triads. If they're more likely to wind up as corpses on some distant battlefield, I'd like to know it."

"So you can be the bearer of bad tidings, the sour voice in the corner that spoils the feast, the pessimist everyone ignores until he's proven right, whereupon everyone hates him for it?"

"Something like that," Malledd admitted wryly.

Vadeviya shook his head. "I don't know what's happened to your townsmen, I'm afraid, or what their fate will be."

"I don't expect you to foresee the future," Malledd said. "I just want an honest opinion of their chances."

"I don't have one," Vadeviya said. "I don't know enough. Rebiri Nazakri is a mystery. It may be that the optimists on the Imperial Council are right, and the army will sweep through the rebels, nightwalkers and all, like a scythe through ripe wheat, and the Nazakri will die there, or be dragged before the

Empress in chains—but for all I know, it may be that the sorcerer's magic will blast the army in a moment, and he'll be at the gates of Seidabar before the snows come."

Malledd frowned. "Doesn't *anyone* know?"

"Only the gods," Vadeviya said, "and they, alas, are no longer speaking to us."

"Does anyone know more than you do?"

"Oh, certainly! I'm no expert on this; my job is to study the gods, not to keep up on the latest war news."

"Who knows more, then?"

Vadeviya considered. "Well, I would suppose the messenger magicians would know the most; they relay all the reports, after all."

Malledd nodded. "I want to talk to them," he said.

Vadeviya blinked slowly and studied Malledd.

"That's not ordinarily permitted, you know," he said. "Only priests and imperial officials, or people who pay an outrageous tribute, are allowed to address the messengers directly. Anyone else must provide his messages in writing, and receive an answer in writing, if he receives an answer at all."

Malledd had never before had any reason to use the temple's communication services, so this was news to him, but it was not entirely unexpected.

"I'm not anyone else," he said, tapping the ivory letter-case. If these priests were going to claim he was the chosen of the gods, then he was going to use that; if they backed down and refused him anything, he would use that as proof that the story was a fraud and would be free of this burden that confounded priest had put on him the day he was born.

"So you aren't," Vadeviya agreed. He stood up and stretched. "Come on, then."

Disappointed that Vadeviya had not given him a way out but nonetheless intrigued, Malledd followed the old man through the temple corridors, down a narrow curving staircase to a lower level that was cool and dim, and then down another set of steps farther along, until at last Vadeviya led him into a round windowless chamber so deep within the temple complex that no sunlight reached it, even indirectly, and the air was almost chilly.

They entered through a broad, open archway. Half a dozen doors were spaced along the curve of the opposite side, barely visible in the light of the single candle that stood on a table in the center of the circular room.

An elderly priestess was seated at that table, reading a codex by candlelight; she looked up, startled, as the two men entered. When she recognized Vadeviya she closed her book and set it aside.

"How can I help you?" she asked politely.

"The divine champion wishes to speak to the magicians," Vadeviya said.

Malledd suppressed a start. Vadeviya had agreed not to reveal his identity. . . .

But then, how else was the old man to convince the magicians to talk to Malledd? And in fact, he had not actually said that Malledd was the champion, merely that the champion wished to speak to the magicians.

"Champion?" she said, startled anew. "Oh!" She looked at Malledd. "Is this really he?"

"So it would seem," Vadeviya said.

That cut even closer to directly revealing the truth. Malledd frowned.

"I'm honored to meet you, sir," she said, nodding her head. "Would you prefer to speak to the magicians individually, or all at once?"

"Individually would be fine," Malledd said, forcing the frown from his face.

She nodded, and turned to scan the doors—seven of them, Malledd realized, not the six he had first thought. Five were closed, two slightly ajar. She rose from her chair and crossed to the first open door, second from the left, and rapped lightly. "Dokar?" she asked.

The door swung open, revealing a tall priest—and perhaps the thinnest human being Malledd had ever seen; he was almost skeletal. His white robe had a light blue band across the chest and around each sleeve; Malledd had never seen such a thing before. Priests sometimes wore other garments while performing their duties, and messengers wore red armbands, but he had never seen any color but white as part of an ordinary robe.

The priest's head was utterly hairless, and he peered out with a quizzical expression.

"Vadeviya tells me that this man is the gods' chosen champion, and that he wishes to speak to you," the priestess explained. Then she put her hands on her hips and added, "And you should eat something—*look* at you! You've forgotten again, haven't you?"

"I've been busy," the magician priest mumbled.

"You've been spending all your time chatting, that's what you've been doing! There hasn't been that much *official* traffic. Aren't you hungry?"

Shamefaced, the priest nodded. "Right now I'm ravenous," he said. "But when I'm in trance I don't feel it. . . ."

"And you forget. Well, here, you talk to Vadeviya and his friend, and I'll go get you something." She turned and marched away, leaving an amused Vadeviya standing to one side while Malledd and Dokar, both embarrassed, faced each other.

"You're the divine champion?" Dokar asked uncertainly. "Did she really say that?"

"*She* really said that," Vadeviya replied.

Dokar glanced at him uncertainly, puzzled by his emphasis. "But it's true?" he asked. "You're the chosen of the gods?"

"So my parents were told when I was an infant," Malledd admitted. "A priest told them that no fewer than three oracles had confirmed it."

Dokar bowed, a trifle unsteadily. When he came back up his expression was awed.

"What was it you wanted, sir?" Dokar asked.

"I want to know what's happening in Govya," Malledd said. "In the war."

Dokar glanced at Vadeviya, who nodded.

"Well," Dokar said, "I don't know where to begin." He looked at Vadeviya and Malledd and found no guidance there, so he sighed and began, "The rebel army captured Ai Varach and held it for a time, then left it and broke through the Shoka Pass onto the plains. Now they're marching west. Rebiri Nazakri has said that he intends to destroy Seidabar—he's issued *proclamations* about it. He says he'll smash its walls to powder and drench its streets in blood, that he'll wipe the Domdur dynasty from beneath the Hundred Moons forever, and apparently that's what he actually intends to do, as he has not bothered to occupy, garrison, or govern the provinces where he has defeated our forces, but has only used them to supply his army for the westward march. He's had some problems with desertion, but he's also been recruiting more, both living and dead—our scouts estimate that at present, he has at least ten thousand nightwalkers and four thousand men, and that those numbers are growing. Our surviving forces in the region are scattered and only lightly armed—about sixteen hundred men in all, mostly the survivors of Ai Varach and the eastern garrisons, all of them nominally under the command of General Balinus but many of them actually in small, independent bands with no communications with Balinus or much of anyone else. For now, they're fighting a hit-and-run campaign of quick raids, always by daylight, when the nightwalkers can't defend—"

Malledd held up a hand, and Dokar stopped abruptly. The brisk recitation was too much for him to take in, with the casual mention of thousands upon thousands of men fighting for one side or another. Malledd could not imagine what a thousand men in one place would look like.

And the calm account of the horrors Rebiri Nazakri had said he would perform in Seidabar . . .

"I think you're going too fast for him," Vadeviya said, smiling.

Malledd realized he didn't need to know all these details. Hearing the numbers and times and places wouldn't tell him whether or not he was shirking his duties. There was a much simpler question he needed answered.

"Who's winning?" he asked.

Dokar blinked, startled. "Why, the enemy, of course. Our defenders are horribly outnumbered, quite aside from Nazakri's magic."

"But . . . but what about the Imperial Army?"

Enlightenment seemed to dawn. "Oh, but you didn't *ask* that!" he said. "You asked about *Govya*. The vanguard of the Imperial Army departed Seidabar two days ago, and ought to be able to reach the Grebiguata River and set up a defensive line there well before the rebel army arrives. The goal is for General Balinus and the vanguard to hold the foe at the river until winter, which will give Lord Kadan time to gather and prepare an overwhelming counterstrike. This vanguard includes some six full regiments of infantry and one company of light cavalry, with priestly contingents providing full magical communications. In addition an elite force of New Magicians, sent by the Imperial College, has preceded them—the garrison at Ai Varach included three New Magicians, of whom two still live, and a few others from the east have also been involved in actions against the rebels, though unfortunately none of those appear to have survived. Balinus has reported the New Magicians to be very effective in both combat and reconnaissance, but distressingly vulnerable to Nazakri's black magic. The bulk of the Imperial force is still forming and training at Seidabar, of course—or really, in the military camps at Agabdal, just northwest of Seidabar. Reinforcements are expected to follow the vanguard to the Grebiguata shortly, while the main body will march east when the roads clear next spring."

"And then what?" Malledd asked.

The magician blinked at him in puzzlement.

"I mean, will the Imperial Army be victorious?" Malledd explained. "Will they be able to stop the nightwalkers?"

Dokar stared at him.

"How should *I* know? I'm a magician, that's all—a messenger, not a prophet!"

"Well, what do you *think*? You know what's happening—by the sound of it, you know better than almost anyone."

"Oh, no," Dokar said, waving a hand. "I just relay messages. I go into a trance that transports my spirit into the Higher Realm, and in the Higher Realm I can talk to other magicians from all over the world, and I've trained myself to remember whatever is said, but I don't know what's happening. I can't see the future—only the gods can do that. And I'm not a general; I can't judge who's going to win a battle any better than you could. And even if I could, I'm only hearing one side—there aren't any magician priests on the other side. The Nazakri had them all slain in any town they captured. I don't know what the enemy's real strength is, and I don't know just how powerful Rebiri Nazakri's magic is."

"But you know how strong *our* army is," Malledd said.

"Well, as much as anyone does," Dokar agreed. "Tens of thousands of hastily trained and poorly armed farm boys, for the most part—some of them are using sharpened graveyard fence pickets for swords or lances. The officers are telling them it's because they're fighting nightwalkers, but the truth is it's because there aren't enough proper blades. We haven't fought a real war in two hundred years; none of our experienced officers have ever been in any fight bigger than the brewery riots of 1099, and half the officers are ordinary soldiers who were promoted specifically for this campaign and have never been in anything worse than a barroom brawl. We have numbers on our side—*huge* numbers, the Imperial Council expects to be able to field half a million men at the Grebiguata in the spring—and the rebel army isn't much more experienced than ours. Our morale is generally excellent, so far, but when actual battle comes, something more than the skirmishes we've fought so far, there's absolutely no telling how well our troops will fight, or what magic the Nazakri may have in reserve."

Malledd frowned. "You can't tell?"

"No one can."

"You said they don't have good swords—what about the Imperial Armory?" Malledd had heard tales about the size of the Imperial Armory, and the fearsomeness of the weapons it held, since he was a boy. "And didn't they call for smiths triads ago?"

"The Imperial Armory was cleaned out equipping that six-regiment vanguard, stripped to the walls. And just because they *called* for smiths doesn't mean they *got* them; it's easy to convince surplus farm boys to leave home, but most smiths know better."

Just then the priestess returned with a platter of food—bread, sliced ham, hard cheese, apples, and cider. She set it on the table and Dokar immediately began to eat, ignoring his visitors.

Malledd stared as the half-starved magician wolfed down bread and ham. He was thinking hard about what he had just heard.

A cough interrupted his concentration. "There's enough for everyone," the priestess said, shyly offering Malledd an apple.

CHAPTER 23

Asari Asakari looked thoughtfully around the rebel camp, then turned back to his companion, who was busily polishing a complex crystal structure. He asked Aldassi, "Do you think it will work?" He spoke in Olnami, not Domdur.

Aldassi looked up from his work, startled, and met Asari's gaze. "Do I think *what* will work?" he asked.

"Your father's plan," Asari said. "Such as it is," he added.

Aldassi turned his head and studied the encampment, just as Asari had, taking in the stacked corpses that were the nightwalkers, the mismatched tents of the living, the patrols marching the camp's boundaries, the mound of dirt around the pit his father had ordered the nightwalkers to dig the night before. He didn't reply immediately.

"I'd say that some of the initial enthusiasm has worn off," Asari ventured. "I don't think most of our people realized how far it is from Matua to Seidabar."

"I know," Aldassi answered. "I don't think my *father* really understood the distance. It's a long way, certainly." Then he shrugged. "But what choice do any of them have?"

"Well, I wondered whether they would still have the necessary enthusiasm to fight, once we reach Seidabar," Asari said, trying to sound casual.

"They don't need to be enthusiastic," Aldassi replied flatly. "The nightwalkers will destroy the city—or my father will, with his magic. All these people have to do is guard the nightwalkers and my father by day, and by night we will advance, and in time we will get there." His pronunciation grew somewhat more elaborate and precise as he spoke. His father preferred the older, more formal dialects, and when he spoke of Rebiri's goals Aldassi tended to shift toward that mode of speaking.

"But do they still want to?" Asari asked.

"Does it matter?" Aldassi shrugged. "If they desert, my father or the night-walkers will hunt them down and kill them. They know that. They've seen it." He swept an arm around, taking in the horizon. "And where would they go, out here?"

Asari had to concede that point; the great plain between Govya and the western hills was not exactly inviting territory. Endless fields of barley and wheat stretched out to the horizon in all directions, sprinkled with the scattered homes of the Domdur farmers—the nomads who had once occupied this land were all long gone, either dead, departed, or become Domdur farmers themselves. Now the farmers were mostly gone as well, having fled before the advancing army of nightwalkers. The army's foragers stripped clean each house they passed, and each field that had not been burned. One such house stood thirty yards away, and they were sitting in one such field, beneath a faded brown awning that fluttered above them in the constant wind.

"Then you think we will reach Seidabar?"

"Of course," Aldassi said.

"And Seidabar will fall?" Asari asked.

"How can it not?" Aldassi replied, now speaking entirely in the archaic formal style, as if he were engaged in one of the ritual tribal debates that were an Olnami tradition. "My family has lived for revenge for three hundred years, and now my father has found the means of that vengeance. We will have it; the gods would not have permitted us to come so far if they did not mean us to succeed."

"The gods favor the Domdur," Asari said, his own pronunciation shifting toward the formal. He had never been trained in the old debating rituals, but he had heard them a few times. "Everyone knows that to be so."

Aldassi frowned. "No more," he said.

"You are certain? I have heard it suggested . . ."

"I *suggest* nothing," Aldassi said. "I *tell* you it is so—a god speaks to my father, directing him, showing him where his destiny lies. It is this god who has seen to it that my father learned the New Magic and found the means to use it for more than its Diknoi inventors ever imagined possible."

"A god . . . speaks to your father?" Asari hesitated. "I know he claims to have a destiny leading him on . . ."

"And he has now learned that it is a god who guides him toward that destiny." Aldassi considered a moment, then said, "Perhaps 'speaks' is overstating the case; this god, for that is what my father now knows it to be, does not openly address him in words, as the gods spoke to the Domdur oracles. Yet it makes its will known."

"You call a god 'it,' not 'he'?"

"We know nothing of this deity's nature. Perhaps it is a god, or a goddess, or some other divine entity." Aldassi shrugged. "It is enough to know that it is divine. The gods have abandoned the Domdur; their oracles are silent, and we have freed the ancient powers of the earth the gods once imprisoned. I know not whether the old, forgotten gods of my people have thrown down the Domdur gods, or whether the Domdur have sinned against their own gods and been cast aside, and I do not care—it is enough to know that the Domdur are bereft of divine favor, while my father has divine guidance in his pursuit of his destiny. With that guidance and the power it has given us we can once again fight the Domdur, and this time we will prevail."

"So Seidabar will fall."

"Seidabar *must* fall."

Asari nodded. "And then what?" he asked.

Aldassi blinked, and stared at him.

Asari stared back. "Then what?" he repeated. "When Seidabar is destroyed, then what?"

For a moment neither man spoke. "Then we have our revenge," Aldassi said at last.

"And what will we do *after* that?" Asari insisted. "The Domdur still rule most of the world, after all, and even when Seidabar is gone their garrisons and governors will be everywhere."

"There will be chaos," Aldassi said. "With the Domdur heart cut out the slaves will rise against their masters, and the Domdur will be slaughtered everywhere. The old nations will rise anew, and my father and I shall return to Olnami in triumph."

"And the rest of us?"

Aldassi shrugged. "I don't know," he admitted, slipping briefly out of the formal mode. "What will come will come."

"Perhaps we could make sure that what comes is what we *want* to come," Asari said, his own accent becoming still more formal. "Why should we allow all the old nations to be restored? Were the Domdur our only foes of old?"

"Pah." Aldassi waved that away. "No one would dare defy my father."

"Exactly my point," Asari said. "Why should you return to Olnami, to be nothing more than the Olnami warlords? Why should you allow the Matuans and the Greyans and the Kashbaanaya to do as they please? Do you not fear that the Domdur might someday recover, even with their Empress slain and their fortresses thrown down?"

Aldassi did not bother to reply in words; he simply stared at Asari.

"I *mean*," Asari said, "why do we not take the place of the Domdur, and rule all the world?"

Aldassi did not answer directly; he turned his head and stared westward, toward Seidabar.

"You mean name my father the Emperor?" he asked at last.

"Why not?" Asari said.

"There are not enough Olnami in all the world to man the garrisons and the governors' palaces," Aldassi said. "And the Olnami are free people, not soldiers."

Asari did not contradict that, though he knew better than to believe that most Olnami were any more devoted to freedom than anyone else. "Are all the Empire's soldiers Domdur?" he asked. "The priests, the messengers, the governors and advisers—are they all of Domdur blood?"

"They serve the Domdur, whatever their ancestral blood," Aldassi replied.

"And most would as willingly serve the Olnami."

"Would they?"

"Most assuredly," Asari said.

Something in his tone made it plain that he meant it. Aldassi cocked his head and looked sideways at Asari. "Have you spoken to my father of this notion?"

Asari shook his head. "I do not have your father's ear."

"And I do, of course," Aldassi said.

"Of course," Asari agreed. "I do not pretend that this conversation has occurred entirely by chance."

Aldassi turned his gaze westward again. "And do you pretend that this idea is solely the product of your own thoughts?"

"No," Asari admitted. "I have spoken with many people."

"Including, perhaps, some among the enemy who hope to be spared, should they agree to serve the Olnami?"

"Perhaps."

Aldassi nodded. "But why should we spare them? What can they offer us?"

"The means to rule the Empire, rather than to simply destroy it—that's what they offer, O Nazakri."

"Can the people to whom you have spoken truly offer us so much, then?"

Asari hesitated.

"In truth, Nazakri," he said, "I have only spoken with messengers. If the signatures upon these messages are authentic, however, I would say that yes, these people can deliver what they promise."

Aldassi considered that. "You call me Nazakri as if it were my title," he said abruptly. "My father is yet the lord of the Nazakri."

"Of course," Asari agreed.

Aldassi shifted abruptly back to modern, colloquial Olnami, the language not of formal challenge and debate, but of the marketplace. "So just who are these people, and what are their terms?"

"First," Asari said, "they want to know whether we will listen to them. They want an honest hearing."

Aldassi nodded. "Fair enough. I'll talk to my father when I get a chance," he said. "I'm not promising anything."

"Of course," Asari said, bowing.

Rebiri Nazakri stared at his son, and Aldassi suppressed a shudder. The magic had changed the old man, Aldassi thought. His father had always been cold and hard, but now he scarcely seemed human. Even when he was not actually holding his staff the Nazakri seemed to be surrounded by darkness, and his eyes, always dark, now seemed to almost possess the black-beyond-black of a nightwalker's eyes.

Ungrateful though the thought was, Aldassi could not help being relieved that he had not himself tried to bind darkness in his power-trapping crystals. His was still the same New Magic that Tebas Tudan had taught, capturing sunlight, and with it the energy of the gods themselves.

That had initially been his father's choice, not his own—Rebiri had told Aldassi that the wise warrior always carried more than a single weapon. Better they should have both the light and the dark in their arsenal than to rely on only one or the other.

Aldassi had not argued. He was comfortable with the light, while the darkness made him uneasy—and he suspected that he had become sufficiently fraught with the sunlit magic that the deep darkness would never come near him. Tebas Tudan had told Aldassi privately, before the two Olnami left the school in Fadari Tu, that he was twice the magician his father was, and there might even have been some truth in it, but Aldassi doubted that he could have handled those dark *things* as well as Rebiri did.

"Are they Domdur?" Rebiri demanded.

"What?" Aldassi asked.

"These people who want to bargain with us," Rebiri said. "Are they Domdur?"

"I don't know yet," Aldassi admitted, "but I think so."

"If they are, they must die," Rebiri said. "I won't let any Domdur traitors survive my vengeance—being Domdur is enough, and being traitors to their own kind dooms them a second time. If they're Diknoi or Matuan or some other such tribe, then they may live, and serve the Olnami if they choose. I have no objection to setting ourselves atop a new empire, if that's what they want—but not if it means sparing any of the Domdur."

"But, Father," Aldassi said, "what if . . ."

Rebiri held up a hand, and his son fell silent.

"I did not say we would not deal with them," the old man said. "If they offer to help us, we will accept that aid. But understand, my son—our word is good, yet the Domdur must die. Say what you must to convince them to destroy their own people, but you must not swear any oaths that would bind us as we would not be bound. My ancestor Basari made that mistake, and we will not repeat it. Speak gently, twist words—make them hear what they want to hear, rather than what we say."

Aldassi nodded. "I understand, and I'll do my best."

"You have your staff," Rebiri said.

"Of course."

Rebiri nodded. "If you must fly to Seidabar to treat with these people, you have my blessing to do so," he said. "But make no promises! Let them fool themselves, Aldassi. Do not lie—but tell only those truths that will aid us."

"Yes," Aldassi said. "As you say."

Three days later Aldassi sat in a small, richly appointed chamber and spoke to a high-ranking Domdur lord. He said, "We can promise nothing before we have seen proof that you are truly on our side."

He did not say that they would promise nothing in any case, or that no Domdur could ever be on the Olnami side.

He said, "We will find places for those who please my father."

He did not say that for some the places the Nazakri would find would be graves, or that no Domdur could ever please Rebiri Nazakri.

His listeners heard what they chose to hear.

The Nazakri's army marched westward, and as it marched there were some who awaited its eventual coming not with dread, but with anticipation.

CHAPTER 24

An hour after their talk with the magicians, Malledd and Vadeviya were back in Vadeviya's study. This time Malledd took the window seat, looking out over the rooftops of Biekedau, while Vadeviya sat at the writing table. Malledd's belly was satisfied, but his mind was not.

He had spoken with three of the magicians in all, and with an aide to the imperial representative in Biekedau who had come in with a message to send. The aide had refused to say anything definite about almost everything—but then, he wasn't a priest, and Malledd had not tried to use Dolkout's letter as leverage with him.

The three messengers had all agreed, though—the army in Seidabar was large and growing, enthusiastic but lacking in training and armament, while Rebiri Nazakri's capabilities were unknown.

"What would happen," Malledd asked from the window seat, "if the Nazakri *did* destroy Seidabar?"

"That would depend on many things," Vadeviya replied. "Are you supposing that the Empress and her court escaped, or not? Are you assuming Rebiri Nazakri would be satisfied by the destruction, or that he would die in accomplishing it? Do you think the gods would intervene?"

"I don't know," Malledd said, looking out the window. The sun was sinking westward, and the town was crisscrossed by lengthening shadows. He had never seen it from this angle before, had never before looked down on *any* town from a window like this. "It's so hard to believe, this talk of a war hundreds of miles away, with nightwalkers and evil magicians."

"I doubt Rebiri Nazakri considers himself evil, Malledd."

"But isn't he evil?" Malledd asked. "He wants to destroy the government that's kept the world happy and at peace for centuries."

"The way he sees it, he wants to destroy the people who defeated and subjugated his ancestors."

"His ancestors are long dead. Destroying Seidabar won't bring them back."

"But it will avenge them."

"What good will *that* do?"

Vadeviya didn't have an answer for that.

"If Seidabar falls," Malledd asked again, "what will happen to the rest of the world?"

"No one knows," Vadeviya replied. "I would guess that other people in various parts of the world will see it as the end of the Domdur Empire, and dozens, or hundreds, of provinces will rebel and reassert their independence. And if the Empress dies violently, there will probably be civil war among the Domdur as various claimants vie for the throne—Prince Graubris's presumed succession is already troubled by the lack of oracular confirmation, and a military disaster would serve to discredit it completely. It won't be very pleasant."

"But how could anyone oppose the Prince's claim?"

"His older sister could easily argue that her seniority is more important than her sex, Malledd, while Prince Zolous, who is, after all, only ten minutes younger, could point out that of the Empress's three children, only he has heirs of his own."

"I hadn't thought about that," Malledd said. "It seems so far away."

"It *is* far away. But there could be a civil war, all the same."

"And if there *is* a civil war, or rebellions in the outlying provinces," Malledd asked, "how far would it spread? Would anything happen *here*? Or in Grozer-odz?"

"Probably," Vadeviya said. "Armies will be marching, and they'll need men and supplies. No place would be entirely safe."

"And the gods would allow it—civil war and rebellion? They would allow the destruction of Seidabar?"

Vadeviya nodded. "As far as we know, yes," he said. "Unless you believe the legends about the days before the Selection of the Domdur, the gods have never really interfered all that much in human affairs beyond guiding the Empire with oracles and champions. Now they don't even do that. Since the oracles fell silent there hasn't been a single documented case of divine intervention."

"But don't they favor the Domdur?"

Vadeviya was slow to answer that, but at last he said, "For a thousand years, they did—but the gods can change. Perhaps they favor us no longer. It might well be that some dark god has granted this Rebiri Nazakri his power specifically to overthrow the Domdur."

Malledd's head snapped around, and he stared at the old priest.

"You're a Domdur priest," he said, "yet you can doubt the gods' favor?"

"I am an honest man, Malledd, even with myself," Vadeviya replied. "Or at least I try to be. The gods will no longer tell us what they want, or what they intend; we don't *know* what they're doing. It may be that they have deserted us—or it may be that they're testing our faith by feigning such a desertion, and they'll save us in the end. I *don't* know. No one does."

"And you don't even know, then, if I am the gods' champion, with the gifts they promised."

"True enough," Vadeviya agreed. "You *were* truly the chosen one when you were born, and in all the thousand years of the Empire no champion has ever been renounced—but never before were the oracles silent. It may be that you are only a smith, and Rebiri Nazakri is now the gods' chosen one—or that some other has been chosen, or that there *is* no champion."

Malledd was silent for a moment. Then he asked, "Such uncertainty does not trouble you?"

"Oh, it troubles me very much," Vadeviya said. "Just as it's troubled *you* all your life. I'm not going to deceive myself to end my discomfort, though, any more than you have. You're here today because you're unsure what you should do, where your true duties lie. You want me to tell you, and to put all my authority as a senior priest behind it. Well, I'm sorry, Malledd, but I can't do that, because I don't know where your duties truly lie. I *believe* that you have a responsibility to the Empire that supersedes your desire to stay safely at home with your wife and children, if only because they'll be in as much danger as any other Domdur family if Seidabar falls, but I don't *know* it to be true—it may be that the gods will strike the Nazakri dead tomorrow. I believe you're still the gods' champion, because while the gods can change, they have never been so capricious as such a change would be—but I don't *know*."

"I never asked to be champion," Malledd said.

"None of us asked to be born what we are," Vadeviya replied. "I did not choose to be a man, but I accept the responsibilities of manhood."

Malledd shook his head. "It's not the same," he said. He sat speechless for a long moment, thinking, remembering what he had told Anva. He had said he would come straight home from Biekedau.

But that was before he had heard the magicians talking about the inexperienced Imperial Army facing this infernal wizard. Hundreds had already died at Nazakri's hand, and hundreds more might die. Seidabar might fall. The whole world might collapse into chaos.

And what would stop the chaos from striking at Grozerodz, at Anva and Neyil and Poria and Arshui?

It seemed much more real, much more immediate, here in Vadeviya's study than it had back home. His own designation as the gods' chosen seemed more believable than ever before when he saw the priests waiting on his every whim; whatever his own doubts, it was clear that the people of this temple believed every word in Dolkout's letter.

He could return to Grozerodz for now—the enemy was still far to the east—but he feared that if he once went back, then all he had seen and heard here would fade, that he would be unable to tear himself away from Anva again.

He had told Anva he would come home to her—but he couldn't yet.

He struggled to convince himself. At last, he said, "I will go to Seidabar—as a smith, though, no more. *You* may believe I am still the chosen of the gods, but I do not."

Vadeviya nodded.

"I would ask one more favor before I go," Malledd said. "Might I have paper and pen, and would someone take a message to my wife in Grozerodz?"

"Is that all?" Vadeviya asked. "You forget, Malledd, that whatever you may believe, you can still command every priest in this temple as if we were your slaves. If you ask, we will send a dozen priestesses to wait on your wife hand and foot, and a dozen strong priests will carry you to Seidabar on their shoulders, singing your praise with every step."

"I am only a smith," Malledd insisted. Then he hesitated. "But if you could send a woman to help Anva with the children, perhaps . . ." He flushed with embarrassment at his own presumption.

"It will be done," Vadeviya promised. "In fact, I'll send two."

"Then I had best be going." He rose from the window seat. "It's a long way to Seidabar."

"Too long to start tonight—we'll find you a bed here and leave in the morning."

"We?" Malledd asked, startled.

"Certainly," Vadeviya said, smiling. "You've never been to Seidabar, have you?"

Malledd admitted he had not.

"Then you'll need a guide, an adviser. I spent three years in the capital as a novice, and I've visited on occasion since; I don't know its every street and building, but I can provide at least a little help."

Malledd hesitated. "But . . . don't you . . ."

"I have no duties here anymore, Malledd," Vadeviya said, his smile fading. "I'm an old man who's finished his assigned tasks, and is kept on out of loyalty. I would like very much to accompany you to Seidabar, to see what happens there—after all, however the war turns out, think what a tale it will be to tell my sister's grandchildren if I am witness to the final battle. To say I saw Rebiri Nazakri slain on the banks of the Grebiguata, or that I watched him march in triumph through the burning ruins of Seidabar—that's a story worth the seeing, and worth the telling, isn't it?"

Malledd had no further arguments to make; after all, he couldn't prevent Vadeviya from coming to Seidabar if the priest chose to do so, and to be honest, a familiar face might be very welcome in a strange city.

"As you wish," he said. "But I do ask that you tell no one—no one—that I am the gods' chosen unless I have consented beforehand."

Vadeviya smiled. "Agreed," he said.

Malledd smiled back, then turned his gaze out the window again.

The shadows were thick in the streets and creeping across the lower rooftops, the sky in the west beginning to redden. In the distance, almost on the horizon,

Malledd could glimpse a sliver of gold that he recognized as a bend in the Vren River, well downstream from Biekedau.

Tomorrow he would cross the Vren for the first time in his life, leave the familiar hills for the plain, and set out for Seidabar, the Imperial City, home of Her Imperial Majesty Beretris, Queen of the Domdur and Empress of All the World.

He shivered at the thought, and turned away.

CHAPTER 25

I don't *care* what Mother says!" shouted Princess Darisei, stamping angrily across the lush Iyaran carpet in a fashion more suited to someone a tenth her age. "Why should an Emperor be preferable to an Empress? *She's* done just fine for the past fifty-five years!" She reached the broad, many-paned window and spun to face the others, the bright summer sunlight pouring in around her.

"The Empire was always at peace then," her brother Zolous said calmly. He was settled comfortably in one of the big tapestry-upholstered chairs, watching his elder sister with brotherly tolerance. He had a rather strong suspicion that her sex was merely an excuse, and that their mother had chosen their brother Graubris for more personal reasons.

"The Empire will *be* at peace," Granzer said, from where he stood beside the unlit hearth. "This stupid rebellion can't last long."

"You're sure of that?" Zolous asked.

"I hope you're right," Graubris remarked. He was slumped into the other tapestry chair, in the shadows beside the window.

"Of course I'm sure, and of course I'm right," Granzer replied, leaning back against the stones. "We're *destined* to rule. The gods aren't going to reverse a thousand years of history."

"*We* are destined to rule," Darisei corrected him from her place in the sun. She pointed a long finger at Granzer. "*You* just married me."

"If you like," Granzer said mildly.

Zolous suppressed a smile—Darisei would not have appreciated it had she seen him smiling, but he could not help being amused, all the same. Here they were, the three siblings bickering over who would rule the Empire when their mother died—as Zolous certainly hoped she wouldn't do anytime soon—when their cousin Granzer, as the President of the Imperial Council, actually ruled the Empire *now*.

Zolous had to admit, to himself at least, that he harbored hopes of somehow taking the throne himself someday; certainly he thought he could do a better job than his hot-tempered sister, and he thought he could match anything Graubris might do. Graubris had been moody ever since poor little Maurezoi died; Zolous suspected that the relationship between Graubris and his wife Gaudiga had never recovered from that blow. Zolous had noticed that Gaudiga was not at the family meeting Darisei had called.

His own wife, Daunla, wasn't there either—but she had never been very concerned with politics, and was at home, three floors below and one wing over, helping their daughter Dallis plan her wedding.

And that brought up a key reason that Zolous was not terribly concerned if he himself had little chance of becoming Emperor. Zolous had surviving children, while neither Darisei nor Graubris did, which meant that whoever succeeded Beretris the chances were very good that it would be Zolous's children who carried on the dynasty in the long run. Darisei was over fifty, too old to have any children of her own; Graubris could theoretically still father heirs, but showed no signs of doing so. That left Zolous, with his four daughters and two sons, as the dynasty's best hope for the future. No matter who succeeded Beretris it seemed inevitable that eventually Darris or Vali or one of their sibs would reign in Seidabar. Zolous smiled, despite trying not to; he might have lost out on the throne by being born ten minutes after his brother, but he had the satisfaction of knowing that his offspring would almost certainly inherit anyway.

Assuming, of course, that the black wizard, Rebiri Nazakri, did not make good his threat to destroy the Domdur. Safe here in the tower of the Imperial Palace it was hard to believe that the mad Olnamian posed a real threat, but all the imperial family had heard the reports from the east, the accounts that made the Nazakri sound almost unbeatable.

The smile vanished, and Zolous looked at Granzer.

Zolous knew his brother-in-law was not stupid. Granzer had used his wife's position to help him secure his own post, but he had administered the Empire well enough; he would have held a council seat even if Darisei had refused him, albeit probably not the presidency. Furthermore, Granzer was a strong-willed man when he wanted to be—in thirty years of marriage he had never allowed Darisei to dominate him, and he had, on occasion, even dared to oppose the Empress herself. Zolous was not sure *he* could have opposed his mother in similar circumstances. Still, Granzer was only human, and had had no divine assistance for many years now; he could make mistakes, could misjudge situations.

Zolous sincerely hoped that Granzer was not misjudging how serious a threat Rebiri Nazakri posed. Placing one's confidence in the gods was all very well, and a very traditional strategy among the Domdur, but the gods had not exactly been cooperative of late.

The Nazakri wasn't the only problem the gods had declined to solve for the Domdur. There was the matter of the succession. For a thousand years, whenever an Emperor or Empress had died, the Domdur had asked which member of the imperial family should take the throne—in fact, usually the question was posed some time in advance, when the monarch fell ill or went to war or otherwise made death seem like a reasonable possibility—and the oracles had told them. Usually, the gods had chosen the Emperor's oldest son—but not always. Daughters had been given the divine blessing; so had younger children, siblings, even nephews or nieces, bypassing more obvious choices.

Beretris had been in perfect health in 1092, when the oracles last spoke. No one had thought to ask who would be her heir.

Her health was no longer good; her digestive problems were obviously serious and growing gradually worse, and the doctors could not agree on the exact cause. The possibility that she might die at any time was very real. The time to name an heir had come.

And no one knew who should do it.

The traditional route would have been for a representative of the imperial family to convene a special session of the Imperial Council and ask them to identify the heir, whereupon the Council would ask the Archpriest to determine the will of the gods. The Archpriest would have consulted the oracles and brought back their answer.

Now, though, Apiris had no one to consult, and nobody wanted *Apiris* to make the final decision. Instead, Beretris, after a particularly bad night, had informed her children and their spouses that she considered Graubris her successor.

Darisei had stewed over that for a triad or two, and had then called her siblings together and announced that she didn't believe the Empress had the right to name her own heir—the Imperial Council should make the choice.

Clearly, she had expected her husband, the President of that Council, to back her up and to push for her own selection. Granzer had not openly rejected the idea—he wasn't stupid, as Zolous had already reminded himself, and had no desire to destroy his own domestic felicity. He had not supported it, either, however; he had instead suggested that the imperial family had best work things out among themselves, so as to present a united front to the other Councillors.

Graubris and Zolous had agreed with that; Graubris had then suggested that perhaps they ought to defer to their mother's far greater experience in these matters.

And that had started the argument.

It seemed to be winding down, though. Darisei had found herself without much support, even from Granzer. She didn't like that, but she couldn't do much about it.

So Graubris would take the throne someday, if the gods did not choose otherwise, and one of Zolous's own children—probably Vali, his older son—would come after Graubris. Darisei would never wear the crown—but her husband was the true power in the imperial government, all the same, and Zolous thought that was fair enough.

That, he thought, was one matter settled without divine intervention.

Now, if only they could settle the others—Rebiri Nazakri and his rebellion being the most serious.

Zolous sighed. What a shame, he thought, that the gods hadn't named a divine champion before they fell silent. Then the Domdur would know who should lead the campaign against the Olnamians.

And furthermore, Zolous would not have had to worry about his *younger* son, Bagar, who was out there with the Company of Champions, on his way into battle.

Zolous didn't think Bagar was the divine champion; the lad was a fine young man, strong and handsome, good with a sword and comfortable on horseback, but the chosen champion? Somehow, listening to the old stories, Zolous had always pictured the champions as a bit farther out of the ordinary run of humanity than Bagar.

But the boy was old enough to make his own mistakes.

Zolous just hoped Bagar would *survive* his mistakes.

He wondered where the boy was at that moment.

Prince Bagar looked over Drievabor as the Company of Champions rode toward it, and was not impressed. There was no great hilltop fortress here, no soaring walls and massive gates, no domes or towers or palaces. The Gogror Highway did pass through an archway that had once been a gate in the city wall, but the rest of the wall was long gone—it had been in the way of the spreading warehouses and markets and granaries, and once the plains beyond the river fell, centuries ago, it had scarcely been needed.

Drievabor itself, discounting the granaries and other artifacts of the grain merchants' trade, was not particularly large; it would have been considered not much more than a couple of neighborhoods in Seidabar's Outer City. Most of the buildings were of brown or yellow brick, a story or two in height, simple and straightforward and relatively unadorned. The three exceptions, rising in a cluster at the far side of town, were the official residence of the Lords of Drieva, the city's temple, and a guard tower at the foot of the great bridge where the highway crossed the Grebiguata.

The current occupant of the manor, Bagar knew, was a Lady Karmaran—he had never met her, but he had heard of her. She was said to be quite formidable. He wondered how she could stand living in such a boring little town.

There was one oddity about Drievabor, Bagar noticed, one way in which it was more than an overgrown village: starting at that archway the highway ahead was paved with dark brick, for as far as he could see. Bagar had seen paved plazas and streets, of course—the area around the Imperial Palace had plenty of them—but they were scarce outside Seidabar, and he had not expected to see one here.

He supposed that it had something to do with the bridge across the river.

That bridge, Bagar knew, was where General Balinus intended to stop the rebels. He had never officially been informed of this, but he had heard enough bits of conversation around his father, his uncle Granzer, Captain Duzon, and the other officers to be certain of his facts. Balinus and his superior officer, Lord Kadan, did not want to meet the enemy on the open plain; they were afraid that the wizard's magic would let the rebels somehow slip around the Imperial forces. The only real natural barrier between Govya and Seidabar was the Grebiguata River, and unless the Nazakri intended to detour almost a thousand miles out of his way, the only bridge across the Grebiguata was here at Drievabor.

There were hundreds of small boats, of course—the river was too shallow for real ships, but rafts and flat-bottomed boats abounded. By imperial decree, all were to be stored on the western side until further notice; any boat found unattended on the eastern side would be confiscated.

The generals seemed to take it for granted that the rebels would not be able to make their own boats; Bagar had not been certain why, but he did notice, as he looked eastward at the town, that there were no forests anywhere in sight—nothing but farms. Olnamians were desert people; they presumably wouldn't know how to make boats from bundles of straw.

That left the bridge.

Bagar turned and looked back up the highway.

The infantry regiments were nowhere in sight; the Company of Champions had long since outdistanced them, even though half the men did not ride well. Still, Bagar knew they were back there, somewhere on the road—six regiments, three thousand men in all, to guard a single bridge.

Surely, that would be plenty. Lord Kadan was gathering a much larger army, back in the Agabdal camps north of Seidabar, but Bagar could not believe he would need it.

He wasn't entirely sure that the six regiments of the vanguard would be needed. After all, even with a wizard prodding them on, would a ragtag bunch of rebels really make it all the way across that vast eastern plain?

Bagar *hoped* they would. He wanted a chance to show what he could do. He envisioned himself standing on that bridge ahead, sword in hand, battling a dozen Olnamians at once and handily defeating them.

His brother Vali might someday be Emperor, Bagar thought, but *he* would be the Empire's champion!

CHAPTER 26

The journey north from Biekedau to Seidabar took four and a half days—for the most part, remarkably boring days, in Malledd's opinion. Vadeviya wore ordinary traveling clothes, keeping his priest's robe tucked away in his pack, so no one remarked on the peculiarity of a priest and a commoner traveling together; most people seemed to assume that Vadeviya was Malledd's father.

That rather annoyed Malledd; Vadeviya was a big man for a priest, but not so big as Hmar, nor possessed of the same calm self-assurance.

The first leg of the journey was by far the most interesting, as the two men took the river road downstream to Nuzedy. Malledd watched the boats working their way upstream or drifting back down toward the sea, the colors of their sails proclaiming their ownership and the banners at the mastheads announcing their intended destinations. All those bound upstream, of course, flew the yellow and green of Biekedau, while it seemed no two of the downstream craft bore the same flag; Malledd had no idea what ports most of the banners represented, but the sheer variety fascinated him.

He watched the morning sun burn the dew from the grass, and saw the children come out to play along the banks of the river, splashing and shouting.

For the entire twenty-odd miles from Biekedau to Nuzedy they were never out of sight of boats, and buildings, and people. A score of inns were scattered along the river road, for those who for one reason or another chose not to make the journey in a single day, each with its own dock, and there were other docks as well, serving farmers, fishermen, and even warehouses. Two of the inns even offered ferries.

Always, to their left were low hills, while to their right lay the river, and beyond it the plain, cut into squares and oblongs by farmers' fields, but otherwise featureless.

Nuzedy was visible from miles away; in fact, it scarcely seemed they were fully out of sight of Biekedau when Vadeviya pointed out a speck on the horizon he said was the Nuzedy watchtower.

Malledd had never come so far from home before, had never seen Nuzedy. He watched with interest as the tower became more clearly visible, and the temple dome beneath it.

Nuzedy was larger than Biekedau, and built on both sides of the Vren, its two halves connected by four great bridges; to Malledd it seemed a marvel, with its broad, straight streets and elegant buildings of multicolored stone and brick. Unlike the far older Biekedau, it had never had a city wall—Nuzedy had been founded long after this region had been fully pacified. This lack of a wall left its edges undefined; it seemed to fade away gradually in every direction, so that Malledd was unable to say just when they had entered the town.

Vadeviya led the way across the first of the four bridges, and at first Malledd thought they might continue on toward Seidabar, though the afternoon was well advanced; but then the priest led the way to an inn on the outskirts of Nuzedy.

"I am not as young as I once was," he explained apologetically. "I'm afraid I need a meal and a night's rest."

Malledd didn't comment, but he thought stopping was quite reasonable. He was not tired himself, but he was a strong man, and could hardly remember ever feeling tired. He looked about the inn with interest; it was much larger than Bardetta's, far more spacious, with more ornate and expensive furnishings, but otherwise not very different.

It was odd to think that for the first time in his life he was on the other side of the Vren. The bridge had made the crossing so simple, with no need for a ferry, or a ford, or to swim, that he felt almost cheated.

For the remainder of the day and evening he strolled casually about the inn and its surroundings, listening to the people of Nuzedy and the travelers, studying their elegant clothing, their elaborate hairstyles, their fine manners, all far more sophisticated than anything he saw in Grozerodz. He heard men talking about women, women talking about men, and everyone talking about business, friends, family, the weather—and the war, though it did not dominate the conversation as much as he had expected.

He did not intrude on any of these conversations; he did not speak to anyone but Vadeviya and, a bit reluctantly, the staff of the inn. He was uncomfortably aware of his village accent.

His conversation with the old priest was entirely about the inn and their journey; no mention was made of why they were going to Seidabar.

The next morning they ate a hasty breakfast and left while the sun was still behind the buildings across the street from the inn. Vadeviya paid the bill—of necessity, since Malledd had brought only a viert and a half, which would scarcely have covered it. The prices in Nuzedy seemed outrageously high, but the locals seemed untroubled by them, calmly passing around more money in a single transaction than Malledd ordinarily saw in a season. Most of the people of Grozerodz never handled large coins at all, and even the smiths saw them only rarely; Malledd had left three vierts with Anva, in case of emergency, and that, combined with the one and a half in his pocket, represented his entire fortune.

They left Nuzedy by the Seidabar road, a highway wide enough for four wagons, most of its length flanked on either side by hedges; the height of the hedges, and their appearance, varied according to the whim and industry of the farmers maintaining them. The road ran perfectly straight; now that they were across the river the countryside was flat and featureless, with nothing to force the highway from the shortest possible line between Nuzedy and Seidabar.

And the view in all directions, once they had left Nuzedy, was completely without interest. The farmhouses they passed were much like any other farmhouses in the region; simply leaving the hills for the plain had not altered the local architecture. The hedges quickly grew tedious. Other travelers paid the two men no heed. There were no children at play, no boats to watch, only scattered farmhouses and endless farms and hedges.

Around noon they passed through the village of Vurs—the highway widened into a square where a small fountain provided water for weary travelers or their mounts, and two inns faced each other across the square. Tempting odors drifted from a bakery's open door, but Malledd remembered how little money he carried and steadfastly ignored them—which suddenly became much easier when he and Vadeviya passed downwind of the village's tannery. They walked on without stopping.

At the next village, however, they stopped for the night. That was, as Vadeviya told him and the innkeeper confirmed, Deu Anafa.

The third day was virtually identical to the second—walking the dead-straight Seidabar road between hedges and fields that extended all the way to the horizon. They passed through the village of Deu Bionda at midmorning, then stopped for the night in a town Vadeviya called Allas.

The morning of the fourth day was the most tedious to date, as there was not even a village to break the monotony, but that afternoon Malledd noticed a certain haziness in the distance ahead of them. Another hour or so and he identified it as smoke, and mentioned it to Vadeviya.

"The forges of Seidabar," the priest said. Then he stumbled, and Malledd caught him before he fell.

"My apologies," Vadeviya said as he straightened up. "I'm afraid I'm no longer accustomed to traveling."

"We can rest, if you like," Malledd offered, though he was not particularly weary.

The priest shook his head. "No," he said. "Come on."

The sun was on the western horizon and the sky's blue deepening around the scattered moons when they finally reached the end of the hedges and saw an inn by the roadside. Far ahead, Malledd could see the final rays of sunlight glittering from towers and a golden dome, half-hidden by the smoke.

"Yes," Vadeviya said, before Malledd could ask, "that's Seidabar. The dome is the Great Temple, and that tower to the right, with the golden spire, is the Imperial Palace. And they're much larger and farther away than you imagine, so you can forget any idea you might have of reaching the city gates tonight. This inn will suit us just fine."

Malledd looked at the distant glitter, then at the sunset spreading red across the western sky.

"All right," he said. "Where are we? What village is this?" He gestured at the inn, and the other buildings along the road ahead.

Vadeviya smiled.

"This place is called Dauzger," he said, "but it's not exactly a village in the usual sense." He refused to explain that further, and instead led Malledd into the inn for supper and a bed.

In the morning they set out again, following the Seidabar road past inns and shops; there were no more hedges, and the few fields they saw were vegetable gardens rather than vast expanses of grain or grazing land for livestock. Even this early, there were many other travelers along the road.

When they had walked for an hour or so, Malledd asked, "Are we still in Dauzger? I would have thought I'd have heard of a town this size."

Vadeviya laughed. "No," he said, "I believe we're now in Nesbur. That's what I meant when I said Dauzger is no village. It's simply the outermost segment of the buildings around the inland side of Seidabar."

The towers of Seidabar and the dome of the Great Temple were now clearly visible ahead, but were still far off; Malledd stared at them for a moment, then turned to Vadeviya. "You mean from here to Seidabar, it's *all* towns?"

"Exactly. At least, along the roads."

Malledd found this hard to believe, but he didn't argue with the old priest; he kept walking.

Another hour convinced him. The highway was now intersected every hundred yards or so by a cross street, and Malledd glimpsed side streets, as well, paralleling the main road, but they were not yet in Seidabar—he could see that clearly, just by looking over the heads of the surrounding crowds. Ahead of them, unmistakably, stood Seidabar.

It no longer appeared directly ahead, but was offset to the right, rising above the shops and houses along the road. The city was built atop a mound—a hill, perhaps, but it wasn't shaped like any hill Malledd had ever seen before; it had sides so steep they were almost cliffs, and yet the top appeared to be almost flat.

He couldn't really be sure what the top was like, though, because it was hidden behind the city walls.

The walls blended almost imperceptibly into the sides of the mound, but there was no question that the rough, rocky, weed-strewn terrain at the base was natural, and the ornate structure of black stone buttresses and wrought-iron walkways at the top was man-made. The division between wall and cliff, as best Malledd could judge, was perhaps a hundred feet above the surrounding plain; the walls rose another fifty or sixty feet above that.

"How do we get *up* there?" he asked.

"The gates are on the northwest side, facing Agabdal," Vadeviya explained. "The road goes around."

"There's only one set of gates?"

"Yes."

Malledd considered that, then remarked, "All my life, I've heard people speak of the gates of Seidabar, but it never occurred to me that there was only one pair of them."

"Oh, yes. Seidabar was a fortress first, and everything it is now came later."

"A fortress." Malledd looked up at the looming walls, the high towers, the elaborate defenses. "You know, in all the stories my mother told she credited the gods and their champions with defending the Empire, but I can't see how anyone could ever hope to take a place like that even without its divine protection!"

Vadeviya smiled. "Well, no one ever has, of course—but Rebiri Nazakri intends to."

It was perhaps half a mile farther along that the highway joined with another and began to curve visibly. Buildings now lined either side in an unbroken wall, save for cross streets and merging highways.

This was no village, no mere town—this was unquestionably a *city*. Malledd had never seen one before, but there was no mistaking it.

"Are we in Seidabar?" Malledd asked. "Or is there some other name?"

"That would depend on who you ask," Vadeviya said. "To all intents and purposes, this is part of Seidabar, but the purists reserve that name for the fortress. Some call this area Outer Seidabar, or the Outer City; others call it Eastern Agabdal."

"Are we so near Agabdal, then?" Malledd had heard of the great port that brought goods from all over the Empire to Seidabar, but had not realized it was *that* close to the capital.

"Oh, yes. You'll see. Can't you smell the sea?"

Malledd could smell a great many things, many of them unfamiliar, but had not identified any of them as being the sea. He shrugged.

The avenue they followed continued on, curving around the base of the great mound, and at last they came in sight of the entrance to the fortress above them.

The avenue, far ahead, ended in an immense plaza that seemed to be packed with people, and a gigantic earthen ramp, a hundred yards wide, led from that plaza up to Seidabar itself. The lower two-thirds of the ramp were built out from the mound, into the surrounding city; the top third was cut into the mound, with the fortress walls towering over either side.

And at the top of the ramp, in the shadow of the walls, the great gates of Seidabar stood open.

Malledd stared at those gates for a long moment, marveling at the sheer size of them—immense panels of gleaming metal, many times the height of a man and each at least forty yards wide. They opened outward, of necessity—given the ramp's slope they could hardly swing in. They hung there, suspended from their monstrous hinges and a web of cables that stretched from the gates back to the watchtowers at either side, above either side of the ramp, reminding Malledd of a bird's wings—but what sort of bird had wings of silver and gold, and so unbelievably large?

"Come on," Vadeviya said. "You'll have plenty of time to look at them."

Malledd realized that he had slowed to a stop as he stared up at the gates; now he trotted onward. Together, the smith and the priest pushed through the crowds into the plaza, and across the plaza to the ramp.

As they marched up the steep slope, in the midst of scores of other people heading up to the Inner City, Malledd could see the gleaming dome of the Great Temple rearing up directly before them, a looming mass of gold framed between those unbelievable gates. Vadeviya noticed him staring at it.

"We'll stop there first, if you don't mind," the priest said, gesturing at the temple.

Malledd, overwhelmed by the crowds, the noise, the *size* of the place, did not argue. The temple seemed as good a place to go as any.

He wondered, though, what possible difference Vadeviya thought one man, *any* man, could make here in Seidabar.

What did a place like this need with a champion?

CHAPTER 27

Apiris, Archpriest of the Great Temple at Seidabar, Spokesman of the Gods and Speaker to the Gods, Councillor to Her Imperial Majesty Beretris Queen of the Domdur and Empress of the Domdur Domains, had a raging headache; it felt as if his entire skull were throbbing and about to burst.

This was no surprise. Sometimes he thought he'd had a headache for the past sixteen years, ever since his title as "Spokesman of the Gods" ceased to be the literal truth. The rest of his titles didn't help much; he did still speak to the gods, but he no longer had any evidence that they listened. And while he still sat on the Imperial Council, he doubted that Beretris—or more importantly, Prince Granzer—really noticed.

Some of the other Councillors noticed, but that didn't mean they wanted him there. Quite the contrary. Lord Orbalir had said openly that if the gods were no longer meddling in human affairs there was no more need for priests and temples, and the Archpriest no longer belonged on the Council.

Apiris knew why Orbalir argued as he did; he didn't care one way or the other who believed what, or who sat on the Council. He simply wanted to put messenger magicians on his ships, instead of keeping them cooped up in temples. He was undermining Apiris any way he could in hopes of prying the magicians loose.

Knowing Orbalir's reasons didn't help Apiris much, though; Lord Orbalir still did all he could to make life difficult for him.

And Lord Kadan didn't help any, with the way he ignored Orbalir in running the campaign against the eastern rebels. While it was perfectly true that as Commissioner of the Fleet Orbalir couldn't do much to help directly with what was, so far, entirely a land war, there was still a standing imperial edict that the two Lords Commissioner were to confer on any military operation. Lord Kadan seemed to feel that by telling Orbalir, before the entire Council, that his services would not be needed, he had fulfilled this edict. That hadn't helped Orbalir's temper *at all*.

And it wasn't as if the fleet really *was* completely superfluous; there were recruits and supplies to be brought to the port of Agabdal if the Imperial Army was to reach its intended size and readiness.

And while Orbalir campaigned against Kadan and Apiris, and Kadan ignored Orbalir and demanded ever better intelligence from Apiris, Lord Gornir was forever bringing in delegations from the eastern provinces with more tales of woe—as if the Empire wasn't already doing everything it could! Lady Mirashan was trying to supply Kadan's army and find alternate trade routes around the Nazakri army, Lord Dabos was constantly worrying about how much damage the enemy was doing to crops and highways, Lord Shoule was seeing spies everywhere and demanding that Vrai Burrai be executed for having invented the New Magic, Lady Dalbisha was questioning everyone's loyalty and competence, Lady Vamia was exacerbating the perpetual internal feuding on the Council with her flirting, Lord Sulibai kept insisting that the Council should try to negotiate with the rebels . . .

And Prince Granzer, the President of the Council, was too busy with his personal affairs and the imperial household to force the Councillors back into line—let alone the various governors, princes, princesses, and others who were cluttering up the capital during the crisis.

At this particular moment, despite the agony in his head, Apiris was trying to compose a reassuring letter to Her Imperial Majesty, who wanted to know whether the gods had forsaken the Empire.

Everyone wanted to know whether the gods had forsaken the Empire, including Apiris, but somehow he doubted that Beretris would take it well if he told her that her guess was as good as his.

It was at this moment that someone knocked on the door of his study.

"Oh, please," Apiris said, dropping his quill and putting a hand to his aching brow. "Samardas, if you hear me, make it stop."

Samardas didn't answer; the knock was repeated.

"Come in," Apiris called despairingly.

The door opened, and young Omaran, the priestess attending him today, stepped in. She bowed her head respectfully.

"Your pardon, Archpriest," she said, "but you have a visitor."

"Who is it?" Apiris said, dreading the answer.

"He gives his name as Vadeviya, from Biekedau. He says he's . . ."

"Biekedau?" Apiris blinked. "Vadeviya? Dallor is the imperial representative in Biekedau, and Danugai is high priest; I don't know any Vadeviya."

"No, Your Holiness, he's not . . . he's a priest, a scholar. He's come about the chosen champion."

"What, is he claiming he's the champion?"

"No, Your Holiness. He just says he knows who it is. He's brought a man with him . . ."

Something snapped. "I don't care," Apiris shouted at her. "It's Lord Graush who wanted to find the gods' champion, not me! Send him away—send them both away, send them all away! I'll see no one, no courtesy calls, no messages, no claimants to the role of champion, no one below the rank of imperial governor! Is that clear?"

"Yes, Your Holiness," the priestess managed. She bobbed in a quick curtsy, then ducked back out the door and closed it quickly but—thank the gods!—quietly behind her.

Apiris turned back to the letter, mumbling angrily to himself.

Outside the study door Omaran hesitated, then shrugged. She had tried. She turned and headed back through the maze of stairways and passages to the anteroom where Vadeviya and Malledd waited.

"I'm very sorry," she told them, "but the Archpriest is terribly busy just now, and really can't spare the time to see you."

Vadeviya frowned. "You told him that I've brought proof of the identity of the gods' champion?"

"Yes, sir, I told him that—but you must understand, ever since Lord Graush first suggested we find the holy champion, we've had people turning up here, or at the palace, claiming to be him."

Vadeviya glanced up at Malledd, but the smith's face was unreadable. If he was thinking "I told you so," he was hiding it well.

Malledd had not wanted to talk to Apiris. He had argued that Vadeviya had sworn not to tell anyone that he, Malledd, was the divine champion, and Vadeviya had countered that he wasn't going to tell Apiris, he was simply going to show him Dolkout's letter and let him draw his own conclusions.

Malledd hadn't thought that would work, and it appeared he might be right.

"I see," the old priest said. "And did you tell him that we have a letter from Dolkout, the Biekedau high priest, confirming our claim?"

Omaran sighed. "I told him everything I could, sir," she replied.

Somehow, Vadeviya doubted that that was literally true, but it didn't really seem worth pressing the matter. After all, if they *had* gotten in to see Apiris, what difference would it have made? It was clear to anyone who had ever seen Seidabar in peaceful times that the entire city was on the verge of chaos, with people scurrying about every which way on mysterious errands; Apiris was probably deluged with matters demanding his attention. He wouldn't have had time to worry about Dolkout's letter.

"All right," he said. "Then should we find this Lord Graush?"

Before the little priestess could reply, Malledd growled, "No. I am here as a smith. The army wanted smiths."

Vadeviya glanced at him and smothered a frown. He had thought that Malledd had gotten over most of his reluctance to acknowledge his foreordained role, but apparently he was suffering a relapse.

Omaran blinked. "Lord Passeil has taken responsibility for arming our soldiers, if that's what you mean—under the direction of Lord Kadan, of course."

"Very good," Vadeviya said with a sigh. "And where do we find Lord Passeil?"

"Lord Passeil is a member of the Imperial Council, sir."

"Yes?" Vadeviya looked politely inquiring.

Omaran looked flustered. "I mean, he isn't going to meet personally with every armorer who volunteers! You'll have to report to the Imperial Armory."

Vadeviya nodded. "And where is that?"

"On Wall Street, beyond the palace."

"Thank you." He turned and beckoned to Malledd.

When they were out of the anteroom and out of Omaran's earshot, in the long stone corridor that led from the priests' entrance out to the street, Malledd muttered, "We could have accomplished just as much by asking any of the guards at the gate, or anyone on the streets, and done it far more quickly."

"If all we wanted was the Imperial Armory, yes," Vadeviya admitted. "I had hoped for rather more."

"Didn't get it."

Vadeviya considered various retorts, but the moment passed before he could choose one—they stepped out of the temple into the plaza, and Vadeviya led the way around the Great Temple toward Wall Street.

The crowds were thick here; Malledd was astonished by the throngs. The brief stop at the temple had let him start to forget the size and density of Seidabar, and now they were plunging into the most tightly packed mob he had seen yet.

It was daunting. He couldn't take a step without bumping against someone, without thrusting an elbow into a woman's face or a boot into a child's knee. People of every size and shape, wearing clothes of every imaginable cut and color, pushing in every direction, filled the street for as far as Malledd could see.

The noise was the worst of it. The jostling wasn't a real problem for someone Malledd's size, and he could see over most of the heads, but the shouting and thumping and unidentifiable other sounds of a thousand people going about their business added up to a roar that was surely even louder than the rumble of the lower falls of the Vren.

Up until then, Malledd would have said that the only sound he had ever heard that was louder than the falls was thunder, and thunder never lasted very long, while the falls sounded constantly.

The sound of massed humanity in the streets of Seidabar was like a thunder that never ceased.

"Who *are* all these people?" Malledd shouted to Vadeviya as he pushed his way through the crowd, the priest following in his wake. "What are they all doing here?"

Vadeviya didn't try to shout over the crowd; he just shook his head and pointed the direction they had to go.

Malledd pushed onward, past nobles and beggars, tradesmen and whores.

When they finally stepped past the guards into the cool dimness of the Imperial Armory, the sound changed—the roar of the crowd was replaced by shouting voices and the clanging of steel, echoing from the stone and plaster walls. It was loud, but nowhere near as overpowering as the hubbub in the streets, and Malledd sagged in relief.

They were directed to a clerk seated behind a table; they crossed the room and stood before the table, waiting, until the man deigned to notice them. He seemed far more concerned with arranging a stack of papers properly, and making occasional marks on them with a short-clipped quill, than in attending to his visitors.

"Your business?" the clerk asked at last, abandoning his papers, capping his inkwell, and looking up at Malledd's chest—he seemed incapable of bending his neck far enough to see Malledd's face. He had a lilting, musical accent, as had the priestess; Malledd knew he had heard someone speak like that before, but he could not remember exactly where or when. A long time ago, certainly.

The guards at the door had already asked his business, and Malledd gave the clerk the same answer he had given before: "I'm a smith."

The clerk nodded. "And you're volunteering to work here, equipping the Imperial Army?"

"Yes."

"Very good." The clerk smiled unconvincingly at the front of Malledd's blouse. "Where are you from?"

"Grozerodz," Malledd answered.

The clerk strained his face a notch upward and looked politely blank. Vadeviya interjected, "It's a village near Biekedau, along the Yildau road."

"Ah, a *village* smith," the clerk said, nodding and bending back down to his papers. "Unspecialized, then?"

It was Malledd's turn to look blank, and the clerk looked up to see why no answer had been forthcoming. He had to crank his gaze much higher than he liked to determine that the applicant had not understood the question.

"I mean, you did general metalwork, rather than any one specialty?" he asked.

"That's right," Malledd agreed.

"Ever make a sword?"

"No," Malledd admitted. "But I learn pretty fast, and I've made a dozen or more good steel daggers." He didn't mention that he'd made at least as many that hadn't come out well at all before he got the hang of it.

"Not the same thing," the clerk said.

"I know that."

"Ever make armor?"

"A pair of gauntlets once." That had been a special order for a farmer named Amaltrur, who had decided to see if iron gloves would do better than leather in protecting his hands from animal bites.

"You said you'd made steel daggers?"

Malledd nodded.

The clerk considered for a moment, then said, "All right, we'll find a use for you. What we really *need* is swordsmiths, and we may not have time to train them up properly, but if you really do learn fast . . . well, if it doesn't work out, we can use you on repair work or making armor." He uncapped his inkwell, found a scrap of unused paper, scribbled a quick note, and handed it to Malledd. "Take this down to the end of that hall." He pointed. Then he turned to Vadeviya.

"And you?"

"I'm Malledd's guide," Vadeviya explained.

The clerk shook his head. "Not here," he said. "Sorry." He beckoned to a guard.

Vadeviya did not wait to be escorted out. "I'll see you later, Malledd," he said.

Malledd couldn't decide whether to thank the old man, to agree to meet later, or to simply say good-bye; in the end, he stood and watched silently as the priest departed.

Then he turned, hesitating.

They didn't need champions here; one good long look at the size of Seidabar, and the scope of its defenses, had convinced Malledd of that. He should probably have stayed home with Anva—in fact, he should probably turn around and leave and go back to her right now. If he did not, there was no knowing how long he would be here.

But the Empire said they needed smiths, and he had come this far. He sighed, and marched down to the end of the hall, the scribbled note in his hand.

CHAPTER 28

The wind howled down from the north, carrying snow in great swirls of white through the camp. Rebiri Nazakri huddled in his black bearskin cloak, crouched on a maroon velvet cushion, shivering and watching as glittering flakes blew in under the black silk sides of his pavilion. The sun was still red in the west and he was already miserably cold.

He could have built the fire up higher, but they were low on fuel; he could not afford to waste it. He could have used the red-glowing end of his staff to warm himself, but he might need that magic later, and renewing it would not be easy in this freezing wasteland. He could move to one of the buildings his army had occupied—they had captured a village that was well equipped with snug, thick-walled stone-and-brick structures—but that would not suit his role as an Olnami warlord.

The rest of his army had taken shelter in the village or the nearby farmhouses—or rather the living portion of his army; the nightwalkers were not troubled by the cold and simply lay wherever they fell when the sun rose each day. Rebiri could have joined Aldassi and Asari and his other officers in what had been the village inn, but as the warlord, as the chosen one of whatever being guided him toward his destiny, he dared not.

Although he did not know what god or spirit was directing him toward his long-sought vengeance on the Domdur, Rebiri did not want to risk losing its favor; it had chosen him because he was the rightful warlord of the Olnami, so he must be, in all ways, a warlord of the Olnami. And the Olnami lived in tents and pavilions, in the living air, ready to move on at any time; they did not huddle inside piles of dead earth and stone.

But nowhere in the Olnami lands did the wind blow so cold as it did on this accursed plain; nowhere back home did the snow sweep down from the sky for days on end, covering the sky in dead gray, covering everything below the sky, for as far as the eye could see, in gleaming white. Rebiri tucked his folded hands between his thighs, trying to warm them.

Winter had come early. Perhaps it always came early here on the plain; the Nazakri did not know, and there were no natives he could ask. Those he had not slaughtered had fled.

Of course, many had become nightwalkers and joined his army, and some of them might have enough of their hosts' memories to answer questions—but it didn't matter. Winter *had* come, and the rebel army would have to survive it and continue the westward march in the spring.

At least the nightwalkers required no food, and only enough warmth that they not freeze into immobility—if that; they could always be thawed later. And the cold kept their stink to a minimum.

And the army had crossed most of the plain. Asakari had managed to coax that much information from somewhere—the Matuan scholars with their maps, perhaps, or the locals before they died, or the nightwalkers afterward. Rebiri did not trouble himself with the source; what mattered was that Asari said they had covered more than two-thirds of the distance from Ai Varach to Seidabar. Perhaps a hundred miles to the west lay the Domdur market town of Drievabor, where a bridge would carry them across the Grebiguata River; two hundred miles beyond *that* stood Seidabar.

They could not advance in winter—the snow and cold would slow them too much. The nightwalkers were stiff and clumsy in the cold, and the living devoted much of their energy to simply keeping warm. They could not break camp, march, make a new camp, and gather sufficient food and firewood all in a single night, even with the shorter winter days. The skies were often cloudy, making the nights too dark to see, and they had no fuel to waste on torches or lanterns. They might manage a few quick moves of a mile or two, but regular nightly marches were out of the question.

At least the thrice-accursed General Balinus and his Domdur would not be able to harass them in the snow. And when spring came another half a season should see them at the gates of Seidabar . . .

No.

Rebiri frowned, unsure whether someone had spoken—himself, perhaps—or whether he had simply *thought* that monosyllabic negative.

But why would he have? He looked around the tent, puzzled. He was alone out here; he had sent his servants to warm themselves and prepare his supper, and they had not yet returned. It must have been his own thought—odd, that it had seemed so . . . so *outside* himself.

He shook himself, as much to shake off the chill as anything else, and returned to his musings. Three hundred miles to Seidabar—perhaps as little as thirty nights' travel . . .

No!

Rebiri started and looked around wildly.

"Who's there?" he demanded, reaching for his staff.

Put that down. It irritates me.

Rebiri stopped with his hand not quite touching the black wood shaft.

He had not *heard* those words; he had *felt* them, in his heart, and he recognized that sensation, though it had never before been so clear, so strong, so explicit. This was the spirit of his destiny addressing him.

Slowly, he drew his hand back and straightened until he was sitting bolt upright, his hands folded in his lap.

"How should I address you?" he asked.

It matters not. I am what I am, and what you call me cannot alter that in any way. Call me whatever you will.

"But you must have a name! The nightwalkers say you are a god, and do not the gods have names?"

I am a god. My name does not matter; it differs in every tongue.

"But which god are you? Are you Olnami?"

I am your god, Rebiri Nazakri, the god who guides you to your revenge. Need you know more?

"No." Whatever it was that conversed with him, he did not need to know any more than that. "Why do you speak to me now, after these many seasons of silence?"

I have not been wholly silent for years, Nazakri—not since your son first brought you news of the New Magic.

"But you never before spoke to me in words, O Lord."

Our bond strengthens. You are ready to hear me—and I have that to tell you which you have failed to heed without my words.

"How have I failed, Lord?"

You plan to push on to Seidabar too fast, Nazakri. You must be patient. You must wait until all is prepared, until the time is at its most propitious and my power greatest.

"But my people have already waited so long, Lord!"

The wait shall not be long. You shall reach Seidabar before another year has passed—but not in the spring. You and those living souls who follow you shall not cross the Grebiguata until high summer.

"But . . . but *why*? Will that not give the Domdur time to prepare their defenses?"

The Domdur have prepared their defenses for a thousand years, Nazakri; to shatter them you must strike when all is in position.

"I don't understand."

You need not.

"But then how am I to obey, if I do not understand? How shall I know when to cross the bridge at Drievabor . . . ?"

You shall not cross at Drievabor. Find another place.

"But there *is* no other place! That's the only bridge!"

You need no bridge. The means shall be there, wherever you choose.

"Boats? Should we build boats?"

The means shall be there when the time is right.

"At high summer."

Yes.

"How shall I know when the time is right?"

You shall know, as you knew to go to Fadari Tu, as you knew to seek out the cave.

"You'll tell me? Will you speak to me often, then? Am I to become your oracle?"

Oracles are forbidden me now. It may be we shall speak again, or it may be that we shall not; I cannot foresee as yet which it shall be.

The Nazakri found that a relief, in truth; he did not care to be a priest or an oracle. It was sufficient, more than sufficient, to be the warlord of the Olnami.

One more thing, Rebiri Nazakri.

"Yes?"

I do not demand you keep scrupulously to the old ways. You endanger yourself needlessly staying in this tent when the storms of winter approach. Take shelter when you must; to perish for the sake of a meaningless tradition, a tradition inappropriate to this land, does no honor to your ancestors.

And then suddenly something was gone, and Rebiri Nazakri was staring straight ahead at the embers of a dying fire, glowing dully at the center of a black tent. The line of daylight beneath the pavilion walls had dimmed away, and streaks of snow melted darkly into the earth where it had been.

The god, or spirit, or whatever it was, was gone, at least for now. Rebiri could not have said how he knew that, but he knew it beyond any possibility of doubt.

He remembered its every word, though. He was to wait, not to cross the river until high summer—he would know when the time was right. He was to cross somewhere other than Drievabor.

He reached for his staff, picked it up, and stared contemplatively into the smoky red crystal.

It irritates me, the voice had said. And, *Oracles are forbidden me now.*

What sort of a god would say such things? How could mere mortal magic trouble a god? What could forbid a god anything?

Was the darkness bound in the staff something more than mere magic? Were there powers higher than the gods? And *why* was he to wait? Why was he to avoid Drievabor?

Mysteries and puzzles. The Nazakri hated mysteries.

Still, whatever the being that spoke to him, it was clearly strong, clearly knew things beyond mortal knowledge, and clearly wanted him to succeed in his quest for vengeance. Perhaps it was one of the Olnami gods, weakened by centuries of neglect and Domdur oppression, and the alienness of the darkness was enough to trouble it in its lessened condition, the edict of the Domdur gods enough to forbid it oracles.

It knew Olnami traditions, certainly—and said he need not follow them all. That spoke well of its wisdom.

He noticed that it had never said *nightwalkers* must not cross the river—only living souls were thus restricted. That was interesting, and presented several possibilities.

He unfolded his legs and stood, straightening his bearskin robe. He lowered the staff, let it hang loose in his hand, and stared unseeing at the fire.

He would, he resolved, do what the being had instructed him to do. He would do whatever was necessary to survive the winter and the spring, and he would then cross the Grebiguata in midsummer, somewhere north of Drievabor.

And before a year had passed, he would be at the gates of Seidabar.

He smiled, a fierce, strong smile, and the staff in his hand quivered and hissed.

CHAPTER 29

So has Apiris spoken out on behalf of Lord Duzon?" Malledd asked, looking at his fellow apprentice Darsmit.

The two men were sitting in the apprentices' common room, in the stony depths of the Imperial Armory, eating their midday meal at the easternmost table. Fires blazed in the hearths at either end of the room, but the winter chill still seemed to seep in through the stone walls and collect in pools around their ankles.

The apprentices ate in shifts, as their work permitted, and on this particular day, the first of Dirva's Triad, Malledd and Darsmit were the only two from their group eating this late. A group of eight or nine younger apprentices were chattering away near the western hearth, but Malledd and Darsmit ignored them.

Darsmit shrugged at Malledd's question and swallowed a bite of chicken. "Not that I've heard," he said. "Apiris hasn't spoken out about anything. He never does." He bit into the drumstick again.

Malledd frowned. He felt stupid here. It wasn't being reduced to a mere apprentice again that was responsible for this feeling; he was learning sword-making quickly enough, and was already turning out a few decent blades. He was a good smith, and it wasn't all that different from some of the work he'd done in the past. It took patience and a steady hand and a good eye and a feel for the temper of the metal, but he had all that, and he knew that with practice he'd be able to make swords as well as anyone.

No, he felt stupid because he knew so little of what was going on around him. The other apprentices all seemed to know all the latest rumors, the hottest gossip, every little detail of what went on in the council chamber and elsewhere in the Imperial Palace, and they all seemed to grasp the implications of each new tidbit instantly, while he, after two dozen triads in Seidabar, was still struggling to keep the names of the Empress's grandchildren straight—especially the four grand-daughters; their names all sounded alike to him! He had no idea where the others heard all the news they brought to the common-room discussions; sometimes it seemed as if they breathed it in with the very air of the city.

He had never had any trouble keeping up with the gossip in Grozerodz, but the city of Seidabar was so utterly different that even now he was still learning the finer points of how to avoid embarrassing himself in the streets. He had had a few visits from Vadeviya, but the old man had brought no gossip or advice; he had insisted on talking about whether Malledd should reveal his identity as divine champion to someone to the point that Malledd had sent him away and refused to see him again.

Malledd knew almost no one else in Seidabar, and that meant that he was as yet unable to pick up the news—except from his fellow apprentices.

Which was, he supposed, as good a way as any to learn what was happening, even if he didn't understand where the reports originated. What was *in* the reports seemed more important—and there was plenty to think about in them.

He had accepted that there were other claimants to the title of divine cham-pion; it had come as a bit of a shock at first when that priestess had said that Lord Graush had suggested they find the holy champion and people had been turning up claiming to be him ever since, but now he thought it shouldn't have been. Hmar had always said there might be others, that the priests might have lied or been misled somehow, and sure enough, the other apprentice armorers knew of dozens of people who were considered possible recipients of divine favor, from the Empress's grandson Prince Bagar to a fellow who had been begging in the streets a year ago.

So perhaps Malledd had come here for nothing—nothing except answering the call for smiths, at any rate. Perhaps he was no more the divine champion than most of the others who had claimed the title. Perhaps Vadeviya was de-luded; Dolkout might not have included him in the hoax, if hoax it was. Perhaps Dolkout himself had believed Malledd to be the true champion—but that didn't necessarily mean he *was* the true champion. One of these others might be, in-stead.

If so, it would lift a great burden from Malledd. He could go home to Anva with a clear conscience once enough swords were made, and leave the Empire to its chosen defenders.

And this Lord Duzon seemed to be everybody's favorite candidate for the job of defender of the Empire. Malledd had never seen him, of course, since Duzon had left the city not long before Malledd's arrival, but he was said to be a handsome young noble of good family and fine reputation, a first-rate swordsman and well-known athlete. He would seem, by all accounts, to be a far better choice than some obscure smith. Malledd wanted very much to believe that Duzon was the chosen one.

But shouldn't Apiris, the Archpriest and foremost spokesman of the gods, have said something, one way or the other, about Duzon's claim? Wasn't it a priest's job to answer questions and clear up doubts?

Malledd chewed on chicken while he mulled over Darsmit's words.

"Has *anyone* endorsed Lord Duzon, then?" he asked. "Any of the priests?"

"What do the priests know of it?" Darsmit asked. He swigged sweet ale, wiped his mouth on his sleeve, and added, "Since the oracles stopped talking the priests don't know any more than the rest of us. At least, that's what Apiris says."

"But was nothing said *before* the oracles fell silent?"

"Not that I've ever heard," Darsmit said. "But then, I don't know everything. My sister's betrothed to a guard who's been posted at the temple, so I hear a lot, but I don't hear everything."

That Darsmit's prospective brother-in-law was in the Imperial Guard at least explained where some of the news came from—but there it was again. None of the other claimants could produce oracular backing for their claims. Dolkout *had* said that three oracles had named Malledd as the champion.

It would seem that he was not going to escape the burden as easily as he had hoped. If the oracles had named no one else, then he *was* the champion—the gods did not lie. And if he was the champion, his duty lay here—or with the army on the eastern plain, but at any rate not back home in Grozerodz.

"Some folks do say," Darsmit remarked, after swallowing another bite of chicken, "that Apiris must surely know the champion's identity, but that he refuses to reveal it, because he does not approve of the gods' choice. Gharman, my brother-in-law-to-be, won't venture an opinion either way on that idea."

"Would the Archpriest dare defy the gods that way?" Malledd asked.

Darsmit shrugged. "Who knows, in these godsforsaken times? Some say that Apiris's impieties are the very *reason* the gods abandoned us! Certainly it wasn't until Bonvas died and Apiris took office that the oracles stopped talking."

Malledd frowned, wondering who this "some" might be. He glanced out the easternmost window of the apprentice hall; two small brownish moons were in sight, moons he didn't recognize.

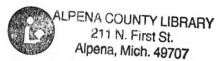
ALPENA COUNTY LIBRARY
211 N. First St.
Alpena, Mich. 49707

The motives of the gods were certainly questionable in recent years. Malledd wondered whether there had ever before been a time when they were so inscrutable. How, he wondered, had he had the misfortune to be born at such a time, and worse, to have this dubious honor of alleged divine favor bestowed upon him?

Why was he here, learning to make swords, instead of home with his wife and children?

Or if he were the true champion, why was he here in Seidabar when the threat to the Empire lay hundreds of miles to the east?

It didn't seem right, either way.

Malledd tossed aside the chicken bones and got to his feet. He was debating whether to find his way outside for a bit of fresh air, or to stay and chat with Darsmit, or to head back to his forge and get started on the afternoon's labors, when a sound from outside the common-room door caught his attention.

Someone was arguing out there—and one of the voices was female.

Women were scarce in the armory; almost all smiths and soldiers were male, and very few people other than smiths and soldiers had any business there. Those who were married generally lived elsewhere and came to the armory to work, and their wives rarely visited. A female voice was an attention-catching oddity.

Furthermore, this voice was *familiar*. For half an instant Malledd wondered if it was Darsmit's sister Berai, but then he recognized it.

"*Anva?*" He shoved aside the bench he had been sitting on, pushed away from the table, and charged toward the door.

The bench went whirling and slammed against the hearth rail. Darsmit froze in astonishment, a drumstick between his teeth, as his dining companion suddenly dashed away, almost upsetting the table in the process—and the table had been built for the use of a dozen smiths, and smiths tended to be large. That table was no delicate little gewgaw.

Malledd threw open the door, letting in a rush of cold air—the armory was remarkable for being stifling hot around the forges but staying cold elsewhere—and found a knot of people in the corridor outside, arguing loudly. Three big men—not Malledd's size, but big—were standing a dozen feet away with their backs to him, facing three women. Two of the men wore the leather aprons of smiths, and the third the red and gold of a soldier; the dark-haired, medium-sized woman at the front wore a good sheepskin coat and a fur cap, while the other two wore white woolen cloaks over the white robes of priestesses.

Malledd recognized the woman in the sheepskin coat instantly.

"Anva!" he called. "What are *you* doing here?"

She looked past the men at him.

"Malledd!" she said. "There you are!" She pushed between the two burly smiths and ran toward him. The men parted, allowing her to pass—which was a good thing for them, because Malledd met Anva halfway, and had they declined to make way he would probably have injured them in getting at her.

Neither of them bothered to say anything for the next few minutes.

The smiths turned and saw Malledd, Anva wrapped in his arms; one cleared his throat.

Malledd and Anva paid no attention.

The smiths looked at one another.

"Well," one of them said, "I guess that must be who she was looking for."

"I'm sure he knows the rules," the other said.

"Then there's no need for us to stay around," the first agreed.

With a shrug, they turned away and trotted down the hallway.

The soldier did not; he stood, watching Malledd and Anva, and waited.

The priestesses stepped up on either side of the soldier and also watched and waited. One of them began blushing.

Behind Malledd, Darsmit came to the door and watched.

Finally, Malledd and Anva released one another, gasping for breath, and stood staring into each other's eyes.

"Excuse me," the soldier said.

Malledd turned his head to look at him questioningly.

"I'm afraid this woman entered the armory without permission," the soldier said. "While you obviously know her, I must still ask her to leave."

"We'll both go," Malledd said, before Anva could object. "We can talk some-where else."

"Very good. Shall I escort you to the door?"

"If you like," Malledd said.

"Malledd!" Darsmit called. "What's going on? Should I come?"

Malledd shook his head. "Finish your lunch," he said. "I'll be back later."

Darsmit hesitated, then turned back into the common room.

The others—Malledd, Anva, the soldier, and the two priestesses—made their way down the corridor, down the stairs, and out through the maze of anterooms and passageways onto the street. The soldier then returned to the armory and left the four of them standing in the street.

Normal traffic had churned the light snowfall from a triad before into the mud of the street, but streaks of dirty white still adorned the stone fronts of the buildings on either side. Because of the cold there were few people on the street, and most of those were bundled up and hurrying quickly to wherever they were bound. The wind gusted occasionally, tearing bits of sooty snow from cornices and windowsills and chilling exposed hands and faces.

Malledd watched the soldier go, then remarked, "Seems like a nice fellow."

"That unpleasant little man at the front door sent him after us, when I wouldn't wait while he sent messengers all over the place," Anva said.

"Ah," Malledd said. He was quite familiar with the officious doorkeeper at the armory entrance. He glanced at the priestesses. "Are these who Vadeviya sent to Grozerodz?"

"She is," Anva said, pointing to the taller one. "Her name is Bezida. The other one, Esgora, is from the Great Temple here in Seidabar."

Bezida was plump and dark-haired; she smiled. Esgora was short and fair, and bowed slightly at the mention of her name.

Malledd nodded a polite acknowledgment of the introduction, then asked, "Where are the children?"

"Back in Grozerodz, where they belong, with your parents and Uncle Sparrak and another priestess, Zadai. Malledd, can we find somewhere warm?" She shivered.

"Of course!" Malledd looked around, then placed his hands on Anva's shoulders and turned her toward a nearby tavern. "And we'll get something to drink. Have you eaten?"

Twenty minutes later the four of them were seated around a small table near a window in the nameless tavern across the street from Lord Graush's palace. The three women had been fed, wiping out Malledd's apprentice allowance for the triad; Malledd himself, having already eaten, had settled for a little bread and cheese and two pints of golden ale.

"Now," he said, thumping his mug down, "what are you doing here?"

"I came to fetch you home, of course," Anva said as she took a final bite of winter apple and dropped the core on her plate. "Baranmel's Triad is just eight days away—you can be home with your children to celebrate, instead of here, living in that crowded, drafty pile of stone they call an armory."

"But I haven't finished," Malledd said. "I'm training to be a swordsmith. The army will need swords for the spring campaign."

"You can make swords back in Grozerodz, if that's all it is."

"They need swords *here*," Malledd protested.

"And *I* need *you* back in Grozerodz!"

Malledd stared at her wordlessly for a moment.

"It's not swordsmithing that's keeping you here," Anva said.

Malledd glanced at the two priestesses, who had both stayed remarkably silent so far.

"They know who you are," Anva said. "Bezida found out from Zadai, and Zadai found out back in Biekedau—she says she met you in the temple porch there, when you showed that letter of yours to somebody. Besides, Malledd, they've been living with me in Grozerodz—*everyone* in Grozerodz knows, you know that. It would have slipped sooner or later."

Malledd frowned slightly, and pointed a thumb at the other. "And Esgora?" he asked.

"I told her," Anva replied.

Malledd frowned more deeply.

"Malledd, if you wanted to keep it a secret, you should have stayed home, not come here," Anva said. "Everyone back in Grozerodz is talking about you, you know—oh, it's mostly whispers when I'm around, since they all know you didn't want anyone to talk about it, but *really*, Malledd, they think you're the divine champion, and you went off to the war! Of *course* they're going to talk about it! They're all waiting for news of you, waiting to hear that you've lopped off this Olnamian wizard's filthy head."

"I came to make swords," Malledd growled.

"You came because that disgusting old Vadeviya convinced you it was your duty," Anva retorted.

"It was my duty to come make swords," Malledd insisted.

"Nonsense!" Anva snapped. "You think you're the divine champion, and so does Vadeviya, and that's why you're both here. That's why I have these priestesses following me around, guarding me and baby-sitting our children and running my errands—because Vadeviya thinks you're the champion. I *asked* him, Malledd—he's still at the Great Temple here, you know. He's the one who told me to look for you at the armory. I went to Biekedau, and Bezida made one of the magicians send a message, and I found out that you and Vadeviya were both still in Seidabar, and I came to fetch you home."

"Maybe Vadeviya thinks I'm the champion," Malledd said, "but nobody else here does—including me. They all think Lord Duzon is."

"I've heard of him," Anva admitted. "He's captain of the Company of Champions, isn't he?"

Malledd nodded. "And if I thought I was really the divine champion, wouldn't I be out there in Drievabor with that company, instead of here in the armory?"

"So you *don't* think you are? You think Mezizar lied, the day you were born? You think the high priest's letter is a fraud?"

Malledd hesitated, then drained the last few drops from his mug before answering.

"I don't know," he said, staring into his empty mug. "No one else has any stories about oracles, or letters from high priests. I've been asking. Lord Duzon sounds like a fine man, and I expect he'll be a hero, but that doesn't mean he's the chosen of the gods." He looked up and met Anva's eyes. "Maybe *nobody* is the gods' chosen anymore."

Bezida looked shocked; Esgora managed to retain her composure, but Malledd could see, from the corner of his eye, a subtle shift in her expression. She was obviously listening just as closely.

"That could be," Anva agreed.

Malledd stared at her, then asked, "Anva, do *you* think I'm the divine champion?"

"I don't know," Anva replied. "I *knew* you'd ask that, so I've been trying to decide—I've been trying to decide for *years*, ever since we were first betrothed. And I can't. I just don't know. Sometimes I see you at work, or with the other men, and you're so big and splendid that I think you *must* be more than an ordinary man, but then other times . . . and there are the stories about Lord Duzon, and why would the gods choose someone in a quiet little place like Grozerodz, if they really chose anyone . . . oh, I don't know."

Malledd smiled gently. "And do you think I *want* to be the divine champion?"

"No," she said instantly.

"So I'm not here because I'm seeking glory, am I? I'm just trying to do what's right."

"But how do you *know* it's right? We want you *home*, Malledd. The children miss you. *I* miss you."

Malledd's throat tightened. For a moment words failed him. He looked out the window to his right, unable to meet Anva's eyes. He reached out to touch the brass-covered leading between the panes; it was cold to the touch and wet with condensation, and he drew a glistening line of moisture down the brass.

"I miss you, too," he said at last, turning back to face his wife. "Maybe . . . maybe you could come *here*? Bring the children here to Seidabar?"

"Bring . . . ?" She looked out the window at the windblown street and the gray stone buildings. "*Here*? Where would we live, in that horrible armory with you?"

Esgora cleared her throat. "My lady, I'm certain we could find room in the temple."

Anva stared at her, horror-stricken.

"Oh, no," she said. "I couldn't live *anywhere* in this . . . this *place*. It's crowded and dirty and hard and ugly, and it stinks."

"You haven't seen . . ." Malledd began.

"I've seen enough!" Anva said sharply, cutting him off. "I'm not going to bring the children here. I want you to come home with me, Malledd!" She slapped her hand on the table for emphasis.

"And I'm not going to, as long as Rebiri Nazakri is a threat to the Empire," Malledd replied mildly. "I'm sorry, Anva—I love you very much, and I miss you, but I can't go home yet."

"Why not? I've heard the news from the temple magicians—that wizard hasn't come any closer to Seidabar in a dozen triads! Maybe he's not coming!"

"He's holed up for the winter, Anva," Malledd said patiently. "He's in a village called Uinaguem with his army, three hundred miles east of here, waiting for the snow to melt. The New Magicians have flown over and seen it. He's there, and in the spring he'll come here—or try to, anyway."

"How do you know that?" Anva asked desperately. "Maybe he won't! Maybe he'll freeze, or starve, or his army will desert him."

"And maybe he won't. If he dies, or his army disbands, we'll hear about it quickly enough, and I'll come straight home. But if they march on Seidabar, and Lord Kadan's army can't stop them, my place is *here*." He hesitated, then smiled and added, "Making swords."

"You *do* think you're the champion," Anva accused.

"I've been told all my life that I am," Malledd agreed. "I'm not *sure*—but yes, I guess I do think so." He was rather surprised at his own words, but all the same, he recognized them for the truth.

"Then why aren't you on your way to that village, whatever it's called? Why aren't you at least in Drievabor?"

"Uinaguem. Because I'm not *sure*—and besides, what would I do there? Walk up to Rebiri Nazakri and order him to surrender? I may be the chosen of the gods, but I'm not a god myself, and nobody ever said the champions were immortal."

"So what will you do *here*?"

"Make swords."

"Ooh! You're impossible."

"Stubborn, anyway. But so are you."

"You won't come home?"

"No. You won't stay?"

"No."

"Not a single night?"

Anva's mouth quirked into a smile.

"I didn't say *that*," she said. "I promised I'd be home by Baranmel's Triad. If it doesn't snow again . . . well, I can certainly stay *one* night."

CHAPTER 30

Aldassi held his bag and staff up before him as he slid down the hard-packed snow into the shadowy porch—which hardly seemed like a porch, with the snow piled man-high on every side, like solid walls of white stone. He would have preferred entering the inn through one of the upstairs windows, but the others insisted on keeping those tightly shuttered.

He couldn't blame them, really.

He glanced at the ice-lined opening that connected the inn to the network of tunnels that linked the whole village together, then stamped across the porch, shaking the snow from his clothes and sending up swirls of glittering white powder. At the door of the inn the snow was only an inch or two deep—but even here, sheltered by a good solid roof and surrounded by drifts, the stone pavement was covered in snow. There was nowhere they could escape it.

At least in Seidabar the streets were kept clear. When the snows had swept down out of the north, half a season before, Aldassi had suggested using the nightwalkers to dig out the village, and for the first few storms the undead had cooperated, but now they were all frozen stiff and buried under ten feet of snow.

The latch was frozen again; Aldassi transferred his sack to his other hand, then pointed his staff and let a tendril of golden light lick out, melting the ice from the door and eerily illuminating the snowed-in porch. Then he lifted the latch and swung open the door.

The thick stink of a hundred unwashed men jammed into far too small a space rolled out at him. Every time he left on one of his father's errands and then returned, the stench seemed worse; he wasn't sure whether it really *was* worse each time, or whether his memory failed to retain its true horror. He took a deep breath—the smell would only be worse if he waited—and stepped inside.

A lone lantern flickered dimly on a hook in the ceiling, a few orange coals glowed on the hearth, and thin gray winter daylight seeped in through the upper portions of shuttered windows; otherwise the room was awash in thick shadows, its occupants mere outlines in the gloom. The glow of his staff, when he swung it inside, was the brightest light to be seen.

"Speak your name," a voice hissed in Olnami from close beside him, and even through his cloak, jacket, and tunic he felt the tip of a knife pressed against his side.

"Aldassi Nazakri," he said. "You know me, Hirini Abaradi."

"And you know *my* name," Hirini said, stepping into the light and sheathing his blade. "That's the *real* proof."

"Proof of what?"

"That you are indeed Aldassi, and not some Domdur magician in his shape," Hirini said.

"Since when are the Domdur magicians shapeshifters?" Aldassi asked, amused and puzzled. "Weren't the last shapeshifters put to death a thousand years ago?"

Hirini shrugged. "So they say," he said. "But the nightwalkers were gone, and your father brought them back. We were talking the other night, and the thought came to us that perhaps the Domdur might find a way to bring back shapeshifters and infiltrate."

Aldassi let out a bark of laughter. "You have been caged here too long," he said. "Your thoughts are bending back on themselves and tying knots. Before long you'll be hearing voices in the wind and seeing spirits in the snow."

"And can you swear there *are* no such voices and spirits?" Hirini asked sourly.

"I can swear that the wind is the wind, and the snow is the snow, just as they always are," Aldassi replied. "Now, where is my father?"

"In his room," Hirini answered. "Go on up." He started to step aside, out of Aldassi's way, then paused. "You didn't bring any food, did you?"

"I could not carry much over such a distance," Aldassi said apologetically, holding out the sack. "I have a dozen loaves of black bread and a wheel of good cheese, nothing more."

"*Cheese?*" A dozen figures stirred in the gloom, suddenly interested.

"Bread and cheese, yes," Aldassi said, pushing the bag into Hirini's arms. "Distribute this fairly, Hirini—see that those who need it most get what they need."

"Yes, O Nazakri," Hirini said, bowing his head as he accepted the bag.

Aldassi smiled bitterly to himself—all it really took to change Hirini's attitude from hostility and distrust to near reverence was the promise of a meal. This northwestern winter was hard on them all. He marched past and crossed to the stairs, stepping over the legs of half a dozen people sprawled in his path.

Rebiri Nazakri had claimed the little room at the southernmost end of the upstairs passage as his own—he was the only person in the entire rebel force who had the luxury of an unshared bed; even Aldassi himself, when he was here in the winter camp, had to squeeze onto a cot with Asari Asakari.

The smell of unwashed bodies did not seem so thick once he got out of the common room and up the stairs. Aldassi marched down the corridor and rapped on the door at the end.

"Is that some accursed Domdur I hear?" Rebiri called from within—speaking Olnami, as always.

Aldassi sighed; habit had gotten the better of him, and he had forgotten that Rebiri did not approve of knocking on doors. Traditional Olnami tents did not have hard doors on which to knock; the custom was to rattle something instead.

"It's someone who has been too long among the Domdur," Aldassi called back.

"Ah, my son! Enter!" The latch slid open, as if of its own accord—his father's magic at work.

Aldassi pushed the door open and stepped in, to find his father seated cross-legged on a velvet cushion. Bundles of tent cloth were stacked against the walls on either side, filling more than half the room; a small rug had been hung over the shuttered window to block drafts, and also shut out what little daylight might have otherwise penetrated. The narrow bed and rickety table that had been the room's original furnishings were pushed behind the door.

And until Aldassi pushed the door wide, all of this was illuminated solely by the smoky red glow of Rebiri's fire-magic crystal, giving it a hellish, unnatural appearance. Everything appeared either red or black; no other colors showed in that light.

Aldassi's own staff vibrated uncomfortably as its golden glow spilled into Rebiri's room; the two Olnami wizards bore incompatible magicks, magicks that could not be kept easily near one another.

"I bring you salt, O Nazakri," Aldassi said in formal greeting.

"And I give you water," Rebiri replied, completing the formula. "Come in, Aldassi, come in! Tell me what you have seen!" He leaned over and pulled another cushion from one of the black tent-cloth bundles and tossed it forward for Aldassi to sit on.

The younger man settled slowly onto the velvet, then placed his staff on the floor behind him, as far from his father as he could reach without rising. He looked Rebiri over, trying not to be obvious about it.

The old man seemed fit; oh, he had lost a little weight, as had all the rebels during this bitter winter, but his eyes were bright and his hands were strong. He had tossed the cushion as casually as if it were a nutshell to be discarded.

That was good.

"It's good to see *you*, Father," he said.

Rebiri smiled, then swiftly erased it, turning the corners of his mouth back down.

"Tell me where you have been, what you have seen, what you have heard," he commanded. "I have been closed away here, and I hunger for news."

"I have been to Seidabar, and to Drievabor, and to Agabdal," Aldassi replied. "I dressed as a Domdur, and spoke as a Domdur, and when asked I professed myself a messenger from the Imperial College of the New Magic. None questioned me closely, and I encountered no serious difficulties nor dangers. The snowfall of two . . ." He paused, realizing he had started to say "two triads," only to stumble over the lack of a word for "triad" in formal Olnami. He *had* been too much among the Domdur. "Of six days ago caught me between Drievabor and Seidabar, and I took shelter in a farmhouse until it had passed. The farmers treated me kindly, and I left them unharmed."

Rebiri nodded an acknowledgment. "The time to end our mercy to the Domdur has not yet come," he said. "What of our supposed allies?"

"All goes well, they say," Aldassi replied. "We have spoken at length of their plans. They know of our whereabouts here—they say this town is called Uinaguem. They will know when we move westward in the spring, just as our enemies will know, and they will begin their attacks when we begin our own. They promise us fear, confusion, and delay, O Father, and in return they ask their lives, and power as our subordinates when we rule in Seidabar."

"And do you believe that they will deliver what they promise?"

"Perhaps not so much as they say, but I believe they will harm our foes, and hinder their army."

"And have you promised them aught?"

"I have spoken with words as twisted as the wind through the rocks of Zedon, Father, and have promised them nothing but the defeat of their Council and the death of their Empress."

Rebiri nodded, and smiled again, allowing this one to linger.

"Good," he said. "And what of our foes, in Seidabar and Agabdal and Drievabor?"

"In Agabdal, the Imperial Army continues to train. Their numbers no longer grow, though the roads of the Domdur heartland have been cleared and traffic flows freely. A quarter of a million soldiers are gathered against us, perhaps more—but the supplies and weapons and transport they need to fight us are still lacking. Our allies have conspired to hide the shortages from Lord Kadan."

Rebiri nodded again. "And Seidabar?"

"In Seidabar, all goes on as before. Nothing has altered since my last report."

"In Drievabor?"

"The Imperial vanguard waits in Drievabor. General Balinus and half a dozen of his staff arrived there at last some twenty days ago. . . ."

"They got past us?" Rebiri's eyes blazed, and his staff hissed; smoke swirled upward, and the red glow brightened momentarily.

"Yes, Father."

"How?"

Aldassi shook his head. "I don't know," he said. "Balinus is a wily old man with many years of experience in the Govya Mountains; he undoubtedly knows tricks that we do not for traveling in snow and surviving the cold. Further, he has with him Tebas Tudan, and a woman I did not recognize who carries a New Magic staff."

"You said half a dozen?"

"Yes."

"He had two or three hundred men when last we encountered him."

"He says he sent them back east, to attempt the recapture of Ai Varach."

Rebiri frowned. "I had not foreseen that," he said. Then he shrugged. "It is of no consequence. Let the beast restore a talon, while we strike at the heart."

Aldassi hesitated, then asked, "Your guiding spirit made no mention of this?"

"My guiding spirit has not spoken to me directly in half a season," Rebiri said, without any display of concern. "I know what I must do; I need no instructions now."

"Yes, Father."

"We must last through this unspeakable winter," Rebiri said. "We must *sur-*

vive. That's enough for now. We must remain alive until the snows melt." He showed his teeth in something that might technically have been a smile, but which showed no trace of pleasure.

"And when the snows melt, and the roads are clear," he said, "then we will strike, and the traitors in Seidabar and Agabdal will strike with us, and if I need guidance then the spirit of my destiny shall undoubtedly provide it. Before the coming summer is out, my son, Seidabar will fall."

CHAPTER 31

For a moment Prince Granzer gazed up at the clerestory windows that circled the council chamber's dome. The snow and ice that had obscured them from Dremeger's Triad until Orini's Triad were long gone, and the late spring sunshine of Dau's Triad poured in, golden and warm, after a winter that had lasted longer than usual. He smiled. "Is the army finally ready to march?" he demanded, turning to Lord Kadan.

"Very nearly," Kadan replied. "However, Your Highness, there is the question of where they are to march *to*."

Granzer's smile vanished. "Are you joking, my lord?" he asked angrily.

"No, Your Highness. I wish I were. However, I suggest you ask him." He jerked a thumb at Apiris. "It seems the Archpriest has received word that the rebels have turned aside."

A stir ran through the room, and all eyes fell on the Archpriest.

"Indeed, Your Highness," Apiris said, unruffled. "That is what the magicians report."

"Which magicians?" Granzer asked sourly.

Apiris blinked. "I received word from our Holy College of Magicians this morning. I believe the magician who made the contact was Rezho—a very reliable young man."

Granzer stared at him. Apiris seemed completely unaware of the significance of any of this; he was carrying out his job, and the fact that the fate of the Domdur Empire might well depend on getting the Imperial Army to the right place at the right time, and that his report on what the magicians said would directly affect whether or not this was done, didn't seem to have registered.

Was the man really so narrow-minded and unimaginative as all that?

"And where did this Rezho hear this?" Granzer demanded.

"I'm afraid I don't know the names of everyone involved, Your Highness," Apiris said, struggling unsuccessfully to hide his surprise and hurt at the tone of the questioning. "This was in the daily report from Drievabor. The New Magicians conduct regular reconnaissance, flying out as close as they dare to the enemy—except when storms prevented it, they've done the same all through the winter, under the direction of Vrai Burrai of the Imperial College and a Diknoi magician named Tebas Tudan who arrived there with General Balinus back in Gol's Triad. It's all in the reports. . . ."

"I've read your blasted reports," Granzer growled. "For triad after triad . . ." He shifted to a high-pitched mockery of Apiris's voice, "No enemy movement was seen." He dropped back to his normal register. "The roads have been clear for triads, but they still just sat there in Uinaguem, according to your magicians. Except for the past two days they *have* been moving. Along the Gogror Highway, straight toward Seidabar."

"Yes, well, last night they left the highway and veered well to the north," Apiris said. "It's in today's report." He held up a sheaf of parchment.

"Which Lord Kadan evidently received before I did."

Apiris shrugged. "I sent your copy at the usual time, Your Highness." He obviously felt that he had done his duty by following the usual routine, and it was no fault of his if no one had pointed out the matter's urgency to Prince Granzer.

"Hmph." Granzer let the matter drop, and turned back to Kadan. "And what do you see as the significance of this change in the rebels' course?"

"I can't explain it, Your Highness," Kadan replied. "My best guess is that they somehow received word of our plans, and decided to cross the Grebiguata somewhere else."

"Ah. And just *how* do they expect to do that? The bridge at Drievabor is the only bridge between Varnor and Diesdenza—are they going to spend the summer marching to Varnor?"

Kadan shook his head. "According to the priests, they're not heading for Varnor, nor any other known crossing."

"Then what *are* they doing?" Granzer demanded, exasperated.

"I have no idea, Your Highness. My best guess would be that they believe they can cross the river without a bridge—perhaps they plan to build their own bridge, or make boats, or even tunnel underneath. Perhaps this black wizard can part the waters and let them simply walk across."

Granzer frowned at Kadan—not because he suspected that the Commissioner of the Army was being sarcastic or deliberately uncooperative, but because there was an uncomfortable truth in his words. They knew so little of Rebiri Nazakri's capabilities!

Not everyone interpreted either Kadan's words or Granzer's expression that way. "Show some respect, Kadan," Lord Shoule hissed from two seats over.

Lord Kadan glanced at Shoule, but said nothing.

"So what should we do?" Lady Dalbisha asked, looking back and forth between Granzer and Kadan.

"That's a very good question, my lady," Lord Kadan replied.

"And do you have an answer, my lord?" Granzer asked angrily. He knew that he was being unfair to Kadan, but he needed to vent his frustration somehow, and Kadan could handle it. "If I understand you correctly, the rebels will reach the river in another two triads. Do you propose to let them cross unopposed?"

"I am at a disadvantage, Your Highness, in being unable to guess how they intend to cross at all."

"So will you just sit there and do nothing?"

"Oh, by no means. I have every intention of ordering the vanguard currently stationed in Drievabor to move wherever may be necessary to keep the enemy from crossing the Grebiguata. However, right now I don't know where that will be, nor do I have a firm plan as to exactly how the enemy is to be defeated. Had they crossed at Drievabor, as we had anticipated, it would have been simple enough—the vanguard was to hold them at the bridge until the main body could arrive, then allow them across into an ambush. The Imperial Army would be arrayed along either side of the Gogror Highway, using the buildings of Drievabor for shelter and concealment, and when the enemy attempted to pass through the town and the country beyond they could be slaughtered easily."

"But the Imperial Army is still in the Agabdal camps," Lady Luzla pointed out.

"True enough," Lord Kadan admitted. "And I concede that that's a disappointment, and they should have been prepared sooner. We have had unexpected problems in logistics. I accept responsibility for these delays—assembling and supplying an army this size has been far more difficult than I anticipated, and that failure in foresight should not have happened. But still, the problems have been dealt with, and the main body should be ready to march in a triad or less. Despite our much greater numbers I believe our forces will be able to move much more quickly than the rebels. Because they rely on nightwalkers the enemy must travel by night, and without so exhausting their human troops that they're unfit to stand guard over the nightwalkers by day; that limits them. They're lucky to cover twelve miles in a day, while we should be able to make twenty on good roads—and the Gogror Highway is a good road. We expected the enemy to reach Drievabor in another five or six days, and our own main body to arrive six or seven days later; the vanguard would be expected to hold the foe off for that interim. If they found themselves incapable of doing so, they were to destroy the bridge. . . ."

Lady Mirashan, the Minister of Trade, let out a yelp of startled displeasure. Lord Kadan paused long enough to glance at her, then continued, "And even if the vanguard were destroyed, which I thought extremely unlikely, the Imperial Army would still be between Seidabar and the foe, and able to maneuver freely to block any attempt to bypass them."

Lord Graush spoke up. "Maneuver freely, you say."

"Yes, my lord."

"You have half a million men in those camps, don't you?"

"Three hundred thousand infantry and at least a hundred thousand men and women in auxiliary and support roles, yes," Kadan agreed.

"Half a million people can't maneuver freely *anywhere*," Graush said. "It's too damn many. They'll trip over each other. How many men has the Olnamian got?"

"Perhaps twelve to fifteen thousand," Kadan said. "But most of them are nightwalkers."

"Nightwalkers or not, we outnumber them twenty to one!" Lord Sulibai declared. "Isn't that a bit excessive? Wouldn't it be wiser to field a smaller, more efficient force?"

"Rebiri Nazakri reportedly took Ai Varach, a major fortress, with three or four hundred nightwalkers," Kadan pointed out. "If I am to err, I prefer to err on the side of caution."

"This is all off the subject," Granzer said. "The point is that Lord Kadan's plans no longer apply, as the enemy is not doing what we expected. We therefore need *new* plans, immediately."

"If I may, Your Highness . . ." Lord Kadan said.

"By all means, my lord."

Kadan rose from his chair and addressed the Council.

"My lords and ladies," he said. "While it's true that we do not know what the enemy intends, he has said that his goal is nothing less than the destruction of Seidabar. I think we do well to believe he means exactly that. So long as we prevent his forces from approaching the city, we cannot fail. I propose to order General Balinus and the Imperial vanguard to use their magical scouts to keep close track of the foe, and to move along the western bank of the Grebiguata to confront the enemy wherever he might attempt a crossing, by any means whatsoever. We will move the bulk of our forces out to the general vicinity, sending reinforcements to the vanguard as necessary and forming a barrier on the path to Seidabar. When and if the enemy succeeds in crossing the Grebiguata, the main body shall sweep down upon him in full force, and obliterate him through sheer strength of numbers."

"Why not put the whole army on the western bank to begin with?" Lady Luzla demanded.

"Because, my lady, it's as Lord Graush says—a force that size, while it can move quickly enough once organized and set on the road, is sluggish and clumsy if any sort of sudden change is called for. If the Olnamian has some clever stratagem in mind the main body might be evaded or penetrated before it could bring its full power to bear. Suppose he does, indeed, somehow intend to cross by boat—and sails fifty miles downstream before we can prevent it. A small, mobile force can follow and impede a landing; three hundred thousand men and their supplies would be left far behind. No, we must first pin the enemy down, *then* demolish him."

The discussion continued for another hour, but little new was said, and at last the meeting was adjourned.

Apiris happened to encounter Lord Kadan in the hallway on the way out of the Imperial Palace.

"A very good plan, I would say, my lord," Apiris remarked.

Kadan turned to him, startled. "What plan?" he asked.

"Why, *your* plan, for defeating the rebels even though they've changed their own plans."

"We don't know that they've changed anything," Kadan said. "Maybe the bastards planned this all along."

"Oh," Apiris said, disconcerted. "Well, it's a good plan, all the same."

Kadan snorted. "It's not a *plan* at all," he said. "It's just the only thing we can do until we know what we're really up against."

Apiris blinked in surprise. He felt a headache coming on. "Then you don't think the vanguard can hold the enemy until the main body arrives?"

"How should I know?" Kadan asked. "They've never fought. For all I know, those six regiments will turn and run at the first sight of a nightwalker. Oh, Balinus is a good man, and his people fought well in Govya, but this is going to be different. These men are mostly raw recruits who just spent a long, boring winter doing nothing in Drievabor. There's no telling what that's done to morale."

"But ... but the Company of Champions is there. They'll rally around the champion, surely."

"If they know who he is, maybe," Kadan said. "And if he's really there at all. If there even *is* a champion anymore."

"Oh, but there *must* be," Apiris said. "And surely he's there."

"Surely," Kadan agreed sourly. "And if he's not, we've got three thousand men against ten thousand nightwalkers, and if they can't use the bridge as a funnel they may be butchered like so many hogs. I just hope they can hold the rebels long enough for the real army to get ready." He pushed past Apiris and stamped away.

Apiris stood for a moment, staring after Lord Kadan.

"Oh, but that can't be right," he said quietly, to no one in particular. "The gods wouldn't allow it." He turned and walked slowly down the stairs and paused in the entry hall, gazing out the open door at the gleaming dome of the Great Temple.

"Would they?" he asked himself.

CHAPTER 32

Lord Duzon shaded his eyes from the first rays of the morning sun as he gazed eastward across the Grebiguata. The fields seemed to stretch on forever—the horizon seemed higher than usual, which added to the effect. Duzon supposed that was actually due to a slight upward slope of the land to the east as it rose out of the river valley.

Far above the eastern plain he could see Vrai Burrai, his staff glittering as he soared through the air.

And now, on the eastern horizon, Duzon could see something dark, something more than the abandoned fields and empty farms that he had seen the day before—not just at one spot, but along a broad band.

That would be Rebiri Nazakri's army, then—Vrai Burrai had said it was approaching, that it was now very near. They had left Drievabor a triad before and had, without undue haste, moved up to this stretch of river, arriving early yesterday afternoon. The New Magician had told General Balinus, the six regimental commanders, and Lord Duzon that this was where the enemy was headed.

It appeared that Vrai Burrai had been right.

He had also said that the enemy traveled only by night. Duzon strained to see whether those dark shapes were moving, or whether they had made camp.

He couldn't tell. He couldn't see movement, but at this distance that didn't mean much.

"Are they coming, Lord?" someone asked.

Duzon turned and looked down at the speaker—though not very far down; it was a big man who spoke, and the folding camp chair on which Duzon stood was not particularly tall.

"Well, they're out there," Duzon said, "but I couldn't say whether they're coming any closer yet. We'll have to wait until Vrai Burrai reports back—or until they move close enough that we can see for ourselves."

He started to step down from the chair, but something caught his eye, and he turned to look eastward again, trying to spot what had distracted him.

"They've got archers," the big man remarked.

Duzon squinted, and realized the other was right. Arrows, invisible at that distance save when their heads caught the sunlight and sparkled briefly, were sailing up around Vrai Burrai.

The New Magician wasn't foolhardy; he was ascending now, and moving westward, back toward the Imperial lines.

"You've got good eyes, fellow," Duzon remarked as he stepped off the chair.

The man ignored the compliment. "I guess the magician's coming back, and we'll get the news, then."

"So it would appear." Duzon folded the chair and tucked it under one arm, then looked at the other.

He was a big man, as Duzon had already noted—roughly Duzon's own height or a little taller, and definitely broader in the shoulder. He wore the scarlet and gold of an Imperial soldier, but didn't seem entirely at home in it; Duzon guessed that this fellow was one of the recent recruits that made up most of the vanguard, not one of the veterans who had been mixed in to provide the newer troops with the benefits of their experience. He had had all winter to adjust to the uniform—but he probably hadn't bothered to wear it much; many of the men had not, during their stay in Drievabor.

"Are you eager to meet the foe, then?" Duzon asked.

The man grimaced. "Hardly, Lord," he said. "I'd rather not meet them at all; I'd rather they all dropped dead of plague, so that I could go home to my village and brag about my heroism without having to actually demonstrate it."

A bark of startled laughter escaped Duzon. "An honest man, by the gods!" he said. "What's your name, fellow? You aren't in my company, certainly, nor the Second Seidabar." The Company of Champions had been attached to the Second Seidabar for the winter. That was one of the adjustments General Balinus had made after he and his staff finally made it through the snow into Drievabor.

"No, my lord," the other said. "My name is Onnell, Third Company, Biekedau Regiment."

"Then you're from Biekedau?" Duzon had heard of the town, of course, long before he ever saw the name on the regimental banner—Biekedau was the river port on the Vren, to the south of Seidabar somewhere. He had never been there; his family's concerns were all to the northwest.

"I'm not really from Biekedau," Onnell explained quickly. "I'm from Grozerodz. But there are only seven of us from there, not enough for our own unit."

Duzon nodded understanding. He had never heard of Grozerodz; it was presumably just another of the thousands of villages scattered through the Domdur heartland. "And you're eager to get home to Grozerodz and regale all the pretty girls with tales of your adventures soldiering for the Empress, are you?"

"Well, yes, sir, since you ask. But I'm ready to fight for the Empress, if it comes to that."

Duzon glanced eastward again.

"It appears that it will indeed come to that, Onnell," he said.

Onnell shrugged. "I'm ready, then."

For a moment the two men stood in companionable silence, gazing eastward. Then Onnell glanced up at the white plume bobbing in Lord Duzon's broad-brimmed hat and said, "They tell me you're Lord Duzon of . . . Snafallia?"

"Snauvalia," Duzon corrected him automatically. He knew it didn't matter, and he was long past the point of taking offense or being amused at mistakes in pronouncing the name of his ancestral demesne, but enough family pride lingered that he couldn't simply ignore the error.

Onnell accepted the correction, and continued diffidently, "Some of the men say you're the gods' champion, sent to defeat this Rebiri Nazakri."

This was the closest anyone in the vanguard had yet come to asking him straight out if he was, indeed, the divine champion, and Duzon hesitated, unsure just how to reply.

He had thought about it, of course; he'd known the question would come. He'd hoped, though, that it would come in circumstances where his reply would be dictated by necessity, where the mood of his audience would tell him what to say.

That wasn't the case here. He had no audience to be swayed by his answer, no troops to be inspired by his example—and as yet he had scarcely had any chance to set an example; the stay in Drievabor had been quiet, almost without incident. There had been a handful of drunken brawls, and one young idiot had gotten lost in a storm and almost frozen to death, but there had been no opportunity for the Company of Champions, or its captain, to show what they could do.

Duzon didn't know this man Onnell, and couldn't read much of his mood. There could be little doubt, though, that whatever he said would be carried back to the Biekedau Regiment, and would spread through all the vanguard from there, and in time, when the main body finally arrived, through all the Imperial Army.

He studied Onnell's face quickly, and thought he saw something hard under the outward friendliness, something challenging, ready to turn hostile. Somehow, he didn't think this man would take well to boasting.

"It's not what any of the *men* might say that counts, though, is it, Onnell?" he replied at last. "It's what the *gods* say that matters."

"True enough," Onnell said. He looked at Duzon expectantly, clearly not content with that response, in and of itself.

The nobleman smiled wryly. "Whatever else I might be, I'm no oracle," Duzon said. "These days even the *oracles* aren't oracles. If I'm the champion, the gods haven't told me—but then, who's to say they would have?"

The look on Onnell's face after that struck Duzon as peculiar; the man appeared positively *relieved,* and that didn't fit Duzon's expectations at all. Thoughtful at the possibility that the champion might not himself know he was champion, yes; disappointed that Duzon was not claiming the title, yes; but relieved?

An explanation occurred to him, and Duzon slapped Onnell on the back. "For all we know, friend," he said, "*you* might be the chosen one!"

Onnell shook his head. "Oh, no," he said. "I know I'm not."

Again, Duzon was puzzled by the response.

"But how can you know it, Onnell?" he asked lightly. "I've forty-one men in my company who all think they might be the champion, and at least forty of them must be wrong; how can you be certain you're not just as wrong in the opposite way?"

"I . . ." Onnell hesitated. "I've promised not to say, my lord."

Duzon stared at him, more baffled than ever.

Promised *whom*? Just what did this man, this common soldier, this ordinary citizen from a backwater village, know about the divine champion that he had promised not to tell?

The sudden curiosity was almost unbearable, but Duzon resisted—to try to coax the information from Onnell when he had promised not to reveal it would be dishonorable. Question after leading question leaped to mind—was there an oracle in this man's village, in Grozerodz, who still heard from the gods? Had someone there had word of the champion's identity from an oracle before the silence?—but he stifled each before it reached his lips.

It certainly seemed that Onnell knew something. . . .

Or *thought* he knew something. He could, of course, be wrong. Duzon tore his gaze away and looked out across the Grebiguata.

Vrai Burrai had fled the arrows and was now over the river, nearing the Imperial camp.

Rebiri Nazakri didn't seem to be worried about any divine champion. He seemed to think he could march his army right up to the gates of Seidabar. It was up to Lord Duzon and the Company of Champions and the Imperial Army to show this rebel the error of his ways! Maybe a real divine champion would emerge, and maybe not—and maybe the army would decide on someone, but not the ones the gods had actually selected. Duzon didn't think the matter was as settled as Onnell seemed to believe.

Still, it might be interesting to find out a little more about this Grozerodz place, once the war was over and Rebiri Nazakri had been dealt with.

Duzon realized he had been staring rudely at Onnell for a second or two. He forced a smile that quickly turned genuine, and turned his gaze to the main Imperial camp.

"Fair enough," he said. "Have you had breakfast yet?"

"No, Lord," Onnell said. "But I . . ."

"Come and eat with the Company of Champions, then," Duzon said. "I'll not pry at your secrets, I promise you."

Onnell hesitated. He glanced out across the river, at the distant enemy.

He wished Malledd were here. Wasn't this where the gods' chosen defender should be? Malledd ought to have come. Onnell had been thinking that all winter; at times he had even thought that Malledd's absence meant that he and the other soldiers of the vanguard were in the wrong place in Drievabor, and the real fight would be somewhere else entirely.

But so far as he knew Malledd was safely at home in Grozerodz, in his tidy little house behind the graveyard with his wife and children, with his parents just across the field, and surely the confrontation with Rebiri Nazakri would not happen *there*.

In fact, the rebel army was out there, across the river, after all. The vanguard had not been misdirected. The battle would be *here*.

Onnell wondered if perhaps he should tell Lord Duzon about Malledd, after all. He had promised Malledd he would not, and a promise should be kept, but Malledd ought to be here, leading the defenders against the rebel army. General Balinus and all these colonels and New Magicians and so on were all very well, but the Domdur ruled because the gods had chosen them to rule, not because of any generals or soldiers. The divine champion was the mark of the gods' favor, their representative to mortals; he should be here. There shouldn't be Lord Duzon and his Company of Champions, all of them pretenders to the title, a bunch of overambitious upstarts playing at the role. Lord Duzon himself seemed like a pretty good man, but the rest . . .

But maybe it was all part of some plan the gods were following. There were no oracles to consult anymore, so the gods' actions were more mysterious than ever; maybe Malledd wasn't here because the gods wanted him somewhere else. Maybe the gods wanted Lord Duzon here in Malledd's stead, even if Duzon wasn't the champion.

Onnell thought he might have liked Lord Duzon if he hadn't heard the stories about how Duzon was probably the champion. As it was, though, he couldn't help thinking there was something false about the nobleman. True, Duzon himself had not claimed to be the champion, but he had left the possibility open. And since he had, Onnell could not trust him with Malledd's story.

Besides, what if all the scurrilous rumors that had been whispered in Grozerodz were true? What if the priests had chosen a hundred "divine champions," all over the Empire? Lord Duzon had not presented any claim of priestly support, but perhaps that was because he knew such claims to be worthless. Onnell didn't really believe that, but he had to admit that the possibility was at least theoret-ically there.

He didn't like it, and didn't believe it—he had always seen something special in Malledd, quite apart from his size and strength, and he didn't *think* it was just because everyone had always *said* Malledd was special.

Still, it wouldn't hurt to ask a few more questions of these people who claimed to be champions. He had started by asking Lord Duzon, indirectly, about the stories that Duzon was the chosen of the gods—Duzon was generally seen by Onnell's companions in the Biekedau Regiment, other than the other six from Grozerodz, as the most likely candidate. Now Onnell had a chance to have breakfast with the entire company of claimants—he could ask more of them about their claims, and could find out whether they had any basis for their boasts.

That would be a very welcome opportunity.

And besides, they probably ate better than the common soldiers in the Bie-kedau Regiment.

"I'd be pleased to join you, Lord," Onnell said.

CHAPTER 33

Malledd had been in Seidabar for some time now, long enough to grow thor-oughly accustomed to the city's sounds, and the shouting outside the armory didn't fit the regular patterns. Malledd couldn't make out the words, but people outside were yelling, almost shrieking, and it wasn't the normal shouting of irate merchants or drunken brawlers or any of the other urban phenomena Malledd had become familiar with. The shouts were mostly a long way off, but coming closer. Malledd could hear them distinctly, despite the clanging of hammers on steel.

Some of the other apprentices had noticed the noise, as well. Three or four of them were looking at the small window, high in the west wall of the forge room, that looked out on the street.

Fresh air suddenly seemed like a very good idea to Malledd. Technically it was a violation of the apprenticeship rules to leave the hall without permission, but Malledd was not the only one who sometimes ignored that particular stric-ture.

The shouts were growing louder, and there were definitely many voices now, not just a handful. Darsmit, who had been sitting cross-legged on the floor sharpening a blade, had gotten to his feet and stood beside Malledd, staring at the window.

"Come on," Malledd said, putting down his hammer. He headed for the steps that led up to the street door.

Darsmit followed without a word.

A moment later the two of them emerged from the alleyway that ran along one side of the Imperial Armory, stepping out onto Wall Street.

Ever since Malledd had arrived in the city, anytime the weather was tolerable, Wall Street had been perpetually mobbed from dawn to dusk, and often long after darkness fell, as well. Cold and snow had driven the crowds indoors for much of the winter, but now that spring had brought back the sun the throngs were thicker than ever.

Today was no exception. This time, however, the crowd was different in that everyone seemed to be running in one of two directions—no one was walking, or standing, or moving in or out of any of the side streets.

The current in one direction seemed to be made up of frightened people, while the current flowing the other way carried a more varied atmosphere—determination, concern, curiosity.

Malledd frowned. He reached out and grabbed the first passing runner he could—one of the frightened ones.

The man started to protest the grip on his arm; then he turned and looked up and saw Malledd's face, and the words died on his lips.

"What's happening?" Malledd demanded.

"The Imperial Palace is on fire!" the man shouted. "Let me go! I have to get out, before the whole city burns down!"

Malledd let him go, then glanced at Darsmit.

"I think he's right," Darsmit said. "Look!" He pointed.

A column of smoke was visible above the roofs to the northwest—Malledd hadn't noticed it before because after all, Seidabar was full of smoking chimneys, its sky perpetually streaked with gray.

This smoke, though, now that it had been pointed out, was clearly not coming from any mere chimney; it was a thick, towering pillar of white against the blue of the sky, one side of it twining around the golden spire of the palace tower.

"Come on," Malledd said again, pushing forward into the street.

Darsmit hesitated for perhaps half a second before following.

As they pushed their way toward the palace he did call, "Malledd, what are we doing?"

Malledd glanced back at him.

"We came to Seidabar to defend the Empire, didn't we?" he asked. He gestured at the smoke. "Well, anything that threatens the Empress or her palace threatens the Empire, and it's our duty to stop it!"

Darsmit did not seem entirely convinced, but he followed Malledd anyway—

by this time it was easier to trot along in the big man's wake than to go anywhere else in the surging mob on the street.

A few minutes later Malledd pushed his way into the plaza before the palace steps, but here even he could not press on farther; the way was blocked by a tightly packed crowd of people standing and staring at the flames that billowed from several of the palace windows. Sparks were showering upward around the towering central spire; the air rippled with heat.

The crowd was jammed back against the walls and streets opposite the palace; the steps and the inner pavement were empty. No one was moving any closer than the plaza's midpoint; in fact, the front lines of the crowd were pressing backward, trying to escape the heat and smoke, but were unable to move because of the pressure of newly arrived curiosity-seekers.

"Why isn't anyone doing anything?" Malledd demanded. "That's the Imperial Palace burning! The Empress might be in there. And if that tower falls, it could smash a dozen buildings!"

Darsmit looked around at the crowd—though he couldn't see much; he wasn't anywhere near as tall as Malledd, and mostly found himself looking at the backs of heads and, above them, the rising sparks and smoke.

"Who should be doing something?" Darsmit asked. "Are there guards?"

"No," Malledd said. He frowned. Surely, he thought, there *ought* to be guards; where were they? Part of the army was off to the east fighting the rebels, and a much larger part was training new recruits in the camps just outside Agabdal, but surely they hadn't left the palace *completely* undefended? And guards or no, why were these people just *standing* here?

Someone had to do something.

"Let me through!" he bellowed.

"Stop shoving!" a man in front of him said.

Malledd reached forward with both hands and grabbed the complainer by the back of his shirt. He twisted the fabric to tighten it, then lifted, hauling the man up out of the crowd as if he were pulling out a rotted fence post.

The man made a strangled squawk of protest, but was too surprised to do any more than that before he found himself held over Malledd's head. He curled up instinctively.

Malledd twisted halfway around and tossed the man out of the plaza as if he were a ball. He landed atop an approaching woman, and both of them tumbled back onto the hard-packed dirt, bruised but not seriously hurt.

"Let me *through!*" Malledd repeated.

The man immediately in front of him had seen what just happened; he pushed aside, even though he would have sworn, a few seconds earlier, that he couldn't move an inch.

Malledd shoved past, bellowing, towing Darsmit in his wake. A moment later he burst through the front line of the crowd, into the open.

The heat washed over him in waves—but he was a blacksmith; the heat of his forge when he was working steel was worse. He ran forward, across the inner plaza, up the dozen broad stone steps to the main entrance, right at the base of the central tower.

The visible sources of smoke and flame were all to his right, in the east wing, Malledd saw; perhaps the fire, despite its ferocity, hadn't yet spread too far.

Behind him the crowd, which had been muttering and shouting, hushed for a moment; then people began to shout, "What's he doing? Where's he going?"

The palace doors were standing open, and beyond them Malledd could see a great marble hall, divided by broad pillars and full of smoke—but no flames were visible, nor any bodies. That was good. The fact that the doors were open meant no one was trapped inside—unless they were in some part of the palace that had been cut off by the flames, and of course, people might have been overcome by smoke.

But the open doors also meant the fire was getting plenty of air. Malledd hesitated, unsure whether it was more important to let air in for anyone who might still be in there, or to shut it out to weaken the flames.

He decided that the doors didn't really matter; there were plenty of windows.

There should have been guards at the doors; where had they gone?

That didn't really matter, either. He turned to face the crowd.

"Water!" he shouted. "Where's a water source? A well, or a spring?" Seidabar's Inner City was generously endowed with water sources, generally attributed to divine beneficence; certainly they made life within the walls much easier. Villagers in Grozerodz often spent a large part of their time hauling water up from the streams on either side of the village; the people of Seidabar had no need to do the same.

But where was the nearest water source? He needed one *now*.

Malledd spotted Darsmit, who had followed him as far as the front line of the crowd and then stopped. "You, Darsmit," he called, "do you know where there's water?"

Darsmit looked blank, but a woman next to him stopped shoving against the people behind her long enough to call back, "There's a pump right here!" She pointed back into the crowd.

From his position atop the steps, Malledd could now distinguish a small discontinuity in the crowd, a row of raised heads in a relatively uncrowded area. He had only visited the plaza a very few times, just walking through, and he had mostly been paying attention to the Imperial Palace, but he remembered now that yes, there was a pump right there, and a horse trough, for the use of visiting nobles.

And those raised heads were because those people were standing in the trough.

"Buckets!" he bellowed. "Boots, hats, anything that will hold water!" He marched down the steps, directly toward the pump, and dragged aside anyone in his way, yanking half a dozen people out into the hot, smoky open space before the others managed to clear a path.

When he reached the trough the people standing in it were unable to climb out in time; Malledd snatched them up, one by one, and heaved them out, tossing them aside.

A woman was leaning against the pump handle; she straightened up as best she could as Malledd glared at her.

"You," he said, "start pumping." He pointed at a man just the other side. "You help. Take turns. Keep that trough full."

The two obeyed as best they could, despite the protests from neighbors who suddenly found elbows or the pump handle poking them. Water spurted, gurgled, then began flowing steadily into the trough.

"Now, buckets!" Malledd bellowed. He looked around.

The crowd looked back blankly—but then someone yelled, a hundred feet away in one of the streets adjoining the plaza.

"Over here!" he called, holding up a bucket. "From the cooper up the street!"

"Good! Get more! Everything the cooper's got!" Malledd shouted back. "Pass that one here! Then find a tinker, or a smith, for more!"

The bucket was passed hand-to-hand over the heads of the crowd until it reached Malledd, who snatched it full from the slowly filling trough. Then he handed it to a man.

"You're first in the chain," he said. Then he grabbed another man and shoved him into position. "You're second."

The first man handed the bucket to the second; a third took his position without being told, and a fourth. By the time Malledd pushed his way back to the front of the crowd the bucket, and the line of volunteers, had reached halfway up the steps—though the last few in line seemed to regret their enthusiasm as they cowered from the heat and smoke.

Malledd turned and looked back at the front of the crowd, then pulled out half a dozen of the biggest, strongest-looking men—and Darsmit. "You come with me," he said. Then he raised his voice again.

"Extend that chain! That bucket's not doing any good on the steps!"

He could see people hesitating, glancing about uncertainly—no one else wanted to walk out across the open to the steps to join the line. He already had the boldest people.

Well, that was no problem.

"Come on," he said, and he led his band of men to the steps.

There he paused to address the last few members of the bucket brigade.

"Good for you, coming this far! But the fire's in there." He pointed. "Take a cloth and soak it, and hold that over your face to cool it and keep out the smoke." He pulled a polishing rag from his belt and demonstrated, dipping it in the bucket and then slapping it over his nose and mouth; it wasn't the best cloth for the purpose, but it served. Then he lowered the cloth. "Better you use up half the water protecting yourself and get the rest on the fire than *none* of it get to where it'll do some good! And if you can't keep a line in there, just run in when you can, then run back out—anything to slow the flames! Now, those cowards out there"—he gestured at the crowd—"they aren't going to come up here; they aren't brave enough. You'll have to show them what courage is. But if *you* go in, and the whole line moves along—well, some of them will find the nerve to join at the back of the line and keep the water coming. So let's get in there and do what we can! For the Empire!" He raised a fist in salute, then turned back to his chosen party of big men.

"You come with me—wet yourselves down, grab a wet cloth, and come on." He splashed himself with water from the bucket—a second bucket was now being passed up the line, he saw—the cooper had presumably cooperated. "We'll see what we can do to keep the fire from spreading!"

"But the fire . . ." someone protested.

"We'll move fast, we'll watch each other's backs—come on! I'm a smith, I know heat and smoke, and I'll keep us safe."

Malledd clapped his soaked polishing cloth over his mouth and marched into the palace, not looking back to see whether the others were following him—if they didn't, bullying them further wouldn't be worth the trouble.

The fire was mostly in the upper stories and off to the right, easily heard and felt, but not seen; Malledd ventured several yards down a smoke-filled grand hallway before he glimpsed the yellow glow of flames spilling down a staircase not far ahead. The air was thick with smoke; the smell almost choked him.

He turned, and found that Darsmit and the others were right there behind him—and even a few of the bucket brigade.

"All right," he said, bellowing to be heard over the roar of the flames, "there's the fire—if you can get that water up there without scorching, go to it. If you can't, don't worry—we'll find a way. Just soak anything that looks as if it might burn. Darsmit, you watch anyone who goes past this point; if anyone collapses, you drag him out, fast! The rest of you, we need a firebreak—grab anything flammable and get it out of here!" He pointed to the ancient tapestries on the walls, which were already beginning to darken from the heat.

That done, he looked around, squinting through the smoke, trying to judge what should be done next.

The wall behind the tapestries was plaster, and he had no way of telling what supported the plaster. The exterior walls were cut stone, but the interior frame, except for the pillars supporting the tower, might well be entirely wood—very old, very dry wood. *Something* was certainly burning enthusiastically up there. The floor beneath his feet was stone, which was good, but the coffered ceiling above was painted wood. The entrance to the stairway was a stone arch—if that wasn't merely ornamentation, then the interior structure was a mix of materials, which would make it hard to know what would burn and what would not.

He wanted to know what was inside those walls. He hadn't brought any of his tools, though—even the polishing cloth that now protected his face had been a lucky accident.

"I can't do it," someone said.

Malledd looked for the speaker, and saw a young man, scarcely more than a boy, crouching at the foot of the stairs, bucket in hand.

"Then don't," Malledd called. He strode over and snatched the bucket away. "Go back for more—we don't need any dead heroes, we need live workers." He looked up.

The flames were licking across the upstairs ceiling; the stairway railings were burning. He flung the water at the banister.

"Just stop the spreading," he shouted. "Don't try to put out the whole thing—just keep it from spreading, and it'll burn itself out!" He remembered when his great-uncle's forge in Duvrenarodz had caught fire; the villagers had stood around, outside the firebreak, and simply watched as the little shed burned down. The stone of the hearth and the metal tools had all survived, somewhat the worse for wear, and no one had been hurt; that was what mattered.

If they didn't save the east wing it didn't really matter, but Malledd didn't want to let the fire spread and maybe bring down the tower; that would be a disaster, especially if anyone was still in it.

The tapestries were gone, carried out and dumped on the plaza; more water was arriving, to be flung on the stone steps and smoldering railings. Malledd snatched a bucket and splashed its contents on the wall plaster, to soften it; then he kicked hard.

Plaster cracked and crumbled, revealing rough stone.

Malledd smiled, and turned to the other side of the corridor; there his boot broke through, revealing oaken timbers.

That was bad; it meant that some walls were safe and others weren't.

His big men were back from removing the tapestries; Malledd pointed to the wood-frame wall and said, "Smash that down! Make a gap the fire can't jump. And someone get some tools!"

The men hastened to obey, pounding on the wall with feet, shoulders, and improvised clubs. Malledd didn't stay to help; instead he moved on to another corridor, then to one room after another, marking which walls were wood and which were stone, drawing a line the fire could not be allowed to cross.

He worked on, tirelessly, through the rest of the day and into the night. He had been at it for about an hour when the first New Magicians from the nearby Imperial College arrived and began clearing away wreckage and cutting a fire-break far more effectively than Malledd and his recruits could. He had been there almost two hours when the first guards and soldiers finally showed up, closely followed by government officials who took charge. Malledd didn't let any of that stop him. He had a job to do, and he intended to carry on until it was done.

The sky was brightening in the east, and a large percentage of the eastern wing of the Imperial Palace was a blackened ruin, when Malledd finally looked around and nodded with satisfaction. Most of the fire fighting had actually been accomplished by the New Magic, but Malledd was still pleased with what he and his volunteers had done.

The northern and western wings of the Imperial Palace, and the central section with its soaring spire, were all intact. The guards were back in place; the crowd had long since dissipated. The New Magicians had exhausted their magic not long after nightfall, and had walked back to their college. Darsmit had collapsed from exhaustion and been carried out hours ago, back to the apprentices' hall at the Imperial Armory. Reports had come in from various places, assuring the safety of the imperial family, the Imperial Council, and the other usual occupants of the palace. The Empress herself had been in the tower the whole time, too ill to move, but had not been harmed.

And the fire was out.

Malledd didn't know how it could have started in the first place, or why the guards hadn't been present, or where all the officials who should have taken charge had been, but none of that was any of his business; he had wanted to save as much of the palace and the surrounding city as he could, and he had done that.

Now he could go home and get some sleep.

Not that he was really tired; as everyone around him had noticed ever since his childhood, Malledd didn't *get* tired. Still, he thought sleep would be pleasant. He brushed off what he could of the ashes and smoke stains, then ambled back out through the main hall, down the steps to the plaza, and back toward the Imperial Armory.

CHAPTER 34

Where were you two yesterday?" the master demanded as he stood in the dormitory entry glowering angrily at Malledd and Darsmit.

Malledd had just awoken, after only an hour or so of sleep, and was not yet fully awake; he sat up in his bed and blinked stupidly at the master in response.

"Fighting the fire at the Imperial Palace," Darsmit said.

The master's expression softened abruptly.

"Oh," he said.

"Malledd here organized the bucket brigade," Darsmit said. "He was magnificent!"

"Oh," the master said again. He took in Malledd's appearance, and didn't doubt the explanation—while smiths and apprentices were often blackened by smoke and metal, Malledd's filthy condition went far beyond anything a mere forge would produce. "Well, clean yourselves up and get back to work, both of you."

"Yes, sir," Darsmit replied. Malledd nodded.

The master departed, and Malledd looked around. The apprentices' dormitory was deserted save for the two of them.

"Where is everybody?" he asked.

"At breakfast," Darsmit replied. "You slept through the call. I stayed to wake you, but then the master arrived . . ."

"I see," Malledd said. He looked down at himself.

His blouse was ruined. His breeches were still serviceable, but black with smoke and ash. His boots were gone completely, and he vaguely remembered discarding them after they had been so damaged by fire, water, and abuse as to be worse than useless. He had walked back to the armory barefoot.

He had another blouse and a tunic, and a second pair of breeches, but no spare boots; he would have to make do with his slippers until he could somehow afford another pair.

"Malledd, what I said to the master just now . . ." Darsmit began. Malledd looked up, puzzled. Darsmit cleared his throat and continued, "I just wanted to tell you I meant it. You *were* magnificent!"

"The magicians did most of it," Malledd said.

"But still, the way you took charge and led everyone to work . . . the magicians would have been too late if you hadn't done that!"

Malledd snorted. "And look what it got me," he said, pulling his blouse up over his head and flinging it aside.

Darsmit looked at Malledd's bare torso and gasped.

"No, I meant the blouse," Malledd said. Then he looked down, trying to see why Darsmit should be so astonished.

"Oh," Malledd said. The lower ribs on his left side were covered by an immense purple bruise, and the red slash of a half-healed burn. "A falling timber hit me there. Hurt like demons' teeth at the time."

"Doesn't it *still* hurt?"

"A little," Malledd admitted, working his left arm experimentally. He noticed Darsmit's expression and said, "I heal fast." Then he pulled his spare tunic from his pack and slipped it over his head—he didn't care to risk his remaining blouse just yet.

"I guess you do," Darsmit agreed. "And you worked on and on for so long without tiring! You took charge of the crowd as if you were Lord Kadan himself—and you say you're a village smith, with no noble blood? I've never seen . . ."

He suddenly stopped dead, and his eyes widened.

"*That's* why you used to ask about Lord Duzon and the others so much!" he said. Malledd looked up apprehensively from straightening his clothes. "I should have guessed," Darsmit said, almost shouting. "Your size, your strength . . . by all the gods, you've come!"

"Shut up," Malledd said.

"But you *are*, aren't you?" Darsmit insisted, lowering his voice. "You're the divine champion?"

"Shut *up*," Malledd repeated through clenched teeth. He stood up, took a step, and grabbed the front of Darsmit's blouse. He yanked the smaller man— though Darsmit was not especially small or frail—closer until their faces were mere inches apart.

"Listen to me, Darsmit," Malledd said, speaking slowly and trying to avoid letting his native accent interfere with the clarity of his speech. "Whether I am the divine champion or not, and yes, I admit others have said I might be, I do not want it *said* that I am he. I don't *know* if I am, and I don't want to deal with it. Do you understand?"

"*No*, I don't," Darsmit said. "If you're the champion, don't you want . . ."

"Don't you worry what I want," Malledd interrupted. "I'm *telling* you what I want. I like you, Darsmit—you're about the closest thing to a friend I've found here in Seidabar—but I swear by Ba'el, if you start announcing that I'm the divine champion I will do my best to crack your skull. *I don't want it said.* Is that clear?"

"Yes, but . . ."

"*No 'buts'!*" Malledd lifted Darsmit up off his feet and held him dangling from one immense hand.

"All right!" Darsmit shouted. "All right. Put me down. I won't say anything."

Malledd lowered him to the floor and released him. Darsmit tugged his blouse back into shape as Malledd fished out his slippers.

"I won't say anything, Malledd," Darsmit said, "but can't you tell me *why* you don't want me to?"

Malledd sat down heavily on his bunk and pulled on a slipper.

"When I was a baby," he said, "a priest told my parents I had been touched by the gods—I had a birthmark that was said to be the mark of Ba'el's claw." He glanced down at his tunic. "I'm told it looked something like that burn, but across my face instead of my side. It faded away."

Darsmit sat down on a nearby bunk and listened raptly.

"The mark was supposed to mean that I was the chosen of the gods, the next ordained champion," Malledd explained. "My parents didn't entirely believe it— or disbelieve it. They said it didn't matter, and they were right, it *didn't* matter when I was growing up. What mattered was that *other* people thought it was important. People from the village would come to my father's forge just to look at me; they'd stare at me while I was playing, or learning my trade. Anytime I did anything good, it would be dismissed—'What do you expect? He's the champion!' And the other children, my sisters in particular, teased me about it. The only way I could have a decent life was to insist that everyone ignore it—I had to beat a few people who were slow to learn."

Darsmit nodded. "But you came to Seidabar . . . ?"

"I don't want to be the champion," Malledd said, "but I'm a loyal Domdur. And maybe I *am* the champion, and even if I didn't choose it I won't refuse to defend my people if the gods insist on it. But I don't *know* I'm the champion, and I don't want to put up with the same harassment here I had as a child. This isn't a village; I can't very well beat up all the slow learners in Seidabar."

"I can see that," Darsmit said. "But how can you not be sure you're the chosen one? You had the birthmark, the priests said you were the chosen, you're bigger and stronger than any ordinary man, you heal as if blessed by Pashima, you never seem to tire . . ."

"Three or four priests have said I'm the chosen," Malledd replied. "Others, including Apiris, say they know nothing about it. Size and strength are scarcely decisive. And I'm just a blacksmith from Grozerodz—wouldn't Lord Duzon or Prince Bagar or Vrai Burrai make a better champion?"

"But they . . ."

"Just forget about it, all right? Or at least keep your mouth shut."

"All right," Darsmit said. "I think you're crazy, but all right." He hesitated, then said, "I'd been meaning to ask you anyway, though maybe you won't believe that, but—listen, my sister's wedding is the day after tomorrow. Her fiancé is probably going to be sent east to fight soon—in fact, we *thought* he'd be gone by now, but Lord Kadan keeps postponing it. Anyway, they're getting married as soon as they can so they'll have a little time together before he goes. I'd be proud if you'd come to the wedding."

Malledd stared at him for a moment.

"You're right, maybe I won't believe you were going to ask me anyway," he said. "What you mean is that you'd be proud to have the chosen of the gods at your sister's wedding. The next best thing to having Baranmel dance for you, I suppose."

"No, honestly . . ." Darsmit began.

Malledd cut him off. "I'll come," he said. "You know why, Darsmit? To make sure you keep your mouth shut about me. I'll be there to keep an eye on you, no matter how drunk you get." He stood up. "Now, let's go wash up, and then see if the rest of those pigs have left us anything to eat."

Reluctantly, wanting to argue further or make further protestations about the purity of his motives, Darsmit followed, limping slightly; he was still stiff from the previous day's exertions.

He really *had* meant to invite Malledd anyway; he liked the big man, and he'd thought that Malledd had gotten to like him in the two seasons they'd been working together in the armory.

Of course, knowing that the divine protector of the Empire was there at the wedding wouldn't hurt any.

Darsmit, as he tried to work the stiffness from his joints, noticed that Malledd, despite the bruise and burn and his prodigious feats, seemed as fit as ever. The man really was more than merely human; he ought to be wincing in pain or staggering with exhaustion, but the only difference in how he walked was that his feet rustled along in slippers, rather than clomping in boots.

A few blocks away Prince Granzer peered down into the smoldering wreckage of the east wing and noticed the remains of Malledd's boots lying in a corner. Even in their present battered condition they were clearly neither a nobleman's boots nor the standard military issue, but the footwear of an ordinary working man.

"Whose are those?" he demanded. "The arsonist's, perhaps?"

"I would think it more likely, Your Highness, that they belonged to one of the firefighters," murmured his aide, Delbur. "Even assuming that the fire was in fact arson, why would the arsonist be foolish enough to leave his boots?"

"You doubt it was arson?" Granzer turned to glare at Delbur. The half-dozen other officials and courtiers in the inspection party moved back slightly, away from the Prince's annoyance; the dozen soldiers paid no attention.

Delbur shrugged. "I don't know, Highness."

"Hm," Granzer muttered. He turned back to the boots. "Find out whose those were. Take them to the temple and see what the magicians can tell us."

"Perhaps the Imperial College . . ."

Granzer shook his head. "No, for information you want the *old* magic, the *Holy* College. If you want something *done*, maybe you call the New Magicians. If you trust them."

"Very good," Delbur agreed. He beckoned to a soldier, pointed out the boots, and whispered instructions, while Granzer continued to study the damage.

"You believe it was arson?" Lord Sulibai asked. "Might I inquire as to your reasons?"

Granzer turned and stared at Sulibai for a moment, then asked, "It's not obvious to you?"

"Humor me, Your Highness."

Granzer pointed out the soldier clambering down a charred timber. "Where was he yesterday, Sulibai? Where were all the guards? The palace servants? The Imperial Council? Where were *you*, Lord Sulibai?"

"I had been called away. . . ."

"Exactly. So had I. So had the guards. So had the servants. So had the other Councillors. And I don't know about your summons, but the call I responded to turned out to be fraudulent. The riot in the Outer City that drew away the soldiery was, according to the ringleaders we captured, bought and paid for by anonymous robed men."

"Priests?" Sulibai asked.

Granzer shook his head. "I doubt it—the robes were dark, and of good heavy fabric. Our prisoners say that the men spoke with the accents of educated Domdur—nobles or wealthy merchants."

"So you think that everyone who might have fought the fire before it became uncontrollable was deliberately lured away? Thus, it must have been set?"

"Exactly."

Sulibai nodded. "I see your reasoning," he said, "yet I would not rule out the possibility of coincidence. Perhaps the diversion had some other purpose."

"*What* other purpose?" Granzer demanded. "And whatever its purpose, it was clearly the work of a hostile conspiracy."

"The rebels?"

"Do you also think it might be a mere coincidence that when this palace has stood unharmed for eight hundred years, it should be burned when we face a mysterious and dangerous new foe?"

"That would be hard to accept, I agree, Your Highness," Sulibai agreed thoughtfully. "But the workings of the gods sometimes *are* hard to accept."

"Then you see the hands of the gods in this?" Granzer demanded.

"No," Sulibai said. "No, I don't. While I do not yet consider it proven fact, I believe it most likely that you are right, and that we are faced with a conspiracy among mortals. Still, I hesitate to blame the rebels. Perhaps they're merely a scapegoat for some faction within our own people. That would not be a coincidence. How could rebels get into the palace? We've had no reports of any of them crossing the Grebiguata, let alone infiltrating Seidabar."

"We haven't exactly been interrogating everyone who sets foot through the gates," Granzer retorted sarcastically. "We don't know who the rebels are or aren't. Yes, we know the names of their leaders, and we can tell nightwalkers from the living, but we don't know who *else* might be working with them."

"The Olnamians," Delbur suggested. "Many of them, at any rate."

"And several Greyans and Matuans and Govyans," Sulibai agreed. "What of it?"

Granzer glanced down; the soldier had retrieved the ruined boots and was making his way back up. "Perhaps there are rebels among us. How many Olnamians and Greyans and Matuans and Govyans are in this city right now?"

"Very few Olnamians," Delbur said.

"But hundreds of Matuans," Sulibai added. "And the rioters, you said, were employed by Domdur."

"Who may have been working for Olnamians or Matuans. I think we may want to ask some of our eastern guests a few questions."

Delbur nodded; Sulibai looked doubtful, but said nothing.

The soldier reached the broken edge of the floor, and two of his comrades reached down to help him up. Granzer and the others watched the operation.

"Those are damned big boots!" someone remarked.

"They are, aren't they?" Granzer said thoughtfully. He glanced down at his own far more elegant footwear. He was not a small man, by any means, but those scorched and blackened boots would have fallen off his feet with the first high step he took.

"Maybe they expanded from the heat," someone suggested.

Several people responded with derisive noises. "Leather *shrinks* when it gets hot!" someone pointed out. "It dries out and shrinks!"

"Not good leather," someone retorted.

"Those aren't good leather."

"And it doesn't *expand*, in any case."

Granzer listened without comment as the soldiers argued; he knew that those boots had to be close to their original size, which meant their wearer was very large indeed—at least from the knees down.

"I'd wager the champion wore them," a soldier said.

Granzer snorted. He'd heard more than enough about "divine champions" ever since this crisis started, years ago.

"They do look like the pair he had on," a second soldier replied.

Granzer started. "What did you say?" he asked.

The soldier turned, startled, and saw the Prince staring at him. He stammered, then said, "I said, Your Highness, that those do look like the boots the divine champion wore last night."

"You saw the divine champion last night?"

"Well, yes . . ." The soldier looked about in confusion. "We all did—Souldz and Garad and I. He was here leading the fight against the fire."

"Who are Souldz and Garad?" Granzer demanded loudly.

Two other soldiers stepped forward uneasily.

The sergeant in charge of the military detachment spoke up. "If it please you, Your Highness, when I received my orders this morning I thought it might be useful to have some men here who were involved in putting out the fire. I chose these three."

"So they were here last night?"

"Yes, Your Highness," the sergeant replied.

"And you saw the divine champion?"

"Yes, sir," the three soldiers replied.

"What did he look like?"

The three glanced at one another; Granzer chose one at random and pointed.

"You," he said. "What did this champion look like? How did you know he was the champion?"

The chosen witness hesitated, then said, "Well, he's big—very tall, and broad in the shoulders, with long, thick arms. A wide face, dark eyes, and hair worn in a braid. He was dressed in an ordinary workman's blouse and breeches, and boots—those boots, by the look of them. He was striding about, giving orders, and working away at whatever needed to be done."

"How did you know he was the champion?"

"Well, we didn't, at the time, but later, on the way back to the barracks, we were talking, and Garad said something and we talked it over, and we all realized that that was who he must be. We . . . we thought you knew, Your Highness; we thought the Empress or the Council must have sent him."

"Hadn't you heard that Lord Graush is still looking for the champion? That all the known candidates are out at the Grebiguata, facing the enemy?"

The soldier looked at his companions for support, then said, "But we *saw* him. We decided that the Empress and Council must be keeping it quiet that he'd been found, so as to take the rebels by surprise."

"Did you get his name?"

"No, sir."

Granzer frowned. "All right, go on," he said. "Get those boots to the priests. And don't say anything about this."

The soldiers hastened to obey. Granzer took a final look at the damage, then turned away.

"Who do you think this alleged champion is?" Sulibai asked as the party made their way back down the smoke-darkened passageway to the grand entry hall.

"I have no idea," Granzer admitted. "Perhaps he really *is* the divine champion, come at last—but why here, in Seidabar, and not at the head of the army?" He shook his head. "Or it could be some trick the conspirators have devised— perhaps they intend to set up a false champion and then kill him, to dishearten our people, or have him betray the Empire."

"What do you intend to do about it?"

"Find him," Granzer replied immediately. "Find him, and talk to him. And see if those rioters recognize his voice—he might be one of the men who hired them. This whole thing might have been staged to convince us he's the champion."

Sulibai said, "That seems improbably complicated."

"Conspiracies often *are* improbably complicated. It's in their nature."

"Is there anything else, Your Highness?" Delbur asked.

Granzer stopped dead in his tracks and stared at his aide.

"Of *course* there is, you confounded idiot," he said. "I want to know *everything* that happened here! I want everyone who was in this palace at any time in the past two days questioned—even my wife's mother!" Delbur flinched at this mention of the Empress; Granzer ignored it and continued. "I want every Olnamian in the city brought in and questioned. I want the priests to send scholars and magicians to go over every inch of the east wing and tell me *exactly* how the fire started. In case it hasn't sunk in, we have an enemy here who has just struck at the very heart of the Empire; we need to identify and *destroy* our foe immediately, no matter what it takes!"

Then he turned and, with a swirl of his red cloak, marched off.

"I've never seen him so angry," Delbur muttered, hanging back from following.

"No one ever tried to burn down his home before," Sulibai replied.

Delbur glanced at the Councillor, then took a deep breath and ran after the Prince.

CHAPTER 35

Onnell stood on a camp chair at one end of his ordained route and peered eastward across the river at the enemy camp.

It seemed very odd that the two camps should be so close together, in plain sight of one another, separated by little more than a couple of hundred yards of brownish water. If the two armies were this close, shouldn't they be fighting?

It seemed natural that they would fight. All through the training back in Agabdal and the long, boring winter in Drievabor, Onnell and his companions had taken it for granted that once the rebel army was within reach, the two sides would immediately begin fighting, and would fight until one side was destroyed.

So far, though, they weren't fighting. Oh, each side would occasionally send a flight of arrows across, or a New Magician would try to fly over and spy, only to be sent scurrying back by either archers or the other side's magicians, but in general the two sides were simply watching each other.

The rebels had arrived and made camp the night before, pitching their tents and digging firepits and so on; Onnell was very glad that the prevailing winds were from the west, because even so the stench of the corpses, the nightwalkers, was ghastly. Only a whiff of it reached the Imperial forces, here on the western banks of the Grebiguata; Onnell thought it must be unbearable to the east.

The rebel soldiers—the living ones—didn't seem to mind the smell. They must, Onnell thought, have gotten used to it during the long march westward, or during the winter spent holed up in Uinaguem, though the cold had probably helped keep it down.

The smell had been one nasty surprise when the rebels got close enough. The fact that they had their own New Magicians had been another. The Imperial Army had a dozen—Vrai Burrai himself, and General Balinus's aide Tebas Tudan, and several of Vrai Burrai's students from the Imperial College—but the rebels had at least two, one wielding the same bright magic as Vrai Burrai's group, and the other . . . well, the other was presumably Rebiri Nazakri, the dreaded evil wizard who was leading the rebellion against the Domdur Empire. Somehow Onnell had not expected to see the Nazakri himself taking part in matters yet, but there he had been, walking along the riverbank in a shimmering, shadowy aura of red fire and black smoke.

That had been this morning. Then, around midmorning, everything over there had fallen silent. The nightwalkers lay in neat rows, as still as the corpses they ought to be; the Nazakri had vanished into his pavilion, leaving it to the archers and his other magician to fend off any intruding Imperial magicians. Living sentries patrolled the camp's boundaries, but there was no shouting, no singing, no orders being passed along.

And the Imperial vanguard had simply watched all this, for the most part.

General Balinus had debated with Lord Duzon and the other six commanders as to whether a messenger should be sent to demand the rebels' surrender; Onnell had overheard part of the discussion as he went about his duties. Some of the colonels had thought that a formal demand for surrender might bring Rebiri Nazakri to his senses, now that he could actually see the Imperial vanguard.

Balinus had pointed out that other messengers sent to talk terms with the

Nazakri had wound up dead. He had challenged his subordinates to name the man they would send to such near-certain doom.

Colonel Imbigai, commander of the Third Seidabar, had suggested sending a magician, and the others had taken up the idea. In the end Vrai Burrai had sent Vimal, one of his students. Burrai himself, as a claimant to the title of champion, was nominally under the command of Lord Duzon, but at the same time, as master of the Imperial College of the New Magic he was in charge of all the New Magicians and answered directly to General Balinus; that unclear chain of command had prolonged the debate, since neither Balinus nor Duzon really wanted to send anyone, but at last Vimal had been chosen and sent. She had gotten about halfway through her first sentence, announcing herself, when the enemy's black magic had sent her fleeing back across the Grebiguata.

That had been shortly before noon. Since then everything had been quiet, and both camps seemed to have already settled into a normal routine despite the proximity of their foes. Onnell had thought that it might have been clever to strike immediately, before the enemy was entirely prepared, but apparently General Balinus preferred to wait and see what happened.

So far, that had been nothing.

The sun was down in the west, though, and the sky dimming. The air, which had still borne the lingering chill of early spring, was turning downright cold. Onnell wondered whether the coming of night would make any difference. He shielded his eyes from the light behind him and stared across the river—just in time to see the nightwalkers start to stir.

He watched long enough to be absolutely sure he wasn't imagining things, then hurried to the lieutenant in charge of the watch—not running, but walking very briskly.

He saluted, hand to chest, then said, "Sir, the nightwalkers are moving."

"Moving how?" the lieutenant demanded, looking up from his papers.

"Just . . . moving, sir. They've been lying still all day, but now they're getting up and moving about."

"Are they preparing to attack?"

Onnell hesitated. "Uh . . . not that I saw, sir."

"Nor shall they," the lieutenant said. "They have no boats, no bridges—what are they going to do, fly across?"

"Swim, perhaps?"

"Assuming nightwalkers can swim, soldier—an assumption I wouldn't hasten to make—I think that would make them fine targets for our archers, don't you?"

"I don't know, sir."

"Fine. Go away. You've made your report." He waved a dismissal.

Onnell turned and left, vaguely unsatisfied. There was something wrong with the lieutenant's thinking; the rebels wouldn't have come all this way just to be stopped by a river. It wasn't as if they hadn't known the Grebiguata was here. Onnell didn't know how they intended to cross it, but he was sure they had a way. They had deliberately avoided Drievabor, after all.

He returned to his post and watched uneasily as the nightwalkers rose and gathered in a great crowd around the black wizard's pavilion.

They didn't seem to be preparing to attack, but they did have weapons—he could see swords and spears. Why would they have weapons if they didn't intend to use them?

He watched as long as he could, staring into the gathering gloom; then, at last, Bousian came to relieve him.

"I hate sentry duty," Bousian said as he slapped Onnell on the shoulder and accepted the ceremonial horn. He slung the horn's leather cord around his own neck, then peered out across the river.

"The one advantage of the night shift," Bousian remarked, "is that it's so dark no one will fault me if I miss a few details in my report."

"I'd rather you didn't miss anything tonight," Onnell said uneasily.

"I can see why," Bousian said. "What are they doing over there, anyway? Bathing? Do they think it'll keep the stench down?"

"What?" Onnell whirled and stared into the night.

"There," Bousian said, pointing off to the right.

Onnell looked. He had been concentrating so much on the main group clustered around Rebiri Nazakri's tent that he hadn't even noticed that roughly a hundred yards off to the south of the rebel camp nightwalkers were crawling one by one down the riverbank and into the water. At least, he assumed they were nightwalkers; it was almost impossible to make out details in the darkness. There were simply man-sized shapes moving awkwardly down into the water.

And he didn't see any coming back *out* of the water.

"Vevanis and Vedal," Onnell muttered. He told Bousian, "Keep a good watch!" Then he turned and hurried to find the lieutenant.

The lieutenant was reluctant to believe that there was any cause for concern, but he did come out of his tent to take a look.

"They're going into the water," he admitted, "but what of it? I don't see any of them swimming across."

"They're staying underwater!" Onnell insisted.

"They'd drown," the lieutenant said derisively.

"Sir, they're already dead!"

The lieutenant had to consider that for a moment, trying to find some way to deny Onnell's conclusion; he had just yielded to the inevitable and begun shouting the alarm when the first nightwalkers rose up from the water on the western shore of the river.

Onnell didn't wait for the lieutenant to give orders; he drew his sword and ran to confront the foe.

The Imperial camp had three sentries posted on each side; the three from the southern boundary and the one from the southern end of the riverfront had confronted the foe, and were now gathered into a tight little knot, back to back, swords flailing. A dozen nightwalkers surrounded them, their wet clothes and weapons glittering strangely in the light of the watch fires behind them and the twoscore moons overhead.

"Aim for their necks!" someone shouted. "General Balinus says they die if you cut off their heads!"

"That's easier said than done," Onnell muttered to himself as he ran.

The commotion was spreading; heads were being thrust out through tent flaps, and soldiers were emerging, some of them still buckling belts or pulling on boots.

Onnell saw one of the surrounded Imperials go down, and he launched himself at the nearest nightwalker, sword swinging in a great sidearm swoop.

The blade bit into flesh and lodged in bone; had the enemy been mortal, Onnell knew he would have been slain instantly.

Nightwalkers were not mortal. This one reached up its free hand and grabbed Onnell's blade even before it turned to face him.

Watery brown fluid dribbled from the wound, and the stink of rotting flesh assailed Onnell more strongly than ever. He grabbed the hilt of his sword in both hands and heaved, pulling the blade free from the nightwalker's neck, slicing bloodless flesh from its grasping fingers. The nightwalker had been a medium-sized man once, no more than that; it was far smaller than Onnell. Still, it took all Onnell's strength to free his weapon, and he had to throw himself off balance to do it.

That left the nightwalker an opening; it brought its own weapon up, a notched and rusted blade in the broad, hook-tipped Matuan style.

If the nightwalker had had a weapon meant for stabbing, Onnell thought, it would have been able to run him through then and there, but the Matuan blade was meant for slashing and chopping, not for thrusting. Instead of jabbing, the nightwalker swung the sword at Onnell with the point of the hook forward, trying to catch and rip. Onnell, with his much greater reach, was able to step back and let the blade pass harmlessly an inch or two from his chest.

"You can't dodge forever," the nightwalker said as it stepped forward for another swing. Its voice was a thin, ugly wheeze; Onnell's earlier blow had cut into its voice box.

Onnell struggled to regain his balance; by the time he had done so, he had retreated three more steps, the nightwalker slashing and hacking at him. Once he was stable he made a feint at the thing's chest, expecting it to parry, which would allow him to chop at its neck again.

It didn't bother to parry, and his intended feint punched the point of his sword into dry, dead flesh. He slashed it free as the nightwalker grinned at him and chopped at his sword arm.

The blow struck and drew blood, but Onnell's arm was already moving away; the wound was a superficial scrape that tore skin, but missed the muscle and bone.

The pain forced Onnell to concentrate even as it angered him. He struck again, this time aiming backhanded for the nightwalker's neck.

It brought its own weapon up to block, and Onnell turned his blow at the last second, chopping down at his foe's arm, instead. Muscles and tendons parted, and the Matuan sword sank out of line.

The nightwalker grabbed at the hilt with its other hand, but too late—Onnell's next blow finished the work his first had started. The nightwalker's severed head rolled across its shoulder and tumbled to the ground.

Something black, something half smoke and half shadow, erupted from the ruined stump of the dead thing's neck and vanished into the deepening night, and the corpse tumbled to the ground at Onnell's feet.

Onnell had no time to admire his handiwork; two more nightwalkers were coming at him with raised weapons, a spear and a sword. A sword came out of the darkness behind one of them, sweeping toward its neck, and Onnell engaged the other.

After that Onnell's view of the fight was confused, at best; he struck at the throat of anyone not wearing Imperial red, dodged or parried any blades headed his way, and tried not to get in anyone else's way.

At one point, when the melee had lasted well over an hour and Onnell was ready to collapse from exhaustion and loss of blood, he glanced across the river and saw the main body of nightwalkers standing there, still on the eastern side of the water. Hundreds of them were lined up in neat rows, watching the battle and grinning.

Even in his wearied, fuddled state, it was at that moment that Onnell realized that despite the blood on his arms and on his uniform and under his feet, despite the screams of the wounded and dying, despite the dozen or more heads he had chopped from decaying shoulders, this was not the great battle that would decide the Empire's fate.

This was just a raid, a skirmish.

Then he slipped in the mud as he dodged a spear thrust, and a comrade's elbow hit him in the ear on his way down, and he rolled, dazed, to one side.

CHAPTER 36

Where were the guards?" Lord Shoule demanded again, gesticulating wildly.

Lord Niniam sighed.

"I've told you, Councillor," he said. "Lord Kadan had reduced the palace guard to an absolute minimum, one-third its usual strength, so that the experienced soldiers of the Imperial Guard could be used in training or sent to fight the rebels. When the riots started in the Outer City, a messenger came from the commander there asking for help, and I sent the guards to help."

"And who was this commander you obeyed so readily?" Shoule asked.

Lord Niniam blinked in surprise.

"Come now, Lord Niniam," Shoule said. "You obeyed his request without question—who *was* he, that a member of the Imperial Council did his bidding so readily? Prince Granzer? Lord Kadan?"

Prince Granzer shifted uneasily in his chair; Lord Kadan glowered. Lord Shoule, Granzer thought, was certainly being enthusiastic in his efforts to get at the truth; he just wished the enthusiasm were a bit more controlled.

"I don't know," Lord Niniam admitted. "I don't believe the messenger gave a name."

"Yet you sent away *every guard in the palace* at this messenger's behest?"

"Well, the Empress and her children were away," Niniam said, "and I had already received reports of the riot. . . ."

"The Empress was *not* away," Shoule corrected him.

"I had been told that she was away."

"By whom?"

"By . . . well, by a messenger."

"The same one who brought word from this supposed commander in the Outer City?"

Shamefaced, Niniam admitted, "I believe it was, yes."

"And how is it you were so certain these reports were genuine, and not mere fabrications to support this messenger's claims?"

"I could *hear* the rioters from the plaza!" Niniam protested. "Why would anyone lie about it?"

"Really, Shoule," Lord Sulibai murmured, "is there any need to harass the man like this?"

Granzer threw Sulibai a quick glance, then focused on Shoule again.

Shoule, standing at his place at the Council's table, turned slowly to glare at Sulibai, three seats away.

"It would seem," he said, "that some of my fellow Councillors fail to grasp the enormity of the crimes committed here, in our very capital."

"I grasp the enormity perfectly well, Shoule," Sulibai said. "I simply see no point in badgering the innocents who were caught by surprise by the conspirators and tricked into doing their bidding."

"And are you so certain, then, that Lord Niniam is truly innocent?" Shoule shouted. "How do you *know*? A conspiracy like this—"

"Oh, come now," Lord Dabos interrupted. "Niniam's a member of the Imperial Council! He has as much to lose as any man alive should the rebels actually harm the Empire—surely, you can't think any of *us* are involved in this plot?"

"And why not?" Shoule said, whirling to face the Minister of the Commonwealth. "True, he has much to lose—but perhaps he has as much to gain! The man who hands the Imperial Palace, or the entire capital, to the rebels can surely name his own price; how do we know we are not looking at a man who hopes to become Emperor Niniam the First?"

"Second," Lord Graush interjected. "Niniam the First was fourth century, younger son of Bederach the First, reigned about eighteen months during the time of the Veruet Campaign."

"I stand corrected," Shoule said. "And was there a Sulibai the First, perhaps?"

Granzer frowned. Shoule was being rather free with his thinly veiled accusations.

"Not that I ever heard of," Graush replied. "It's not a traditional Domdur name."

Lady Dalbisha rapped on the table with her cane. "Who *cares*?" she demanded. "We're here to find out who set the fire and why, not to bicker about names or pedigrees, or throw around a lot of foolish accusations!"

"Are you calling me a fool, Dalbisha?" Shoule shouted back. "*Someone* betrayed the Empire to arrange this fire!"

"Who says so?" Dalbisha replied angrily. "I see trickery at work, yes, but no treachery!"

"And how did our rebel tricksters know what to do, where to go, who to deceive?" Shoule said. "*Someone* must have instructed them in the workings of the palace routine!"

Dalbisha frowned, lifted her cane, and tapped one end thoughtfully against her cheek.

"Perhaps," she said, "you have a point."

"Lady Dalbisha," Sulibai said, "don't listen to this nonsense!"

"*Is* it nonsense?" Dalbisha asked, turning to face him. "Lord Shoule may or may not be a fool, I'll reserve my judgment on that, but he asks a good question—how *did* our foes know so much?"

"Is it so secret, then?" Sulibai said, spreading his hands. "Does not every soldier here know the routines?"

"Damn!" Dabos said, slamming a fist on the council table. "*Is* it that easy? I don't know who to believe! I've never meddled in palace maintenance."

"If there *were* secrets known," Lord Gornir ventured, "that still doesn't mean treachery—what if we were spied upon by magical means? We know the rebel leader is a wizard—could he have observed us from afar, perhaps, or listened in on our conversations?"

"I should think that the province of the *old* magic," Lord Passeil said. "Isn't this wizard using the *New* Magic?"

Several eyes turned toward Apiris.

"We don't know *what* he's using," Apiris said.

"Can't you find out?" Graush barked.

Apiris sighed wearily. "You have already demanded that our temple magicians devote their attention not only to whatever they can do to aid General Balinus against the rebels, and to restore order in the eastern provinces, but also to Lord Kadan's efforts at recruiting and supplying the largest army the Empire has fielded in two hundred years; when that's added to their usual duties for the temples, and their services for the public, they have no time . . ."

"*Blast* their services to the public!" Lord Graush bellowed. "Do you mean to tell me that you still have them sending messages and enchanting lovers just as if we were at peace?"

Apiris blinked at him in surprise.

"Of course," he said. "How else are the temples to raise the money they need?"

For a moment no one spoke; half a dozen Councillors glared angrily at Apiris, while the rest looked variously embarrassed, confused, or sympathetic. Apiris was simply bewildered.

"Your Highness," Graush said, turning to Prince Granzer and breaking the silence at last, "will you tell this . . . this *priest* that . . . that . . . oh, blood and death!"

"Calm yourself, Councillor," Granzer said. He turned his attention to Apiris.

"It seems to me," he said, "that if the Imperial Treasury can afford to equip and feed an army, we can also keep our priests fed. Your magicians would be better used elsewhere; your customers can wait until the rebels are defeated."

"But, Your Highness . . ." Apiris protested.

Granzer held up a hand.

"If we can't feed you, then you can sell off some of your temple treasures," Granzer said. "You don't seem to appreciate the gravity of the situation, Apiris. Maybe you think the gods would tell you if you were supposed to do anything out of the ordinary—but when was the last time the gods told you or your oracles *anything*?"

"Sixteen years ago," Apiris mumbled, eyes downcast.

"Then isn't it time you started listening to *somebody*?" Lord Shoule demanded. "Or is this deliberate?"

Apiris looked up, astonished. "Deliberate?"

Shoule didn't address him directly; instead he turned and spoke to the Prince.

"Your Highness," he said, "while at first it might seem unthinkable that we might distrust the Archpriest himself, the gods' own representative beneath the Hundred Moons, I ask you to consider the situation. By his own admission, Apiris has done as little as possible to advance the war effort...."

"That's not what I said!" Apiris objected.

Granzer held up a hand, then told Shoule, "Go on." He didn't think Shoule was right in accusing Apiris of disloyalty, but he wanted to hear the reasoning, so that he could judge for himself whether it was sound.

"Very well, by his own admission our Archpriest no longer has any more contact with the gods than the lowliest farmer praying to Vedal as he works in his field," Shoule said. "But surely, he's had many years to form theories about this. What if he's concluded that the gods have abandoned the Domdur? I'm sure you've all heard such pessimistic theorizing and dismissed it—but here we have a man who devoted his entire *life* to serving as the link between the Domdur and the gods, only to find himself cast aside by the gods he has sworn to serve! Might he not have more cause than any of us to believe that the gods no longer favor us, and that, as the gods' servant, he no longer has any duty to the Empire? Might he not see this eastern wizard's black power as a sign of divine favor?"

"That's absurd!" Apiris shouted.

"Then perhaps he knows the gods still favor the Domdur," Shoule suggested, "but *he* no longer chooses to serve the gods! In petty revenge for their silence he seeks to side with those who defy the divine will...."

"This is nonsense," Apiris said, getting to his feet. "I'm not going to listen to this."

"Yes, you will," Dalbisha said, rising as well and brandishing her cane. "Sit down."

Apiris sat, but turned to Granzer.

"Your Highness, is this the sort of behavior I can expect in the Imperial Council's chambers henceforth?"

"Until we know whether there are traitors among us, and who, if anyone, they are," Granzer said, "I don't know *what* to expect. Now, can we get back to reviewing what we actually know?"

"Your Highness, I am no constable," Apiris said. "I know nothing about investigating anything. If I'm to order my magicians to new duties, snooping out the enemy's secrets, might I not do better to get on with it? I have nothing to contribute here. I was in the temple throughout yesterday's unfortunate events."

Granzer considered for a moment, glancing at Graush, Shoule, and Dalbisha.

"Oh, let him go," Graush said. "As he says, he's no help here."

"Should he be permitted to leave alone?" Shoule asked.

"Lord Kadan," the Prince said. "Would you accompany the Archpriest back to the temple? And perhaps you might station a few trusted soldiers there, to guard the temple against any such misfortune as struck the palace."

Lord Kadan bowed his head in acknowledgment, then pushed his chair back and rose. "Your Holiness?" he said.

Apiris got to his feet and looked around at the other Councillors. "You're all being ridiculous," he said. "Mistrusting me, accusing one another—it's insane! The gods will protect the Domdur Empire; we're their chosen people. We need only use our plain common sense, and this Olnamian warlord will be defeated in due time."

"How do you *know*?" Lord Shoule countered.

Apiris stared at him for a moment, then cast a glance at Prince Granzer. He saw no sympathy on the Prince's face.

The Archpriest turned on his heel and marched out without answering, with Lord Kadan at his elbow.

CHAPTER 37

So you still believe the gods will ensure our triumph?" Lord Kadan asked as he escorted Apiris down a long stone corridor in the Great Temple. The muffled echoes of their footsteps thudded from the gray walls.

"It depends," Apiris said. "When I think about it I know it might not be true. When I think about it I can envision all sorts of horrors; I can imagine that the gods have, indeed, deserted us—but then, if I *don't* think, for even a moment, I always believe again."

Kadan smiled crookedly. "So you weren't thinking at the meeting just now."

"No, I wasn't," Apiris agreed. "I couldn't believe what I was hearing! All that bickering, the casual accusations of treason—what's *wrong* with them all? Whatever the gods want, we're still the rulers of the world—why should we distrust one another?"

"They're frightened," Kadan said.

"Of what? Of some eastern magician? Of nightwalkers?"

"Of the unknown," Kadan replied. "That's what every man fears. Didn't you just say that you envision horrors because you no longer know the gods' will?"

"It's not the same at all," Apiris protested.

Kadan shrugged. "Something has struck at us where we thought ourselves safe. That's frightened them, and they need to strike out at something. They have no foe visible, so they strike at each other."

Apiris glanced at him with interest. "You speak as if you were no part of the Imperial Council."

"Oh, I'm very much a Councillor, Apiris—more than you, I think. It often seems your heart isn't in it, that you'd much rather be here in the temple than there in the palace."

"Well, that's true enough," Apiris agreed. "I chose to be a priest, not a politician. It wasn't I who decided the Archpriest should automatically have a seat on the Council."

"But you're *there*, as I am—and I chose to be a soldier, not a politician. You might as well use the opportunity. As you say, we are the masters of the world, Apiris. . . ."

"No," Apiris objected. "I correct myself. The gods are the masters of the world."

"Well, the gods aren't doing much about it right now, so far as I can see," Kadan said, "and we're the masters of the mortal world. We should behave as such, and act assertively, decisively, courageously. Bickering among ourselves and hurling accusations is pointless—those others are fools to give in to their fear this way. If there *is* a traitor among us, he'll reveal himself eventually; we won't find him by shouting at each other."

"It seems to me that I've heard you shout a few times in the council chamber," Apiris remarked. "Usually at Lord Orbalir."

"*That* fool," Kadan said. "Yes, of course I've shouted at him—it's a natural response to idiocy. But that was when it didn't matter. You didn't hear me shout today; there's too much at stake."

"I heard you growl, perhaps. . . ."

"At myself. For not having considered the possibility of a strike at the Imperial Palace itself."

"We were all shocked."

"I shouldn't have been."

"You have no gift of prophecy, Kadan."

"But I'm supposed to have an understanding of strategy. And speaking of prophecy, where are these magicians of yours? This passage seems to go on forever!"

"We're almost there." He pointed. "That door ahead leads to the Master Magician's chambers."

Kadan nodded, and stayed back a step as Apiris knocked on the indicated door.

The door opened, and Bishau himself, Master Magician of the Great Temple, thrust his head out. He squinted in the dim light and brushed a lock of unruly white hair out of his eyes.

"Ah, Your Holiness," he said when he recognized Apiris. "Come about those boots? I was just about to send a messenger to the Prince."

"Boots?" Kadan asked.

"I don't know what he's talking about," Apiris said. He glanced at Kadan. "I suppose you'll want to hear whatever we say."

"I'm afraid so," Kadan said, not sounding at all sorry. "If only so I can tell the others I did so."

Apiris sighed. "Let us in, Bishau. There's no point in standing out here."

"Certainly, Holiness," Bishau agreed, swinging the door wide.

The two Councillors entered the apartment; Kadan looked around at the rather austere interior with mild interest. He had noticed before that magicians—the traditional magicians, not Vrai Burrai's upstarts—tended to be unworldly, more involved in their so-called Higher Realm than in everyday reality; this room reflected that. It was bare of ornament, furnished with a desk, two small benches, and little else. A half-eaten meal of bread and fruit was on the desk beside a bit of parchment. A door on the far side stood slightly ajar.

"What's this about boots?" Apiris asked as he settled on one of the benches.

"You don't know?" Bishau looked surprised. "I know Prince Granzer said to keep it quiet, but I thought the Council would have heard. A pair of boots was found in the ruins of the east wing of the Imperial Palace, and eyewitnesses to the fire say that they belonged to the divine champion. The Prince sent them to us, to see what the diviners could tell us."

Apiris and Kadan looked at one another.

"I thought all the supposed champions had gone east," Apiris said.

"They have," Kadan replied. "At least, all we knew about."

"Then who's this person with the boots?" Apiris asked, turning to Bishau.

"The witnesses say he was a giant of a man who led the volunteers in fighting the fire," Bishau replied.

"He claimed to be the gods' chosen?"

Bishau waved a hand. "No, no," he said. "He didn't make any claims. The others just decided that he must be the champion, based on his actions."

"Do you suppose he might be the *real* champion, come at last?" Kadan asked Apiris.

"I have no idea," the Archpriest replied.

"Is there any way to tell?"

"No," Apiris and Bishau answered in unison.

"Not by divination," Bishau added.

"Nor by external signs," Apiris said. "Lord Graush has researched that—you know that."

"So what about these boots, then?" Kadan asked. "Can they tell your magicians anything?"

"Oh, yes," Bishau said. "They retain their owner's aura, and his recent experiences can be read. He's a blacksmith from somewhere in the southern hills, but recently he's been staying in the Imperial Armory. I'd guess he's one of the volunteers come to make swords." He gestured at the desk. "I was just writing that down for the messenger . . . now, where did I put it?" He stooped and picked the parchment off the desk. "Here," he said.

Apiris glanced at the parchment, but it didn't say anything beyond what Bishau had just told them. "So some people think the divine champion was fighting the fire?" he asked.

"It would seem so," Bishau agreed.

"And it would seem reasonable," Kadan said. "For after all, if there *is* a divine champion, shouldn't he be defending the Empire from saboteurs and traitors, as well as from the enemy's army?"

"As Prince Greldar fought the Red Traitors," Apiris said. "I suppose so."

"Shall I send the message, Holiness?" Bishau asked.

"Of course," Apiris said. "No need to keep Prince Granzer waiting."

"And if you don't, he'll start believing Lord Shoule's suggestion that the Archpriest's turned traitor," Kadan said with a grim smile.

Apiris winced; Bishau's jaw dropped.

"Lord Kadan's joking," Apiris said hastily. "Go, find a messenger, send your message. Then come back; we have new orders for the Holy College of Magicians. The Council wants you to learn more about the Nazakri's black magic."

"As you command, Holiness," Bishau said. He bowed, and hurried through the inner door, parchment in hand, calling for a messenger.

"A blacksmith from the southern hills," Apiris said thoughtfully as he and Kadan waited for the Master Magician's return.

"Why not?" Kadan said. "Better an honest workman than that confounded Diknoi troublemaker."

"I don't think Vrai Burrai was ever a serious contender," Apiris said. "I rather thought that the heir of Snauvalia might be the genuine article, though."

"Duzon?" Kadan shook his head. "He's not the heir; he has an older brother. He still might be the champion, though. For all we know this smith is a fraud—or maybe *he's* the traitor who set the palace ablaze!"

Apiris glanced at Kadan. "Didn't Bishau say the smith was seen *fighting* the fire?"

"And how better to get into our good graces?" Kadan asked with an unpleasant smile.

"Do you really think so?"

"No," Kadan admitted. "But is it any more absurd than some of the theories Shoule was shouting about?"

Apiris didn't reply. Instead he repeated to himself, "A smith from the southern hills . . ." The mention of the southern hills in connection with the divine champion reminded him of something, but he couldn't quite place it—and then he remembered.

"Biekedau," he said.

"What?" Lord Kadan asked.

"Biekedau," Apiris said. "That's in the southern hills, isn't it?"

"More or less," Kadan agreed. "It's on the Vren just below the falls. A pretty town. What about it?"

"Someone from Biekedau, a priest, came to the temple last summer, claiming to know who the true champion was," Apiris explained.

"And did he know?"

"I don't know," Apiris admitted, shamefaced. "I wouldn't see him, told him to go tell Lord Graush, not me."

"And what did Lord Graush say?"

"I don't know." Apiris hesitated. It seemed to him that he had heard that the priest from Biekedau had stayed in Seidabar, right there in the Great Temple. He had never petitioned for an audience, though, and surely if he knew anything important he would have. . . .

But why would he stay in Seidabar if he did not?

Just then Bishau returned, and the two Councillors forgot about the mysterious smith and the priest from Biekedau as they settled down to work out what the temple magicians might do to aid in the Empire's defense.

CHAPTER 38

Malledd!"

The master's bellow was audible even over the clanging of a dozen hammers on metal, and Malledd looked up from the sword he was shaping. He knew he finally had this one right, that it was going to be one of his best blades, and he hated to be interrupted—if he permitted the steel to cool before it was finished it might lose its temper.

The master was the master, though. "Yes, sir?" he called.

"Come here!"

Malledd looked helplessly down at the rough-shaped blade. He held it up with the tongs for the master to see.

The master immediately recognized the situation.

"Let someone else finish it," he ordered. "I know it hurts your pride, but do it."

Reluctantly, Malledd looked around, and saw that Darsmit had just tossed away a ruined blade, to be melted down and forged anew. The smaller apprentice was glowering at his anvil in disgust.

"Here," Malledd called, "take mine."

Darsmit needed a few precious seconds to take in what was happening, but once he understood he hurried to obey, and Malledd was free to leave the forge room at the master's behest.

"What is it, sir?" he asked as he stepped up to the antechamber. His heart was pounding; it had to be bad news, surely. A message from home, perhaps? Anva was ill, or little Arshui, or Neyil had injured himself?

The master was not alone in the antechamber; four soldiers in scarlet and gold stood behind him. That puzzled and relieved Malledd; had a message come from Anva or anyone else in Grozerodz, he would have expected Bezida or one of the other priestesses to be there, rather than Imperial soldiers.

"Are these yours?" one of the soldiers demanded, holding up the battered, filthy remains of a pair of boots.

Malledd stared for a moment. Was *that* what this was about? Was someone angry at him for littering the palace ruins?

"They look like mine," he admitted. "I lost mine when I was fighting the fire in the Imperial Palace."

"In that case," the soldier said, "Prince Granzer would like to speak with you."

Malledd blinked. He felt his jaw sag, and in response snapped his mouth shut. "Prince Granzer?" he said.

"That's right," the soldier said. "He's investigating the fire, and he wants to talk to you."

That made sense enough, Malledd supposed, but it was still terrifying—he was being asked to speak to a *prince*, the Empress's own son-in-law and President of the Imperial Council.

He would have thought that the matter would be handled on a much lower level than that, but it was not his place to question; if Prince Granzer chose to handle the matter personally, Malledd could hardly object. He gathered his nerve to speak, but glanced back into the forge room at first to see whether Darsmit was ruining that blade.

So far, he seemed to be handling it well. Malledd turned back to the soldiers and asked, "When?"

"Now," the soldier replied.

"Now?" Malledd asked. "You mean, this very minute?"

The soldier nodded.

Malledd glanced at the Master Swordsmith, who shrugged.

"All right," Malledd said. "Should I bring anything? Will it take long?"

"That wasn't in our instructions," the soldier said. "We were just told to fetch you. I'd suggest you come along immediately; if you need anything else, someone can be sent for it."

Malledd nodded, and followed, a bit dazed.

Half an hour later he was seated in a waiting room in the central tower of the Imperial Palace, looking out a window to the east and realizing that the word "immediately" had applied only to himself, not to the Prince. Granzer's aide had told Malledd to make himself comfortable, and the Prince would see him "presently."

From the window he had a view of the city wall, with its black stone parapet and elaborate iron bracing. Beyond that, he knew, lay the plains, stretching from Seidabar to the Grebiguata, where the Imperial Army—including Onnell and Bousian and the other volunteers from Grozerodz—faced an army of night-walkers.

He should be back at the armory, forging swords for those men—either that, or he should be out there with them. . . .

But he wasn't a soldier, and he didn't want to play the champion. Leading men into battle did not appeal to him at all. Let Lord Duzon do it.

Besides, weren't there threats right here in Seidabar, as well?

He stood up and looked down from the window at the burned-out ruins of the east wing.

He'd done the right thing there, unquestionably—those fools in the crowd would have let the whole palace burn down if someone with some sense hadn't gotten them moving! If anything he might tell Prince Granzer would be helpful in finding the traitors responsible, or in preventing a recurrence, then it was well worth his while to sit here and wait on the Prince's pleasure.

That, at least, was what he told himself then. When his wait had stretched to almost two hours he was no longer quite so certain. He had discovered that he couldn't simply walk out, as there were guards at the outer door, but he was seriously considering trying to talk his way out; perhaps if he claimed to be ill, they'd let him go back to the armory, where he was at least accomplishing something.

And that was when Delbur, the Prince's aide, reappeared and said, "This way."

Malledd followed him down a short passage and into the Prince's study. There, amid a clutter of scrolls, parchments, tokens, and weapons, Prince Granzer stood reading a letter.

He put it down when Delbur bowed and announced, "The smith Malledd, of Grozerodz, Your Highness."

"Ah," Granzer said. He turned and looked Malledd over—starting with Malledd's neck, apparently having expected his face to be at that level. He worked first up, then back down to Malledd's slippers.

"So you're the fellow who lost those boots?" he asked.

"I didn't so much lose them as dispose of them, Your Highness," Malledd explained. "They were so badly damaged I was afraid I might trip over them."

"But they are, in fact, your boots?"

"Yes, Your Highness."

"And you're the one who organized the bucket brigade and started cutting the firebreak?"

"Yes, Your Highness."

Granzer leaned back against a table and folded his arms across his chest.

"Might I ask how you came to do that?" he said.

Malledd hesitated, unsure what the Prince was actually asking. "Someone had to," he said.

"Tell me about it," Granzer said.

Malledd hesitated further. He was no storyteller. "I don't know what to say, Your Highness."

"Start at the beginning," Granzer suggested. "How did you happen to be near the palace when the fire broke out?"

"Oh, I wasn't! I was working in the armory when I heard shouting outside, so I went to the door and looked out and saw smoke. . . ."

Once he had started, Malledd found that it wasn't really difficult to keep going. He described the entire sequence of events from his first glimpse of the smoke to finally falling into his own bunk back at the armory.

"And no one had instructed you to take action?" the Prince asked when Malledd had finished his tale. "You didn't feel, perhaps, the hand of the gods in your fortunate presence at the right time and place?"

"No, Your Highness," Malledd said, uneasy at the direction the question seemed to be pointing. "I felt nothing but the ordinary urge to put things right when one sees them going wrong."

"It's been suggested by some of the soldiers who saw you," Granzer said, "that you might be the divine champion of the Domdur, come at last to aid in the current crisis."

That was a statement, not a question, so Malledd made no reply; he looked politely blank.

He didn't doubt a question was coming, though, and he tried to prepare equivocal answers. He couldn't *lie* to this man—this was Prince Granzer, the son-in-law of the Empress, President of the Imperial Council! But he didn't want to admit too much of the truth, either. If Granzer believed he was the champion he would surely be sent to the Grebiguata and put in command of the army there, and he knew nothing about commanding armies. He was a *smith*, not a warrior!

"*Are* you the divine champion?" Granzer asked.

"Me?" Malledd said, trying hard to sound surprised by the question. "Well, I suppose I don't really know. After all, how can I be entirely sure?" He smiled nervously.

"Did you tell anyone at the scene of the fire that you were the champion?" Granzer asked.

"No, of course not!" Malledd said, quite sincerely. "Why would I tell anyone that? I didn't want anyone thinking anything of the sort!"

He hated this. He hoped his voice wasn't betraying him. How could he try so hard to deliberately mislead the Prince this way?

Shouldn't he *admit* his identity? Shouldn't he show the Prince Dolkout's letter?

But he didn't *have* Dolkout's letter, of course; it was back at the armory with the rest of his belongings. And he didn't want to show it to anyone. He was doing his part for the Empire. He'd left his wife and children to come here to make swords; wasn't that enough?

Still, it seemed almost treasonous to be standing here dissembling to the Prince, and he wished it were over, that he were safely back at the armory and away from the palace and everything connected with it.

"So you just did what you thought had to be done? You had no ulterior motive?" the Prince asked.

"That's right, Your Highness," Malledd said.

"You're a brave man, then, Malledd of Grozerodz. I congratulate you on it." The Prince smiled warmly.

That made Malledd feel even worse about his deception. "Thank you, Your Highness," he murmured.

"Well, now—you were the first person in there—did you see anything that might indicate how the fire started?"

Malledd shook his head.

"No, sir . . . I mean, no, Your Highness, I didn't. I don't even know *where* it started, let alone how—half a dozen rooms were already ablaze by the time I set foot in the palace."

Prince Granzer nodded. "I see," he said. "Tell me, Malledd, have you ever spoken to any of the other members of the Imperial Council?"

The question caught Malledd off guard. "I don't think so," he said.

"You haven't spoken to, perhaps, Lord Niniam? Or Lord Sulibai?"

"Not that I know of," Malledd replied, baffled. "What do they look like?"

Prince Granzer waved the question away. "The Archpriest Apiris, perhaps?"

"He wouldn't see us," Malledd said, without thinking.

"Oh?"

"Yes, well, when we first arrived in Seidabar, Vadeviya wanted to talk to the Archpriest," Malledd explained, wishing he had just said no—but the Prince's question had surprised him, and he hadn't thought quickly enough to limit his reply. "But he wouldn't see us. So I've never spoken to him."

"Who's Vadeviya?"

"A priest from Biekedau," Malledd answered. "We traveled together, from Biekedau to Seidabar."

"Ah. And he wanted to speak to Apiris, but was refused?"

"Yes, Your Highness."

"Interesting. Where's this Vadeviya now?"

"I don't know, Your Highness. At the Great Temple, perhaps—don't they have accommodations there for visiting priests from elsewhere?"

"Indeed. So he might have spoken to Apiris by now, after all, eh?"

"Uh . . . I suppose so, Your Highness."

"Have you ever met the Lady Vamia, Malledd?"

"No, Your Highness," Malledd answered. The simple answer seemed to be best when he was confused, and he was certainly confused now.

"Lord Kadan?"

"No, Your Highness." At least he knew who Lord Kadan was; he'd never heard of Lady Vamia or the others.

"Lady Luzla?"

"No, Your Highness."

"Can you read and write, Malledd?"

"A little, Your Highness."

Granzer nodded. "Good," he said. "Then I want you to do something for me."

"If I can, Your Highness."

"If you're approached by any of those people—by Vamia or Kadan or Luzla, but most particularly by Apiris or Niniam . . . no, if you're approached by *anyone* who wants to talk to you about the fire, or about the idea that you might be the divine champion, I want you to write me a letter at once, and send it along. And I want you to refuse to answer any questions if you can do so without endangering yourself."

"Ah . . . but why, Your Highness?"

"There are strange things going on in Seidabar, Malledd," Granzer said gravely. "Things you need not concern yourself with, but which I must pay careful attention to. I'm asking you to help me do that."

"As you wish, Your Highness."

And with that, Prince Granzer turned away, and Delbur beckoned for Malledd to depart.

Malledd obliged.

The entire interview puzzled him. He had expected closer questioning about the fire, and about why he did or didn't believe himself to be the chosen of the gods; the questions about various nobles he had never met didn't seem to make any sense. He mulled it over at length on the way back to the armory.

When he had gone, Granzer asked Delbur, "What did you think?"

"About what, Your Highness?"

"About his veracity, first of all."

Delbur pursed his lips and considered that. He rocked back on his heels for a second.

"I saw no sign he was lying," he said at last. "He was nervous, yes, but the man's a common villager—of course he was nervous speaking to you!"

"You think he was involved by chance, as he says? That he had no reason beyond patriotism for taking action?"

Delbur shrugged. "Why not?"

"And you don't think he's the gods' chosen?"

"As to that, I couldn't say—he said he doesn't know, and neither do I."

"Mmm." Granzer gazed thoughtfully out a window at a dozen moons hanging in the afternoon sky, faint and pale against the blue.

"Should I have him watched, Your Highness?"

"Yes, I think so," Granzer said. "And this priest from Biekedau, Vadeviya—keep an eye on him, as well."

"Should I have him brought in for questioning?"

"No," the Prince said, picking up a letter. "No, not yet. Let us just see what he does. In particular, let us see if he succeeds in making contact with Apiris after all."

"Then you think that the Archpriest might truly be involved in a conspiracy of some sort?"

"I have no idea, Delbur," the Prince said, holding the letter but not reading it. He looked out the window for another second or two, then turned to his aide. "Perhaps Apiris refused to see his fellow conspirator Vadeviya for fear that this Malledd would become suspicious. Perhaps there is no such person as Vadeviya. Perhaps I've contrived this entire scene to delude *you*, as a step in a plot to take the throne from my mother-in-law—or to mislead you, because I suspect *you* of being a conspirator against the crown. Once you start theorizing without solid information you can make up anything you please, and incriminate anyone at all. I'm trying to collect enough facts to prevent that; I only want to incriminate the actual criminals. When this is all done I expect to see heads on the spikes atop the wall, Delbur, but I want them to be the *right* heads, and only the right heads."

"I see," Delbur said, unconvincingly. He hesitated. "And the divine champion . . . ?"

"Delbur, I don't know who the champion is. I don't know whether there *is* a divine champion at this point. I'm inclined to think there isn't. If there is, I wouldn't mind if it's this Malledd, or if it were Duzon, or some other more or less sensible fellow—but I'm not going to worry about it. By Ba'el, we rule the *world*—do we really need some visible sign of divine favor to defeat a few thousand rebels?"

"Um." Delbur didn't reply beyond that, but as Granzer began reading the rest of the letter he had interrupted to speak to Malledd, he could guess what his aide was thinking.

A few thousand rebels were nothing. The Empire could handle a few thousand rebels easily.

A few thousand rebels with a horde of undead monsters out of ancient myth at their beck and call, a few thousand rebels under the command of a mysterious wizard of unknown abilities, a few thousand rebels who were the first the Empire had faced in two hundred years, a few thousand rebels who might inspire millions more throughout all the lands beneath the Hundred Moons, a few thousand rebels who apparently had the willing aid of traitors in Seidabar itself . . .

A sign of divine favor would be very welcome.

Granzer didn't think they were going to get one, however, and had to act on that assumption. Any admission of doubt would make it even worse.

He looked up from the letter.

"Well, Delbur?" he said. "Go on, fetch the next one!"

CHAPTER 39

Onnell stared up at the yellow fabric of the tent, trying to remember where he was. It looked like the tent he shared with Orzin, Timuan, and Bousian, but he didn't remember returning here. He remembered the battle, and his slip in the mud. He had struggled to rise, had slit open a nightwalker's belly and been struck from behind . . .

After that he couldn't recall.

"Oh, good, you're awake," someone said.

He turned his head and found Orzin standing beside the cot, smiling down at him. Behind him Onnell could see a heaped blanket on Timuan's bunk.

"What happened?" he asked.

"You took a whack on the head," Orzin replied. "We don't know what hit you, but it wasn't a blade—maybe an armored fist, or a club of some kind. They found you lying there when we cleaned up the mess. You're lucky you didn't have any visible wounds, or they might've chopped your head off just to be sure—none of the men sorting corpses came from Grozerodz."

"We won? It's over?"

Orzin's smile vanished.

"We won," he said, "but nothing's over. That was just a beginning—something to shake us up, the officers say. A few score of nightwalkers came over and started hacking, and we hacked back and killed them all—or destroyed them all, or rekilled them, or whatever's the right way to describe what you do to nightwalkers. We lost a lot of men doing it—I don't know how many—but we cut the head off every nightwalker that crossed the river."

"Good," Onnell said, managing to sit up.

"It's good, yes—but the main body's still out there on the other side, stacked up like firewood in autumn."

Onnell looked up at the cloth over his head. It glowed with sunlight.

"They're all asleep? Or dead, or dormant, or whatever?"

Orzin nodded. "That's right."

"We should go destroy them while we can, then. Before sunset."

Orzin grimaced. "Of course we should," he said. "Everyone knows that, from General Balinus down to the whores up in Drievabor. The trick is getting across the river to do it."

Onnell blinked in confusion; his head was still not entirely clear.

"Not *all* the rebel army is nightwalkers, Onnell," Orzin reminded him. "We'd have to swim across the river, or use boats, and either way they'd see us coming. We'd have archers shooting at us the whole way, and we'd have to fight through their men to get ashore. *We* can't just walk across underwater!"

"Oh," Onnell said, feeling stupid. Then he asked, "Can't we go downstream and cross at Drievabor, then come back here along the other side?"

"Lord Duzon's taken a dozen men and horses to check on whether that might work," Orzin said.

"Oh," Onnell said again. "So we might try it?"

"We might," Orzin agreed. "But it's a long march, and we'd be outnumbered if we did."

"Would we?" Onnell asked, startled. "Are there that many of them? I mean, living rebels, not nightwalkers."

"So the magicians say."

"I didn't see that many tents," Onnell said. "Did more of them arrive after dark or something?"

Orzin sighed. "No," he said. "I mean, yes, there were stragglers, and they're still arriving over there, but a lot of those men don't *have* tents—they're just sleeping on the ground. They're not a real army, after all."

"Then we ought to be able to beat them even if we *are* outnumbered!"

"Maybe," Orzin said. "But I don't know how much of a soldier I really am, even if I did have a few triads of training and I do have a tent and a uniform. They've already fought their way all the way across the plain from the far side of Govya, Onnell. . . ."

"The *nightwalkers* fought their way across the plain!" Onnell protested.

"The mortals fought, too," Orzin said. "You know General Balinus harassed them from Ai Varach halfway across the plain, right up until the first snows—don't you think he'd have had the sense to attack by daylight?"

"But he didn't have enough men."

"But the men he did have were professional soldiers, not farm boys and street sweepers who volunteered a few seasons ago and got sent out here half-trained, then sat through the winter in Drievabor getting fat and lazy."

Onnell glared at his friend. "We hardly got fat on what they fed us there," he said. "You make it sound like you think we'll *lose*."

"No," Orzin said. "No, I don't think that. But I don't think we'll win until the whole Imperial Army gets here. When we can send the entire army at them, and not just six regiments, I think we'll be able to cut right through them. So *our* job is to hold them until Lord Kadan marches the main body out from Seidabar."

"When will that be?"

Orzin shrugged. "Do I look like an officer?"

"I want to see," Onnell said. He looked about and spotted his helmet at the foot of the bed; he reached over and picked it up, then got to his feet.

He wasn't quite as steady as he had expected; he stood for a moment, re-collecting himself, before he crossed the wheat-straw matting to the tent flap.

The sun was bright, and the water of the Grebiguata glittered in its light. A lone picket stood at the water's edge, staring across at the camp on the far side—where, as Orzin had said, the nightwalkers were stacked like firewood.

Onnell stepped out and looked around. The lines of golden yellow tents stretched off in either direction, and he could see a few other sentries . . . but no one else. There were no troops drilling, no soldiers lolling about.

"Where is everybody?" he asked aloud.

No one answered. Onnell turned and stuck his head back through the flap.

Orzin was on his own cot, clearly settling in to sleep.

"Where is everyone?" Onnell demanded.

"Sleeping," Orzin said. "And you probably should be, too, if you can get back to it after being out for so long."

"But it's the middle of the day!"

"And we were fighting all night," Orzin said, "and we'll probably do it again tonight, so we're resting while we can."

"But . . . then why were you up?"

"I was on watch," Orzin said. "Bousian just relieved me, and when I came in I saw you were waking up."

"But what . . ." Onnell looked around the tent, and realized for the first time that the blanket on Timuan's cot had Timuan under it. The boy was sound asleep.

Bousian's bunk was empty.

Onnell decided that he wanted to talk to Bousian. "All right, then," he said. "Sleep. I'll see you later." He dropped the tent flap and turned away.

The camp was eerily quiet as Onnell marched along the riverbank; he could hear the wind in the stubble of the abandoned wheat fields that still stood around the perimeter. Shading his eyes with one hand he looked eastward.

The enemy camp wasn't as still; people were moving about, and cookfires were burning. A group of men was digging at something near the center of the camp—Onnell would have assumed it was a latrine, if not for the location.

The wind was from the northwest, carrying away the stench of the night-walkers' decomposing flesh, but their stacked bodies were quite gruesome enough without it. Onnell shuddered; where had the Nazakri gotten so many corpses to reanimate? Had he killed that many?

Something caught his eye, and he stared, trying to make it out. One of the bodies, one near the top of one heap, was dressed in red and gold. . . .

The red and gold of an Imperial uniform.

Onnell hadn't noticed that before, but now he began looking for them and quickly spotted three more.

It shouldn't be a surprise, he told himself. After all, the nightwalkers were stolen corpses, and the rebels had been fighting General Balinus for seasons, and a dead soldier was no different from any other cadaver.

It wouldn't be pleasant in battle, though, to find himself facing a nightwalker who had once been an Imperial soldier like himself.

And the possibility that not only might he die fighting, but his *own* body might wind up in those stacks over there, was more than just unpleasant. It was nauseating. He leaned against a tent pole, suddenly unsteady. He tried to tell himself that it was just the aftereffects of the blow on the head he'd received, and perhaps that was truly all it was. When he had recovered sufficiently he walked on, through the camp.

As he walked he noticed a buzzing sound, and followed it, curious as to its origins.

When he found the sound's source, though, he had to stop and, since he could find nothing to lean on, sit down. He sat, legs folded under him, and stared out at the field behind the camp.

Again, it was something that shouldn't have surprised him. Orzin had said the previous night's battle was over and that the mess had been cleaned up, but he hadn't said everything that had to be done was done. He had also said everyone was resting.

Apparently the officers had considered rest more urgent than burying the dead. The buzzing came from swarms of flies that seethed around the corpses left by last night's fighting.

At least they weren't stacked up like the nightwalkers across the river—but on the other hand, at least the nightwalkers over there were still each in one piece. Here, the bodies were laid out in rows, and the heads were in separate rows.

And it wasn't just the remains of the nightwalkers that had been so treated; the bodies of the Imperial soldiers who had died in the fighting had also been decapitated, presumably to ensure that they would stay dead and not themselves become nightwalkers.

Onnell stared at the rows of the dead and realized that with their heads removed he couldn't even tell whether he had known any of them. He couldn't bring himself to look closely at the sagging, distorted faces of the severed heads.

This was ghastly, far more horrible than he imagined war would be—but then, this was no ordinary war. They were fighting nightwalkers and black magic.

This wasn't something for ordinary men, Onnell told himself. He should be home in Grozerodz, working the family farm and courting little Sezuan, not sitting here on the plain among headless corpses awaiting a night of horror.

Someone had to stop the nightwalkers, of course, or someday the village square in Grozerodz might be strewn with the dead just as this place was—but it shouldn't be *him*, Onnell told himself. This was a job for the New Magicians, or the priests, or the divine champion, not ordinary men.

The magicians were here, some of them, and doing their best—Onnell could see someone with a glowing staff in the sky to the east, keeping an eye on the enemy camp, even now. The priests were undoubtedly praying and working their own magic, as well.

But the champion—why wasn't Malledd here? Was he *that* determined to reject his appointment?

Maybe he didn't know, didn't believe, just how dangerous the Nazakri and his nightwalkers were.

Someone had to tell him. Someone *had* to.

Onnell looked up to the west.

If he slipped away and began walking, he thought he could reach Seidabar in six or seven days, and Grozerodz in five more. He could go to Hmar's forge and *tell* Malledd that he was needed here. Malledd might not listen to priests or recruiters, but if he, Onnell, told him, surely the champion would heed the call?

Onnell had always respected Malledd. The chosen of the gods was quiet, slow to choose sides, reluctant to involve himself in other people's business, but he was a good man, strong in more than just body. Surely, if he knew he was needed, he would come.

Twelve days to Grozerodz—at least; it might be more. And that was assuming he wasn't caught and punished for desertion.

In twelve days the entire Imperial vanguard might be destroyed—or the main army might arrive and wipe out the rebels. Even the vanguard might find some way to defeat them, if it could be done by daylight.

And Malledd might already be on the way here, Onnell realized. Slow to decide, yes—but he might have reached his decision, and seen that he was needed.

And meanwhile, the vanguard needed every man it had. Onnell couldn't desert his friends.

But he thought that when he had the chance, he wanted a word or two with a priest about when a man might break a promise without shaming himself, and after that a word or two with Lord Duzon about just who the true divine champion was.

CHAPTER 40

Malledd followed Darsmit through the huge gold-plated doors into the Great Temple warily. He didn't like this; the temple was the domain of the gods, and right now he didn't want to attract the attention of any divinities. He had a feeling his presence in Seidabar wasn't what the gods wanted—though he couldn't say why he thought so. After all, hadn't he helped the Empire by fighting the fire in the Imperial Palace?

He was probably just letting all the stress of the past few days get to him, he told himself. He should be home with his wife and children, not here in this great roaring city of strangers, talking with princes and battling blazes.

"Where are we going?" he asked as Darsmit turned down a side passage.

"The wedding hall," Darsmit replied. He pointed to a small crowd ahead. Malledd heard high-pitched laughter echoing from the stone walls. "It's right next to the marriage altar."

The feasting hall in Biekedau wasn't in the temple itself; it was a separate structure owned by an enterprising townsman. Couples who couldn't afford to rent it held their wedding feasts at home. For anyone from Grozerodz a home celebration meant a ten-mile walk for the bride and groom, so Malledd and his sisters—the four who had gotten properly married, at any rate—had all used the hall in Biekedau, despite the expense.

Apparently things were different in Seidabar, and the feasts were held right in the temple.

Next to the marriage altar? "The altar's not under the central dome?" Malledd asked.

"Not the one Berai is using." Berai was Darsmit's sister.

"There's more than one?"

Darsmit didn't bother replying, and Malledd didn't blame him; it was a stupid question. This was the *Great Temple at Seidabar*—of course it had more than one marriage altar in it! There might be dozens in a place this size. After all, if there was room for a feasting hall . . .

"Darsmit!" someone called. "You made it!"

"Of course!" Darsmit shouted back, smiling. "You think I'd miss my own sister's wedding?"

"Not without a pretty reason," came the reply.

"She'd have to be more than just pretty," Darsmit said. He didn't have to shout anymore; he and Malledd had reached the crowd at the door of the wedding hall.

"Who's your friend?" someone else asked. "Or is this your bodyguard, to fight off all those outraged husbands?"

"Ah, this is Malledd," Darsmit said, reaching up to clap Malledd on the shoulder. "He's one of the other smiths training as an armorer with me—and he's a brave man and a hero; he organized the bucket brigade at the palace."

"Ah, I thought I'd seen him before!" a woman called as she sidled nearer through the crowd. "Malledd, you say? I'm Breduin."

For the next few minutes Malledd was the center of a circle of faces. Introductions were made all around, but Malledd was quite certain he wouldn't remember most of the names. In the press of people he wasn't entirely sure when or how he got through the door, but he found himself inside the hall where a golden cloth covered a long table, awaiting the feast. Barrels were tiered along one wall. A small shrine at the far end held small statues of Vevanis and his sister-wife Orini, similar to those found on the marriage altar in Biekedau—and presumably on the marriage altar here in Seidabar, as well. A dozen vases of red flowers were arranged around the shrine—not roses, as Malledd was accustomed to seeing at weddings back home, but an unfamiliar variety, with very large, open blossoms. Other vases, holding various red flowers, were set here and there throughout the room.

The food wouldn't be brought out until the happy couple made their entrance, but a preliminary keg of wine had been tapped; Malledd accepted a glass and endured a dozen more introductions as Darsmit worked his way down the table toward the shrine, pulling Malledd along.

They had almost reached the end of the table when a white-robed priest stepped out from behind a curtain near the little shrine; that was clearly a signal that the ceremony at the altar was almost over, and the real party about to begin. The babble of conversation died away, and the guests turned to watch the priest.

The man in the white robe raised his hands and began the invocation, first of Orini, goddess of love and beauty, and then of her brother Vevanis, god of love and duty—not that anyone actually expected the deities in question to manifest themselves, but they were presumed to be listening.

"We understand it to be the will of this holy pair that Gharman and Berai shall be bound together in marriage, and we have seen Gharman and Berai pledge themselves accordingly," the priest concluded, "and so it is as husband and wife that they join us here now, to celebrate their union!"

The guests shouted their approval as the bride and groom stepped out through the curtain, both of them grinning foolishly. Berai was brushing nervously at the full skirt of her crimson gown; Gharman's wedding robe, made of the same fabric, didn't seem to fit him terribly well.

That didn't matter, of course. Friends and family rushed forward to embrace them both, and on cue a piper began playing the traditional Domdur wedding song.

Malledd wondered whether anyone ever remembered the lyrics to that cheerful tune; he had heard them sung once or twice. He didn't recall all the words, but he knew they included something about breeding new Domdur to serve the gods. That seemed a bit archaic now.

Guests moved away from the door to allow the delivery of the feast itself—a hired baker and his apprentice, alerted by the music, had appeared with trays of cakes and filled pastries. A man who bore a strong resemblance to the groom— probably a brother, Malledd guessed—led a group of men in tapping the waiting barrels of wine and ale.

"Come on, Malledd," Darsmit said. "I want Berai to meet you!" Reluctantly, Malledd allowed himself to be dragged over to meet the bride.

She was a comely young woman, despite a definite resemblance to her brother; she was smiling, happy and nervous, constantly fiddling with her red dress and darting glances around the room.

"Berai, I've got someone I want . . ." Darsmit began.

"You're Malledd," she said, interrupting him and grabbing Malledd's hand. "Darsmit's told me about you. I thought he'd exaggerated, but you really are as big as he said!"

Then she blushed and glanced at her husband, who was grinning foolishly, paying no attention to what she was saying. He had an arm around Berai's waist, but was talking to one of the other guests.

"I'm pleased to meet you," Malledd said awkwardly. "May all the gods smile on you and your new husband."

Berai smiled up at him. "Thank you," she said. "I'm so pleased to meet *you*, too!"

They had scarcely had time to exchange a dozen more words, though, when someone else demanded Berai's attention, and a cousin began talking loudly to Darsmit about their shared boyhood adventures, allowing Malledd to step away, into a corner by the shrine.

He wasn't comfortable here. He didn't know anyone but Darsmit, and who wanted a stranger at a wedding? And when Darsmit introduced him to anyone, he always mentioned the fire—if Malledd was going to be here at all, he wanted to be just one of the revelers, here amid the red flowers that represented new life to celebrate Berai and Gharman finding each other. He didn't want to play the hero, or distract attention from the bride and groom.

Besides, he didn't like being in the Great Temple; he was afraid Vadeviya would turn up and say something, take his presence as a sign his resolve was weakening, get him involved in something. He didn't even want to be in Seidabar anymore, let alone the Great Temple—if his resolve was weakening at all, it was in favor of going home to Anva. He had missed her painfully ever since her brief midwinter visit.

Someone who looked like another of Gharman's relatives pushed a glass of wine into Malledd's hand, then turned and called, "Does everyone have a drink?"

"I don't!" a voice bellowed, and a figure appeared in front of the curtain just to the other side of the shrine from where Malledd stood—but Malledd hadn't seen the curtain move or seen this figure emerge. He stared, puzzled.

The chatter faded suddenly as half the fifty or so people in the hall turned to see who had shouted, then died away completely as the other half turned to see why their friends were staring silently. The music missed a beat as the piper, too, spotted the new arrival—and recognized him.

"Baranmel," someone whispered loudly in the unexpected quiet.

"It *is*!" another said, somewhat louder.

Berai let out a piercing shriek of delight.

The new arrival smiled broadly and raised his hands in acknowledgment, but didn't speak.

And then the silence vanished in cheering and applause. Baranmel shouted over the racket, "Where's my drink? Why aren't we dancing?" He swept forward into the room, snatching up a beer in one hand and a young woman in the other as the piper began a new tune, a song of welcome.

Malledd shrank back in the corner by the shrine, staring at the god's back. The uneasiness that had been nagging at him since he set foot in the Great Temple bloomed into outright fear—he was in the presence of a *god*.

There was no possibility of doubt or deception. Baranmel wasn't particularly large or overwhelming—he was perhaps the second-tallest person in the room, after Malledd—but he was still unmistakably more than human. His face was oddly undefined, so that Malledd could not describe any part of it when the god was facing away from him, but it left an impression of supernal beauty; he moved with grace and smoothness even in such vulgar actions as gulping beer. The giggling woman he held under one arm seemed stunningly beautiful merely because he was holding her.

And there was no darkness anywhere about him. It was not so much that he seemed to radiate light as that the rest of the world seemed shadowy in contrast—his blouse was so brilliantly white, his breeches so richly golden, that the people around him in their bright wedding clothes seemed dim and dull. His hair and beard were a light brown that seemed to shift hue as Malledd watched—and maybe it did; after all, this was a god. His physical form was whatever he wanted it to be.

The other guests were clearly delighted with his presence; they cheered when he kissed the bride, a kiss that was rather more emphatic than would have been appropriate from anyone else but the groom. They cheered again when he swept the woman under his arm upright and set her back on her feet, and swirled into a dance with her, somehow managing to swing his just-refilled beer mug about wildly without spilling a drop. The piper was playing far better than he had before, and someone had begun drumming, using the various kegs and barrels as his instruments.

They were all overcome with joy, and Malledd knew that that was as it should be—after all, this was Baranmel, the god of festivities, whose presence was a sign of good luck for years to come. "May Baranmel dance at your wedding" was the most widely used blessing beneath the Hundred Moons; Berai and Gharman were assured by his presence that they would love each other as long as they lived, that their lives together would be long and full and rich, that they would have fine children. Not one couple in a thousand was so fortunate, and the guests were all sharing in their friends' happiness.

All but Malledd.

He didn't know Berai or Gharman, after all—and the presence of a god raised too many issues for him.

It wasn't that he hadn't believed the gods were real; he had never doubted their existence. He had, however, doubted just how involved they were in mortal affairs. His father Hmar had always been suspicious of gods and priests, had sometimes wondered aloud whether the oracles actually heard the words of the gods or merely gave sensible advice on their own, had even accused the priests of trickery of various kinds. Hmar had always maintained that the gods weren't any of his concern—he would deal with the world as he found it, and he hadn't found any gods in his forge. Dremeger had put the ore in the earth and given mankind the skills to work it, and Hmar had given thanks for that annually, but he hadn't expected the gods to interfere in his life, nor did he try to interfere in theirs.

Malledd had picked up that attitude as far as he could, but his own life had been marked by the gods from birth—according to the priests, anyway—and he hadn't appreciated it. The gods *had* interfered in his life, as they hadn't in Hmar's, and not for the better. Since boyhood he had been trying to escape that interference, to have as little to do with the gods as possible. He had taken the silence of the oracles as a sign that the gods were not meddling anymore. He had taken the fact that Baranmel had not attended his own wedding as a sign that the gods had no more interest in him. The oracles had abandoned the Domdur, and that suited Malledd just fine; it meant he could make up his own mind about just what duties he might have as the chosen of the gods, since the gods weren't telling him.

But here was Baranmel, not a dozen feet away, not three days after the Imperial Palace burned, in the midst of the greatest crisis the Domdur had faced in centuries. Could it really be a coincidence?

Malledd had heard, often enough from his more religious or mystically inclined friends and companions, that there are no coincidences, that everything is part of the plans of the gods. Certainly being dragged to a stranger's wedding where Baranmel just happened to appear would seem awesomely unlikely.

But if it was not a coincidence, just why was he here? Were the gods angry with him for not revealing himself as the defender of the Empire? Were they going to remove his recognition and declare that the Domdur had lost divine favor? Would Baranmel strike him dead for failing to make his way to the Grebiguata to confront Rebiri Nazakri?

Malledd was not afraid of much, but he feared the gods. They were inscrutable and all-powerful—how could he not fear them?

He hung back, wishing he were anywhere else. He couldn't get to the door without pushing his way through the crowd and passing even closer to the dancing god.

The first dance ended, and Baranmel changed partners for the next, whirling an aging redhead across the tiny dance floor. Malledd stood and watched, accepting the wine someone passed him and downing it quickly.

Berai danced the third dance with Baranmel; for the fourth the piper played an old marching tune, the volunteer drummer beating it out on the barrels. Baranmel flung his arms over the shoulders of Gharman and Darsmit, and the three of them drunkenly bellowed the words as they reeled through a traditional Domdur war dance.

When that ended, the musicians announced they were taking a drinking break—"I haven't enough spit left for another note," the piper gasped. That was the cue for most of those present to tackle some serious eating and drinking, as the pastries vanished rapidly and the barrels were "retuned."

Baranmel clapped his winded fellow dancers on the back, fetched himself a mug of ale, and then turned.

"Ah, Malledd," he said as he strode over to the corner by the shrine.

Malledd backed up until he was leaning against the curtain and could feel the cold stone beneath the cloth, but there was nowhere he could go, no way to avoid the god.

That inevitability forced him to think, to consider what he could say, and despite his fear he saw that this was his chance to finally get some straight answers, clear instructions on what, if anything, the gods expected of him. That gave him the courage to straighten up and look Baranmel in the eye.

"What do you want of me?" Malledd said.

"I? I want you to cheer up!" Baranmel said. "Have a drink! Smile! Dance! I see at least a dozen pretty girls here, and your wife won't mind if you just *dance* with one!" He grinned and handed Malledd a cup of wine.

Malledd took it, but didn't drink.

"Is that all?" he asked.

Baranmel cocked his head to one side. "Malledd, I am the god of joyful celebration—what *else* would I want of anyone?" He smiled a charming, ingratiating smile, then gulped beer. He wiped foam from his lip with the back of his hand.

"Am I just anyone, then?" Malledd asked warily. "You know my name."

"I know *everyone's* name!" Baranmel shouted, flinging his arms wide. "I'm a *god*, Malledd!" He turned and, without looking, tossed his empty mug aside; a man by the nearest beer barrel caught it and refilled it, but Baranmel didn't wait for its return, but instead snatched another that was being passed nearby.

"Thanks!" he called, hoisting the mug in salute. Then he turned back to Malledd and said, "No, you're not just anyone, Malledd. Forget your doubts— you are, indeed, the chosen defender of the Domdur. And isn't that something to celebrate? Drink up!"

Malledd sipped wine and stared at Baranmel's dripping beard as the god emptied his mug again.

He *was* the divine champion, then. It wasn't a priestly hoax or an error. And Baranmel had said "are," not "were."

"Then why weren't you at *my* wedding?" he asked.

Baranmel lowered his mug. His perpetual smile faded.

"I think you can figure that out," he said. "You know what my presence here means."

"It means Berai and Gharman are going to live long, happy lives together. And Anva and I . . ."

Malledd didn't finish the sentence.

"Well, let's just say that your future isn't as certain," Baranmel said. "Don't think I'm telling you you're doomed, or Anva is; I don't mean that. I just mean you aren't inevitably fated for long-term marital bliss. After all, Malledd, you're here, and Anva . . . ?"

"She's back in Grozerodz."

"Exactly." That winning smile reappeared.

Malledd decided not to press further about his marriage; he wasn't sure he wanted to know. Instead he said, "You must know the future, if you can foretell happiness—so tell me, will Rebiri Nazakri reach Seidabar?"

Baranmel laughed. "Is that anything to talk about at a wedding?"

"Yes!" Malledd shouted. "Yes, it is, blast you!"

Then he stopped and looked around, expecting to see shocked faces—but he didn't; the wedding celebration was continuing undisturbed.

"That's my doing," Baranmel said, waving his beer at the other guests. "I thought you'd prefer our conversation to go unnoticed. So it will."

"They can't hear us?" Malledd asked, looking at an old woman standing not three feet away who was paying no attention to them at all.

"They *won't* hear us," the god said. "It's not quite the same thing."

"You did that?"

Baranmel nodded.

Malledd hesitated, embarrassed by his presumption, but then asked, "Did you come here, to this wedding, because you wanted to talk to me?"

The god smiled and winked. "Let's just say that matters were arranged so that we might meet."

"Do you ever give a straight answer?" Malledd demanded, annoyed.

"Yes," Baranmel said, grinning broadly. "But you have to ask the right questions."

"All right, then just tell me why you're here, and what you want to tell me."

"Ah, that's not the right question. I'm here because I dance at the weddings of the blessed, Malledd—it's part of what I am. Why *you're* here, why this particular couple is blessed, that's another matter."

"Ba'el! Can't you just tell me what's going on?"

Baranmel's smile vanished. "Not if you invoke my half brother again," he said.

"Your . . ." Malledd stopped. He had forgotten that particular relationship, but yes, Ba'el was said to be Baranmel's older half brother. Malledd glanced at the shrine; the gods' relationships, as exemplified by the double idol of Vevanis and Orini, could be complicated.

But what did that have to do with anything?

"Baranmel, please," he said. "Just tell me what the gods want me to do."

Baranmel smiled wryly.

"Which gods?" he asked.

CHAPTER 41

Malledd stared at the god's face, puzzled—and fascinated by his beauty, as well. For a moment he was unable to think clearly enough to respond, but then he tore his gaze away and said, "The gods of the Domdur, of course—what other gods would I concern myself with?"

"Ah, but *which* gods of the Domdur?" Baranmel asked. "We aren't in agreement."

Malledd blinked in confusion. "What?"

"We aren't in agreement," Baranmel said. "Did you think we always are?"

"Well . . . yes, I suppose I did," Malledd admitted.

"Haven't you heard the tales of how we failed to choose a king?"

"Of course I have," Malledd said.

Baranmel didn't have to comment further on that; now that he had pointed it out, Malledd saw that it was implicit in the stories that the gods didn't always agree with each other. Malledd had somehow never thought about it—he was so accustomed to hearing people speak of "the will of the gods," in the singular, that he had almost forgotten the gods were plural.

But that complicated everything. If he was the chosen of the gods, and the gods disagreed . . .

He needed to have this explained, and Baranmel didn't seem willing to explain it. He had to find the right questions. He wished he could speak to an oracle, instead of Baranmel—the old stories said that *they* would give direct, simple answers. Sometimes, anyway.

Of course, sometimes the answer had been, "That's not for you to know."

Most of the oracles had been devoted to Samardas, not Baranmel—maybe that was the problem. Most gods had had at least a few oracles scattered about, but Malledd had never heard of any devoted to Baranmel. Baranmel wasn't the god of wisdom, or answers—he was the god of celebrations.

But maybe there was a way to use that. After all, what was a party without a storyteller?

"Tell me a story, Baranmel," Malledd said. "Tell me the story of how I came to be here, at this wedding."

Baranmel grinned more broadly than ever, more broadly than humanly possible. "I thought you'd never ask." He turned and leaned back against the edge of the shrine, tossed his beer mug away to be miraculously caught, then spread his hands in a storyteller's gesture.

"Long ago," he said, "the world was home to a thousand squabbling mortal tribes." He pointed. "Over here, the Veruet Isles were home to pirates and plunderers. Over there, the Farista idea of a good time was burning enemy villages. The Greyans fought the Matuans, the Sautalans fought the Dradieshna. And among the Hundred Moons above, Ba'el, god of war, was chief among the gods, mightiest of them all, for was not all the world below a confusion of little wars? The farmers might worship Vedal, and the hunters might worship Barzuar, but everyone who fought was serving Ba'el, and the war god laughed with joy when he saw mortals slaughtering each other. The wars went on and on, and the gods often sided with their favorites; if a tribe of farmers fought a tribe of hunters, then Vedal would favor one side with her blessings and advice, and Barzuar would support the other, and the strife would thus spread to the heavens themselves."

Malledd had not expected the tale to begin so far back in time, but he nodded and listened.

"In his place among the gods, Samardas looked at this world below, at its constant warring and all the needless death and suffering that the wars brought, and said, 'This is stupid.' For that reason, if no other, he despised it, for Samardas is the god of wisdom and cannot abide stupidity," Baranmel continued. "He resolved to put an end to the wars—but how could he do that when Ba'el had fed on the strife and become the strongest of the gods, and Ba'el wished the wars to continue? So Samardas, in consultation with his allies, devised a plan to fool Ba'el into destroying his own power."

This was not quite how Malledd remembered the tale. He had always heard that the gods simply decided that they were tired of war, not that Samardas had tricked anyone. He leaned forward attentively.

"Samardas went to Ba'el one day and said, 'What a shame the wars are so small. If the tribes were larger, then the armies would be larger—what carnage you would see then!'

"And Ba'el listened, astonished; he had never thought of such a thing. 'How could we make them larger?' he asked.

"And Samardas said, 'Why, if one tribe were able to conquer another, and then another, it would become large and mighty, able to wage much better wars.'

"Ba'el agreed that this was so, and looked down at the world, and said, 'We must allow one tribe to conquer others!'

"More than that,' Samardas said. 'We must *aid* one tribe in conquering the others! Come, let us talk to the other gods, and see to it!'

"So together, Ba'el and Samardas went to the other gods in their convocation and presented Samardas's plan." Baranmel paused and smiled a cockeyed smile. "My brother was never all that bright," he said.

A snort of laughter escaped Malledd.

"So," Baranmel continued, "the rest of us listened to the plan that Samardas and Ba'el presented, and we looked at one another in wonder that Samardas had convinced Ba'el, for by then we were all save my brother weary of war and eager for peace, but could not see how it might be achieved. And Samardas told us, 'We must choose one tribe, and remove our favor from all others,' and we agreed—but how to choose the tribe? Vedal favored the farmers, Barzuar the hunters, Sheshar the fisherfolk; other gods each had their favorites; but at last we chose the Domdur, who lived on this hill where we now stand and in the lands to the north and west, who farmed on the plain and hunted in the forest and fished in the sea, and who favored no god over the others but praised us all equally. And we withdrew our favor from all the world save the lands between Seidabar and Rishna Gabidéll, so that no magic worked outside those bounds save the black spells of the ungodly powers in the earth. Of old we had sometimes granted special favor to warriors among the many tribes, but now we agreed that there would be but one divinely favored champion, a Domdur chosen according to certain rules, so that there might be no disputes among us. And Ba'el, eager for the holocausts Samardas had promised, supported our efforts."

Baranmel paused, grabbed a beer from a nearby hand, and drank before continuing.

"For eight hundred years, then, the Domdur throve under our mutual auspices, and Ba'el had his wars as the chosen champions led the Domdur in the conquest of each other tribe, one by one, until all the world was subdued, united beneath the Empire. And at last the rest of us looked down at a single peaceful nation and applauded, our goal accomplished.

"But my brother, cursed be his name, looked down and slowly realized that he had been cheated—he had traded away an eternity of minor wars for a few centuries of pillage and bloodshed.

"He went to Samardas and protested, but Samardas merely laughed. He complained to us all, and we shrugged our shoulders or turned away—the new peace pleased us!

"But Ba'el was not yet finished. Power shifts slowly among the gods, and he was still mightiest of us all, though his prominence was waning. Further, he had been defeated by stealth, and he saw that any victory must likewise use more than simple brute force—war is strategy as much as strength. He summoned his allies, for he has never been wholly without his supporters, and began a subtle campaign.

"Through his allies, he suggested that we begin to withdraw from our involvement with the Domdur. He argued that Samardas was using his prominence among the oracles to gain undue influence over humanity, and was able to raise suspicion and gain enough support for his accusations that we, the gods in our councils, ruled that there would be an end to *all* oracles, to prophecy, to visions or divine guidance of any kind.

"Through Dremeger, who cares not at all whether we have war or peace but only that things be built, my brother inspired the Diknoi to discover what you call the New Magic, to create a weapon with the potential to overthrow the Domdur.

"And finally, in what I can only consider an act of treason, he guided Rebiri Nazakri to bargain with the ancient dark powers the gods long ago cast down, and to draw upon the darkness in the earth to destroy Seidabar."

"But he hasn't," Malledd protested. "Seidabar still stands."

"If Ba'el has his way it won't for much longer," Baranmel said. "You asked me to tell you the story of how you came here, and I haven't quite finished, though perhaps you can guess the rest."

"No, tell me," Malledd said.

"It's simple enough," Baranmel said. "Those who see what Ba'el intends and oppose it wish him to be stopped; we want Rebiri Nazakri defeated and slain, the nightwalkers destroyed and the darkness again buried, Seidabar and the Domdur strong and united. We cannot speak to mortals through the old methods; our councils forbid it, and we cannot defy them. But it is in my nature to go among mortals and share their celebrations; Ba'el cannot prevent it even if he thought to, nor can any other among the gods. If it happens that I meet you here and speak to you, why, that's no violation of our covenants. If it happens that incidents have guided you here to Seidabar to meet me, that fate has seen fit to place you at the Imperial Palace when traitors have set it ablaze, that breaks no agreements. The gods are entwined in fate and always have been. But beyond this, Malledd . . . beyond this, you're on your own. Ba'el cannot tamper with the mechanisms of the championship, but neither can we—we set it up that way a thousand years ago. You're free to do as you please with the gifts of strength and endurance and leadership that we've given you. If you fight for the Domdur, all well and good; if you don't, we can't force you."

"If I do fight, what happens?" Malledd asked.

Baranmel shook his head. "I can't tell you that," he said. "I can make no prophecy outside the blessings that are mine to give—and you, I'm afraid, are not to receive those. But I can say that the forces involved are very nearly in balance. Ba'el grew very, very powerful during the years of the Domdur expansion, and his allies are many. Rebiri Nazakri may indeed have the power to destroy Seidabar and throw the world into renewed chaos and endless war— Ba'el will not allow him to rule in the Domdur's stead if he wins, as that would defeat the whole purpose. If he wins the coming battles, then the Empire will be destroyed, and the world will know no peace for centuries, if ever. But you may indeed have the power to stop him. Ba'el will do everything he can to prevent you from doing so, yet you might prevail."

" 'May,' " Malledd said. " 'Might,' you tell me?"

"Yes, 'may' and 'might.' Beyond that I cannot say. But you *are* the champion—not of all the gods, but of the Domdur."

"That's not a great comfort," Malledd said.

Baranmel shrugged. "It's the truth. The wise don't seek comfort in the truth." His serious expression vanished as he dropped his storyteller's guise and stood up straight. "*I* seek it in beer," he said. "Over here!" He beckoned, turning away from Malledd. "My mug's empty! And where's the music?"

The piper smiled and raised his pipes, and the drummer jumped up on a chair by the barrels as Baranmel swooped out into the room, grabbing a girl in each arm.

Malledd watched him go.

It was plain, now, what the gods wanted him to do—most of them, at any rate. He could no longer claim ignorance or uncertainty. He *was* the divine champion, chosen defender of the Empire, and they *did* want him to fight Rebiri Nazakri.

But he was free to refuse—and he was not going to rush off to join the battle. He was a smith, not a warrior.

Furthermore, Baranmel had not said *where* he was to fight, here in Seidabar or out on the eastern plain. The god had clearly implied that Malledd's presence at the time of the fire had been arranged; shouldn't he stay in Seidabar in case there were further attacks from within?

He hesitated, debating whether he should run after Baranmel to ask more questions.

The god was gulping ale, pouring with one hand and tossing a giggling young woman in the air with the other.

If Baranmel had had more to say, he would surely have said it. How could Malledd expect to coax any more sense out of him now?

Besides, what had the gods done for him to earn his devotion? He was no mere underling, begging to know what he could do to please his masters; he was a free man. When his duty was made plain, he would do it. If the gods did not tell him to go, then he need not go. After all, the Imperial Army's main body was still encamped in Agabdal. Would he be of any use without them?

He needed to think about it all. There was no need to hurry.

CHAPTER 42

Lord Duzon, seated astride his horse, looked along the line of soldiers, then down at the torchlit water. "Stand ready!" he called. "Here they come!"

Onnell, fifty feet to Duzon's right and a hundred feet to the left of General Balinus and the Biekedau Regiment's Colonel Blodibord, shifted his feet uncomfortably and lifted his sword. He was wearing his boots, despite standing knee-deep in the river, so that nightwalkers would not be able to chop at his unprotected feet—but he was beginning to wonder if he'd made a mistake, since the boots had filled with water and made his movements slow and awkward. That was probably just as dangerous as wading barefoot.

He wondered whether he could step back out of line long enough to pull off the boots. He glanced up at Lord Duzon. . . .

Then a nightwalker's head burst up through the surface of the Grebiguata, flinging water in Onnell's face—the monster had knelt down and crept up much closer than Onnell had expected, then stood up suddenly, splashing his foe.

Onnell chopped blindly back and forth with his sword while he blinked muddy water from his eyes; he swept his left sleeve across his face and opened his eyes just in time to see the nightwalker grinning through rotted lips as it swung an ax at Onnell's chest. Onnell's sword had hacked into the nightwalker's left side between two ribs, and there wasn't time to pull it free and parry; Onnell ducked to his right, yanking at his sword, and felt the ax pass over his left ear.

The sword came free, but Onnell had lost his balance. He fell sideways into the river, catching himself with his right hand, his sword slapping down through the water to the muddy bottom, his face just a few inches above the rippling surface.

The nightwalker's two-handed grip on his ax shifted, and he swung again, chopping straight down.

Onnell gulped air as he let his elbow collapse. He fell down into the water, beneath the ax's swing, and rolled blindly down the underwater slope, holding his breath.

He stopped abruptly when he slammed against the nightwalker's legs, throwing the undead creature off balance and sending it splashing back into the water.

Onnell shoved himself on top of the thing, grabbed the point of his sword in his left hand while his right still held the hilt, and rammed the blade down onto the nightwalker's neck as if he were chopping vegetables.

Thick fluid spilled out into the water, blinding him, but he could tell that the water had slowed him, the blade hadn't cut deeply. He chopped again and again as the nightwalker flailed about, the ax bursting up out of the water and then back under as its wielder tried to cut at Onnell's back.

Then Onnell felt his sword strike bone. The pressure in his chest and the burning in his water-filled nostrils told him he had no time to spare. He threw his weight onto the sword, feeling the blade cut into the palm of his left hand.

The nightwalker's neck parted with a snap, and Onnell was lying facedown atop a headless, lifeless corpse in two and a half feet of water. He pushed himself upward and gasped for air as his head cleared the water.

He shook water from his hair and eyes as he rose to his knees and looked around.

To left and right, his companions were battling the nightwalkers—and ahead another nightwalker was practically on top of him, this one in a woman's gaunt, decaying body, wearing the tattered, dripping remnants of a Matuan courtesan's silk gown, with long black hair hanging in wet ropes, a heavy sword held incongruously in one of its tiny hands. It was raising the sword as if to plunge it into Onnell's chest.

Onnell ducked sideways again. With his left hand he snatched the ax from the hand of the corpse beneath him, and with the right he jabbed his sword at his new foe.

The dead courtesan's sword scraped down Onnell's left side, while his own sword punched up through her chest.

Onnell on his knees was almost as tall as the nightwalker was standing upright, and the sword through her body held her so that she couldn't dodge; as she raised her sword for another blow, Onnell chopped left-handed at her throat and lopped her head off with the ax.

He stood, kicked the corpse off his blade, and turned to face a third attacker.

Pin with the sword, chop with the ax—Onnell found that to be an effective method for disposing of nightwalkers. Most of them were not particularly good swordsmen; after all, they were evil spirits, who would scarcely have had a chance to learn swordsmanship, and most of them occupied the bodies of civilians, who would not have had any training, either. Onnell was no master, but he handled a blade far better than any of the nightwalkers he encountered.

Of course, the nightwalkers didn't have to be good to be effective, in most cases. They had the advantage of being immune to pain and unconcerned with their own destruction. The black force that animated a nightwalker wasn't destroyed by beheading; it was merely inconvenienced, freed of physical form until Rebiri Nazakri could capture it and install it in a fresh corpse.

By the fifth attack Onnell had switched the ax to his right hand, the sword to his left, and was trying to fight his way to the left, where the nightwalkers seemed to be making their best progress.

Although he had little time or energy to spare for thought, that didn't seem right to Onnell. Lord Duzon and the Company of Champions were to the left; surely, they should be more effective against the nightwalkers than ordinary volunteers! Still, it was to the left that he saw nightwalkers splashing ashore, saw soldiers in red and gold falling back, heard men screaming—and nightwalkers never screamed. As often as not they smiled as they died, which Onnell found unnerving at first.

He got used to it quickly, however.

"Fall back!" he heard someone yell, but he didn't recognize the voice, didn't know if the order was meant for the Imperial vanguard or the nightwalkers. He ignored it as he jammed his sword through a nightwalker's back and chopped at its neck, then ducked a blow from another of the undead.

This wasn't going the way it was supposed to. The idea had been that by showing they were ready and waiting, the Imperial soldiers would discourage the nightwalkers from making a serious assault. Then, in the morning, the vanguard would march back up to Drievabor, cross the bridge, and destroy the enemy once and for all—though it would have meant a fast forced march after an almost sleepless night; the bridge was fifteen miles to the south. Fight, march thirty miles, and fight again, all before sunset—that hadn't been a very appealing prospect, but it would have meant victory.

But that had assumed the nightwalkers would be discouraged. No one could expect the vanguard to march thirty miles and fight again after a serious night-long battle.

The nightwalkers didn't *seem* very discouraged. In fact, they seemed to be making their way ashore despite the best efforts of Onnell and his companions.

He swung the ax wildly to clear himself some room, then turned to find his next foe.

The nightwalker behind and to the right had ducked under Onnell's swing, just as Onnell had avoided its attack; now the two of them stood crouching, knee-deep in the churning black river, and faced each other.

"Ready to give up?" the nightwalker asked, grinning—a grin exaggerated by its shriveled, rotting lips. Its voice was rasping and harsh. Water ran unheeded from its river-soaked hair across its unblinking black eyes.

"Go back to your wizard!" Onnell muttered—he didn't want to waste energy in shouting. "You're not getting past us!"

"Maybe not tonight," the nightwalker agreed. "Come Midsummer's Day, though, we'll be at the gates of Seidabar, and you'll either be lying headless in the Grebiguata, or marching with . . ."

Onnell struck without warning, moving as suddenly as he could, plunging forward with his left arm extended, impaling the nightwalker just below the ribs.

". . . us," the thing concluded as it made its counterstrike, only to meet the blade of Onnell's ax. Bone snapped, and the nightwalker's curved sword flailed wildly upward as the ax shattered the creature's wrist.

Something cut at Onnell's shoulder from behind; he ignored the pain long enough to dispatch the squirming enemy his sword had pinned, then whirled to find Timuan and a female nightwalker in combat mere inches away. Both their swords were red; he couldn't tell whether the nightwalker had taken a swipe at him in passing, or whether Timuan's blade had struck him unintentionally.

And it didn't matter; he tore his sword free of the headless corpse beside him and rammed it through the throat of Timuan's opponent.

She made a hissing sound—probably all she could do with her windpipe severed—and turned, slicing her own neck further. Onnell's ax then scissored with the sword to finish her off.

"Thanks," Timuan said. He was shaking with the madness and exhaustion of battle. Both men then turned, looking for fresh opposition.

They found none—the lines of nightwalkers advancing out of the river were gone. Instead, the enemy had pushed up from the river onto the bank and coalesced into a mass, a walking graveyard, clustered around Lord Duzon and the Company of Champions.

The champions were afoot, Onnell saw, their horses cut out from under them. There didn't seem to be as many of them as there should be.

"Come on," Onnell said, advancing toward the massed foe.

"Are you *crazy*?" Timuan asked. "Look at them all!"

"And look at our men in there!" Onnell said.

Timuan looked, and saw blades flashing in the torchlight, saw blood on arms and blades and faces. He looked away, and saw the river black with whorls of blood, bodies bobbing and drifting in the churned-up water. He looked farther, and saw men standing here and there along the river, some on the shore, some in the water, all of them looking dazed and weary.

"What about them?" he said, pointing.

Onnell turned, and thought at first that Timuan was pointing at the opposite shore, where neat lines of nightwalkers stood watching the battle.

The enemy still had reserves.

Then he realized that Timuan had meant the other Imperial soldiers.

"Come on!" Onnell cried to them, waving his sword and gesturing toward the surrounded champions. He sloshed up the bank.

A few of the others followed him—but Timuan did not; he stood and watched, too stunned and weary to fight anymore.

And then the enemy broke. A shout came from somewhere, and the night-walkers turned away and headed for the river. Onnell stopped in his tracks and lowered his weapons.

Then he saw the struggling figures the nightwalkers were carrying.

"They're taking hostages!" he called. He turned to head off the enemy.

An immense nightwalker in rusted armor seemed to appear from nowhere in front of him, and Onnell swung his ax. The nightwalker threw up an armored fist to deflect the blow and jabbed with its own short sword.

Timuan, his fatigue vanishing when he saw Onnell stagger back away from the thrust, leaped forward.

The fight was too confused for clear description, but a long moment later the nightwalker was down, its skull shattered and its brains spilled. Onnell and Timuan turned to see what had become of the others, on both sides.

The great mass of nightwalkers had marched down into the river, carrying screaming, struggling men with them—had marched down, and down, and down, under the river, carrying their captives with them. Now they were starting to emerge on the far side, in the safety of their own camp.

The screaming still came from the western bank, though, where Lord Duzon and several others stood hip-deep in the water, bellowing with rage.

There was no screaming from the east. The captives no longer struggled when they arose from the water; they hung limp in their captor's hands. Timuan stared in horror.

"Why did they do that?" he said. "Why capture them if you're just going to *drown* them?"

Onnell swallowed.

"They want the bodies intact," he said, too tired to try to disguise the truth as he saw it.

Timuan looked up at him in shock. "Why?" he asked.

"For reinforcements," Onnell replied grimly.

CHAPTER 43

Lord Kadan turned at the sound of jingling spurs, and saw Lord Shoule trotting into the courtyard of the training-ground headquarters astride a fine gray. Behind Shoule were three more riders, these three hooded and wrapped in brown wool cloaks—Lord Shoule's bodyguards or servants, Kadan guessed.

"Oh, Ba'el," he muttered. He did not need any more delays at this point. He put the map down on the stack of letters and reports on the barrel head and waved a greeting.

"Ho, my lord!" he called. "What brings you to Agabdal?"

Lord Shoule peered down his long nose at Kadan, then swung from the saddle in a graceful dismount before replying, "I've come in part to see why your army is still here, Kadan. I see them lined up in the fields here, standing or sitting about—they hardly seem to be training or preparing themselves."

Kadan suppressed his urge to shout angrily. He glanced at the other three horsemen and said quietly, "The preparations are almost complete, my lord, and they but await the final command. Had you come an hour later you would have found us gone."

Shoule brushed dust from the skirts of his powder-blue riding coat, then looked up at Kadan. "You say 'us,' my lord? Were you intending to accompany them?"

Kadan blinked in surprise. "Of course," he said. "I intend to lead them into battle. I could hardly ask anyone else to undertake so important and dangerous a task."

"Ah," Shoule said, nodding. "And of course, you would take command from General Balinus, despite his long experience against this dire foe we face."

Kadan felt his face redden. "I intend to listen very carefully to Balinus's advice, but the final responsibility for any military venture is mine and mine alone."

"Yours and yours alone," Shoule said. "Any military venture." He turned and called to the foremost of the other three, "You heard that, my lord?"

The horseman threw back his hood, revealing Lord Orbalir's face.

"I heard it," Orbalir growled.

"Oh, by Barzuar's bloody spear," Kadan muttered. "This is a land war, my lords," he said aloud. "The Imperial *Army* marches to this fight, not the navy."

"You go to fight across a river," Orbalir said. "We may yet see boats involved. And in any case, Kadan, by imperial edict you're to consult with me."

"All right, then!" Kadan shouted. "Come and consult, if you want! Are you ready to ride? We leave for Drievabor within the hour!"

"I think not," Shoule said.

"What do you mean, you think not?" Kadan said, astonished.

"I mean, my lord," Shoule said, smiling unpleasantly, "that the Imperial Council does not intend to allow you to march the entire army off to the east under no one's control save your own, leaving Seidabar undefended and incidentally taking with you every single soldier who was involved in quelling the riot in Outer Seidabar three triads ago, before any of them have been properly questioned about those events—and about *your* part in them."

"My part in what? What are you talking about, Shoule?"

"Your part in the riots, Lord Kadan," Shoule replied. "And perhaps in other events, as well—such as the fire that broke out during those riots."

Kadan stared at Shoule for a moment, then up at the horsemen. Orbalir was grinning fiercely; the other two were still hooded. What other surprises did Shoule have there?

Kadan's anger drained away. This was suddenly too important to let his temper play a role. These fools, whether misguided or malicious, were making serious accusations against him.

Anyone could make accusations, of course, and Kadan was sure that in time he could clear himself of any wrongdoing—but he might not have any time. There was a real enemy out there to the east, and probably real traitors in the capital itself.

"I had nothing to do with the fire," Kadan said.

"So you say," Shoule said. "We have our doubts. *Someone* sent that messenger to Lord Niniam, luring away the guards—and you were in the Outer City, were you not?"

"I was here, in Agabdal."

"A mere half-hour ride away. And you have hundreds of messengers here, already in their fine red uniforms."

"This is stupid, Shoule," Kadan said, losing his grip on his temper for a moment. "Why would I want to burn the Imperial Palace, or harm the Empress?"

"Because you're an ambitious man, perhaps? Because you think the Empire needs a younger, stronger hand at the helm?"

"That's nonsense!"

"Oh?" Shoule turned to one of the hooded riders. "Your Holiness?"

The second hood was thrown back, revealing Apiris's unhappy face.

"I'm sorry, Kadan," he said.

"Apiris?" Kadan was baffled by this new surprise—what was *Apiris* doing among his accusers? At the last meeting of the Imperial Council Lord Shoule had been denouncing the Archpriest as untrustworthy, and here he was at Shoule's heel?

"Tell us, Your Holiness, what *Lord* Kadan said to you in the Great Temple a few days ago," Shoule said, never taking his eyes off Kadan.

"He said . . . he said that being on the Imperial Council is a great opportunity, and we should use it. He said we're the masters of the world, and we should act like it. And that there was no use looking for a traitor on the Council."

"And what did you make of this?" Shoule asked.

"Well, nothing, at the time," Apiris admitted. "But later, when I thought about it, I wondered whether maybe when he talked about being assertive he meant we shouldn't yield so much to the imperial family, and to Prince Granzer. I thought maybe there was some resentment there."

"And why would he suggest there was no point in looking for a traitor, when there almost certainly is one?"

"Well, he said that the traitor would reveal himself if we waited, but I couldn't help wondering if he didn't want us to look because *he's* the traitor."

"That's ridiculous," Kadan protested. "I merely meant that left to his own devices, anyone who could be so foolish as to betray the Empire must surely make mistakes that would show us who it is!"

Apiris stared miserably at him; Orbalir and Shoule grinned with satisfaction. "I think he has," Shoule said. "To speak so freely to the Archpriest—were you trying to bring him into your conspiracy, Kadan?"

"There *is* no conspiracy!" Kadan shouted. "Or at least, if there is, I've no part in it!" He glanced up as the light changed; one of the larger moons, perhaps Barzuar's, was moving across the sun's face.

That reminded him that time was passing, the day going to waste.

"My lords," he said, "the army awaits my command. If you forbid me to accompany it alone, then I welcome your presence on our journey. If you forbid me to go at all, I question your authority to do so, unless this last mysterious figure you bring with you is Prince Granzer or the Empress herself, but I will postpone my own departure and go with you to the council chamber to have this matter out. In either case, I have orders to give—if you will excuse me . . ."

"No." The final horseman threw back his hood.

For a moment Kadan failed to recognize the face thus exposed; he had expected to see another Councillor. At last, though, the features registered.

The final horseman was Prince Graubris.

"Your Imperial Highness?" Kadan said.

"My mother is too ill to leave her chambers," Graubris said, "and my brother-in-law refuses to take the accusations against you seriously. Thus it fell to me to come here and ensure that you do not endanger the Empire."

"I have no *intention* of endangering the Empire!" Kadan shouted in reply.

"I wish we could believe that," Graubris said. "Alas, we cannot be sure.

Therefore, the army shall not march until we have settled the matter. The men who put down the riot must be questioned; if one of your soldiers carried the false message to Lord Niniam, he must be identified."

"But . . . but, Your Highness, we have almost half a million men here! Are you going to have Lord Niniam look at *all* of them, one by one, seeking to identify this messenger?"

"If that's what it takes," Graubris said.

Lord Kadan looked up at him despairingly, and saw blind determination. He turned his gaze to Apiris; the Archpriest refused to meet his eyes. Orbalir was only too glad to meet them and smile mockingly, and Shoule was positively gloating.

Kadan looked down at the map, and the letters of instruction to his subordinates, and the duty rosters and other forms that were not going to be needed right away after all.

"I hope you four know what you're doing," he said. "Very well; I'll postpone the departure. *Again.* And I'll go to the Imperial Palace and discuss this with the full Council." He looked up. "Unless you were planning to arrest me, and throw me in a dungeon somewhere?"

Shoule hesitated, and glanced up at Graubris.

"I must say, I would be impressed by the courage of anyone who dared to arrest me while surrounded by soldiers sworn to my service," Kadan added. He did not glance at the archway behind the horses, where four armed guards stood ready, nor at the doorway behind himself where half a dozen officers awaited his next command.

"That won't be necessary," Graubris said with a frown at Shoule. "If you'll accompany us back to Seidabar there need be no talk of arrest."

Apiris looked relieved, and Orbalir disappointed.

Ten minutes later five horsemen rode out of the Agabdal camps, up through the broad avenues toward Seidabar.

At that moment Prince Granzer emerged from his mother-in-law's chambers, striding heavily across the antechamber. He left the door open, and the sickroom stench of medicines and human waste wafted after him.

"Send in the rest of the doctors," he ordered the nearest attendant. "Her Imperial Majesty is unwell."

That was an understatement, as everyone present understood; Beretris was dying. How much longer she would last no one knew, but any hope for an actual recovery had faded away over the course of the winter.

Granzer stopped in the middle of the broad Dradieshnan carpet and stood for a moment, watching the servants and physicians as they hurried to attend the Empress. Then he turned to his own aide, Delbur.

"Where's Graubris?" he asked. "He should be here; I'm not sure, but this might be the end."

"He left the palace some time ago, with Lord Shoule," Delbur replied unhappily. "I believe they were bound for Agabdal."

"To see the army off?"

"Uh . . . I think they wished to speak to Lord Kadan."

Granzer stared at Delbur, his expression darkening.

"Lord Shoule," he said.

"I believe so."

"Was Orbalir with them?"

"And the Archpriest, yes."

"Apiris? *He's* involved, now?"

"Involved, Highness?"

Granzer didn't answer; instead he turned and strode quickly out of the room, almost running.

He found his way to the tower's central staircase and climbed rapidly up three flights, then threw open a door and stamped across a sitting room, startling his niece, Princess Derva, who had been curled up in a rocking chair, picking at half-finished embroidery.

Granzer marched to the window, which faced northwest, but remarked as he passed, "Your grandmother's worse. You might want to go see her."

"Oh." Derva took the hint; she put the embroidery aside and pushed herself up out of the chair—a task that took some doing, as she was half a year pregnant. She almost collided with Delbur by the sitting-room door; he stepped aside and let her pass, then followed his master inside.

"Highness?" he asked.

"They're still there," Granzer barked. "Look for yourself." He gestured at the window.

Delbur obediently looked out the window, unsure what he was supposed to see. "Who, Highness?"

"The army," Granzer growled. "They're still in Agabdal. They were supposed to leave today."

Delbur peered out through the age-distorted glass. They were near the top of the palace tower, the tallest structure in the Domdur heartland, and one of the few in Seidabar that gave a view over the walls; Delbur could see the rooftops of the Inner City, the black barrier of the city wall, and off in the distance, almost lost in smoke and haze, the jagged skyline of Agabdal. Beyond that, right on the horizon, a thin line of sea shone silver.

To the right of Agabdal's center he could make out the great military camps as a confusion of mud brown and dull yellow sprinkled with tiny specks of red— red tunics on the soldiers, red banners flying.

How Granzer could take one quick glance at that and determine that the army had not marched Delbur did not know, but he wasn't about to argue.

"I don't understand," he said.

"It's that idiot Shoule," Granzer said wearily. "He's finally convinced that Lord Niniam isn't a traitor, so now he thinks Lord Kadan and Lady Vamia are conspiring to overthrow the Empire."

"Lady Vamia?"

Granzer nodded. "Haven't you noticed that her explanation of her whereabouts keeps changing? I assume the truth is that she was trysting with someone else's husband, but she's not about to admit that. And she *was* the one who got Prince Zolous out of the palace."

"Oh," Delbur said. "Then you think . . ."

"*No*, I don't!" Granzer bellowed. "*Shoule* does. Shoule's seeing traitors everywhere. He's tied up half the city guards hunting for Olnamian spies—and now he's decided, with Orbalir's connivance, that Lord Kadan is in Rebiri Nazakri's pay—or perhaps the reverse—and that the Imperial Army's marching into a trap." He turned away from the window and began pacing angrily around the room. "It's nonsense. Lord Kadan's no more a traitor than I am, and the delay this will cause is unconscionable. The vanguard can't hold the enemy forever; they're outnumbered, they're fighting magic. . . ."

"But what if it *is* a trap?" Delbur asked.

"If it is, it's not Kadan's doing," Granzer replied. "But it *might* be one. And the Empress . . ." He sighed, and stopped pacing. He rubbed his temples wearily.

Delbur waited silently.

"I thought this was going to be a *good* day," Granzer said at last. "I thought the army would finally be on its way, and we'd be on our way to ending this crisis. I thought the Empress was resting well, and we would have time yet before Graubris had to worry about accepting the crown. I was looking forward to taking care of some old business, getting caught up, looking into the fire some more. And then Beretris started coughing over breakfast."

Delbur made a sympathetic noise.

Granzer sighed. "I'll need to talk to them," he said. "We all will. Convene the Council, Delbur. And you might mention . . ." A thought struck him. "Did anyone ever tell Lord Graush about that smith?"

"I don't know, Highness."

"Well, someone should. Graush is still looking for our divine champion, isn't he?"

"I believe so, Highness."

"Well, tell him to look at the armory, then."

Granzer marched out the door, headed for the stairs, with Delbur close on his heels.

CHAPTER 44

Malledd?" The shout was not up to the master's usual standards, and Malledd had barely heard it over the pounding of the apprentices' hammers, but he looked up from his forge without thinking.

He thought he had finally gotten the knack of swordsmithing; the trick was in tempering the edge, getting it hard but not brittle, and he was sure he was getting the feel of it. The blade he had just finished was, he thought, a good one—definitely worth keeping, at any rate, and he wanted to test it. He wished he could have pretended he hadn't heard his name, but the master had caught his eye, and he couldn't defy the master. He put down the blade and the polishing cloth and crossed the hall.

Last time the master had come in here shouting his name had been three triads ago, when Malledd had been hauled off to the Imperial Palace. He hoped this new summons wasn't the start of another interview with Prince Granzer.

In fact, as he neared the door, a thought struck him and he almost stumbled.

If it *was* Prince Granzer, and the Prince asked him again if he was the chosen of the gods, he could no longer truthfully say he didn't know. He couldn't explain why he was still in Seidabar when the champion's proper place was almost certainly out at the Grebiguata.

He didn't even *know* why he was still in Seidabar. The latest rumors said that the Imperial Army had been delayed again, and that the Council was now debating whether or not to send it at all, but people were dying out there fighting the nightwalkers. He knew that, and for the past few days it had been gnawing at him. Baranmel had not *told* him to go, but it was plain now that the Grebiguata was where the battle was being fought.

But right now he had more immediate concerns—an unfinished sword and the master's call.

"Yes, Master?" he asked when he was near enough to be heard without shouting.

"Malledd, I've been asked to send you to Lord Graush, for questioning," the master explained.

Malledd stared at him, momentarily puzzled. "Lord Graush?" he asked. He didn't place the name immediately.

Then he remembered. Lord Graush was the Councillor who had taken a particular interest in identifying and locating the divine champion. He had been studying the matter for years and was considered the greatest authority on the subject in Seidabar, perhaps in the world.

And if there was anyone it would be impossible to deceive, now that he *knew* he was the champion, it would surely be Lord Graush.

"Oh," he said.

"No mention was made of any great urgency," the master said. "However, I think that you had best present yourself at his palace within a day or two."

"Thank you, Master," Malledd said.

"That's all. If you need to leave . . ."

"No." Malledd shook his head. "You said there was no urgency."

"As you will, then. But don't forget—if they need to send me another message, you'll hear about it and not like what you hear." The master waved a dismissal, and Malledd turned, trying to think over the clamor of the apprentices' hammering and cursing. Ordinarily he could ignore the noise easily, but now his head seemed to ring with it, vibrating so that he couldn't hold a thought steady.

He made his way slowly back to the forge, turning the situation over in his mind.

Baranmel had told him that yes, he was the gods' chosen, protector of the Domdur. Baranmel had also hinted broadly that it had not been mere happenstance that Malledd was here in Seidabar, and that he had been involved with the fire at the Imperial Palace.

That fire had brought him to the attention of the Imperial Council. First Prince Granzer, and now Lord Graush, had wanted to speak to him—the Prince had asked him if he thought he was the divine champion, and Lord Graush would undoubtedly want to investigate the same possibility—after all, that was what he *did*, what he was, by all accounts, obsessed with.

Then did the gods want him to reveal himself? Should he take Dolkout's letter and present himself to Lord Graush, proclaiming that yes, he was the champion, and here was the proof?

Well, what would happen if he did? He tried to picture the scene, and couldn't quite manage it.

Would his divinely ordained role be trumpeted abroad? Would he be paraded through the streets as if he were some great protective amulet? Or would the Council prefer to keep his identity a secret, to be held in reserve until needed?

Would Lord Graush even believe him? There were no witnesses to his conversation with Baranmel; a hundred people could attest to the god's presence at Berai's wedding, but no one had heard anything that Baranmel had said to Malledd—Baranmel had seen to that. Had the gods wanted Malledd's identity widely known, wouldn't Baranmel have simply proclaimed it to everyone at the wedding? The letter from Dolkout might well be pronounced a forgery, and Vadeviya's corroborating testimony a lie. No one else in Seidabar would speak out for him if that happened. Oh, there were those who had guessed the truth, such as Darsmit, but they had no proof.

Perhaps Lord Graush had some way of knowing the true champion, though—some secret he had found in his studies. Suppose that Lord Graush was convinced, and the Council did accept him as the champion—what would they do with him? He wasn't a nobleman or a soldier; he was just a smith. They wouldn't exactly turn the army or the city over to him; from everything Malledd had heard about Lord Kadan during his stay in Seidabar, the Commissioner of the Army was not about to entrust any peasant, divine champion or no, with the defense of the capital.

And right now there were rumors that the rest of the Council wouldn't even trust *Lord Kadan* with that defense, let alone some outsider. What if the Council couldn't reach agreement on how to handle him? If the gods themselves couldn't agree on Malledd's role, how could he trust the Imperial Council to be of one mind? He might find himself enmeshed in their intrigues and conspiracies, mistrusted by the various factions, forbidden to take any action lest it shift the balance of power within the government.

That thought seemed strange to him—even after half a year in Seidabar, what did he really know of government intrigues? How had he thought of that?

Perhaps, he thought, in what he recognized as an equally alien inspiration, the notion was planted by Samardas. The god of wisdom could surely do such things.

He almost stumbled as he brushed against another apprentice's workbench; he was so lost in his own thoughts that he wasn't watching where he was going.

He didn't want to talk to Lord Graush, he realized. None of the possible outcomes appealed to him. He didn't want to tell lies to a Councillor. He didn't want to be openly identified as the champion, perhaps trotted out like a prize bull to impress the citizens of Seidabar. He didn't want to be involved with the nobility in any way, didn't want to be caught up in their feuds and follies.

But what else could he do? Lord Graush knew who he was, and where he was, and Lord Graush could call upon the entire Imperial Army to enforce his will, if he so chose. So long as he remained here in the armory, he could not avoid Lord Graush.

And where else in Seidabar could he go? He didn't know anyone outside the armory except Vadeviya and a handful of Darsmit's friends, and he wasn't about to try hiding in the Great Temple, with all those magicians, with all those people Vadeviya might have told about him, and he could hardly impose on any of Darsmit's people. . . .

He would have to leave Seidabar.

He reached his own station and stood for a moment, staring blindly at his hammer and at the hiltless blade he had made.

If he left Seidabar, where would he go?

Home, of course. He could go home to Grozerodz, to Anva and the children. He could go back to his own hearth and forget all about Seidabar and Baranmel and Rebiri Nazakri.

And if he did, Nazakri would reach the gates of Seidabar, and the Domdur Empire might well be destroyed, the world plunged into centuries of warfare and chaos.

He reached out for the hammer, closed his hand on it.

"Anva," he said. He swallowed hard and felt tears start in his eyes. "I'm sorry, Anva," he said, releasing the hammer and reaching for the sword.

There was somewhere else he could go, of course. Somewhere men were fighting and dying, waiting for him.

He looked up.

"Darsmit," he said. "I'm going to be going east tomorrow, to the Grebiguata, to join the Imperial vanguard. Care to join me?"

Darsmit turned, startled.

"You're what?" he said.

"I'm going east," Malledd repeated. "That fire at the Imperial Palace made Seidabar too hot for me. I thought I'd go cool my heels in the Grebiguata."

Darsmit stared at him.

"You're going to fight the rebels? You've heard the nightwalkers have been crossing the river, and there's been fighting?"

Malledd nodded. "I've heard. And I'd guess they need smiths there, to keep their swords sharpened and their helmets polished."

"But you haven't . . . I mean . . ."

Malledd had been smiling; now, suddenly, he wasn't.

"I haven't quite finished my apprenticeship, you mean," he said. "No, I haven't. And I'm not going to. There isn't time." As he spoke, he knew that was true. He didn't know *how* he knew . . .

But he could guess. This was presumably divine guidance at work—or divine interference, at any rate.

"The army's still in Agabdal," Darsmit pointed out. "You're going to go alone?"

"I'm better than nothing, which is what they have now," Malledd said. "I'm leaving first thing in the morning. You don't have to come; you're right, you should probably stay here and learn swordsmithing."

"I'm coming," Darsmit said.

"No, I . . ."

"I'm coming with you!" Darsmit insisted.

Malledd's smile reappeared. "I'd appreciate the company," he admitted.

"Then it's settled," Darsmit said. He looked around and spotted the master instructing one of the younger apprentices. "But if I'm going," Darsmit added, "I have a few calls to make first. Family matters. If anyone asks, I'm just making a stop out back." Then he slipped away quickly.

Malledd watched him go, then picked up the sword. It needed a hilt, and he hadn't yet learned how to make one properly, but he thought he could manage something. It would be a way to pass the rest of the day.

And he might need that sword before very long.

CHAPTER 45

They'll wear us away, little by little!" Lord Duzon shouted, flourishing his cloak with one hand and his hat with the other. "They killed Gomiugitar last night—he was the *last* of our magician priests, sir! Prince Bagar panicked and ran, and if he's not lost he's probably halfway back to Seidabar by now. We have to strike back, before they wear us *all* away!"

General Balinus winced at Duzon's bellowing; his head ached with exhaustion. He marveled that the well-meaning young fop had not yet lost either hat or cloak—though that confounded plume was gone, at any rate. At least for the moment; Balinus suspected the man had packed more.

"We can't," he said. "We can't get across the bridge and back to their camp and still be fit to fight before dark, not in our present shape. We'd lose any such battle, Duzon."

"We're losing our battles here, too!" Duzon insisted.

"I know we are," Balinus said. "This is just a holding action. We're only the vanguard, my lord—the Imperial Army has not yet arrived."

"So we're to let ourselves be slaughtered?"

"No, we'll fight, and we'll hold them, and we'll have reinforcements soon. But we don't have the force we need to cross the river by daylight and destroy them."

"We should *try*. . . ."

"No, we should not!" Balinus snapped, his voice suddenly stronger. He glared up at the younger man, then continued in a lower tone, "Listen, my lord, I know you mean well. I know you're brave and eager, and I likewise appreciate that you aren't a fool—you haven't said we should swim the river to get at them, or anything else idiotic. It's *possible* that if we struck now, we could destroy them—not likely, but possible.

"But what if we failed? Even if I were utterly certain we could defeat the living rebels—which I am not, by any means—what if the wizard were to find some way to hold us off until nightfall, and we found ourselves facing the entire force of nightwalkers? Their raids across the river have never committed all of them; you know that, you've seen their reserves standing on the other shore as clearly as I have—probably *more* clearly, with your younger eyes!"

Duzon admitted, "I've seen them. Some of them stand and watch us; others go down into that hole they've dug."

"Have you thought about why they're there, my lord, instead of attacking us?"

"I have heard it said that they draw strength from the earth, and the pit helps them in this. . . ."

"I meant why they haven't attacked, not why they dig," Balinus said wearily. "The ones who simply stand and watch, Duzon—why are they *there*, instead of over here fighting?"

"I can only guess . . ."

"Well, I've made a few guesses of my own, and while I may have no more wits than you, I do have greater experience. Remember that what the Nazakri wants is not to destroy *us*, but to destroy Seidabar—that's why he raised those corpses, why he's led them all the way across the plains from Matua. If he merely wanted to defy us he could sit safely in the fortresses at Pai Shin or Ai Varach and laugh at our attempts to pry him out."

"I know that," Lord Duzon said.

"Do you? Good. Then consider why he's held back much of his force. Those are the nightwalkers he intends to send against Seidabar. He's not committing them to the battles against us because he doesn't care to risk them. He's keeping them on his side of the river because there, they have *protection* during the day. They won't come across the Grebiguata until their living guardians do, and those guardians aren't going to come as long as we stand in their way. That's *my* guess."

"Um," Duzon said. "I had thought he meant to torment us with our own ineffectuality—to tease us by showing us that a mere fraction of his force was enough to defeat us."

Balinus shook his head. "That might be part of it," he said, "but I don't think it's the whole."

"Perhaps you're right," Duzon admitted. "But then isn't it all the more urgent that we cross the river and destroy the force he intends to use against Seidabar?"

"And let us return to my previous suggestion, my lord. Suppose we attempt this attack, and fail? Then what will the enemy do?"

"I don't . . ."

"He'll *march on Seidabar*, of course! Those nightwalkers will cross the river with their protectors, and there won't be anything between here and the Outer City to stop them."

"What about the rest of the army? And the city walls?"

"We don't know where the army is—with Gomiugitar dead we're out of touch with Seidabar until we can get another magician out here from Drievabor, or send one of the New Magicians back for news. We don't know what's happening there, or when the army will arrive—I assume they're on the road by now. We don't know the nightwalkers will *follow* the road, though. They might go around the army somehow, or *through* it, by night. And while I don't know what Nazakri has planned for dealing with the city walls, can you really think he hasn't prepared something?"

"No," Duzon admitted. "The walls of Seidabar are legendary."

"Exactly." Balinus sat back on his folding camp chair, which creaked under his weight. Duzon stood thoughtfully for a moment.

"Sir," he said at last.

"Yes, my lord?"

"You say we are holding Nazakri here until the main army arrives."

"Yes."

"And when the main body arrives, a portion will be left here to guard this section of the bank, while another will cross at the bridge?"

"That's certainly what I intend, but it will, of course, be up to Lord Kadan to assess the situation and make the final decisions."

"And the numbers will be such that the enemy will be totally crushed in a single day, and the nightwalkers then disposed of?"

"I would think so."

"So we're waiting for this, and holding our position until then."

"Yes."

"And the Nazakri, meanwhile, is raiding across the river each night, holding his main force in reserve but harassing us, striking at specific targets to demoralize us."

"Yes."

"But why does he bother? If he were to launch an all-out assault by night, with his living forces securely guarded by the nightwalkers while they made the crossing, couldn't he cut right through us and head for Seidabar?"

"Perhaps he could. That he has not done so would imply he doubts it."

"Or perhaps he's been testing us, and will try it tonight."

"It's possible," Balinus admitted.

"In which case, all of us might well be slaughtered."

"It's possible," Balinus repeated.

Duzon shuddered. This was not how he had pictured the campaign proceeding. Not even counting Prince Bagar and the other two deserters, the Company of Champions had already lost twenty-six horses and eleven men, including a duke's son—and six of the men had been dragged into the river and drowned. Those six would presumably be fighting for the enemy when next they were seen. For a triad the enemy had targeted priests, and had killed all four of the traditional magicians in the vanguard; another triad's raids had been directed against officers, killing five of the six colonels, leaving only Duzon, Balinus, and Daudenor's Zavai of the original eight commanders and forcing several rapid promotions. The Company of Champions, already singled out in one of the early raids, might again be the nightwalkers' next special target—or they might choose the New Magicians next, or some other element of the vanguard. Each Imperial soldier faced the possibility that the next raid might be aimed specifically at *him*.

That uncomfortable anticipation was certainly part of what the Olnamian wizard had intended.

The question was, what *else* did he intend?

"General," Duzon said, "surely Nazakri knows we expect reinforcements."

"Surely he does," Balinus agreed.

"Then why should he wait? The longer he waits, the better our position."

"Perhaps he simply isn't yet prepared to risk all on a single battle. Remember, if he is to succeed, he must get his nightwalkers *and* their protectors past us before dawn, and must leave us so reduced that we cannot counterattack. There will be no river protecting him if he once brings them across."

"But what can he gain by waiting? Nothing, surely!"

Balinus shrugged. "Then perhaps the final battle will come tonight," he said. "But I think he may prefer to wear us down for a few more nights first—after all, we tire, and the nightwalkers do not; we are weakened by wounds, and the nightwalkers are not."

Duzon considered that. It did make sense—but sooner or later, the rebels would have to strike across the river in full force. If they waited too long they were doomed; surely the Nazakri saw that.

Of course, doomed or not, the enemy might well wipe out the vanguard if the main body of the Imperial Army did not arrive soon.

"We need those reinforcements," Duzon said.

Balinus nodded. "I've sent messages by magicians new and old, requesting that they make all possible haste. Gomiugitar said yesterday . . ." Balinus paused and swallowed as he remembered that Gomiugitar was now a decapitated corpse. "He said he had done everything he could to emphasize the urgency. And Vrai Burrai left for Seidabar this morning, not an hour ago."

"Good," Duzon said.

"Get some sleep, my lord," Balinus said. "You'll need it."

Duzon could hardly argue with that; suddenly he was overcome with fatigue. He had, after all, fought all night. He saluted, then turned and staggered out of the tent.

The midmorning sunlight was almost blinding; he blinked, and squinted across the river.

There they were, the stacked corpses and their scruffy guards. If only there were some way to reach them without that thirty-mile march down to the bridge and back!

Perhaps there was, Duzon thought muzzily. Perhaps the New Magicians could find a way across the river . . .

But not today. Not when there would certainly be a battle tonight. They all needed to rest.

And tonight's battle might be another bloody skirmish, or it might be the all-out assault that was to begin the march on Seidabar. Duzon hoped it would only be a skirmish; he was in no hurry to die, and time was surely on the Empire's side.

But if Nazakri knew that, as he surely did, why would he wait? Balinus's explanation suddenly seemed inadequate. Duzon stopped at the flap of his own tent and stared across the river at Rebiri Nazakri's black pavilion.

What was the wizard *really* waiting for?

Duzon didn't know. He hated that, but he didn't know.

"Samardas, I could really use an oracle's counsel now," he muttered.

Then he ducked into his tent and fell onto his cot, where he was asleep in seconds.

CHAPTER 46

You know, I think this ramp is even more impressive from up here than it is from the bottom," Malledd remarked as he started down the slope.

Darsmit shrugged. "It's big," he agreed.

Ahead of them the gates towered on either side, framing a tall indigo slice of the western sky where three moons shone almost full. Below them lay the Outer City, much of it lost in darkness—the sun was still very low in the east, as they had made an early start, and the shadow of Seidabar itself lay across the streets and buildings at the foot of the immense ramp.

Beyond the Outer City, its taller buildings glittering in the distance, lay Agabdal, where the Imperial Army still lingered.

The day was already warm, but Malledd shivered. The scene before them seemed unnatural—the sky trapped vertically between the gates, the dark, almost empty streets, the broad highway sloping down steeply as if the entire world had tipped away and was trying to fling them off. Distant Agabdal seemed almost to be hanging in the sky, waiting to fall upon them when they reached the bottom.

And he was doing something that seemed very, very foolish. He was going off to fight a wizard and an army of the undead, and doing so in direct defiance of Lord Graush's will.

He was the chosen champion of the Domdur, appointed defender of Seidabar—he knew that, and could no longer deny it—but he was also still just Malledd of Grozerodz, son of Hmar, a journeyman smith who tried to mind his own business, a man with a wife and children waiting for him at home.

This vista before him, this tilted, shadowed world, made him very aware how small he was. Oh, perhaps he stood head and shoulders above most men, but compared to this city, or to all the wide world beyond, he was an insignificant speck. How could he expect to do anything truly important? Even with the gods' favor, he was just a mortal, a man caught up in matters far larger than himself.

"Malledd!"

Startled, Malledd stumbled and almost went tumbling down the ramp. He caught himself and turned to see who had shouted his name.

It hadn't been Darsmit; the voice was wrong. And it hadn't been the guards on the gates or the wall; they were still ahead, and the voice had come from behind. Had Lord Graush sent someone after him?

The figure coming swiftly down the ramp, waving a hand in the air, wore white; the sunlight spilling over the city walls and the dome of the Great Temple limned him in pale gold fire and hid his face in shadow, but Malledd knew who it was. He hadn't seen him for a dozen triads, but he still recognized that figure instantly.

"Vadeviya," he said. He stopped and waited for the hurrying priest to catch up.

"Who?" Darsmit asked as he, too, stopped and turned.

"The priest who came with me from Biekedau," Malledd explained. "He knows who I am; he was the one who talked me into leaving home." Then he called out, "If you're going to tell me I should stay in Seidabar, priest, you can save your breath."

Vadeviya slowed from a trot to a walk and called back, "Whether I argue with that depends on where you're going, and why."

"And what business is it of yours, in any case?" Malledd demanded as the priest drew near enough to make shouting unnecessary.

"Oh, I think that's obvious," Vadeviya answered. "I feel responsible for you—after all, it was my temple that was charged with your care."

"My *family* was charged with my care, old man, not your temple."

Vadeviya shrugged as he drew alongside the two smiths. "As you will," he said. "Nevertheless, I feel a certain responsibility where you're concerned."

"You needn't."

"But I do."

Malledd frowned, frustrated. "Where I go and what I do is between myself and the gods," he said.

"And are not priests the intermediaries between mortals and gods?"

"Not anymore," Malledd growled. "I think I've had more direct contact with gods than *you* have in the past sixteen years!"

Vadeviya shrugged. "Well, you could scarcely have had less," he acknowledged, "but I would say that none is no more than none."

"Malledd met a god just a couple of triads ago," Darsmit interrupted.

Vadeviya turned, startled. "*Did* he? Who?" The tone of sarcasm or doubt that might have been expected in reply to such a claim was utterly lacking; all three men knew that if anyone was likely to meet a god, Malledd was.

"Baranmel," Darsmit said. "At my sister's wedding."

Vadeviya peered down at Darsmit thoughtfully. "Ah," he said. "So that was your sister? Berai, wasn't it?"

It was Darsmit's turn to be startled; he nodded, and the priest turned back to Malledd. "And Baranmel spoke to you there?"

"Yes," Malledd admitted.

"The magicians didn't report that."

Malledd's brows lowered. "What magicians?" he growled.

Vadeviya smiled. "Oh, now, surely you didn't think it was merely coincidence that I caught you here before you left? The temple magicians have been spying on you, Malledd, ever since the day after the palace fire. It wasn't even my idea. You caught the attention of the Imperial Council, and Apiris was told to keep an eye on you."

"The Archpriest?" Malledd glanced up at the golden dome of the temple. "Watching me?"

Vadeviya nodded. "Well, at any rate his magicians are watching you," he said. "Or they're supposed to be. They observed the wedding from the Higher Realm, but didn't mention that you'd spoken to anyone there."

"Baranmel probably didn't want them to," Malledd said. "It's no one's business but ours."

The corner of Vadeviya's mouth twitched with amusement. " 'Ours'? Ah, you and Baranmel? Are you such fast friends now, then?"

Malledd made a noise of disgust and turned away. "Come on, Darsmit," he said, leading the way down the ramp, trudging steadily.

Vadeviya waited for a moment, expecting them to stop and turn for further conversation, then realized that Malledd had no intention of doing so. His smile vanished. "Wait!" he called, hurrying after them.

"No," Malledd said, without turning.

"Malledd, wait," Vadeviya insisted. "I can't run on this slope."

"Then go back to the temple," Malledd said, still not looking back. "I have no wish to speak with you further."

Darsmit glanced up at his companion. "Maybe we should hear him out," the smaller man said. "After all, he's a priest."

"He doesn't know anything," Malledd growled.

Darsmit glanced uneasily back at Vadeviya, who was gaining slowly—Malledd was matching his pace to Darsmit's shorter stride, which allowed the priest to better their speed. "Why are you so angry with him?" Darsmit asked. "He's just trying to be helpful."

"Helpful?" Malledd snorted. "Spying on me? Mocking me? That's helpful?"

"The magicians were ordered to spy on you by the Council, he said."

"Nobody ordered *him* to find out what the magicians saw," Malledd said, jerking a thumb over his shoulder at Vadeviya.

"Well, he was concerned," Darsmit said. "He knows who you are, doesn't he? Of course he takes an interest!"

"And mocks me to my face," Malledd retorted. "I don't need that sort of interest."

"What mockery?" Darsmit was genuinely puzzled.

"You and Baranmel, are you such fast friends now?" Malledd said, speaking through his nose in a vicious parody of Vadeviya's slightly nasal voice.

"That was nothing!" Darsmit protested.

Malledd stopped dead in his tracks and turned to face his companion.

"Listen, Darsmit," he said angrily. "You don't understand. Ba'el marked me *at birth. All my life*, since the day I was born with his claw's imprint on my face, I've had to live with people telling me that I have a special connection to the gods. My sisters hated me for it. My father was constantly telling me how un-important it was—I think he was jealous, and all he did was remind me that it was there, which made it *more* important. My playmates were all a little scared of me—maybe they would have been anyway, because of my size, but I was the *chosen of the gods*, on top of that. My mother-in-law is forever telling my wife not to anger me, lest the gods curse her. Even my wife is nervous about it sometimes; the only people in Grozerodz who ignore it completely are my own children, and that's only because we've never told them about it. All my life I've had this hanging over me, marking me, cutting me off from everyone around me!"

"Um," Darsmit said, leaning away from Malledd's fury.

"And what good does it do me?" Malledd demanded. "Do I really live with the gods' favor? No! Sometimes I thought I did, when life was especially good—when Anva agreed to marry me, and at our wedding, where, I would point out, my supposed friend Baranmel did *not* deign to dance, and again when our children were born. But those were just the ordinary blessings that anyone might have; I never saw any great benefit from this *destiny* I was given. Oh, I suppose I have miraculous strength and endurance—so what? How often does that matter? Does that make me a better smith, or bring me customers, or make my wife love me any better?"

Darsmit couldn't stop himself; he said, "Well, if you really don't tire, maybe she . . ."

"Shut up," Malledd told him coldly.

Darsmit shut up immediately.

Malledd glanced up and saw that Vadeviya had caught up to them and was standing nearby, listening.

"Come on," Malledd said. "I'm not done, but we have a long way to go. I'll talk as we walk."

Darsmit agreed, and the two of them continued down the ramp, through the open gate; the world opened out on either side, the Outer City covering most of it, as they passed beyond the walls.

Vadeviya followed close behind, studiously ignored by the two smiths.

Malledd continued, "I never got any good out of being the divine champion. Instead I have an obligation to go out and fight and maybe die for the sake of the Empire, and I'm expected to be a great leader, as well, if the occasion arises. But how? What do I know about fighting? I'm no soldier. What do I know about being a leader? I'm just a village smith, not a nobleman; I've never led anyone anywhere in my life."

"You did a fine job at the palace," Darsmit pointed out.

"That was all just using common sense," Malledd said dismissively.

"Maybe that's all you need," Darsmit suggested. "Nobody *else* seemed to have it."

"True enough," Malledd said. "That's a sad thought." For a moment the two of them walked in companionable silence, down the ramp to the level of the surrounding rooftops; then Malledd continued, "Anyway, it seems to me that this supposed gift I've been given is all price and no pleasure—and Baranmel certainly didn't disprove that. He tells me that Ba'el wants me dead, Seidabar cast down, and the Empire destroyed—so much for divine favor!"

"What?" Darsmit stumbled, and would have fallen if Malledd hadn't caught his arm. "Ba'el *what?*"

"That's right," Malledd said.

Darsmit gaped up at him. "But . . . but . . . but the gods *created* the Empire! They *chose* us!"

"And most of them still favor us," Malledd agreed. "But Ba'el is god of war, and for the past two hundred years the Domdur have brought peace. He hates us. He favors the Olnamian wizard and his rebels."

"But then . . . but you . . ." Darsmit stared around wildly, out at the city and then down the broad avenue that led to Agabdal. "But he's the god of *war*—doesn't the side he favors always win in battle?"

"I don't know," Malledd said, resuming their downward walk. "I don't think even Ba'el's favor can necessarily overcome *every* obstacle. I'm still the chosen champion, after all, still charged with the defense of the Empire, and Ba'el can't take that back. I intend to use what he and the others granted me to be an obstacle for the Nazakri, and while Ba'el is against us, most of the gods still favor us." He sighed bitterly. "Of course, even if Ba'el can't take his clawmark 'gift' back, maybe he can do other things."

"Like what?" Darsmit asked, walking alongside.

Malledd shrugged. "Baranmel didn't know, so I don't."

Darsmit glanced back at Vadeviya, who was following close behind and had obviously been listening with intense interest. "And you still don't want anything to do with priests?" he asked Malledd.

"It's not priests I mind," Malledd said. "I just don't want anything to do with anyone who thinks that being noticed by the gods is something to be *pleased* about."

"Oh," Darsmit said. He saw the shame on Vadeviya's face, but then turned his own gaze resolutely forward. "I understand," he said.

CHAPTER 47

Vadeviya followed the two smiths with amazing tenacity. He was able to keep up only because Darsmit was there; Malledd alone, as big and tireless as he was, could easily have left him far behind, but Darsmit's legs were short and his endurance unexceptional, allowing the priest to stay close as the three men wove their way through the mazelike streets of the Outer City and onto the Gogror Highway.

He didn't speak, didn't try to intrude; he simply followed silently.

At suppertime, as Darsmit and Malledd stepped into the common room of an inn in a village whose name they didn't know, Darsmit asked, "Are you planning to try to slip away tonight, and leave the priest behind?"

Malledd glanced back at the old man, his white robe now filthy with the dust of the road. "No," he said. He had, in truth, been feeling ashamed of himself for several miles now. "Care to join us at table?" he called to Vadeviya.

"If you'll have me," the priest replied.

Malledd's answer was to hold the door open for the old man.

Their meal was not a jolly one; Darsmit and Vadeviya were both exhausted, and each wary of the other, while Malledd was lost in his own thoughts, contributing only grunts and monosyllables to what little conversation there was. The food offered was not particularly encouraging, either—the bread was coarse and almost tasteless, the stewed mutton tough and gristly, the lentils and carrots overcooked.

The beer, however, was excellent—dark and thick and strong. Malledd finished off a quart, and had started a third pint when he suddenly said, "Why did you come?"

Darsmit and Vadeviya both looked at him, startled, unsure at first who the champion was addressing.

"I mean you," he said, jerking his head toward Vadeviya. "After I left you there at the gates, why did you follow us?"

The priest hesitated, and then answered, "I had to."

"Why?"

"Well, for one thing, I've wronged you, Malledd, and I owe you something in return. I can't hope to pay my debt sitting in the Great Temple."

Malledd waved a hand in dismissal. "It was just a little joke. You didn't need to go to such lengths."

"I didn't only mean my mockery at the gates," Vadeviya said. "I meant everything I've done—visiting your forge, talking you into leaving your home and family, driving you to accept the gods' will when I didn't even know what it was."

"You were doing your job," Malledd said gruffly, before gulping more beer.

"No," Vadeviya said. "I wasn't. Not really. Years ago, Malledd, the Archpriest sent a message asking for any information any priest might have about the identity or whereabouts of the divine champion. I not only didn't reply myself, I made sure that no one at the temple in Biekedau did. I pretended I did it because you had asked us not to tell anyone—but then I convinced you to go to Seidabar, and I went with you, so that I could present you to the Archpriest myself. I acted as if I *owned* you, Malledd, as if you, the chosen of the gods, were my own special property, not to be shared with anyone else unless *I* could present you in person."

"Ah," Malledd said, lifting his mug for a final draft. "And you followed us today to keep an eye on your belongings?"

Vadeviya flushed. "Yes," he said.

Malledd stopped his mug in midair and stared past it at the priest. "Really?" he asked. "I thought I was joking."

"Really," Vadeviya said. "I am ashamed to admit it, but that is, indeed, one reason I followed you. It's hard to give up a habit, even when one knows it to be evil."

Malledd's mouth quirked. "I'm a habit?"

"An *evil* habit," Darsmit pointed out mischievously.

"No," Vadeviya said quickly, aware that Malledd was feeling the effects of the alcohol he had consumed. The big smith had a temper, one he usually kept tightly leashed—but alcohol might loosen that leash. "*Harassing* you is an evil habit, but one I can't entirely abandon. Yet."

"Ah." Malledd finished off his beer, wiped his mouth, then looked at Vadeviya's face. "Is there more?"

"In a way," the priest said. "Haven't you wondered *why* I should be so concerned with you?"

"I assumed you wanted to make sure that the champion will do his part for the Empire," Malledd said.

Vadeviya shook his head. "It was more than that," he said. "I wanted to *be* the champion. Why do you think I became a priest? Because the gods have *power*, Malledd, and I wanted a taste of that power—but among mortals, only the defender of the Domdur is granted a portion of that divine power."

Malledd snorted. "Divine power—ha! You can have it."

"No, I can't," Vadeviya said somberly. "I tried—I tried to coerce you, control you, direct you. I wanted to be able to tell myself that it was *I* who saved the Empire, by bringing the champion to Seidabar."

"Perhaps it was, then."

Vadeviya shook his head. "No," he said. "You chose for yourself—or perhaps the gods guided you. Baranmel spoke to *you*, not to me."

Malledd blinked, considering that.

"I was jealous of you, you know," Vadeviya said. "I imagined you reveling in the gods' favor, assured of your own blessedness—I thought you demanded anonymity because you felt yourself above the petty concerns of lesser mortals, too mighty to be bothered by anything but the direst of threats to the Empire. And then this morning, when you spoke of how worthless the gift has been to you, I knew you were speaking the truth, opening your heart, and I felt utterly ashamed of myself. I had thought you this arrogant beast, when in truth you were just struggling to lead an ordinary life. I couldn't let you just walk away; I had to make up for wronging you in my thoughts all these years."

"Um," Malledd said, staring at the priest. That quickly grew uncomfortable, and he looked down at his empty mug, as if preparing to order another. He wasn't thirsty anymore, however, and another pint, he suddenly felt, wouldn't *fit*.

At least, not unless he made room for it. The discomfort he was experiencing wasn't entirely in his heart; some of it was in his bladder.

"Excuse me," he said. He pushed back his chair and arose.

Darsmit and Vadeviya watched him make his way out the back of the inn, toward the latrine; then the little smith asked, "So, now that you've unburdened your soul, will you head back to Seidabar? Or to Biekedau?"

"I've come this far," Vadeviya said, "I might as well go on."

"Really? To the battlefront?"

The priest nodded.

"Won't that be dangerous?"

"Quite possibly," Vadeviya acknowledged. "But as I said, it's a habit—and having come this far, I'd like a chance to see the champion in action. I missed his appearance at the palace fire, you know."

"He was magnificent there," Darsmit said. "Truly magnificent."

"So I heard. I'd like to see for myself."

Darsmit nodded. "And I want to see it again. There's something about him when he's . . . when he's being the champion."

"He's godlike?"

Darsmit shook his head. "No," he said. "No, I saw Baranmel at the wedding, and that was different. Baranmel is a *god*, and you can't forget it for an instant when you're in his presence; he squeezes out everything else, and you're constantly aware of him and what he wants, and whatever he wants, you want, too. What he's doing, you want to do. Malledd's not like that; Malledd's not overpowering or awesome, he's *inspiring*. He's what a *man* can be. He makes you more aware of *yourself*, and what you can do, and what *you* want. You want to be *like* him, not to do what he wants. And you want to do it yourself, not to have him do anything."

"I really do want to see that," Vadeviya said.

"Well, you probably will," Darsmit said. "If you don't get killed first."

Vadeviya lifted his own beer. "Here's to not getting killed first, then," he said. The two of them drank the toast together.

That night the three men shared a room—Vadeviya and Darsmit crammed themselves together on the narrow bed, while Malledd settled for a blanket on the floor. In the morning they ate a hasty and rather stale breakfast, then headed east while the sun was not yet clear of the horizon.

On the way the three of them spoke at length of the events of recent days. Vadeviya, through his contacts in the Great Temple, was able to tell the two smiths a great deal about the upsets and concerns in the Imperial Council—though some of the gossip seemed contradictory. Lord Shoule seemed to be suspicious of the Great Temple and its occupants, even while he tried to gain their cooperation in his investigations.

"Maybe he's hoping you'll stumble over your own collective feet and let him in on your treachery," Malledd suggested.

"Maybe," Vadeviya said, unconvinced.

By the end of the day Malledd was somewhat impatient with his companions' need for rest, and almost refused to stop at the inn the other two chose. At last, when both Darsmit and Vadeviya refused to take another step, he gave in.

This inn was less crowded than the last, and as they finished their supper the innkeeper took the time to ask them, "Have you come from Seidabar?"

The three admitted that they had, indeed, come from the capital.

"Most people are going the other way now," the innkeeper said. "Even the ones who went east to sell supplies to the soldiers are going back, now that the fighting's getting bad."

Malledd made a noncommittal noise.

"If you're planning to sell anything, you'll probably find a good market, not much competition."

"We're not selling anything," Darsmit said. He glanced at Malledd. "Though maybe we should."

Malledd glowered at the little smith.

"Will the army be coming soon?" the innkeeper asked anxiously. "From what I hear the vanguard has been suffering heavy losses."

"We don't know anything about it," Malledd growled.

"Perhaps we should," Vadeviya suggested. "What have you heard, landlord?"

"Well, the people heading west have told me that the nightwalkers have been wearing the vanguard down, and they haven't the strength to counterattack. They're waiting for Lord Kadan to come with reinforcements. I thought perhaps you'd heard something about when he might be expected."

"I'm afraid not," Vadeviya said.

"The Lord Commissioner of the Army doesn't generally confide his plans to ordinary smiths," Darsmit remarked.

"Well, I hope he comes soon," the innkeeper said, taking a step back. "I don't want those nightwalkers coming *here*. I tell you, I'm not sleeping well these days, thinking I hear them moving about out there."

Vadeviya said something sympathetic, but Malledd wasn't listening anymore. The innkeeper's words had settled into his brain and jarred old memories loose.

Nightwalkers. He was on his way to fight nightwalkers.

He remembered the stories Seguna had told him when he was a boy, the nightmare stories of beloved, peaceful people coming back from the dead and slaughtering their friends and family, of rotting corpses that refused to lie down, of unspeakable *things* digging their way out of graveyards and attacking innocents with teeth and nails and bare bones, garroting children with hanks of their own dead mother's hair.

He was on his way to *fight* these things, with nothing but a sword he'd made himself and barely knew how to use. He shuddered.

And he'd seen no sign that Lord Kadan was about to march the Imperial Army anywhere. According to the gossip back in Seidabar, Lord Kadan seemed more concerned right now with spies and traitors and accusations than with the fighting at the Grebiguata.

Lord Kadan, as a soldier, almost certainly considered Ba'el his patron deity, Malledd realized. Could Ba'el really be guiding him? Could Lord Kadan, perhaps unknowingly, be working for Seidabar's destruction? Might he himself be the traitor on the Imperial Council? From what Vadeviya had overheard, Lord Shoule and Apiris had discussed the possibility and not dismissed it.

What if Lord Kadan left the vanguard to die, and Malledd with it?

Well, then Malledd would die, he told himself, shaking off his momentary fear. He had come this far, and he had the silent support of *most* of the gods. He could die anywhere, anytime, if his luck was bad enough.

"Bring me another ale, would you?" Malledd said. "No point in going to bed thirsty."

"Or leaving beer for the nightwalkers," Darsmit joked.

No one laughed.

At the third night's inn they were the only customers in the place, and the food was almost inedible.

On the fourth night the only inn they found was locked and barred; a farmer saw them standing baffled at the door and called to them, inviting them to take shelter in his barn—for a modest fee, of course.

Malledd found himself glad to have Vadeviya along; the priest had brought money, and Malledd's own funds were exhausted.

On the fifth day they saw two New Magicians flying over, from east to west. The three men paused and stood watching as the glowing figures soared overhead.

"Fleeing, do you think?" Vadeviya asked.

"Or just carrying messages," Darsmit suggested.

"They have *real* magicians for that," Vadeviya protested.

"Old magicians, you mean," Malledd said mildly.

"I mean properly trained priests," Vadeviya insisted. "Not a bunch of glass-blowers playing with things they don't understand."

"Maybe the messages weren't getting through that way," Darsmit said.

"Why wouldn't they?" Vadeviya demanded.

"Perhaps they're dead," Malledd suggested.

Vadeviya glanced at him sharply, then upward to the west again, to where the pair of golden specks were dwindling in the distance. "More likely those two just lost their nerve and fled," he muttered.

The inn they found that night stood open, empty, and deserted; this time there was no nearby farmer to help them out. They took shelter at the inn, scavenging through the cellars and cupboards for their provender and finding nothing but hard cheese and wine that was little better than vinegar.

The following night found them at an inn that was still occupied, though every door was barred and every window shuttered, with iron spikes driven into the frames and flowers twined about them. The innkeeper inspected them carefully before admitting them, and insisted on putting her ear to each man's chest to hear a heartbeat before she would allow them to stay.

"I've never met a nightwalker," the landlady said, "and I don't want to."

"But you aren't leaving?" Malledd asked.

"Where would I go?" she replied. "This is my home, and I'm too old to travel. Besides, I'll be safe. The gods will protect me; I'm a faithful subject of the Empire and three-fourths Domdur by blood."

"Have you heard anything about the fighting at the river?" Vadeviya asked.

She shook her head. "I haven't spoken to a living soul for the past five days now—until you three arrived. I haven't heard a word." She sighed. "I hope the champion's turned up by now."

Darsmit and Vadeviya glanced at Malledd, but said nothing; it was Malledd who asked, "You don't think the champion was with the soldiers?"

"Oh, maybe. I don't know. The officers came in here once, you know, but they didn't say anything about the champion, and if he were there, wouldn't they have been talking about him?"

"Maybe," Malledd agreed.

On the seventh day they saw two more New Magicians flying westward—and later, a different pair flying east.

"*Something*'s going on," Malledd muttered.

"At least that means the vanguard is still there," Vadeviya pointed out.

"Somewhere," Malledd agreed.

They found no inn that night, but stayed in an abandoned farmhouse, foraging in the kitchen garden and making a meal of underripe vegetables.

And around midmorning on the eighth day they crested a low rise and came within sight of Drievabor. At first they kept on walking, but as they drew nearer they slowed, and at last stopped, staring.

"That *must* be the Grebiguata," Darsmit said. "There aren't any other rivers that size around here."

"So that must be Drievabor," Vadeviya agreed.

"It's so small," Darsmit said.

Malledd glanced at him. "Small?"

The town ahead was not small at all; it was many times larger than Grozerodz, perhaps on a par with Biekedau. Of course, it was nothing compared to Seidabar or Agabdal. . . .

And it appeared deserted. The streets were empty; nothing moved anywhere. No smoke rose from the chimneys. That was why they had stopped; deserted inns and farmhouses were one thing, an entire deserted *town* quite another.

Malledd stared past the town at the broad water, glittering silver-blue in the morning sun wherever the brown brick homes and granaries did not hide it, stretching across the whole width of the world before them. Three buildings rose above the rest ahead of them—the dome of a temple, a balconied upper story, and a watchtower.

"We should go *there*," Malledd said, pointing at the tower. "There should still be someone there, shouldn't there? Guards or someone?"

"I would think so," Vadeviya agreed.

"Come on, then," Darsmit said, and the three marched on down the slope, through the archway and onto the paved streets of Drievabor.

The empty streets were unsettling. There were no armies clashing here, no nightwalkers committing atrocities—just empty buildings and deserted countryside, bisected by the river.

They came at last to a plaza at the western end of the bridge. The guard tower stood on the riverbank, beside the stone pillars and wooden arch of the bridge itself; the domed temple was just to the south, the other large building to the north.

No one was in sight. Malledd shouted up at the tower windows, then pounded on the door, but no one replied.

"Where is everyone?" Malledd asked. "Shouldn't there be guards? Could the rebels have gotten past us somehow, and be headed for Seidabar?"

"Perhaps the vanguard has crossed the river and driven them back east," Vadeviya suggested.

"I don't see any signs of a battle," Darsmit pointed out.

Malledd had wandered around the base of the tower to look across the river to the east; now he held up a hand to shade his eyes and stared for a moment, then said, "I do. Look." He pointed.

"Look at what?" Darsmit asked, puzzled.

"That," Vadeviya said, following Malledd's lead. "In the water, caught against the bridge."

Darsmit stared and made out a black lump. "What is it?" he asked.

"A body," Malledd said. "Floating on the current until it snagged there. They must be upstream." He studied the patterns of light on the water, then turned left, toward the north.

They had gone scarcely a hundred feet from the plaza when they spotted the sentry on the balcony overlooking the river; he had been invisible from the west, but Darsmit happened to glance up just as the sentry leaned on the railing at the southeast corner. "Look!" he called.

The others looked, and saw the soldier, in his red tunic and with a horn slung across his chest.

Perhaps more importantly, the soldier turned and saw them.

CHAPTER 48

Malledd looked about uneasily as he and his companions followed a sentry through the gate in the earthen wall and into the camp. They had left Drievabor the afternoon before, slept in an abandoned farmstead ten miles to the north of town, and arisen at dawn to cover the final five or six miles to the vanguard's encampment.

The place looked almost deserted; tents flapped noisily in the warm breeze, and the muddy paths between them were empty. They could hear distant voices, and a dull thumping, and a tower of smoke rose from somewhere ahead of them, but the camp itself was lifeless. No cookfires burned, no soldiers idled. The only living people the new arrivals had seen were three sentries—the one who had brought them from Lady Karmaran te-Drieva's manse in Drievabor, and two others they had met on the way in, one of whom now guided them.

The enemy's camp, across the river, was visibly more active—Malledd could see people strolling about, going about their business, apparently undisturbed by the proximity of their foes. He had a moment's uneasiness as the possibility occurred to him that the Imperial vanguard had been entirely destroyed and both camps were now rebel strongholds, despite the sentries' dusty red-and-gold uniforms and traditional horns.

The soldier who had escorted them on their long hike from Drievabor had turned them over to one of the sentries, then turned and headed back south while their new guide had led them on down the riverbank into the camp. Now he stopped in front of a tent and called, "Lord Duzon?"

Malledd recognized the name instantly, and blinked in surprise. He straightened up. It seemed he was about to meet one of the foremost false claimants to the title of divine champion; he smiled in ironic amusement.

Lord Duzon was welcome to the title, as far as Malledd was concerned.

"I thought General Balinus was in command here," Darsmit said.

"He is," the sentry replied. "And Colonel Zavai is second, but they're both asleep; Lord Duzon is the officer of the watch right now."

"Is *everybody* asleep?" Vadeviya asked.

The sentry didn't answer; instead he called, "My lord?"

The tent's flap opened and a head thrust out—a handsome, dark-haired head that despite some dishevelment was unmistakably that of an aristocrat. He started to say something to the sentry, then spotted the three new arrivals and instead asked, "Who are these?"

"Strangers, sir," the sentry said. "Poz just brought them from Drievabor. They just came walking down the road into town yesterday. These two claim to be armorers sent from Seidabar; Poz said the priest didn't explain himself."

Lord Duzon stepped out of the tent. He wore the red tunic and gold insignia of an Imperial captain, somewhat the worse for wear, and bore a sword on his belt. His hair had obviously been trimmed and curled some time ago, and left untended more recently. He was almost a head taller than Darsmit, slightly taller than Vadeviya, and the top of his head came to the level of Malledd's nose.

He looked the three newcomers over from temple to toe, giving the oversized Malledd particular attention, then told the sentry, "Anyone Lord Kadan sent would have papers, and probably an escort. Did they?"

"No, sir," the sentry admitted.

"Then is there any reason to believe them?" Duzon demanded. "How do we know the Nazakri hasn't decided to send a few spies to take a closer look at us?"

"Well, he's a priest, sir," the sentry said hesitantly.

"He's an old man in a white robe," Duzon answered. "We don't know he's a priest."

"Poz said they came down the road from the west, not across the bridge."

"Poz can be fooled. They could have circled around."

Malledd spoke up. "Lord Kadan didn't send us," he said. "We came on our own. We were apprenticed at the Imperial Armory, but we thought we'd be more use here."

Duzon looked up and met Malledd's gaze for a moment, then asked, "And the priest?"

Malledd shrugged. "He can speak for himself."

Duzon turned to Vadeviya. "Well?" he demanded.

"Thank you *so* much, Malledd," Vadeviya said. "My lord, I am indeed a priest, from the temple in Biekedau. I came because I believed the gods wished me to come." He grimaced. "Some of them, anyway."

"Biekedau—perhaps we can test that," Duzon said thoughtfully. "Gars, who's awake from the Biekedau Regiment?"

"I don't know, sir," the sentry said unhappily.

"It wouldn't prove anything if they don't know me," Vadeviya said. "I was a temple scholar; most of the ordinary citizens wouldn't know me."

"You have some men from Grozerodz, don't you?" Malledd said. "They'd know *me*."

"Grozerodz?" Duzon eyed Malledd with renewed interest. "Name them."

"There were six or seven, I think—Onnell, and Timuan, and Bousian, and Ozerga, and Orzin . . ." He frowned, trying to remember whether Nedduel had gone.

"I know Onnell," Duzon said. "If he'll attest to your identity, I'll believe you." He smiled. "They grow them *big* in Grozerodz, don't they? I thought *Onnell* was big."

"He is," Malledd said. "I'm just bigger."

Duzon chuckled. "Indeed," he said. Then a thought struck him; his smile vanished, and he cast a sideways glance at Malledd.

Malledd noticed this, and waited, dreading the inevitable question—"What did you say your name was?" Onnell must have told this Lord Duzon who Malledd was. If the two knew each other, and Duzon claimed to be the divine champion, that was hardly surprising.

The question didn't come. Instead Duzon turned away and ordered, "Wake up Onnell and bring him here."

"Yes, my lord," the sentry replied; he turned and hurried away.

"He's asleep?" Darsmit asked.

"*Everyone's* asleep," Duzon answered. "We're fighting nightwalkers, remember? Fight all night, sleep all day—that's been our schedule for some time now."

"Um," Malledd said.

"Poz didn't tell you?"

"Poz was the guard who brought us from Drievabor?" Malledd asked. "He didn't even tell us his *name*."

"Indeed," Duzon said. "But you're here."

Malledd nodded. "He took us to see someone who claimed to be Lady Karmaran te-Drieva's housekeeper. When we said we'd come to help against the rebels, she sent us here, with him as our escort."

"And how are matters in Drievabor? We've had no word in triads."

Malledd hesitated, and glanced at the others.

"We don't know," Darsmit said. "The guard and the housekeeper were the only living people we saw. She said Lady Karmaran was asleep—and everyone else, too."

"We weren't sure there really *was* anyone else," Malledd remarked.

"Oh, there are still people there—or at least there *were*," Duzon said. He frowned thoughtfully. "Some ran, of course, but there were still plenty. So they're on a nocturnal schedule, too? Maybe they've had nightwalkers raiding. We'll want to send someone to check on that." For a moment he sat, thinking, and the three newcomers waited silently. Finally, Malledd cleared his throat.

"Ah," Duzon said, looking up. "Sorry. So you've come to help?"

"Yes," Malledd said.

"We can use all the help we can get, so I hope you three are who you claim to be." Duzon frowned. "You wouldn't happen to have heard any rumors about just when Lord Kadan intends to send reinforcements, would you?"

"No," Malledd said. He glanced at Darsmit.

"Nothing helpful," the little man said. He glanced at Vadeviya.

"I'm afraid not," the priest said. "There were *rumors*, of course, but nothing one could trust about exactly when. The stories contradicted each other."

Duzon sighed.

"We're eager to help," Malledd said. "Is there a forge in operation for your armorers?"

Duzon let out a harsh bark of laughter. "No," he said. "We've no forge, nor armorer, nor any use for one. Our only armorer was killed three days ago."

"Then we'll have to build . . ." Malledd began.

Darsmit put a hand on Malledd's arm, silencing him, and asked, "What do you mean, no use for one?"

"We take our weapons from the dead," Duzon explained. "We have no time to spare for forging new blades when the riverbanks are strewn with old ones. After all, our numbers aren't increasing."

"But you said you could use our help," Malledd said.

"Of course—as soldiers," Duzon explained. "We need anyone who can *swing* a sword, not men who can make them."

"We're not soldiers," Malledd protested. "We're swordsmiths."

"Stay until sunset," Duzon said, "and take a look at our troops. Most of *them* aren't soldiers, either. We have a few real soldiers, but most of our men are half-trained farm boys, and we've made up our losses with cooks and camp followers and conscriptees—we've called in every man in the area who hasn't run west. And not just men—we've recruited some of the wives and daughters, too. Hell, we've given bows and swords to the stronger whores who followed us up from Drievabor!"

Malledd was about to protest when he heard someone call his name. He turned, startled, to see Onnell approaching.

"At last!" Onnell shouted, striding up. "At last you're here, Malledd! I knew you'd come!" He flung his arms around Malledd, embracing him—and catching him completely off guard; Malledd could do nothing but stare in astonishment.

"Then you do know him," Lord Duzon remarked sardonically. "At least, I haven't seen you hugging any other strangers."

"Of course I know him," Onnell said, releasing Malledd. "This is Malledd, son of Hmar, one of the two blacksmiths in Grozerodz."

"And these others with him?" Duzon asked, gesturing.

Onnell glanced at Darsmit, then at Vadeviya, then shook his head. "I've never seen them before," he said. "If Malledd says they're trustworthy, though, then they're trustworthy."

"You seem to put great faith in an ordinary smith," Duzon commented.

Onnell stammered and Malledd almost thought he was going to blush. "I've known Malledd since we were children," he said. "He's a good man. I'd trust him with my life."

"You may well be doing exactly that tonight," Duzon said.

"And I'll do it gladly," Onnell said. "Malledd, it's been looking bad for us—they're wearing us down, and all we've been able to do is hold out and wait for reinforcements that haven't come. But now *you're* here!"

"I'm just one man," Malledd muttered unhappily. Onnell wasn't coming out and proclaiming Malledd the chosen champion, but he was doing just about everything short of that—and how could Malledd hope to live up to such expectations? Despite his divine gifts he was just a man, not even a real soldier.

"One man?" Darsmit protested. "One of three, rather."

"Um," Malledd said.

He stepped back to make room for his companions, but before he could speak to make introductions Darsmit stepped forward and said, "I'm Darsmit." The little smith held out a hand for Onnell to clasp. "This is Vadeviya, from Biekedau."

"I'm honored to meet you," Onnell said, taking the hand.

This seemed like an excellent opportunity to divert the discussion away from himself; Malledd asked, "What about Timuan? Is he here?"

Onnell's face fell.

"Timuan is dead," he said. "We don't know exactly how it happened, but we found him among the slain the night before last, and beheaded him."

Malledd blinked in surprise. "Beheaded?"

Onnell nodded. "It's necessary," he said. "If the head is left attached to the body the spirits can turn the corpse into a nightwalker. Cold iron and flowers won't keep them out, not with Rebiri Nazakri guiding them, but a nightwalker needs both heart and brain."

Malledd stared at Onnell's calm, grim face. This was his old compatriot, the rowdy troublemaker who never meant anyone any harm, talking about nightwalkers and corpses as if they were his everyday fare—and here, they presumably *were* his everyday fare.

What had Malledd let himself be talked into? He should be home with his family, or back in Seidabar making swords, not here in this forlorn sleeping camp.

Darsmit shuddered. "So there really are nightwalkers?"

Onnell nodded. "About eight thousand of them by our latest count, and so far as we know we're all that stands between them and Seidabar."

"You are," Malledd said. "The countryside is largely deserted. The army was still in Agabdal when we left." He hesitated, then asked, "Timuan is really dead?"

"Blast," Duzon muttered. "Still in Agabdal?"

"Yes, he's dead," Onnell said unhappily. "So is Ozerga. Orzin lost a leg—an ax hacked his thigh open, and there was no way to save it. He may live, but we don't know for sure yet; he was feverish and sick last I saw. Bousian got a slash across the face that may cost him an eye, but he's otherwise still fit. Nesalas deserted—we haven't heard anything since he left, so we don't know whether he got home safely or got ambushed somewhere. Delazin and I are still fine— or as fine as anyone can be here, fighting those things night after night."

"It's bad?" Malledd asked.

"Very bad," Onnell confirmed.

"I told you we needed men more than swords," Duzon said wearily.

Darsmit looked up at Malledd. "Are we going to stay? Maybe we should go back to Seidabar . . . ?"

Malledd shook his head. "You know better than that. *I* can't go back. If you want to, I won't stop you."

Darsmit hesitated. "Maybe I could get in to see Lord Kadan, tell him how bad it is. . . ."

"He knows," Vadeviya said.

"We've been sending messengers," Lord Duzon said. "New Magicians."

"We saw them," Darsmit said. "When we were traveling."

"And you've used the magician priests," Vadeviya said.

"When we still had them," Duzon agreed. "They're all dead now. I suppose it happened while you were on the road. We'd hoped to get more from Drievabor, but the high priest there won't send anyone."

Vadeviya made a strangled noise. Darsmit looked uneasily from Malledd to Vadeviya and back, but said nothing.

Malledd studied Onnell's face, then glanced at Duzon.

He had known all along that he was going into danger; was he going to give up now? He had come this far to carry out his duty to the Empire; why should he turn back? He had known all along that the gods hadn't appointed him to be their chosen swordsmith; the champion's job was to fight, not equip others.

"I'm staying," Malledd said. "And fighting."

"As am I," said Vadeviya immediately.

Darsmit sighed. "This wasn't what I planned," he said. "I thought I'd be making swords, not fighting."

"You can go, if you like," Duzon said. "We don't ask anyone to stay whose heart isn't in it—those are the ones the nightwalkers kill."

Darsmit swallowed. "No," he said. "If Malledd stays to fight, so do I."

"And Malledd's staying," Onnell said. "Then we'll need to find weapons and armor for all of you. Come on." He beckoned, and started to lead the three new arrivals away.

"Wait," Lord Duzon said.

Onnell stopped dead, turned back, and bowed. "My apologies, my lord. I thought we were dismissed."

Duzon hesitated, looking from Onnell to Malledd and back. Malledd watched the nobleman's face; Duzon was clearly debating with himself about what, if anything, he was going to say.

Malledd thought he could guess what the captain was considering. He waited.

"Onnell," Lord Duzon said at last, "you say this man Malledd is a black-smith?"

"That's right," Onnell said quickly. "Our village smith. One of them, any-way—his father's the other."

"And is he, perhaps, anything *more* than an ordinary smith?"

Onnell hesitated, glanced at Malledd, then said, "If he is, I'm not the one to ask, my lord."

Duzon studied Onnell thoughtfully for a moment, but Onnell didn't flinch; he stood calmly, waiting. Malledd smiled to himself; Onnell had kept his promise after all.

"Go," Duzon said, waving at Onnell. "All of you—except Malledd." He turned to the big smith. "If you would step into my tent for a moment, Malledd, that we might have a word in private, I'd be in your debt." He lifted the tent flap.

For a few seconds the six men—Duzon, Malledd, Onnell, Darsmit, Vadeviya, and Gars the sentry—stood motionless. Then Malledd shrugged; if he was going to be a soldier he'd have to follow orders.

"As you wish, my lord," he said. He ducked down, bending almost double to get into the tent.

Duzon followed him. The other four hesitated a moment longer, then drifted away.

CHAPTER 49

Duzon gestured toward a folding chair, and Malledd cautiously lowered him-self into it. The wood and canvas scarcely looked strong enough to hold him, and in fact the wood did creak ominously, but the fabric held and the seat was surprisingly comfortable.

There was only the one chair; the tent's other furnishings were a table, a cot, and two large chests. Duzon settled himself on one of the chests and contem-plated his guest.

Malledd gazed back, trying not to stare rudely. At last he asked, "May I inquire, my lord, why you wished to speak to me in private, yet haven't said a word?"

"A fair question," Duzon acknowledged, "and one I might ask myself, if the truth be told. I'm not sure I have a sound reason; I have, rather, a suspicion, one that may perhaps be utterly foolish."

Malledd suppressed a sigh. Was it really as obvious as all that? This man had only just met him, and apparently had already guessed the truth. Darsmit and others had figured it out during the fire, Onnell and Vadeviya had been told, but this Lord Duzon seemed to have divined it by magic.

He knew he should ask what Duzon suspected, but he couldn't bring himself to do it. He didn't want to carry the conversation any further; if Duzon wanted answers he'd have to work for them. Instead he simply sat.

For his part, Lord Duzon was fascinated by this stranger. He was huge, perhaps the biggest human being Duzon had ever seen, yet he carried himself with grace, with none of the puppy-dog clumsiness so many big men displayed. He was somehow appealing in appearance without being truly handsome; of course, he was hardly at his best just now, with the dust of the road on him, his hair and beard shaggy and ill kept, his braid crooked and trailing loose wisps. Perhaps were he properly cleaned up and more elegantly attired he *might* be called handsome.

And from Onnell's reaction to his arrival . . . well, Duzon had noticed when he first met Onnell that Onnell seemed to think he knew something about the divine champion, and he had greeted Malledd as if the smith were salvation made flesh.

Was this, then, the chosen of the gods?

And if he was, just how did one ask a divinely appointed savior to affirm his role without sounding like a player in a bad melodrama?

"You heard what I asked Onnell," he said at last, watching Malledd's face closely. "Are you anything more than an ordinary smith?"

Malledd shrugged. "I'm a husband and father, my lord—I have a beautiful wife and three fine children, and I'm sure that to them I'm not just the village smith. I try to be a good son to my mother and father."

"And what are you to the gods, Malledd?"

Malledd replied slowly, "Which gods? What would I have to do with gods? I'm no priest, if that's what you mean."

Duzon frowned. The man was being evasive—but why?

The obvious answer was that he wanted people to think he was the divine champion while he did not actually make any such claim; Duzon could hardly fault him for that, since he had attempted the same thing often enough himself. A corner of his mouth twitched upward at the realization. Interesting, how annoying that game could be when one was on the other end of it.

However, he wasn't at all sure that this Malledd was, in fact, playing the same game. Malledd had brought a priest with him—that might be significant. And clearly, Onnell thought Malledd was something special, presumably the divine champion—but he had not said so, even when offered the opportunity.

It seemed almost as if Malledd was deliberately hiding that he *was* the chosen one.

But was he? Why would he arrive *now*? Why hadn't he been here all along? Walking in now, after Duzon and Balinus and the others had fought and bled and died for so long . . . that was *unfair*. If this Malledd was the divine champion, and he defeated Rebiri Nazakri, *he* would receive all the credit, and Duzon's own efforts would be forgotten—he'd be just an obscure noble who had fought unsuccessfully, only to be rescued by the champion.

That wasn't *fair*.

But maybe he wasn't the champion at all; maybe his evasiveness was all a maneuver, an assumed modesty intended to make his eventual "revelation" more effective. Many nobles assumed that commoners were incapable of such subtlety and intrigue, but Duzon knew better.

Well, there was always a way to put an end to the evasion game, one that many people had found by asking Duzon outright whether he was the gods' choice; he had always answered honestly that he didn't know.

"Malledd," he said, "are you the gods' chosen defender of the Domdur Empire?"

Malledd grimaced, and didn't answer immediately; Duzon met his gaze and stared, waiting for a reply.

"What makes you ask that?" he said at last.

"Don't play with words," Duzon snapped. "Answer me! Are you the divine champion?"

"Why? What answer do you want me to give?"

"I want the truth!"

"And what if I don't know the truth?"

"Then tell me what you *do* know."

Malledd sighed. "I am," he admitted.

For a moment Duzon couldn't parse that simple statement. "You are . . . are what?"

"I am the chosen of the gods," Malledd said. "I was born with the mark of Ba'el's claw across my face, and three of the oracles in Biekedau told the priests there who I was. A priest named Mezizar was sent to verify the birthmark and inform my parents, so of course everyone in Grozerodz knew."

"Onnell, for example," Duzon said, two fingers stroking his chin thoughtfully.

Malledd nodded. "Onnell, and Bousian, and the others."

"But Apiris claimed he didn't know anything of the champion's whereabouts," Duzon said.

"He didn't," Malledd said. "The temple at Biekedau kept it as quiet as they could, and Dolkout, the high priest there, died without informing the Archpriest. Telling people didn't seem important; after all, nobody cared about the champion then, and the priests all assumed that when they needed to know they could ask an oracle."

"But *some* of the priests in Biekedau knew," Duzon said. "When the search began, why didn't they speak up?"

"I . . ." Malledd began. Then he paused, took a deep breath, and said, "I'd ordered them not to."

Duzon's fingers stopped their stroking, and he blinked, once.

"Ah," he said.

Malledd looked desperately unhappy, but said nothing.

"Would you care to explain that?" Duzon asked.

"I have a letter Dolkout had left with my parents," Malledd said. "It says that any priest anywhere has to obey me, because I'm the gods' chosen. So when Vadeviya came to see me, when the first trouble began in the east, I ordered him to make sure that none of the priests told anyone."

"But *why?*"

"I didn't want to be bothered," Malledd said.

Duzon lowered his hand and leaned forward, elbows on his knees, staring at Malledd.

"You didn't want it known you were the champion?" he said.

"No," Malledd said. "All it ever brought me was trouble."

"What sort of trouble?"

Malledd almost blushed. "My sisters teased me," he said. "Everyone in Groz-erodz treated me as if I were some sort of freak, like Nedduel's six-legged hog. I just wanted to be left alone to be myself and do as I pleased. Everyone always said that the wars were gone for good and I'd never be called on, and I'd believed that—that made it possible that I could live a normal life, if people would just forget about the whole thing."

Duzon marveled at that. "But you didn't want to be something more, something greater?" he asked.

Malledd shrugged. "Why should I?"

"So you might have anything you wanted," Duzon said. "So that men would look at you with respect and envy, and women with desire."

"I'm married," Malledd said. "I have the respect of my neighbors—I'm a good smith already, and in time I'll be as good as my father. What more do I need?"

Duzon realized he had reached a point of mutual incomprehension; if this man didn't understand ambition, Duzon had no idea how to explain it to him. For himself, Duzon couldn't imagine *not* wanting more, more power, more status, more women. Satisfaction was fleeting, and greed the normal state of being.

But Malledd plainly didn't see it that way.

"Look at me," Malledd said. "I'm big and strong; strangers stare when they first meet me, and no one ever dares insult me or trouble me. My wife doubts there's a woman alive who doesn't think about what a man my size would be like in bed. With all that, why would I *also* need to have the gods' favor?"

Duzon smiled wryly. "I suppose I see your point," he said, and in fact he did—a man Malledd's size didn't need any competitive instinct in order to flourish. Duzon was reasonably tall, reasonably muscular, reasonably handsome, reasonably rich, with a title and a proud, ancient family. He knew himself to be a very fortunate man in many ways—but he was not so outstanding that strangers stopped to stare at him. At least, not unless he had dressed even more flamboyantly than usual.

"Still," he said, "you *have* the gods' favor."

Malledd shrugged. "I didn't ask for it," he said.

"And you're here, to fight for the Empire," Duzon said. "But *why* are you here, if you've no interest in being the champion of the Domdur?"

Malledd frowned. "I thought it was my duty, if I am truly the chosen. I'm a Domdur born and bred; I was raised to honor the gods and the Empress, and if there's a danger to the Empire, and the gods want me to fight it, then I thought I should fight it."

"Fair enough," Duzon acknowledged, "but why are you only arriving *now*, when we've been fighting for so long?"

"Because I don't *want* to be here," Malledd retorted angrily. "I said that if the gods want me to fight, I'll fight; well, it's taken this long for the gods to make their will known clearly enough to coax me here."

"The gods?"

"Yes, the gods!" Malledd shouted. Then he subsided and added quietly, "Some of them, anyway."

"Are you claiming to be an oracle, then? I hadn't heard that that was a gift the champions received. . . ."

Malledd cut him off with an angry chopping motion. "I'm no oracle," he said. "I met Baranmel at a wedding."

"Ah," Duzon said with sudden understanding. That made sense; the gods no longer spoke to humanity through the oracles, but Baranmel still danced at weddings. If the gods truly wanted to give orders to their servant, that would be a way to do it without breaking their self-imposed silence.

But if this man was the divine champion, why had he *needed* those orders?

Obviously, because he was reluctant to fulfill his appointed role. He had said as much.

That was so horribly unfair! Dozens of men, Duzon himself among them, desperately wanted to be champion, yet the one man the gods had chosen would have preferred to have declined the honor.

Duzon tried to conceal every trace of bitterness as he said, "So Baranmel told you to come here and take command?"

"Baranmel told me that if I didn't fight, Rebiri Nazakri stood a better chance of bringing down the Empire. That's all. Nobody forced me—and I'm not about to take command of anything! I'm a blacksmith, not a general. General Balinus is in command, isn't he?"

"He is indeed," Duzon said.

"Then let him command. I'd rather not have anyone else find out I'm anything but another volunteer. I'm here, and I'll do what I can, but don't expect miracles."

Duzon considered that. He studied Malledd's face closely.

The man was incomprehensible. At first appraisal Duzon would have said he was a coward, bereft of honor, to have refused to declare himself—yet he was here, ready to face the foe. He was willing to fight, and presumably to die—yet he still didn't want it known that he was the Empire's divinely appointed defender.

The very rewards that Duzon sought—recognition, glory, power—seemed to be what Malledd feared more than he feared death or pain.

Duzon hardly knew what to make of such a man, and such a champion; he wondered whether the gods were displaying a streak of cruelty, or perhaps just a twisted sense of humor, in their choice.

But he didn't think Malledd was what the Imperial forces needed right now. Another sword arm was welcome; a reluctant champion who refused command and proclaimed himself no warrior was not.

"Expect miracles?" Duzon said. "Don't worry, Malledd; we won't."

CHAPTER 50

They have an advantage over us in the water," Onnell explained, gesturing at the river. "They don't breathe. Besides, this way we can see them coming."

Malledd nodded as he looked over the earthen parapet. The strip of bare ground along the riverbank made sense, now that he thought about it.

"We tried it the other way at first," Onnell continued. "We fought them right in the water, trying to keep them from even touching the western shore. It didn't work."

Malledd glanced at Onnell; something in the other man's voice conveyed a little of just how much was signified by those simple words, "It didn't work."

"This is better?" he asked, gesturing across the earthworks at the empty area between the barrier and the river, and the long row of torches that lit that area.

"Definitely," Onnell said.

Malledd looked thoughtfully at the black river. "The living rebels never cross?"

"No," Onnell said. "If they ever did we could slaughter them and put an end to all this."

"And the nightwalkers . . . what would they do if we didn't oppose them at all? What if we let them pass? They couldn't reach Seidabar in a single night, and at dawn we could destroy them all."

Onnell snorted. "Lord Duzon suggested that to General Balinus once. The general decided to try an experiment; he pulled back and let them pass. Only they didn't pass; they turned and attacked us. They cross in hopes of destroying us, so that their live allies can cross, and the whole army march on to Seidabar."

"But they haven't destroyed us."

"Not yet," Onnell agreed. "They're working on . . . Look!" He pointed at a ripple in the water.

Malledd looked as the ripple was joined by another and another and another. Then the first erupted out of the water and stood revealed as a soldier in the red and gold of the Empire—but a soldier with his chestplate gone, his tunic slashed open, and his chest pierced by a deep, dark wound. Any blood that might once have stained that puncture had been washed away by the Grebiguata, and the opening was black in the torchlight.

The walking corpse grinned. It shook water from its long hair and shouted at the barricade, "Ready to dance for another night?"

Behind it, others rose up dripping. They didn't speak, simply advanced toward shore, swords and axes and spears held ready. Two or three others wore Imperial uniforms, but most wore rags that had once been civilian garb—farmers' home-spun, Matuan robes, Govyan vests. Ugly wounds gaped bloodlessly on several of them, and at least one was missing most of an arm.

"Do we have any archers?" Malledd asked, noticing how exposed the night-walkers were as they rose from the water. They were monstrous, ugly, terrifying—but now that he actually saw them they weren't quite as bad as he had imagined them. Having faced them, he could put his fear behind him and think again.

"Arrows don't do any good," Onnell reminded him. "You need to cut their heads off to kill them."

Malledd grunted acknowledgment; he had forgotten that detail. He watched the approaching nightwalkers intently.

Then, without warning, the undead creatures broke into a run, and charged straight up the sloping dirt wall. Malledd had no time for thinking about anything but survival as they poured over the top—two of the creatures were coming straight at him, swords thrusting down and forward like spears.

He dodged clumsily sideways, remembering too late to raise his own blade.

Onnell, the veteran, moved far more efficiently; where Malledd ducked low and leaned sideways, throwing himself off balance, Onnell simply took one step back and to the side while he brought his sword sweeping up in a well-timed parry. A single nightwalker had lunged for him, trying to impale him; the deflected blade passed harmlessly over Onnell's shoulder. Then the ax in Onnell's left hand swung around in a ferocious overhand chop, cutting deep into the nightwalker's flank.

Malledd saw that much in an instant, then turned to regain his balance and confront his own foes.

One had stopped dead while the other circled around, trying to trap Malledd between them; Malledd knew that maneuver from childhood battles with his sisters, and scrambled up the barricade, not worrying where that took him, ignoring the fact that he was exposing himself to the enemy. It didn't occur to him until too late that perhaps the nightwalkers had archers, even if the Imperial vanguard did not.

Then he was atop the parapet, and the two nightwalkers were trying to climb up after him. He backed away and slid down the slope toward the river.

He scrambled to his feet and looked around, just as more nightwalkers rose up from the water; Malledd heard the sloshing, more than saw them. Despite the torches and a dozen moons that peeped through gaps in the clouds, the darkness made it hard to see details.

The nightwalkers that had attacked him had followed him back up over the wall, and were sliding down toward him. Fear and anger and determination mingled and merged, and something new swept over him, a combination of them all. He stopped thinking; he lifted his sword with both hands, swinging it up above his right shoulder, then charged bellowing at the two.

They turned to meet him, one moving right, the other left, their own swords at the ready—and Malledd hacked right through both their blades. One sword snapped; the other was torn from its wielder's hand and flew aside.

Malledd chopped back again, and took off a nightwalker's hand. His third swing took off a nightwalker's head.

The surviving opponent stepped back, stooped to retrieve the fallen sword—and tumbled to the ground in two pieces.

Onnell's ax had lopped off its head. He had disposed of his own foe and come over the wall to Malledd's aid.

"That wasn't so bad," Malledd said, his chest heaving as he tried to calm himself.

"Of course not," Onnell said. "It's still early. They send the beginners first, to tire us out." Then he turned to fend off a nightwalker that was preparing to ram its sword into Malledd's back.

Malledd turned, astonished; he had been completely unaware of the enemy's approach.

It hadn't been alone; half a dozen more nightwalkers were charging up the bank. Malledd turned to meet them while Onnell pinned and decapitated the leading figure.

Side by side the two men scrabbled back up the earthworks, fighting off nightwalkers as they did so. When they tumbled back over the top the nightwalkers came close behind.

At that point Malledd knew that he had destroyed one nightwalker. By midnight he had destroyed at least eleven, and had had a sword thrust through his left arm; he was standing amid chaos and disaster, tents burning to one side, men and women screaming in the darkness. The nightwalkers were still coming over the walls.

By dawn he had lost count how many he had destroyed, and was staring about madly, looking for the foe. The Imperial soldiers had been driven back from the barricades into the open, where they had collected into knots, standing back to back, fending off the enemy; Malledd, Onnell, and three others Malledd didn't know formed one such knot. Most of the soldiers were far too tired to do any more than try to stay alive, but Malledd was still ready to charge any nightwalker that came within reach, still able to swing his sword like a woodsman's ax at any nightwalker's neck.

No more necks were available, though; the surviving nightwalkers were now fleeing back into the water, not because the Imperial vanguard had defeated them, but because the sun had. The eastern sky was lightening rapidly.

Onnell relaxed, lowering his ax. He massaged his right arm and glanced around.

There were losses, of course—including at least one very important one, as Onnell thought he had seen Colonel Zavai go down under a nightwalker's ax. Still, most of the corpses scattered through the camp were the headless remains of nightwalkers, not Imperial troops, and Onnell hadn't seen anyone being carried back to the river to be added to the enemy's ranks.

That was good. The attack had been a fairly heavy one, and the Imperial forces had done well. That thought reminded him of Malledd, who had fought well for a new recruit. He turned and looked at his companion.

Malledd was still staring about wildly, sword held high.

"Malledd, relax," Onnell said. "It's over. Now it's time for a meal and a day's rest."

Malledd threw him an uncertain glance. "You're sure?"

"Absolutely. The nightwalkers can't move in sunlight, and their support troops can't cross the river."

Slowly, Malledd lowered the sword, and looked around.

"May all the gods protect me!" he said as he took in the strewn bodies.

"I'm sure they will," Onnell said, amused by Malledd's use of the common-place oath—if the gods were going to protect *anyone*, it would be Malledd.

"So many dead," Malledd muttered.

"Most of them were *already* dead," Onnell pointed out. "We'll need to drag them all to the pyres, but first let's get something to eat—I'm exhausted and half-starved."

Malledd realized then that the other three men in their group were already on their way toward breakfast, their weapons dragging behind them or simply dropped.

"Of course," Malledd said, shaking his head. "I'm hungry, too." He sheathed his sword and followed as Onnell led him away from the river and the barricade, toward the field kitchens and supply wagons at the western edge of the camp.

As they walked, Onnell glanced around to make sure no one else was in earshot, then remarked, "You fought well for a beginner, from what I saw."

"Thanks," Malledd muttered.

"That's all it was, though—good for a beginner. The gods didn't give you any magical skill with a sword?"

"Not that I could tell," Malledd said unhappily. "I did the best I could."

"It wasn't bad," Onnell said. "A little wild. But you kept it up well, especially toward the end. You hardly looked tired at all."

"I'm *not* tired," Malledd said. "I don't tire."

Onnell glanced up at him and saw he was completely serious. "*That's* interesting," he said.

Malledd shrugged.

Onnell went on, "I assume you came out here to be the champion you were born to be, and lead us against the rebels?"

"I came out here to do whatever I could to stop them," Malledd replied.

Onnell nodded. "That may not be all that much," he said. "I can't see some of these people accepting a new arrival as a leader—not unless he's something *really* special. You're big and strong, but you're still just a promising beginner. Maybe if you'd gotten here when the rest of us did, and learned along with the rest of us . . ."

"I should have been here," Malledd admitted, "but I didn't know it yet. And

I didn't *want* to be here." He thought briefly of Anva and the children and quickly suppressed the thought; he had to concentrate on winning, on destroying Rebiri Nazakri and defeating Ba'el's scheme to overthrow the Empire. That was the quickest way to get home to his family; thinking about them would only distract him and delay him.

"I can understand that," Onnell said.

Malledd studied his companion. "Why are *you* here?" he asked. "Couldn't you have left if you wanted to? Lord Duzon said there have been many desertions."

"There have been," Onnell agreed. "I don't blame them. But I'm staying, at least for now. Someone has to. Someone has to keep those *things* out of Seidabar."

Malledd nodded. "I was chosen for it at birth," he said. "I think you're the nobler of us, Onnell."

"I don't have a wife back in Grozerodz," Onnell answered. "It's easier for me. I have less to lose."

"Isn't your life more than enough?"

Onnell grimaced. "Apparently not," he said, "or I wouldn't be here."

Malledd didn't pretend to understand that, and the two big men walked on side by side until they reached a table where three women were handing out hard bread and thick beer.

"No cheese? No fruit?" Onnell asked. "I know meat's too much to ask, but . . ."

"No cheese," the nearest woman snapped back. "We ran out. And the beer's low, so don't spill any."

"We've got some onions," the second woman said, pointing out a small heap of scraggly brown lumps.

"Better than nothing," Onnell muttered, grabbing one from the pile.

Malledd accepted his bread and beer, then followed Onnell off to one side, where the two men settled to the ground.

A moment later Bousian joined them; he wore a thick brown patch over his left eye. "Malledd!" he called as he approached. "I heard you'd arrived!"

Malledd found himself smiling so hard he couldn't speak; it was good to see another familiar face.

"Survived another night, Bousian?" Onnell asked.

"As far as I can tell I have," Bousian replied. "Or perhaps my soul is dreaming this as it's carried to the heavens."

"I'd hope for better dreams than this," Onnell retorted.

"So would I," Bousian agreed, "but we don't always get what we hope for."

Onnell and Malledd both grunted agreement to that.

"It's good to see you, Malledd," Bousian said as he seated himself. "Perhaps we'll live to see the end of this after all."

"I'm just one man," Malledd said. Then he relented. "Even though I am who I am, I'm just one man. The gods haven't made me unbeatable."

Onnell nodded. "He fights like a talented rookie, and no more," he said.

Bousian frowned. "Really? That's not good."

"That's what I am," Malledd said.

"If I might speak freely . . ." Bousian hesitated.

"Go ahead," Malledd said. "We all know what I am."

Bousian nodded. "Well, then, you're the divine champion, protector of the Domdur. You're supposed to lead us all against the nightwalkers and the Nazakri."

Malledd grimaced. "Maybe," he said. "I'm the champion, yes, but I don't know if I'm destined to lead you anywhere."

"It *is* the traditional role," Bousian pointed out.

"These aren't traditional times," Malledd replied, "and Rebiri Nazakri is not a traditional foe."

"Surely the will of the gods hasn't changed. . . ."

Malledd held up a hand. "Bousian," he said, "you don't know what you're talking about. Since you saw me last I have spoken to a god, face-to-face, and I know what my situation is far better than you do."

Bousian hesitated. If any other man, excluding priests, had made such a claim he would have dismissed it as lunacy, but this was Malledd, the chosen one. "You spoke to a god?" he asked.

"Baranmel," Malledd said.

Bousian blinked. "You spoke to Baranmel?" That did add a certain believability to the claim, but on the other hand, what would a frivolous deity like Baranmel have to say about such weighty matters as wars and empires and destinies?

"At a friend's wedding in Seidabar," Malledd said. "He told me a story, one that Samardas wanted me to hear."

Bousian had to admit that did make sense, for another god to use Baranmel as a messenger. He had never heard of such a thing happening before, but on the other hand, until the oracles fell silent, the gods had all the messengers they needed without relying on Baranmel.

"Samardas," Bousian said thoughtfully. "Interesting. I'd have thought you'd be of more interest to Ba'el. Wasn't it his mark you wore at birth?"

"It was," Malledd said. "But he wasn't the one who wanted Baranmel to speak with me."

"Ba'el presumably isn't much for words," Onnell suggested. "He's more interested in action."

"Well, he's given us plenty of that here, these last hundred nights," Bousian said. "His days at the sun are almost upon us; maybe then he'll smile on us and give us a victory."

Malledd glanced at the rising sun, a golden half-circle atop the earthworks. He felt suddenly cold.

Bousian was right—midsummer was almost upon them. In just three days, on Midsummer's Day, Malledd would turn twenty-seven and Ba'el's power would be at its peak.

And Ba'el favored the Nazakri.

Lord Duzon had mentioned that it seemed as if the enemy were waiting for something; suddenly Malledd thought that while he might not know *what* the enemy was waiting for, he knew *when* it was expected.

CHAPTER 51

Get some sleep," Duzon said as he trudged toward his own tent. "We can talk this evening."

"No, my lord," Malledd insisted, following close at his heels. "This is urgent; it can't wait."

Duzon turned, still walking, and looked at Malledd curiously.

The man showed no sign of the exhaustion everyone else felt. Right now Duzon wanted nothing so much but to fall onto his cot and let the world go away for a few hours; it had taken an effort even to force himself to eat, though his stomach had been as empty as a nightwalker's soul, and he hadn't bothered to clean himself properly, but had merely wiped off the worst of the gore. This was normal; he'd felt like this every morning for half a season or more. Everyone who fought for the Empire here felt the same.

Malledd, though . . . Malledd was just as battered as anyone, with blood and filth streaked and smeared on his arms and face and clothes, with scrapes and cuts everywhere, his tunic torn a dozen places, yet his eyes were bright, and his shoulders did not sag, and he was here demanding to talk to Duzon.

"Aren't you tired?" Duzon asked.

"A little," Malledd lied.

"Gods!" Duzon said. A laugh escaped him as he realized what he had said. "It *is* the gods' doing, isn't it?"

"I suppose. It's not important right now. My lord, I really *must* talk to you."

They were at the flap of Duzon's tent, which had not been among the twenty or so burned by the nightwalkers during the night's assault. He paused there and turned to face Malledd.

"Then talk," he said.

Malledd glanced about uneasily.

"No one's listening," Duzon said. "They're all too tired. *I'm* too tired, but I'll do my best to hear you out."

"It's about the gods," Malledd said.

"Have they spoken to you?" Duzon cocked his head and tried to decide whether to believe Malledd if he said "yes." He didn't really doubt that Malledd was indeed the chosen of the gods, but that didn't mean he accepted as true everything the man said. He had never heard anyone assert that the divine champion couldn't be a liar or a madman.

Malledd shook his head. "No. Not again; this is part of what Baranmel told me, but I didn't think about it until now."

"Ah," Duzon said. "And what was this revelation?"

"It's about Ba'el," Malledd said.

"Mighty Ba'el, god of war and conquest, the particular patron of soldiers." He gestured at the great red moon that hovered on the western horizon, still plainly visible despite the dawn. "What about him?"

"Midsummer is coming, and Ba'el's Triad," Malledd said.

"So it is. A favorable omen for us, I assume?"

Malledd shook his head vigorously. "*No*, my lord," he said. "It's a very *bad* omen. Ba'el favors the enemy!"

Duzon stared at him for a moment, then lifted the tent flap.

"Would you care to come inside and explain that?"

Malledd ducked into the tent and Duzon followed; Malledd found a place on the cot while Duzon took the folding camp stool, and the two men sat facing each other.

Malledd quickly ran through Baranmel's explanation of how Ba'el had realized he had been tricked, how he had set out to destroy the Domdur Empire so that wars would again spread throughout the world.

"The other gods still favor us—most of them, at any rate," Malledd concluded, "but Ba'el is our greatest enemy and Rebiri Nazakri's strongest ally, though the Nazakri may not know it."

Duzon stroked his beard. "And why did you not mention this sooner? We spoke before at some length, and you said not a word of this."

"I didn't want to spread needless worry. Why tell soldiers that the greatest of all the gods, their own patron, wants to see them fail and die?"

"So Ba'el has been working against us?"

"Definitely."

"And he's aided the Nazakri?"

"I think he gave the Nazakri his black magic."

"And the unrest back in Seidabar? The bickering within the Imperial Council? Your priest friend told me about that."

Malledd shrugged. "Probably," he said. "I don't know about that."

"And yet he chose *you* as the champion, did he not?"

Malledd blinked in sudden realization, and he said, "Of course he did—and where was I these past forty triads? Am I a soldier, or a leader? I'm just a *smith*."

"You can fight," Duzon said. "And from what Darsmit told me, you can lead. Ba'el is not the only god involved in making a champion."

"Of course not. But I don't *want* to fight or lead, and that may be Ba'el's work."

"The gods make us what we are, Malledd, but then we make our own lives. You're here now." He waved that away. "So you think that Ba'el's Triad will be an evil time for us?"

Malledd nodded.

"Do you have any idea what form this evil might take?"

"None. But hasn't it seemed as if Nazakri was waiting for something, biding his time? If so, isn't it likely that *this* was the time he was awaiting?"

"Ba'el's Triad," Duzon mused. "The longest, hottest days of the year, when Ba'el stokes the sun's fires. Shouldn't that be when the nightwalkers' power is least, when the nights are shortest?"

"That's what I'd expect," Malledd agreed.

"Yet you think it's when Nazakri will finally make his move?"

Malledd nodded again.

"And what would you do about it?"

"We must destroy him *before* then!"

Duzon, weary as he was, managed a laugh. "We have been encamped here for more than a season, Malledd, trying to find a way to do just that. How can we achieve in two days what's eluded us for so long? We can't destroy the rebels with what we have here; we must await the arrival of Lord Kadan and the Imperial Army."

"And what if they never come? Vadeviya tells me that Lord Kadan is caught up in palace intrigue, and under suspicion of treason. We can't just wait for him!"

"What choice do we have?"

"If we could just get across the river and into the enemy camp by daylight, when the nightwalkers are powerless . . ."

"How? That's why the enemy is camped so far north, Malledd—there's no way for living men to cross the water here against armed opposition."

"Then how does the Nazakri intend to get *his* men across?"

Duzon shrugged. "I don't know. I've wondered about that for many a triad."

"We can't swim?"

"They have archers, and swordsmen who would meet us at the bank. And the river is wide—we'd be exhausted as we waded ashore, easy prey for them."

"Boats?"

"Archers and swordsmen, and Rebiri Nazakri's magic—and rowing is almost as much work as swimming."

"A bridge?"

"That would take days. The nightwalkers would burn it before we could get it halfway built."

"What if it were stone?"

"Then they would tear it to pieces."

Malledd frowned thoughtfully. "We have magicians," he said.

"Indeed we do," Duzon agreed. "New ones, anyway."

"Can't they cross the river?"

"Yes, but when they do cross they're met with arrows. When those are dodged or deflected they have only the magic to destroy a handful of nightwalkers—and not the time to do even that much, for the sentries will have awakened Rebiri Nazakri, whose black magic can easily counter a dozen of our New Magicians. Then they flee back across the river—and the weaker of them may well fall in the river and have to swim the last few yards."

"Could they carry soldiers across? The living rebels are a small force, and one man with a sword can lop off a hundred nightwalkers' heads in a matter of minutes by daylight."

"He can if he's not killed first," Duzon replied. "And each magician can only carry one or at most two soldiers. We have no more than a score of New Magicians—I haven't counted lately, it may be no more than a dozen by now. What could thirty men do against the rebel army?"

"Thirty men," Malledd mused. "No more?"

"I'm not even certain we could manage that many; you'd have to ask Vrai Burrai or Tebas Tudan."

"And can't the New Magicians renew their power from the sun?"

"Of course—but not instantly; it takes time. Malledd, we've been over all this. . . ."

"Suppose," Malledd said, "you were to build a bridge in sections, not in place, but here in camp—perhaps disguise it as wooden walls—and then have the New Magicians carry the pieces into place. They could renew their power when it ran low, and have the entire bridge in place within a single day. Then we could charge across, and lay their camp waste."

"They'd burn it."

"No, have it assembled in the water, weighted to rest ankle-deep—no one can burn wood underwater."

"It couldn't be an ordinary bridge—more like a series of rafts."

"Exactly!"

Duzon mulled that over silently for a moment.

"It might work," he admitted. "They'd see us coming, of course; we'd have to fight through archers and swordsman."

"We'd carry shields, of course, to stop the arrows. And not all of us would survive—but *none* of the nightwalkers would reach Seidabar."

"Um," Duzon said. "We'll have to talk to Vrai Burrai."

"*You* can talk to him," Malledd said.

Duzon looked at him sharply.

"My lord, I will be there with my sword, and I will fight as best I can for my people and my Empress, but I'm not the one to lead this; the men don't know me, they know *you*. Vrai Burrai doesn't know me, he knows *you*. General Balinus and all the rest, they trust *you*, not me. Bring them this as *your* idea."

"You don't want the credit?"

Malledd shook his head.

"You don't want to be in charge?"

"My lord, I was marked at birth by Ba'el, who is now our foe; I'm not the one to lead here."

"You're the chosen of *all* the gods."

"And *you*, my lord, are the chosen of the Domdur—I've heard my companions talk about you."

Duzon stared at Malledd for a moment, and felt the blood rush to his face as he stared. He turned his head slightly, to look at the cot on which Malledd sat.

He let out a long sigh. It appeared he would not be able to *use* that cot for quite some time yet.

CHAPTER 52

Our people are being butchered!" Lord Kadan shouted, pulling against the guards who held his arms. He stood at the center of the council chamber, facing the fifteen other Councillors—and Prince Graubris, who had taken Kadan's own customary seat. "They're being slaughtered, and it's *your* doing, Shoule!"

"No!" Shoule shouted in reply, rising to his feet behind the Council's semicircular table. "It's *yours*, you traitor! You sent them to die!"

"*You* kept me from sending help! You and your . . . your *puppet*, the Prince!" Kadan could not free his arm to point, but he spat in the direction of Prince Graubris.

Several Councillors gasped; a shocked silence fell over the chamber.

Prince Granzer rose to his feet. Speaking in his deepest, most commanding voice, he said, "Lord Kadan, you forget yourself."

"No, Highness, I do not!" Kadan replied. "I know that Graubris is to be the Emperor when his mother finally succumbs, and that that could be any moment now; I wouldn't be surprised if a messenger walked in this minute to tell us the Empress is dead. I don't care, Highness—I'll speak the truth, and the truth is that Lord Shoule has manipulated your brother-in-law for his own ends, and that I'll not serve any empire ruled by such a fool. When Her Majesty dies and Graubris takes the throne my time on the Imperial Council is done, either way; I might as well go out speaking the truth, and if it means my head on the city wall rather than an honorable exile, I'll accept that. It'll be worth it!"

"Granzer, I . . ." Graubris began.

"Shut up," Granzer snapped. He glared at his brother-in-law. The man ought to know better than this, Granzer thought—but then, he had never troubled himself with the Council's business, or bothered to learn the Council's rules. Arresting a Councillor on his own authority, taking that Councillor's seat . . . "You're not Emperor yet, Graubris, and you're not a member of this Council; you speak in this room only when invited to do so."

Graubris stared at him, shocked. Lord Shoule, who had settled back in his chair, leaped to his feet again.

"Your Highness, I must protest . . ." he began.

"You shut up, too, Shoule," Granzer said, cutting him off. Shoule's behavior had been even worse than Graubris's. The most favorable interpretation Granzer could put on it was honest stupidity and a sincere conviction that Kadan was a traitor, but anyone who knew Shoule would think it much more likely that Shoule was attempting to curry favor with his Emperor-to-be.

And of course, it might be that Shoule was himself a traitor, trying to stir up trouble and keep the Imperial Army from marching. Granzer had his own opinion on that. He glowered at Shoule for a second, then turned back to Kadan.

"My lord," he said, "if you will give me your word to commit no violence, nor to leave this chamber without my permission, I will have the guards release you."

Kadan stared at him; everyone present could see him struggling for control.

"I will attempt to restrain myself, Your Highness," he said.

"Good," Granzer said. "Excellent." He gestured to the guards, and Kadan was free.

"May I speak, Your Highness?" Shoule asked sardonically.

"No," Granzer snapped. "I think we've heard enough out of you for the moment, you and my esteemed brother-in-law. Arresting a member of the *Imperial Council* without my leave, and bringing him here as a prisoner? By what right do you two presume to take such an action? Graubris?"

"Someone had to do it," Graubris muttered. "Mother's dying, we all know that, and you weren't acting—*someone* had to take charge."

"So you nominated yourself."

"I am the heir to the throne, Granzer—this very Council rejected my sister's claim."

"And I am not asserting my wife's claim to the throne, Graubris," Granzer replied. "I am telling you that you exceeded your authority, usurped the Council's power, by your actions."

"But the man's a traitor!" Graubris protested, gesturing at Kadan. "He had to be stopped!"

"Who names him a traitor?"

"I do!" Shoule immediately announced. He looked at the other Councillors for support, particularly Orbalir and Apiris.

"He's made some bad decisions," Orbalir said.

"I don't know anything about it," Apiris said.

"Of course he's the traitor," Graubris said. "Who else could it be?" He, like Shoule, looked about for support.

"Just about anyone," Lord Sulibai said dryly. "Have you any *evidence*, Your Highness? Lord Shoule?"

Graubris turned to Shoule.

"Well, look at it!" Shoule said. "He let this Olnamian wizard conquer half the east almost unopposed! *He* commands the army, and the army did nothing!"

"The army in the east fought . . ." Kadan began.

Granzer raised a hand. "Let Lord Shoule make his case. You'll have your turn."

"Thank you, Your Highness," Shoule said with a bow. He pointed at Kadan. "*He* was charged with gathering an army that could destroy the rebels—and did he? The rebels are still alive, still fighting, no more than two hundred miles from here! He sent three thousand of his supposed best against them, and what did they do? *Nothing!* They sat all winter, and now they're still just sitting there while the nightwalkers cut them to pieces!"

Lord Kadan opened his mouth, looked at Granzer, and closed it.

"And now that it's too late, *now* he wants to march the rest of our defenders out onto the plain, where the enemy can slaughter them all! Is he manning the city walls, preparing the ancient defenses? *No!* Despite everything, he still insists we can beat the foe in open battle! He wants to send our unprotected men up against nightwalkers! Have you looked at the maps, my lords and ladies? Our army cannot reach the Grebiguata, or the shelter of Drievabor, in less than two triads, even with the most strenuous of forced marches. In two triads, if the Nazakri chooses, he can have his undead hordes past the river, past Drievabor, onto the open plain, where they can easily evade any attempts to hold them, to keep them away from Seidabar. Moving the army east before the enemy reached the river would have made sense; it would have given us a forward line of defense; but Lord Kadan did not *do* that! He waited until it was too late, until the army could not possibly arrive in time to do any good—and *then* he proposed to send them to their deaths, leaving us to the black wizard's mercy!"

"Your Highness . . ." Kadan said.

"And what's more," Shoule said, interrupting before Kadan could say any more, "has he moved the army to the east of the city, to form a barrier between the enemy and the capital? No! He keeps them in the camps to the *northwest* of the city!"

"Agabdal is where their *supplies* are!" Kadan protested angrily.

Granzer held up a hand.

"And is there any more, my lord?" he asked Shoule. "Have you any evidence that Lord Kadan had any part in the riots in the Outer City, or the burning of the east wing of this very palace in which we meet? Can you demonstrate that Lord Kadan's strategy is indeed suicidal and treasonous?"

"It's plain enough, Your Highness!" Shoule exclaimed.

"Perhaps to you," Granzer said. "To me, sending reinforcements to the troops who have held out this long seems a very sensible thing to do."

"It will leave Seidabar undefended!" Shoule shouted, so overwrought that spittle flew from his lips. "The enemy will march right to the gates!"

"The enemy has not demonstrated any ability to do so," Granzer replied coolly. "The vanguard, outnumbered as it is, has held them for several triads now. Why should we assume they could not hold them long enough for the reinforcements to arrive?"

"That's what the wizard is *waiting* for! When our troops are irrevocably committed, he'll bypass them. . . ."

"How do you know that?" Granzer demanded.

Shoule's mouth opened and closed. "Why . . . why, it's self-evident!" he said, a bit less certainly. "The nightwalkers could pass the river at any time, if they chose; they're just waiting until the army leaves. . . ."

"And how would the wizard *know* when the army leaves?"

"Well, he's a *wizard*!" Shoule cried.

"In short, Lord Shoule, you are *assuming* that the enemy would act in certain ways, and basing your accusation of treason on the fact that Lord Kadan does not make those same assumptions?"

Lord Shoule struggled wordlessly.

"In fact, my lords and ladies," Granzer said, turning to the rest of the Council, "while Lord Kadan has been doing his best to get the army on the road to confront the foe, and Lord Shoule has been harassing him by every means possible while accusing Kadan and myself of doing nothing, I have not been completely inactive. I have been investigating the riots, and the fire, and I have made some interesting discoveries." He looked along the row of Councillors, from one end to the other.

"Go on," Lady Dalbisha said.

Granzer nodded an acknowledgment. "Your Holiness," he said. "A few triads ago, you and Lord Shoule and Lord Orbalir and my wife's brother rode out to Agabdal to confront Lord Kadan, and to ensure that the army did not depart the camps. You remember?"

"Of course," Apiris said.

"And you may recall that you wore brown cloaks, though the day was not particularly cool."

"That's right. Lord Shoule insisted. He said Lord Kadan might do something reckless if he saw the four of us approaching together."

"And where did those robes come from?"

Apiris glanced at Shoule. "Well, Lord Shoule had them. He loaned them to us."

Granzer nodded, and turned to the other side of the table. "Lord Dabos," he said. "Tell us what you know of the beginnings of that infamous riot."

"I don't know what you mean," Dabos said. "Three well-spoken men went about the Outer City, recruiting troublemakers and instructing them to create as much disturbance as possible at a prearranged signal."

"And what did these three men wear?"

"Brown robes, so no one could see their faces. But, Your Highness, if we were to suspect everyone in Seidabar who wears a brown robe . . ."

"I merely seek to point out an interesting coincidence," Granzer said. "I own a brown cloak myself."

"It seems to me you seek to accuse me without saying so," Shoule objected.

Granzer smiled. "Not yet, my lord," he said. He turned. "Lord Niniam," he said.

"Yes?"

"You sent the palace guards to the Outer City at the behest of a messenger who claimed to come from a military commander in Greldar Square, did you not?"

Niniam squirmed. "I did," he said.

"And no such commander existed."

"Apparently not," Niniam admitted.

"But the *messenger* existed."

"Yes, of course! I have witnesses . . ."

Granzer gestured. "That won't be necessary." He beckoned to one of the guards. "Bring the silver box from my closet," he ordered.

The guard bowed and vanished out the door, and Granzer continued, "After he gave you the message, Lord Niniam, where did the messenger go?"

Lord Niniam blinked in surprise. "I have no idea," he said.

"He did not accompany you to the Outer City?"

"Why, no—it took me several minutes to rouse the guards . . ."

Granzer nodded. "And you never saw the messenger again?"

"That's right."

"And we have, through intensive questioning, determined the whereabouts of everyone who should have been in the Imperial Palace at that time, have we not?" Granzer said, turning to Lords Graush and Sulibai.

"I believe so, Your Highness," Sulibai said.

"You *trust* him?" Shoule protested, pointing at Sulibai.

"We asked about everyone," Lord Graush growled.

"And none of them could have started the fire?"

"The palace guards were gone," Graush said. "Anyone could have walked in and done it."

"And what if someone saw this mysterious arsonist walk into the unguarded palace?" Granzer shook his head. "It's possible—but wasn't the false messenger *already in* the palace?"

"Oh, very good, Your Highness," Sulibai said quietly.

"But it still doesn't tell us who this messenger was," Graush said.

Granzer nodded. "I'm hoping Lord Niniam can help us with that."

The door opened, as if on cue, and the guard stepped back in, carrying a large, ornate silver box.

Delbur, Granzer's aide, came close behind.

"Ah, very good," Granzer said. He directed the guard to place the box on the table before Lord Niniam.

"I'm afraid, my lord," he said, "that this is not going to be pleasant. However, I must ask if you recognize this." He gestured, and the guard lifted the box's lid.

Niniam rose and peered inside.

His face went white, and he sat down again.

"Gods!" he said. "Close it!"

The guard obeyed.

Delbur cleared his throat.

"In a moment, Delbur," Granzer said. "Lord Niniam, do you recognize it?"

"That's him," Niniam said, nodding. "That's the messenger."

"In that *box*?" Lady Vamia said incredulously.

"It's his head," Lord Niniam said with his hand over his mouth. He looked ill.

"Granzer, I must protest . . ." Graubris began.

"Shut up," Granzer told him.

Delbur winced.

"Guard, would you be so kind as to show the contents of the box to Lord Shoule?" Granzer said.

"That won't be necessary," Shoule said quickly. "*I* never saw this messenger. . . ."

"Ah, but I think you have," Granzer said. "You see, we identified the body before removing the head for transport."

"I don't . . . really, I . . ."

"Look," Granzer said. The guard opened the box.

Lord Shoule did not turn as pale as Niniam had, but he did lose color.

"Really, Your Highness, what are you attempting to prove?" Lord Orbalir protested.

"Tell them," Granzer directed Shoule.

Shoule hesitated, then said, "It's my steward. His name was Asgibur."

"Your *steward*?" Niniam said, astonished.

Shoule nodded. "He maintained my ancestral estate in Daudenor. Where did you find him? How did this happen?"

"Are you saying you aren't behind this?" Kadan shouted. "Are you saying you didn't order him to set the fire, and then kill him so he couldn't tell anyone what you'd done?"

"Of course I didn't!" Shoule said, a trifle shakily.

"His body was found behind an inn, a day's journey toward Daudenor," Granzer said. "He was wearing a brown robe."

"That's terrible!" Shoule said. "What was he doing there? He should have been in Daudenor!"

Granzer stared at Shoule. He sighed.

"I had hoped that I would not need to present any of this until I had further proof of just who was behind your steward's actions, Lord Shoule; alas, you forced my hand by arresting Lord Kadan. However, I ask the Council to consider this carefully—where do you find more evidence for treason, in the actions of Lord Kadan, or in the circumstances surrounding Lord Shoule?"

"You haven't proven a thing, Granzer," Prince Graubris said. "Lord Shoule's been trying to find the traitor! Maybe he was wrong about Lord Kadan—or maybe Lord Kadan suborned this steward in order to incriminate Shoule—but even if he was wrong about Kadan, that doesn't mean *Shoule's* untrustworthy!"

Granzer spread his hands. "I merely ask that the Council consider all the evidence presented," he said. "We are in no hurry. . . ."

Delbur cleared his throat, very loudly.

"What is it, Delbur?" Granzer asked, annoyed.

"We may be in a hurry after all, Highness. The doctors say that Her Imperial Majesty is failing rapidly now, and will most likely be dead before morning. I was sent to see if you or any of the other Councillors wished to attend her in her last moments. . . ."

Graubris was already on his feet and headed for the chamber door.

"This session of the Imperial Council is adjourned," Granzer said quickly. "By my own authority as President, Lord Kadan's arrest is hereby vacated, and all charges against him suspended until further notice." He started around the table toward the door.

He paused long enough to point at Lord Shoule, however, and say, "This is not over, my lord."

CHAPTER 53

Midsummer is almost here," Rebiri Nazakri said, speaking into the fire. He sat alone in his black pavilion, cross-legged on a well-worn velvet cushion. But he could sense another presence.

"I know you're here," he said.

The silence remained.

"I had expected more guidance," he said. "How am I to know what to do? I don't understand how my men are to cross the river. . . ."

They need not.

Rebiri started. He had expected a response, but all the same, it had startled him. "Of course they do," he said. "How else can I reach Seidabar?"

The nightwalkers can cross beneath the water. Your magic can take you over it. You need no one else.

"I don't? And what's to prevent the Domdur from butchering the nightwalkers during the day? Am I supposed to defend them from Kadan's entire army all by myself?"

There will be no need to defend them.

"Why not?"

Have faith in me. There will be no need, if you move quickly, without rest, without hesitation.

"Have faith in you? Why should I?"

I have led you this far. You must trust me. I desire to see Seidabar destroyed, and the Domdur cast down, as greatly as you do.

"But you won't even tell me who you are!"

For a moment there was no reply; then the voice said, *I am known to the Domdur as Ba'el of the Red Moon, Deathbringer, Lord of Battle.*

"Ba'el?" Rebiri caught his breath for a moment. "*Ba'el?* The god who sent the Domdur their stinking champions?"

No more. They have their champion in Malledd, son of Hmar, but he is no more any of mine.

"The Domdur all swear by you!"

They know not what they say. They have betrayed me, and I have turned my face from them.

"Betrayed you how?"

That is not your concern. Do you doubt me? Do you doubt my power?

Rebiri struggled to think that one through.

Ba'el, the chief god of the Domdur, claimed to have turned against them— or at any rate, this being that said it was Ba'el claimed as much.

On its face the idea was preposterous; the Domdur's gods had led them to become rulers of all the world, had favored them in every enterprise. The Domdur lands gave forth the best crops, their waters yielded the finest fish; for a thousand years they had been unbeatable in battle. The gods advised and comforted them, sent champions to lead them, chose their Emperors.

But the oracles had fallen silent. Rumors said that the Empress's children were fighting over the succession, and the Archpriest would take no side in the debate. No champion had yet emerged among the Domdur—Lord Duzon was a dashing, heroic figure, but hardly of mythic stature, and while the spirit had just named Malledd, son of Hmar, Rebiri Nazakri had never heard of such a person; if he existed, he wasn't visible at the forefront of the battle.

And Rebiri Nazakri had defeated the Domdur in skirmish after skirmish.

How could this happen, if the gods still smiled on the Domdur? Why was Rebiri faring any better than his father, or his father's father?

It must be true, then. Something had happened to alienate the Domdur from their gods. Ba'el had forsaken this Malledd, and the gods had chosen a *new* ally.

They had chosen *him.*

A great swelling bubble of emotion rose in his chest, threatening to choke him—pride and joy and wonder, all commingled.

The gods had chosen *him.* The Olnami would be the new chosen people, and he, Rebiri Nazakri, would lead them to victory.

He had believed for years that he had a destiny, that he would bring down the Empire, but until now he had believed that he would do it despite the gods.

Now he knew that he would do it *because* of the gods, and that changed everything.

"Of course," he said. "Of course I believe you, believe in you. Doubt you? Never again!"

The voice was gone; Ba'el was not there.

But he had been. Ba'el had spoken to him.

He still did not know how the god intended to ensure that the nightwalkers could make the long march to Seidabar without being caught defenseless in the sun, but he no longer doubted that the god would do so somehow.

And soon, very soon.

They would have to be ready.

He had a sudden inspiration—he didn't know how or why, but he suddenly knew that there were things he must do, preparations he must make. He arose from the cushion.

"Aldassi!" he bellowed. "Asari!"

The carpenters, most of them volunteers from Drievabor, grumbled about constructing the "barricades," but at Lord Duzon's urging they assembled them quickly and skillfully.

General Balinus had agreed to the plan readily enough, and had left the implementation to Duzon. "You thought it up," Balinus told him. "You know how it's supposed to work. So *you* get it ready. I intend to go into this final battle rested and ready, not worn out from worrying about details. You give me that bridge, Duzon, and I'll lead the men across it."

Duzon protested. "Sir, it would seem to me that as the . . . well, as the captain of the Company of Champions, that I should be . . ."

Balinus cut his objections short. "You thought it up; you make it work. If you're truly the champion and blessed with supernatural endurance, you'll still be fit to join me in leading the attack. If you're not the champion, then you have no grounds for complaint, do you?"

Duzon could find no way to counter that—he thought for a moment of revealing Malledd's presence to Balinus, but could not quite bring himself to do so, since it would wreck his own claim forever, and Malledd wouldn't appreciate it anyway. Instead, Duzon set about harrying the carpenters.

The construction preparations quickly used up all the small remaining stock of timber in the camp; when it became plain that that would not be sufficient Duzon sent the carpenters to their beds, and woke other men to serve as laborers, using the few surviving horses to rush them to Drievabor and haul back salvaged beams and planking from anywhere they could be found.

Duzon had wanted to discuss the plan's feasibility with the New Magicians, but Vrai Burrai and Tebas Tudan were both out of camp, flying another mission to Seidabar, carrying messages both ways and bringing back whatever medical supplies they could carry. None of the others would commit themselves to anything without the approval of their seniors. Duzon, his nerves frayed by lack of sleep, left their enclosure in a state of barely controlled fury at their obstinance and at his sleeping superior's decisions. He returned to his own tent and forced himself to sleep until dusk.

Collecting the materials took the entire first day of Sheshar's triad; in fact, the men and women and horses returning from Drievabor arrived after the nightly cross-river raid had begun. Defending the horses from nightwalkers while unhitching them was a fearsome job, one that cost three good soldiers and a female volunteer their lives.

The word from Drievabor was not good; at least half the town's population had fled west, and most of those who remained stayed behind locked doors, terrified of nightwalkers. The only consolation was that there were no confirmed reports that nightwalkers had actually been there.

On the second day the actual assembly of the raft-bridge sections began, using the carpenters who had slept that first day. Balinus reviewed the latest reports from the New Magicians' aerial reconnaissance, but again took no interest in the construction, leaving it to Duzon. Duzon, wearing his best remaining cloak and hat in an attempt to encourage the troops, moved quickly through the camp, observing the work closely.

"You don't need 'em so tight as all that," one man complained when Duzon reiterated the requirement that each panel be watertight. "They can't put a blade or an arrow through so small a space as all that!"

"Don't be too sure," Duzon said. "And whether they can or not, I want these watertight!"

"But . . ."

"Humor me, my good man. Pretend I might have reasons you don't know."

"But . . ." The carpenter looked at the barrier again, then at the river, then back at Duzon.

"Oh," he said. "Very good, my lord."

Duzon nodded in acknowledgment, setting the rather bedraggled replacement plume in his hat bobbing, and as he did he noticed two shapes descending from the heavens—undoubtedly the messengers to Seidabar were returning. He walked on to the little enclosure where half the surviving graduates of the Imperial College of the New Magic huddled, intent on getting a straight answer this time.

He found Malledd already there, deep in discussion with Vrai Burrai.

That simplified Duzon's errand; he didn't need to explain what was planned, since Malledd already had.

"Can you do it?" he asked.

"We can do it," Burrai replied.

"How quickly?"

Burrai considered that, scratching an ear thoughtfully. "Depends on whether we need to recharge, and how bright the sun is, and how much trouble we get from the other side. An hour at best, half a day at worst."

"And if we have the sections ready at dawn tomorrow?"

Vrai Burrai shrugged. "Sun's dim at dawn. Given a clear sky and no distractions, two hours. If it's raining and the Nazakri takes an interest, we should have it by noon—but I can't promise we'll be able to keep it intact very long if the Nazakri decides to destroy it."

Duzon nodded, and glanced at the cloudless, moon-speckled sky. "That should do fine," he said.

"There's only one more day," Malledd pointed out. "We need to cross *tomorrow*."

"I know that," Duzon snapped. "We'll be ready." He looked eastward, at the earthworks that blocked his view of the river—and the enemy camp. "We'll finally be able to return the visits they've been paying us!" He hurried to inform the general.

Balinus had been on the verge of sleep, but received the report.

"Excellent, Duzon," he said. "Revenge will be sweet, won't it?"

The two men smiled at one another; then Balinus rolled over on his cot and began snoring, while Duzon headed for his own tent.

That night, though, when Duzon saw the number of nightwalkers that marched down into the river, he wondered whether enough of the Imperial vanguard would survive the night to carry out their grand design. Heretofore perhaps at most a thousand nightwalkers, usually fewer, had crossed on any given night, leaving many times more standing idly on the eastern banks, but on this, the night between the second and third days of Sheshar's Triad, the marching ranks of nightwalkers seemed to go on forever, and the numbers left behind were far smaller than usual.

And of the surviving Imperial forces—perhaps eight hundred soldiers, and two hundred assorted volunteers, including a dozen women and nine members of the Company of Champions—fully a hundred and fifty had already gone a day and a night without sleep in making their preparations for the upcoming surprise assault.

The nightwalkers burst up from the Grebiguata at a run, and stormed up the barricades. The new wooden panels, rafts disguised as fortifications, were battered and then shoved aside, and the undead foe, still dripping wet from their walk beneath the river, poured over the earthworks and into the camp.

There the Imperial forces met them with sword and ax.

Duzon himself was in the thick of it, chopping at necks with his borrowed broadsword. He ignored the taunts of the nightwalkers, the mocking comments on his ancestry, the questions about why the gods hadn't struck down the foes of the Domdur, and hacked away.

He found himself confronted with an open-chested horror, once a big, burly farmer, who wore a crude, heavy collar made of an old ox yoke to guard his throat.

Duzon had seen that stunt before. It did make the nightwalker harder to kill, but cutting out its heart or spilling enough of its brain would still dispose of it.

"Ah, lordling!" the nightwalker called to him, raising the mace it bore. "Are you the one who thinks he's the chosen of the gods? Don't you know that Rebiri Nazakri has Ba'el's favor, not any of you decadent Domdur?"

Duzon didn't bother replying as he dodged the blow of the mace. The collar made things difficult; instead of simply beheading his enemy he chopped at its head. The torn flesh and exposed ribs of its chest made the heart a tempting target, but the head was still the easier.

The mace swung in a horizontal arc, and Duzon dropped to one knee to get beneath it. He thrust his sword upward and punched the point up through the nightwalker's throat and into its skull.

That didn't kill it, but it did pin it in place and keep it from speaking. "A hand here!" Duzon called as he held the sword steady and dodged the blind flailing of the mace.

Someone obliged; an ax came down on the nightwalker's head and splattered brains and bone in all directions. Duzon shut his eyes against the spray of rotting gore and therefore did not see at first who had come to his aid. When he opened them again he saw only his helper's back, but the man's size made Onnell unmistakable; Malledd was visibly larger, and no one else came close to either of them.

Half the nightwalker's head was gone, but Duzon realized it still wasn't defeated. Onnell had been distracted before he could be sure of the thing's demise, and the mace was still swinging. The nightwalker's eyes were both gone, along with most of its brain and skull, leaving it blind and stupid.

Duzon ripped his sword free, then reached up and yanked the heavy protective collar off over the ruined head, then quickly lopped off what remained.

The nightwalker collapsed at last, the mace missing Duzon's foot by a fraction of an inch.

He stared down at the ghastly mess for a moment.

The thing had said that Ba'el favored the Nazakri—exactly what Malledd had said. Either it was the truth, or Malledd himself was part of the enemy's scheme.

He looked up and scanned the battle for Malledd, and found the big man bellowing in rage as he chopped the head from a nightwalker.

It was the truth.

Duzon had agreed to Malledd's scheme because it seemed like a sound idea for a counterattack, quite apart from any other consideration. This larger-than-usual assault, though, and the nightwalker's words, now convinced him that

Malledd was right, that Ba'el's Triad was what the Nazakri had been waiting for for so long.

But Ba'el's Triad was when the night was at its *shortest*, when nightwalkers had the least power.

Then what did the Nazakri plan? What was he going to use *instead* of nightwalkers?

Was Ba'el himself going to intervene on the rebels' behalf?

But no, Ba'el would be stoking the sun; surely, this would be the time when he could *not* interfere directly, even while his more generalized influence was at its zenith, his strength and courage spread throughout the world in the rays of the sun itself.

His strength, his courage—and his other traits, as well; everyone knew that midsummer, Ba'el's Triad, was when the most fights took place, when the most murders were committed. And this year, it would apparently be when the key battle of this campaign was fought.

Then Duzon spotted a nightwalker coming up on a soldier from behind and forgot about gods and grand strategies; he ran for the foe screaming, his sword swinging up to strike.

On the far side of the river Rebiri Nazakri stood atop a crude wooden tower, watching the battle avidly. The staff in his hand whined eerily, and smoke swirled about it.

"This is the last," he said.

"Father?" Aldassi said, puzzled. He was standing at the foot of the tower, waiting. Beside him Asari Asakari leaned idly on one of the tower supports.

"This is the last of these raids," Rebiri explained. "Tomorrow night we march onward, across the river to our final triumph!"

Asari looked up. "We'll be taking Drievabor?"

Rebiri glanced down. "You can if you choose, Asari," he said. "I leave the living to you. I shall be leaving you, leading the nightwalkers to Seidabar; I'll have a few more orders in the morning, and then the rest of you are free to do as you choose. You've served me well, and I shall ask no more after tomorrow."

Asari blinked up at him, thought better of asking any questions, and began to look contemplatively around the camp.

Rebiri looked at Aldassi. "You have your magic," he said. "Stay with the others here, where you'll be safe—there's no need to risk your life at the gates of Seidabar. I've been promised victory, not security; I may die, and I would not have my line die with me."

"But, Father . . . !" Aldassi began.

Rebiri held up a hand. "When victory is won, and Seidabar is fallen, you can come seeking me," he said. "If I still live, I should not be difficult to find."

"I . . . are you *commanding* me not to accompany you, Father?"

"I am, my son. You may *follow* me, at a safe distance—but no more, please."

Aldassi stared up at him for a long moment, then looked down.

"As you wish, Father."

Rebiri nodded. "Your friends in Seidabar," he asked. "Are they ready for our arrival?"

"They're not my *friends*," Aldassi growled. "And they'll do what they can, as they have all along."

"You haven't given your word that they'll be spared, have you?"

"No, Father. Of course not. I've never promised a thing."

"I *won't* spare them," Rebiri said warningly.

"Good," Aldassi muttered.

He had never liked Lord Shoule anyway.

CHAPTER 54

The bodies and pieces of bodies were strewn thick across the open area behind the earthworks when at last the nightwalkers scrambled back out and headed for the water. Duzon had been standing and fighting in a morass of mud and blood for the last hour or more, unable to find more secure footing; now he kicked aside a severed hand and a dropped dagger to stand on a dry patch no bigger than a man's chest. His sword hung loose in his hand and he trembled with exhaustion as he peered to the east, at the brightening sky and the fleeing enemy.

He couldn't rest, though. This was the day, the final day of Sheshar's Triad, when they would build their raft-bridge, scatter the Nazakri's living followers, and butcher the dormant nightwalkers.

The sky was clear; there were no clouds to hamper the sunlight the New Magicians needed. A thin line of smoke trailed up the eastern sky—the rebels were lighting their cookfires, he supposed, or perhaps a watchfire hadn't yet burned out—but that was all.

His own people wouldn't have time to cook, Duzon realized. They would barely have time to eat; they needed to get the attack under way *now* if they were to be sure of having time to drive away the guardians and behead most of the nightwalkers.

"Where's the general?" he called.

"Dead," a woman answered, pointing at a bloody heap sprawled against the earthworks. Her voice was unsteady.

"Oh, gods . . ." Duzon hurried over and looked down.

General Balinus, the wily old soldier who had fought Rebiri Nazakri all the way from Matua, lay staring blankly up at the moons. His tunic had been slit across the chest, and the red fabric was covered with a darker red, already fading to brown.

Duzon used his own sword to lift one edge of the cut and look at the wound beneath. He swallowed.

There was no possible doubt. Balinus was dead.

And all six colonels had died in previous battles. That left Lord Captain Duzon as the highest-ranking officer alive, and meant that he was in full command of the Imperial forces in the area.

He had wanted command, but not now, and not like this. It seemed grossly unfair that Balinus had survived so long, and died so soon before the end.

"Cut his head off," Duzon said quietly. "We'll bury him after the battle; we don't have time now."

"We...but..." The woman hesitated.

Duzon looked at her face, and took pity on her.

"I'll do it," he said. "You don't have to watch."

"Thank you," she said, turning away.

Balinus's head was already flung back, exposing his leathery throat, but it was still one of the hardest things Duzon had ever done to bring his sword down on it.

The first blow was not enough; he cursed himself. "I don't have time for this," he said, and swung again.

That did it; the head rolled free.

"Now let's get on with it," he said. He turned to the woman. "Are you fighting today, or staying?"

"I'll fight," she said.

"You're from Drievabor? What's your name?"

"Kiudegar."

"Good." He clapped her on the shoulder. "Go get ready, Kiudegar. Today it's all or nothing."

Then he turned to face the rest of the camp. "All right," he shouted, "where are those barricades we built?"

"There," a familiar voice said. Duzon turned to find Onnell pointing.

"Oh, gods..." Duzon said as he stared in dismay.

Most of the raft-barricades had been knocked down, pushed back from the earthworks, and thrown flat to the ground. There they had served as platforms, and atop them, avoiding the mud, men (and a few women) had fought the invading nightwalkers.

The rafts were buried in the dead. Several bore the marks of blows from blades and clubs, and at least one had been battered to pieces.

"We need those!" Duzon shouted. "You men, get those rebuilt! *Now!*"

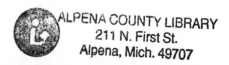
ALPENA COUNTY LIBRARY
211 N. First St.
Alpena, Mich. 49707

No one responded; Duzon turned and found himself staring at faces that were blank and sagging with exhaustion, the faces of men too tired to tackle anything more.

For a few seconds no one moved, no one spoke; then, fifty yards away, Malledd stood up and bellowed, "He's right! Lord Duzon's right! Come on, all of you—for the Empress! For your homes and your families! One last battle, and we can rest all we want!"

"We're doomed," someone said. "The gods have forsaken us. The general is dead, and we have no champion."

"What do you mean, we have no champion?" Malledd roared, marching forward. "We have Lord Duzon, right there! Now, come on!"

From the corner of his eye Duzon saw Onnell's jaw drop. Onnell looked from Malledd to Duzon, then back to Malledd, his astonishment plain on his face.

Duzon was gratified, but not astonished; he knew Malledd hadn't wanted the job, and what's more, he recognized that Malledd hadn't lied. Malledd had never said Duzon was the *divine* champion; he had merely pointed out that Duzon was there, available for a champion's role.

"Come on!" Duzon shouted, raising his sword.

Gradually, men started to move.

When the reassembly of the damaged rafts was under way, Duzon turned his attention to the New Magicians. He found them gathered in their compound, conferring quietly among themselves.

"Are you ready?" Duzon demanded.

Vrai Burrai frowned. "We'll do our best," he said. He waved a hand at the eastern sky. "We weren't expecting that."

"Weren't expecting . . . ?" Duzon turned.

He had not consciously noticed that the sky was brightening more slowly than normal, but now he realized that although it was well after dawn the sun was still dim.

The reason was simple enough—smoke was pouring upward from the enemy's camp in great billowing clouds, filling the sky and darkening the sun to the color of an old copper coin. A small moon was brushing against it in a partial eclipse, as if one side were notched, but the major reason for the lack of light was the smoke.

The light penetrating that smoke was enough to immobilize the nightwalkers, enough to constitute daylight—but not enough to fully power the New Magicians' crystals.

"What are they doing?" Duzon asked no one in particular.

"Burning their own camp," Tebas Tudan replied. "They started at dawn, putting the torch to their tents and pavilions. Now the grass and crops are afire, as well."

Indeed they were; the entire eastern bank of the river seemed to be lined with fire, spilling a torrent of smoke into the open air.

"Their soldiers, and the nightwalkers, are gathered on the bare earth or down in that hole of theirs, safe from the flames," Tebas Tudan added.

"But *why?*" Duzon asked.

No one answered that, but Duzon knew part of the explanation without being told. This long campaign of attrition, of two armies facing each other and raiding one another, of strong defenses and unchanging positions, was over; whatever happened now, Rebiri Nazakri and the nightwalkers would not be staying in that camp any longer.

And the smoke would weaken the New Magicians who fought for the Empire. Until now, the band under Vrai Burrai's command had been sufficient to neutralize much of the Nazakri's own black sorcery. This smoke was only a temporary measure, something that could only be used once and that would last only a few hours, but while it endured it might be enough to give the Nazakri a decisive edge.

Malledd had been right; Ba'el's Triad was when everything would be resolved, one way or the other. Duzon still didn't know just what Rebiri Nazakri planned, but he could no longer doubt that the old Olnami planned *something*.

That made it more urgent than ever to strike *now*, while Sheshar still controlled the sun, while there were still a dozen hours of daylight remaining.

"Do your best," Duzon said. "Start whenever you can; get that bridge built!"

"We'll try," Vrai Burrai said, holding up his staff and staring critically at the rather feeble glow of the crystals.

"Go to it, then!" He clapped Burrai on the arm, then turned and marched out, to oversee preparations elsewhere.

An hour later he headed back to the magicians' enclosure; none of them had yet emerged, and not a single panel had been moved to the river. Repairs were well under way on every raft that needed any, but the rafts were useless without the magicians. Duzon struggled to hide his frustration, fury, and genuine fear at this unexpected delay in the start of assembly.

"What's wrong?" he demanded when he stepped inside. "Why isn't the bridge started?"

"This smoke!" Vrai Burrai shouted. "We can't get enough light!"

"Well, then, do what you can, but do *something!* We have men who can help haul, if that would speed things up."

"It might," Burrai admitted.

"Then get on with it!" Duzon spun on his heel and marched back out.

Many of the soldiers were snatching a little sleep while they could; others were standing or sitting in small groups, talking, many of them staring at the ominous columns of smoke that still rose steadily from across the Grebiguata.

"You," Duzon said, pointing at one of these idlers, "get in there and offer to help." He jerked a thumb at the gate to the enclosure.

The man hesitated; then Malledd, who was among the idlers, said, "Come on, let's get at it." He marched into the magicians' area, and reluctantly, the other followed.

"The rest of you, too," Duzon said.

He stamped on, through the camp, cursing under his breath as the delays continued.

Finally, though, when the sun was almost overhead and clear of the worst of the smoke, the rafts that were to make up the bridge were arrayed along the riverbank, ready to go. The New Magicians emerged, crystals glowing atop their staves, and went to work.

The work still went slowly. The sun passed its zenith and crept down to the west.

On the far side of the river the fires had largely burned out now—that was a relief for Duzon, who had feared that the smoke might become thick enough that the nightwalkers would awaken early. That horror, at least, had been avoided; the eastern sky was gradually clearing.

The western sky was clouding up, though, and that was almost as bad.

Across the river, surrounded the desolation that had been the enemy camp, the possessed corpses were still stacked in their neat rows, untouched by the flames. Their living guardians prowled between the rows and along the riverbank, watching the Imperial preparations. Duzon thought that a large cluster of them near the rim of the great pit was probably Rebiri Nazakri and his staff.

He wished he had some way to strike directly at that group, but the New Magicians were busy with the bridge, and no one else could possibly reach the foe.

Besides, he knew that any attack would be countered by the Nazakri's own black sorcery. The New Magicians had tried any number of magical assaults over the past two seasons, and the Nazakri had countered them all easily.

Something flared red as he watched—the wizard's evil magic, undoubtedly, though Duzon could not see what it accomplished.

One of the New Magicians who had been hovering over the assembling bridge turned and swept toward Rebiri Nazakri, crystal blazing—and smoky red light flared up to meet him. Golden sunlight clashed with baleful crimson for a few seconds, then dispersed, and the New Magician tumbled from the sky, landing in the river with a tremendous splash.

For a moment all work on the bridge ceased as the other New Magicians hurried to aid their fellow, and Duzon cursed this new delay. He also realized that the Nazakri could undoubtedly destroy the bridge if the New Magicians weren't there to defend it; in past encounters Vrai Burrai's band had always been collectively powerful enough to counter every magical assault Rebiri Nazakri attempted, and the Nazakri in turn had had the power to resist all attacks—but the smoke and the clouds had left the Imperial College low on energy, and the assembly of the bridge was consuming what was left.

The army would need to get across *fast*, while the magicians were still functioning. And the Nazakri himself might be more dangerous than all the rest of his rebel force put together, if there was no sun-powered New Magic to oppose him.

They had no choice, though; this was their last opportunity to defeat the rebels before ...

Before Ba'el's Triad, whatever that meant.

The living, fully human rebels were beginning to organize now; the group that had clustered around their commander was now marching down toward the river, and others were collecting around them.

"Malledd!" Duzon called, turning away. "Onnell!"

CHAPTER 55

The Imperial Army was marching at last; Prince Granzer had slipped away from the Empress's bedside long enough to look out the tower windows at the long columns of red and gold moving out of the Agabdal camps and passing around the northern side of Seidabar on the Gogror Highway.

Lord Kadan was at their head, by Granzer's own order.

Prince Graubris would be furious when he found out, of course—Granzer knew that. Graubris was still in the imperial bedchamber, by his mother's death-bed, awaiting the inevitable; he had not noticed when Lord Kadan left the Imperial Palace. One Councillor among sixteen would not be missed; in fact, Councillors and family members drifted in and out constantly. No one could be expected to stand there, silently waiting for the inevitable, indefinitely.

The doctors had been too pessimistic; old Beretris was still clinging to life, two days after they had pronounced her death sentence. For two days, courtiers and Councillors and the entire imperial clan had been clustered in the tower, watching over their Empress, awaiting that final breath, and it hadn't yet come.

Graubris had watched most closely of all, the devoted son—and the others had all watched Graubris, watching for any sign of impatience, any wish that his mother would get it over with and leave him Emperor. Graubris had, so far, disappointed them—he had hovered at his mother's side, displaying nothing but the most sincere concern.

That close attention had made it easy for Granzer and Kadan to act unnoticed elsewhere.

When he *did* notice, Graubris would be furious. He might well, as Emperor, insist upon Granzer's removal as the Council's President, perhaps expel him from the Council entirely.

At this point, Granzer didn't think he cared. Graubris was being a fool. All the evidence pointed to Kadan's innocence, and Shoule's involvement in the treacherous conspiracy—if Shoule was not himself the ringleader, he was at the very least a dupe of whoever was plotting against the Empire. Kadan had said he would rather die than serve such an Emperor as Graubris; Granzer would not go that far, but like Kadan, he had no desire to serve a fool.

He hoped his brother-in-law had merely been distracted and upset, and would recover his senses once the crisis was passed and he was installed upon the throne.

Not that Granzer was eager to see Graubris become Emperor Graubris IV. He had tried very hard to stay out of any disputes about the succession, if only to ensure his own marital harmony—he knew his wife would make an abominable Empress, and had had no strong preference between her twin brothers. Now, though, the more he saw of Graubris's attempts to act authoritatively, the more he favored the idea of putting Zolous on the throne. Darisei was still out of the question, but Zolous . . . Zolous had, so far, behaved admirably. And Zolous had six healthy children—or at least five, since Prince Bagar's current whereabouts was unknown. The idea of Emperor Zolous III looked better all the time.

Of course, Granzer didn't dare say so when his wife was listening. And he wasn't planning to contest Graubris's claim to the throne; even a bad Emperor was surely better than risking civil war, especially with the rebel wizard still out there at the head of an undead army.

A bad Emperor . . . the Domdur had never had one, of course. The gods had made sure of that, even if it meant sometimes skipping over several candidates for the throne and choosing an obscure cousin.

What a shame the gods had left the decision to mortals this time.

The marching lines, partially obscured by intervening structures, now stretched from Agabdal to the eastern horizon; as Granzer watched, the last of them left the camps, and the gates swung shut behind them. He turned away.

"Your Highness," someone said.

Startled, Granzer turned to find Lord Passeil standing at his side. He quickly suppressed the urge to take one final glance out the window; if he did, Passeil might look as well, might see the marching troops, might know what Granzer and Kadan had done. It was too soon; the army could still be stopped, if Graubris chose to stop it. Passeil could *probably* be trusted, but there was that slight uncertainty.

"What is it, my lord?" Granzer asked, trying to move to block Passeil's view without making his intent obvious.

"Her Imperial Majesty's breathing has become uneven; her heartbeat is weak and erratic. I fear she has but minutes remaining."

"I'll come," Granzer said.

Passeil put a hand to Granzer's chest to halt him. "A moment, first," he said. "A word about the succession."

Granzer looked down at the beringed hand pressing at the front of his blouse; Passeil dropped it.

"What about the succession?" Granzer asked. "I believe we had settled that."

"And I believe we have not," Passeil replied. "The Empress expressed a preference, but by what right does she choose her own heir? Ancient tradition says that the imperial family must ask the Council, and the Council must consult the gods. If the gods do not answer—as we must anticipate they will not—then it falls to the *Council*, not the Empress, to name the heir."

"I can see how you might reach that conclusion," Granzer said slowly.

"I can reach no other," Passeil replied.

"And how does this alter anything, my lord?" Granzer asked.

"I should think it would be obvious. The Council must meet and choose a new Emperor—or Empress, Your Highness. The matter has *not* been decided."

"Do you think that a majority of the Council would choose to oppose Her Imperial Majesty's wishes in this matter?"

"Indeed, I think they might," Passeil said. "I have not come entirely on my own initiative, Your Highness; I speak for Lord Graush and Lord Niniam, as well as myself, when I say that we would be pleased to vote for *you* as the heir to the throne."

Granzer's jaw dropped.

"*Me?*" he said. "Are you mad? When the Empress has three children and six grandchildren yet living, and I'm no closer in blood than a dozen others?"

"You're first cousin to the three heirs . . ."

"On their *father's* side, my lord—my uncle was Prince Consort, not Emperor. That's not imperial blood."

". . . and married to the eldest."

"And how can I possibly claim the title for myself, when she has a claim so much greater?"

"Because you are who you are, Your Highness. You've served long and well as President of the Council; we have faith in your abilities."

"It's absurd," Granzer said.

Passeil sighed. "We thought you might say that. In that case, we are willing to support your wife's claim to the throne, rather than your own."

"My wife, much as I love her, can be thoughtless and intemperate; I cannot believe she would fill her mother's role well."

"Can you believe her brother would do better? You saw him in the council chamber yesterday...."

"The day before," Granzer corrected. "Yes, I saw him. No, I do not honestly think he'll be as good a ruler as his mother, or most of his other predecessors. Still, I can't see Darisei doing any better, nor any of them accepting my own claim, should I be foolish enough to make one."

Passeil hesitated. "There is at least one other claimant," he said at last.

"Zolous?" Granzer sighed. "If he were to make a claim, I *would* support it. But how can he? He's the youngest of the three."

"And the only one with heirs of his own," Passeil pointed out. "The age difference is only ten minutes, after all. I think the Council can make a case for him very nicely, on that basis."

"And would Lord Graush support this? Would the others?"

"Graush and Niniam and I would indeed back such a choice, Your Highness; we discussed this at some length. We would prefer you, and then your wife, but Zolous would be acceptable as a third alternative, and preferable to his brother. Alas, I can't speak for the rest of the Council on this."

Granzer stared at him.

Graush, Passeil, Niniam, and himself—that was one-fourth of the Council right there. Five more would be enough.

He could be certain that Shoule and Orbalir would oppose any such scheme. Kadan would almost certainly support it.

He glanced at the window before he could catch himself.

"We know," Passeil said, seeing that glance. "We approve. But I suspect Prince Graubris will not."

Granzer let out a bitter bark of laughter. "I suspect you're right," he said. He turned and looked openly out at the long lines marching eastward.

Those were the people who would really save the Empire, he thought. He and the other Councillors might concern themselves with ensuring that the best available Emperor took the throne, but it was Lord Kadan and his soldiers who would ensure that the throne still stood.

He frowned.

And were they really ensuring anything? What if Graubris refused to accept the Council's decision? What if the Council were to split, eight to eight? The law called for the Empress to act as a tiebreaker—but there would *be* no Empress. Could they count her expressed preference for Graubris as her vote?

Could he and Passeil and the rest be driving the Empire toward civil war? Would they defeat the Nazakri, only to destroy themselves?

Would they defeat the Nazakri at all? Was he doing the right thing, sending Kadan eastward and leaving Seidabar almost unguarded?

He looked up, as if seeking a sign in the heavens, and saw one moon hanging high in the sky above, dominating the view—Ba'el, clearly visible even by daylight. The sun was in the east, and Ba'el showed only a red crescent, like a bloody grin.

Granzer shuddered and turned away.

CHAPTER 56

The bridge was ready. The magicians had arranged it and weighted it so that an inch or so of water flowed across it, making any attempt to burn it useless—at least, any attempt to destroy it with natural, everyday fire; no one knew what the ghastly red stuff used by Rebiri Nazakri could do.

Most of the New Magicians had collapsed, their power spent; the last few had had to swim ashore while rebel arrows splashed around them, as their companions could no longer spare the energy to assist them. Only Vrai Burrai and Tebas Tudan still flew, and they did so only intermittently as they hurried back and forth along the bridge, checking the seams.

"Need we wait any longer?" Malledd asked as he stood on the brink, at the head of the disorderly column of Imperial troops. Having come this far he was eager to get it all over with, one way or the other—and with the sun sinking in the west, every moment was precious.

"No," Lord Duzon said from astride his charger—the last horse left to them, as the others had all fallen during the night's fighting. He rose up in the stirrups and shouted, "For our Empress, for the gods, for the Domdur—and for our dead, forward!" He shook the reins and kicked his heels, urging his mount out onto the bridge.

Malledd ran at the horse's left side; to the right came Kodeida and Manenobar, the last of the Company of Champions besides Duzon himself. Behind these four ran Onnell, Darsmit, Kiudegar, and the rest of the surviving Imperial vanguard, splashing onto the wooden causeway.

They charged across the bridge, gathering speed, sweeping past the startled Tebas Tudan and the unsurprised Vrai Burrai, and plunged off the eastern end into knee-deep water; they didn't hesitate there, but continued up the bank to smash headlong into their waiting enemies.

There was no possibility of subtlety or surprise in this assault; the bridge had made their intent obvious from the first, and the rebels had had hours to prepare. Surprisingly, they had done little—the Imperials were not met with pikes, nor locked shields, nor any barriers other than men with raised weapons.

Even as Malledd ran forward, and as little as he knew of warfare, he marveled at this—shouldn't they have dug ditches, thrown up earthworks, set traps? They hadn't; he knew that, as the Domdur had watched from across the river and would have seen any such activity.

Nor did the wizard himself confront them; he was nowhere in sight.

"Break through them!" Duzon shouted, his sword raised; his mount's greater speed had carried him ahead of the others. "Get the nightwalkers!" He suited his own actions to his words, sending his horse trampling over the enemy, slashing at anyone in reach.

Malledd let out a wordless bellow of approval and swung his own sword at the nearest foe. The rebel ducked, screaming, then tried to turn and flee but collided with his neighbor, sending them both sprawling.

These weren't the grinning, mocking nightwalkers, unafraid of death; these were mortal men they faced now, men who had watched the nightly battles for triad after triad but who had never had to fight in them. Seasons of battle had hardened the Domdur troops into ruthless veterans, while those same seasons spent in inaction had left the rebels a disorganized, cowardly mob. Many shrieked and ran the first time a hostile weapon came near.

Malledd slashed at the legs of both downed rebels, leaving them helpless and bleeding but still alive, then looked up just in time to see Duzon and his mount vanish.

Malledd blinked in confusion; where had Lord Duzon gone? He hurried forward, heedless of his own safety, trying to see what had become of the horseman.

"Look out!" Manenobar shouted, and Malledd turned to fend off a wild, reckless blow from a plump Matuan who was already panting with exertion. The two men locked swords, and for a moment Malledd stared into the rebel's face and saw anger, terror, and sweat.

Then, swords still locked, he punched the Matuan in the nose with his free left hand. The Matuan crumpled, and his sword clattered to the ground.

Malledd turned his attention eastward again and pushed his way forward, through the rebels, trying to find Duzon, trying to get through the rebel lines so as to get at the inert nightwalkers.

Then he was clear of the press, nothing but open space before him—and the ground crumbled beneath him. He tumbled forward, into darkness, and landed hard on rough ground.

He remained alert, though, and scrambled quickly to his feet. He was in a hole, facing a tunnel.

"Malledd," someone said.

Malled turned, and found Lord Duzon standing beside him in the mouth of another tunnel, holding the charger's bridle.

"They've mined all through here," Duzon said. "It's a maze—there must be at least a dozen tunnels!"

Malledd looked up, at the gray sky far above; the sounds of battle were still audible, but muffled. The surface of the ground was a good four feet above his head; a hole had been dug in the tunnel ceiling, not quite all the way up into the open air, and his own weight had broken in the last thin layer of soil.

There had been traps after all. Malledd didn't know when they had been prepared, but they had been here, ready and waiting.

"We have to get out of here," he said.

Just then someone shrieked, and light appeared in one of the tunnels—another booby trap had been triggered, another thinned roof had collapsed beneath someone.

"How did they dig these without our seeing anything?" Duzon asked of no one in particular.

"We *did* see them," Malledd said, suddenly realizing. "The pit they kept digging in, the pit where the Nazakri dug up whatever it is he uses to make nightwalkers. They tunneled out from the pit!"

"You're right," Duzon said. He turned. "And that's our way out."

Another soldier broke through and tumbled into the tunnels in a rush and roar of earth, a second man falling on his heels. Duzon's horse whinnied in fear.

"We have to find a way to the pit," Duzon said. "We can climb out there."

"Right," Malledd said. He looked around, trying to orient himself; the slant of the light from the openings overhead told him which way was east and which west. "That way," he said, pointing in the direction he judged to lead toward the great open pit at the heart of the rebel camp.

Another hole opened, and someone cried out in surprise—a cry that was abruptly cut off by impact with the hard-trodden tunnel floor.

A voice groaned in pain.

"I'll help them," Malledd said. "You go find the pit. Show yourself, rally our troops."

"Yes, of course," Duzon said. He hurried down the passage Malledd had pointed to, pulling his protesting mount after him.

Malledd turned to gather the others, and tend to any who had been injured in the fall. Fortunately, the daylight served to spotlight each of them; he need merely go to each illuminated place in turn and find who was there.

At the first he found two men, one down with a twisted ankle and the other guarding his fallen companion. Malledd asked, "Can you walk?"

"Limp, maybe," the man on the ground replied. "I can't fight."

Malledd frowned. "These tunnels open off the big pit in the center of the enemy camp," he explained. He pointed. "The pit's that way, and you can climb out there—but you might need to fight, I don't know."

"We'll try it," his companion said, glancing uneasily at the darkness of the tunnels behind them. "We don't know what surprises they might have for us down here."

Malledd hadn't really given that much thought—if there had been enemies waiting down here, he thought they would have already attacked by now. . . .

Another scream sounded amid a rush of falling earth; Malledd had lost count of how many people had been caught in these pitfalls.

So far, though, all had survived the experience, and most weren't even injured beyond a few bruises and scrapes. Surely the enemy hadn't expected the Imperial troops to be killed by so short a drop. Perhaps they *did* have soldiers, or monsters of some sort, or some other dire menace, waiting to see how many would fall into their trap before they attacked.

Or perhaps the enemy's soldiers were waiting at the pit, perhaps with archers posted around the rim.

Or perhaps the tunnels had been dug for some other purpose entirely, and converted to traps at the last moment—the nightwalkers were said to draw their power from beneath the earth, and that was generally believed to be why the Nazakri had dug a pit in the first place. Maybe the tunnels had been where the nightwalkers renewed their strength.

There was no way of knowing, however, either why the tunnels had been dug or what might be lurking in them, and heading for the open pit seemed the safest course of action.

"Be careful," Malledd said, before moving off toward the next fallen ally.

He had directed four more toward the pit and Lord Duzon, and was heading for another, when he heard the dry, hideous laugh from the darkness of a tunnel. Malledd froze, sword raised.

"Go ahead," a rasping voice said. "Get them back aboveground if you like. The sun's going down, Domdur, and when it's gone we'll have them all."

"Oh, no, you won't," Malledd replied. "We'll have *you*."

The nightwalker's only reply was another long laugh, this one fading as if the creature was retreating deeper into the subterranean maze. Malledd considered pursuit, then discarded the idea—nightwalkers could see in the dark, he was fairly sure, and he had no way of knowing how many of the foul things might be lurking there in the dark, or what traps they might have set.

Besides, the nightwalker had a point—sunset was approaching all too rapidly, and he had to get as many of the Domdur soldiers out as he could before night fell.

More seemed to be falling as fast as he could reach them; at one point a long stretch of ceiling crumbled all at once, dumping more than a dozen combatants from both sides into the tunnels. The rebels seemed as surprised as the Domdur, and with Malledd rallying them, the Imperial troops were able to make short work of their foe.

"How goes it above?" Malledd asked one of the victors as he wiped blood from his ax—fresh human blood, Malledd noted uneasily, not the half-clotted ichor of a nightwalker.

"They fight like children," the soldier replied contemptuously. "Much shouting and posturing, but half of them flee at the first blow, and the rest flail about wildly, with no skill at all. After the nightwalkers, these people are nothing!"

"Then we've taken most of the camp?"

The man hesitated. "No," he admitted. "We've held back, for fear of traps. We saw our people disappearing, and didn't know what had become of them. We've cleared everything between the river and the first holes, but dared not advance farther."

"But the sun's setting!"

"I know," the soldier said unhappily.

Malledd looked up at the sky overhead; the tunnel they were in had become more of a trench, thanks to the collapse of so much of its roof. "Here, let me boost you up there," he said. "Tell our people to press on, that the traps aren't dangerous!"

The man nodded. Malledd knelt, and the other clambered up his back until Malledd could grab his ankles and hoist him upward. When the man's arms reached the rim of the opening, Malledd shifted his grip and shoved him farther up, so that he sprawled out onto the ground.

Then he clambered to his feet and ran off; Malledd could hear his voice as he shouted encouragement to the others.

"It's not dangerous down here?" another of the Domdur troops asked.

"Not if you stay in the light," Malledd said. "There are nightwalkers in the darkest places—I don't know how many, but at least one or two. And the pit in the center of the camp is that way—Lord Duzon was trying to find a way out there."

Just then a great shout sounded above them; Malledd and the others looked up, startled.

"Duzon!" someone above them called. "It's Lord Duzon! The champion!"

"It would seem he's found one," Malledd said, smiling broadly. "Come on!"

Together, the little band headed into the tunnels in the direction Duzon had taken. Malledd took the lead, sword held ready.

The path led them into utter darkness for a hundred feet or so, as they felt their way through turning, twisting tunnels that seemed to be designed to shut out the light—as, Malledd realized, they undoubtedly were, since it was sunlight that immobilized nightwalkers. Then a faint glimmer appeared ahead, and moments later they emerged into the open pit.

The sounds of battle crashed down on them as they stepped out into open air; the rebels and the Domdur were fighting along the rim of the pit. Malledd glimpsed Duzon's horse rearing, and an arrow flying near it, and that was all he needed.

"This way!" he shouted, charging up the crumbling slope to Duzon's aid.

The others followed him, bellowing war cries. Malledd heard bowstrings twang, heard a yelp, saw a flash of blood red—and then he was too busy hacking at the unguarded side of someone in rotted Greyan robes to pay any further attention.

As the soldier in the fallen tunnel had said, these rebels were not veterans, not nightwalkers; they were, in fact, no match for the battle-hardened Domdur, and the major factor slowing their retreat from the Imperial assault was their own clumsiness and confusion. Everywhere that the Imperial vanguard managed to form a line and advance without tumbling into the tunnels beneath, they made steady progress, driving the rebels back or scattering them completely.

Malledd took a fierce, unreasoning delight in this, but as the western sky turned from blue to red and daylight began to fade, a sliver of worry drove itself into his heart.

Where was the black wizard? And would there be time to behead the nightwalkers?

He shoved aside a man who had fallen against him, blinked ashes from his eyes, and looked about.

Domdur soldiers were at work among the stacked corpses, chopping through throat after throat with ax and sword—but there were so *many*!

And where was the wizard?

Then a flash of light drew his attention—just minutes earlier he might have missed it, but as the sky darkened it stood out more. He turned, pushed aside a dazed Imperial soldier, and peered across a great expanse of bodies at the remains of the black pavilion that had served as Rebiri Nazakri's headquarters.

There amid the fluttering tatters was the Nazakri, standing atop a smoking mound of rubble, surrounded by the New Magicians. Bolts of golden fire were being flung at him from every side—but they were feeble things, weakened by the magicians' earlier efforts in creating the bridge and striking aside lesser foes, and drawing on reserves that had been kept low by the heavy smoke of the camp's destruction.

The Olnamian wizard's staff absorbed each burst, countering it with a smothering darkness from the smoking crystal at the raised end; the Nazakri seemed untroubled by the assault, though his expression was calmly intent. Both sides fought in determined silence, without war cries or shouted bravado.

An Imperial soldier—not a magician of any sort, but an ordinary swordsman in Imperial red—was creeping up behind the Olnamian; Malledd glimpsed him briefly. He clearly intended to take Rebiri Nazakri from behind.

Then the wizard turned, ever so slightly, though Malledd had no idea how he had known the skulking foeman was there; red fire lashed out from the glowing end of the staff, and the would-be assassin screamed in agony, a scream clearly audible over the roar of battle despite the distance. He fell back out of Malledd's sight; the smith only had a glimpse of a blackened, smoking ruin where the man's face had been.

Clearly, it would take magic to defeat the wizard's own dark magic. The New Magicians would have to handle him—and Malledd prayed that they could.

The ordinary soldiers, though, and the nightwalkers—*those* could be defeated by more ordinary means. Malledd turned his attention elsewhere, spotted a cluster of terrified rebels trying to rally, and charged toward them, bellowing and swinging his sword above his head.

They scattered.

Moments later, as he looked around for new foes, Malledd realized that he could find none—fading shadows stretched across the bloody ruins of the camp, the gathering dusk bleached out much of the color, and smoke and sweat had dimmed his eyes, making it hard to be sure what he was looking at, but it was clear that all armed resistance had collapsed. The wizard was still holding off the New Magicians, and only a tiny fraction of the nightwalkers had been disposed of, but the living rebels the Olnami warlord had recruited were now in full flight, eastward across the plains.

The battle was won.

Malledd smiled triumphantly—but an instant later the smile vanished as a tiny movement caught his eye. He turned and stared.

He hadn't imagined it. A dozen feet away a corpse was beginning to twitch.

Malledd whirled and stared at the western horizon. The sun was gone; the afterglow was already starting to fade.

And on all sides, the nightwalkers were stirring—not the few hundred the vanguard had fought every night for so many triads, but *all* of them.

Thousands of them.

Asari Asakari crouched on the blackened, half-burnt grass, peering back toward the camp.

His part was over. Rebiri Nazakri had said so. One more day of burning everything that could be burned, so as to hide the sun with smoke—and then, when the old wizard had realized what the Domdur were up to with their wooden constructions, digging at the tunnel ceilings to create pitfalls that would hamper their advance, and a final desperate defense, keeping the enemy away from the nightwalkers until the sun had set.

And now the sun was down, the sky dark, and the nightwalkers stirring. Asari had done everything the Nazakri had asked of him. He was free to go—to return to Matua, or Olnami, or anywhere he chose.

And what would he do there—beg? The Nazakri had abandoned him, and left him no better off than before. Worse, really—he was no longer in Hao Tan, but instead out on this vast, empty plain.

At the very least, he decided, he should stay and loot the bodies when the nightwalkers had finished.

CHAPTER 57

Hold fast," Malledd shouted. "Retreat if you need to—anything to stay alive until dawn!"

The little knot of men clustered about him closed together more tightly, preparing for the onslaught. On all sides of them nightwalkers were sitting up, getting to their feet, picking up weapons.

Most of the scattered Domdur troops, who had spread out across the plain pursuing their fleeing foes or chopping the heads off corpses, were now forming into groups like this one, and retreating slowly toward the makeshift bridge. All of them understood the situation—they had put the living enemy to flight, and if they could hold out until the sun rose again they would win. Dawn would drop the nightwalkers in their tracks, leaving them so much dead meat to be butchered.

But dawn was hours away.

It was midsummer, when the nights were shortest, but nine long hours still lay before them before they could expect to see new light in the east.

Nine hours of hell. Malledd saw several of his companions shuddering in weary anticipation. They had already fought one full night and a long afternoon with only a brief morning's rest in between, and now they would have to fight on.

Malledd himself was not tired—he never tired, and knew now that this was his divine gift. Those around him, though . . .

It struck him that most of them would probably die tonight—perhaps all of them. They were outnumbered almost ten to one by creatures that felt no pain, that could only be killed by decapitation.

The nightwalkers were upright now, upright and armed, a great seething mob of them; thousands of dead staring eyes turned toward the retreating Domdur.

Red light flared to one side, and Malledd looked quickly for its source as a scream rose, then cut off in a dying gurgle.

The wizard, of course; a burst of his baleful fire had broken through the defenses of one of the New Magicians and burned the man's chest to smoking black ruin.

The crystals of the other New Magicians all seemed dim, scarcely sparkling, let alone glowing with their usual golden fire. Their power was draining away, while Rebiri Nazakri seemed as strong as ever.

The New Magicians were falling back—and as Malledd watched, the black wizard stepped down from his place atop the heap, a heap that Malledd now saw was largely made up of severed heads. They weren't the fresh remains of Domdur, but the half-rotted skulls of decapitated nightwalkers—the wizard's staff had been reabsorbing their dark essence.

The Nazakri was advancing toward the bridge, Malledd realized. The New Magicians milled about, confused and exhausted, and did not pursue.

"He's going to blast it!" someone shouted. "He's going to trap us on this side of the river!"

At that, a mad rush for the supposed safety of the western bank began, but Malledd held up his arms and held back his own little party. "Wait and see," he shouted. "We don't want to be caught *on* the bridge!"

The nightwalkers still hadn't attacked—not Malledd's band, nor anywhere else—and that made him wary. Something strange was going on here.

This was the night Rebiri Nazakri had been waiting for, the night when Ba'el's Triad began, the night when whatever dire scheme the Olnami had devised was meant to be put into action; this move toward the bridge might be part of that scheme. Malledd had no intention of falling into any more traps.

Perhaps threescore Imperial troops reached the bridge before the wizard and fled across it in disorder, while the rest stood and waited, surrounded by the horde of waiting nightwalkers. Then Rebiri Nazakri reached the water's edge and turned to face them all. He raised his staff above his head, smoking red flame to his right and utter blackness to his left, and spoke.

His words rang out like the beating of a great gong, in a voice that was no longer human, a voice that carried easily to every corner of the rebel encampment and out onto the plains beyond.

He spoke in Olnami; Malledd could not understand the words, but he recognized the tone as that of command. The wizard was issuing instructions to his undead followers.

Then one word rang out clearly—"Seidabar." A moment later Malledd caught another, "Domdur," and then "Seidabar" again.

And then the Nazakri turned to face the west and marched out through ankle-deep water to the bridge.

And behind him, ten thousand nightwalkers turned to face west and began marching.

They didn't attack; they didn't fight; they marched due west, pushing around or climbing over anything in their path. The Domdur in that path hacked and slashed and cut their way through the oncoming masses, meeting no active resistance, but merely the steady press of more and more bodies pushing westward, pushing past or over them.

"Destroy the bridge!" Lord Duzon shouted. Malledd turned to see the commander swinging back up into his saddle and spurring his mount toward the river. "Destroy it, before he can cross!"

Soldiers turned in confusion; several of those who had escaped across the bridge paused and looked back. A few of the New Magicians moved halfheartedly toward the crossing.

"How?" Malledd heard someone ask.

That was a sound question; how could they destroy the bridge? It couldn't be burned, sunken as it was two inches below the surface, nor was there any easy way to break apart its component sections. It was a solid, sturdy construction.

And Rebiri Nazakri was marching relentlessly westward across it.

Someone screamed, and Malledd turned to find a wall of nightwalkers approaching his own position. None had raised their weapons; none of them bothered to spout their usual mockery; they simply marched westward, and looked ready to trample anything in their path.

"Into the holes," Malledd said. "Into the tunnels!"

Indeed, the nightwalkers were moving around the openings, not allowing themselves to drop back down into the earth from which their dark spirits had been pulled. Hurriedly, the Domdur retreated and slid down into the openings.

Above them on all sides they could hear the unceasing tread of the night-walkers. The ground seemed to shake beneath them, and clods of earth tumbled down around the cowering Domdur.

At last, after what seemed like hours, the army of the undead was past; Malledd led his little band quickly through the tunnels to the pit, and back to the surface.

There they looked around at a scene of untold devastation.

The rebel camp had been reduced to rubble and ash and the remains of the dead. Countless bodies lay scattered across the landscape—Domdur, and rebel, and the headless remnants of hundreds of nightwalkers. The surviving Imperial forces wandered among the dead, dazed and weary.

But to the west, beyond the Grebiguata, an undead horde was marching away, following the smoky red glow of the wizard's staff.

"I don't understand," someone said. "Where are they going?"

"Seidabar," Malledd replied. "Didn't you hear the wizard say that?"

"I didn't understand any of it," the other answered.

"Malledd!" someone called, and Malledd heard the jingle of harness. He turned to find Lord Duzon riding up.

"Your lordship," Malledd said, bowing.

When he arose from his bow he looked up to find Duzon grinning.

"We've beaten them!" he said.

Malledd made no answer; he frowned thoughtfully.

"We'll follow them," Duzon said, "and when dawn comes we'll slaughter them all. They'll be defenseless."

"The wizard doesn't sleep as they do," Malledd said. "I'm not sure he still sleeps at all."

"True enough," Duzon admitted, "but our own wizards can match him once the sun's up, match him magic for magic, wear him down and eventually destroy him!"

"Maybe," Malledd said. "When the sun comes up." He glanced westward. "But I think he said they would destroy Seidabar."

"Seidabar is more than a hundred miles away," Duzon said. "They can't possibly reach it before dawn!"

"Then why would he try?"

"He must be hoping we're too tired to pursue him," Duzon said.

"Some of us *are* too tired to pursue him," Bousian replied from behind Duzon. He wiped sweat from above his one remaining eye.

"Well, some of us aren't," Duzon retorted. "We'll pursue them, and we'll finish them! Come on—who's with me? For the Empress! For the Domdur!" He raised his sword in a dramatic gesture.

Malledd wasn't tired, but he couldn't find the spirit to join the ragged cheer that answered Duzon's flamboyance.

Something was wrong here. Rebiri Nazakri could not have fought so long, and waited so patiently, only to let himself be conquered as easily as Duzon predicted.

And dawn would bring not just any day, but the first day of Ba'el's Triad. Ba'el favored the Olnami, not the Domdur. Could they really expect to triumph under Ba'el's fiery gaze?

But what could the Nazakri be planning?

When Duzon led his cheering band of volunteers back across the bridge, in pursuit of the nightwalkers, Malledd followed reluctantly.

Asari whirled at a sound behind him, raising his sword.

"Don't!" a voice called. "It's just me!"

Asari recognized the voice even before he saw the golden glow beneath Aldassi's cloak, and lowered his weapon.

"Aldassi," he said, "what's going on?"

"I don't know," Aldassi said. "My father never confided in me."

"Where are they going?"

"Seidabar, of course. I know *that* much."

"But . . . but they can't reach it before dawn, and they left the Domdur alive!"

Aldassi shrugged. "This is what Ba'el told my father to do. Perhaps he knows more than we do, and all will be well—or perhaps my father has been betrayed, and Ba'el is still a god of the Domdur."

"Don't you care?"

"Of course I care!" The glow brightened, and for a moment Aldassi shone like a candle on the darkened plain. Then the brilliance faded again. "But what can I do against the gods?" Aldassi asked.

Asari glanced to the west, where the Domdur soldiers were carrying torches in their pursuit of the nightwalkers.

"What do we do now?" he asked.

"We find shelter, find food," Aldassi said. "My father will succeed or fail without us. If he succeeds, we will hear, and go to join him; if he fails, we have a choice—avenge him, or get on with our own lives."

"And which will it be?" Asari asked. "Vengeance?"

Aldassi paused before answering, "My family has pursued vengeance for a very long time. It would be hard to give it up; I have little else left. Sometimes, though, one must give up all one has in order to survive and begin anew. It's not a matter to be decided in haste—and besides, can you doubt that my father will triumph?"

Asari didn't answer; instead he followed as Aldassi led him away in search of food and shelter.

But in truth, he found it quite easy to doubt.

CHAPTER 58

Lord Duzon looked up at the sky for what was surely the hundredth time, studying the moons; he glanced once again at the eastern horizon. Malledd saw the action and gritted his teeth.

All of them, all the determined little band that was still pursuing the Olnami wizard and his undead warriors, had done the same. All of them had noticed the wrongness, though no one had yet said anything about it above a whisper.

The moons were fading.

The Domdur knew more than a hundred moons; in the ordinary course of events the sky would hold anywhere from a dozen to ninety or so at a time, moons great and small, scattered or clumped together, their colors ranging from the drying-blood color of Ba'el to the cool blue of Sheshar, from the intense white of Samardas to the dim dull brown of Dremeger. On very rare occasions the sky might be completely moonless, or the entire complement might gather in a single part of the heavens—such gatherings usually meant fierce storms, earthquakes, and other upheavals.

The movements and interactions of the many moons were far too complex, too intricate, for anyone but an astrologer to track. Even so, the presence of so many moons, day and night, made it almost impossible for anyone in the Domdur Empire to *not* learn certain basic facts.

One of those facts was the relationship between sunlight and the phases of the moons. When one could observe a sunset and simultaneously see a scattering of moons above it ranging from the thinnest smiling slivers in the west to full round circles on the eastern horizon, it was hard not to recognize that moonslight was reflected sunlight.

And when a score of moons gradually faded out, full and half-moon and crescent alike, dimming like dying embers while still far above the horizon, and while the stars stayed clear and bright, almost any Domdur with any wit at all would know it meant something was wrong with the sun.

The Domdur rarely bothered with lanterns or torches when traveling long distances by night; moonslight was usually sufficient. This time, though, even though it meant losing ground in the pursuit of the nightwalkers, Duzon had called a halt so that torches could be prepared and lit.

The distant glow of the wizard's staff vanished in the west as the soldiers struggled to get tarred rags tied onto whatever scraps of wood they could find; they would need to make up that lost ground. At least, Malledd thought, the wizard and nightwalkers had veered to the south and were now following the highway, rather than trampling cross-country through fields and over fences; that would make the going easier, and he was fairly certain that it would be more of an advantage for the Domdur than for the nightwalkers.

Many people muttered and cursed as the lights were prepared and distributed, but still, no one spoke openly of the strange phenomenon overhead. Finally, though, as the last torch blazed up and the weary warriors prepared to march on, someone could keep quiet no longer.

"Lord Duzon," Kiudegar called, "what's happening? Has that wizard shut out the sun somehow?"

"I don't know," Duzon replied unhappily. "It doesn't matter; whatever he's done, we still need to follow them, to be ready when the sun appears."

"But what if it *doesn't*?" someone with a Seidabar accent demanded.

"Then it's the end of the world and we're all dead anyway!" Duzon retorted, momentarily losing any pretense of calm. He glanced eastward again. "The sun will rise, just as it always has."

Malledd wasn't so sure. The moons had begun to dim shortly after midnight, and this was to be the first day of Ba'el's Triad—the three days of the year when Ba'el's power, and his power alone, kept the sun burning.

And Ba'el wanted Rebiri Nazakri and his nightwalkers to win.

It was hard to believe that any god could so completely abandon his duties, could allow the well-ordered world to be so deranged, but those dying moons, faint brown shadows where they should be bright and golden, were an irrefutable sign that *something* was wrong in the heavens.

Three days until Ba'el's Triad ended, and Vedal could restore the sun. Three days of darkness, when untiring nightwalkers could march on, not stopping to rest for even a moment, unhindered by any sort of packs or baggage, untroubled by living escort, along Gogror's Highway where there were no obstacles to slow them.

Three days.

Malledd knew he could easily cover four miles in an hour by walking briskly. At twenty-four hours a day, and with half a night at either end, that would mean the relentless nightwalkers could almost certainly cover more than three hundred miles before the sun rose on the first day of Vedal's Triad.

And Seidabar lay only slightly more than two hundred miles from the Grebiguata.

This was Rebiri's plan, clearly; this was the revenge he had schemed for, the plot he had somehow connived with Ba'el to devise. He and his horde of nightwalkers would march to Seidabar in the unnatural darkness and lay waste to the city, destroying the seat of Domdur power and plunging the world into chaos and conflict.

Ba'el would have his wars, and the Nazakri would have his vengeance.

But what of the main body of the Imperial Army? What about the defenses of the fortress, those great black walls that guarded Seidabar? Could the nightwalkers overwhelm them all in the single night that would remain to them at the end of their march?

Undoubtedly Ba'el and the Nazakri thought they could, and so far those two seemed to have known what they were doing. Perhaps they believed the extinguished sun would panic the Domdur into leaving the city undefended.

And in fact, Malledd thought, the darkness might do just that, if no one was able to rally the defenders.

Someone like the divine champion, for example.

And he was here, on the wrong side of the nightwalker army, pursuing them instead of confronting them.

Perhaps he should never have left Seidabar at all.

With that thought he patted Onnell on the shoulder and told him, "I need to go talk to Lord Duzon." He waved to Darsmit and Bousian and Vadeviya and Kiudegar, and then ran forward.

The others stared at him in amazement; they were all far too exhausted to do more than trudge stolidly on, and they knew they were losing ground in their pursuit of the nightwalkers. In fact, with every mile, more of the Imperial van-guard dropped behind and collapsed at the side of the road, too tired to take another step. Vadeviya, who had not fought at the river but had joined the pursuit, was the only one of them not on the verge of such a collapse, and even he was weary just from the hours of walking.

"How does he *do* that?" Kiudegar asked, staring after Malledd.

"I don't know," Onnell said. "For years I thought I did, but I'm not sure anymore."

Bousian glanced at Onnell, but said nothing; Darsmit coughed discreetly. *He* hadn't fallen for Malledd's distractions. He knew that Malledd was the divine champion, and Malledd's deferral to Duzon a mere ruse. All of them but Kiu-degar knew it, really, or ought to; if Onnell chose to doubt it, Darsmit wasn't going to argue, but he thought it foolish.

At the head of the shrinking band of diehards Lord Duzon rode on, waiting for his horse to die beneath him; he knew that he was driving the poor beast far too hard, and that she would almost certainly break down soon if he didn't allow her food, water, and a long rest.

But he couldn't. The nightwalkers were already well ahead of them. . . .

"Lord Duzon!"

Duzon blinked and started awake, realizing he'd been dozing in the saddle. He turned to find Malledd walking alongside.

"What?" he asked, still fuddled.

"My lord, we need to go faster!" Malledd said, his tone urgently pleading. "We need to catch up to the nightwalkers and destroy them! We need to send messengers, warn Seidabar!"

"We'll catch them at dawn . . ." Duzon managed.

"My lord, look up at the moons," Malledd said. "The sun won't rise during Ba'el's Triad—or if it does, it will be dark. The sky should be rosy *now*, Lord, and look at it—black as fired iron."

"Then we'll catch them on the fourth day!" Duzon insisted. "Look at us, Malledd—we're in no shape to fight them by night."

"But we *have* to, my lord—we can't let them reach Seidabar! At the very least, we need to warn the city, so they can prepare the defenses. . . ."

"Seidabar is at least *six* days from the river, Malledd," Duzon replied angrily. "They won't even reach the outlying towns in a single triad!"

"My lord, they have three days *and four nights*! They don't stop for the night. They don't stop for food, or water, or rest. They don't pause for *anything*, not for so much as a moment!"

Duzon stared mazily down at Malledd for a moment, then looked to the west; he could make out a faint reddish glow on the horizon, miles away, a glow he knew from its color to be the wizard's staff.

"Oh, gods preserve us," he said despairingly. "You're right!" He turned to look at the ragtag remnants of an army marching in his wake. "We can't do it, though. Look at us! We can barely hobble onward, let alone fight."

"*Someone* has to fight, sir. If we can't, we must send a messenger to Seidabar."

Duzon shook his head. "Who could we send? None of the surviving New Magicians can stir so much as a flicker in their crystals; they used it all in the battle. And no one on foot can possibly outrace that horde."

"What about *old* magicians, then?"

"The priests?" Duzon blinked owlishly as he considered that. "Ours are dead—but there were still two in Drievabor, I believe."

"Then send someone back—they can still give Seidabar at least a day's warning."

Duzon nodded. "You're right. Someone they'll trust. That priest of yours, Vadeviya—we'll send him."

"Good," Malledd said. "And the rest of us must do what we can to harry the foe from behind."

"What we can, yes," Duzon said. "But don't expect it to be much, O Chosen One—we're not as tireless as you."

Malledd's brows pulled down and his lips tightened angrily.

"I'm still a man," he said. "Not a god. And as far as most of these people are concerned, my lord, *you* are the divine defender of the Domdur Empire, not I."

"Thereby demonstrating that popular belief is not certain truth," Duzon retorted, growing angry in his turn. "*We* know the truth, you and I, and let us not pretend otherwise."

"Let us not confuse anyone unnecessarily, either," Malledd said. "Please *act* like a champion, my lord—don't let them be disappointed."

"Don't you presume to order me, Malledd . . ." Duzon began. Then he stopped and looked at Malledd, startled.

"You know, I never really thought about it," he said. "*Do* you have any authority over me? Is that a part of the gods' gifts?"

"You're a free man, my lord," Malledd replied. "As am I. We both serve the Empress, and she's given *you* a commission as captain, not me. I don't think the gods come into it."

"Fine. Then do as you see fit, Malledd, and may the gods who favor you prove wiser than those you oppose. Send Vadeviya back to Drievabor, and then go on ahead, if you choose and you can. I'll lead these others as best I can, and do what I can to aid you—but I can't promise much."

Malledd nodded. "I understand," he said. He turned and waited for Vadeviya.

When the situation had been explained to the old priest's liking and the message delivered, Malledd turned westward again and trotted. He passed Lord Duzon and hurried on toward the nightwalkers.

CHAPTER 59

She's dead," Prince Graubris said. He reached down and touched his mother's eyelids, making sure they were closed, then leaned over and kissed her cheek. Her skin was already cool, so dry and lifeless it hardly felt like skin at all.

"Her Imperial Majesty Beretris is dead," the chief physician agreed.

"The Empress is dead," Lord Shoule proclaimed. "Long live the Emperor!"

Graubris straightened up and looked around the room at a dozen frightened faces—maids, doctors, and attendants. Lord Shoule was the only Councillor present; Princess Darisei was asleep in a chair.

"Wake my sister," Graubris ordered. "Let her see."

One of the maids hurried to obey.

Just then the door opened and Prince Zolous hurried in. Before he had taken a third step toward the bed he saw the expressions, saw his brother's face and posture.

"Am I too late?" he said.

"Yes," Graubris said as he pushed past Zolous toward the door.

"Grau!" Zolous called after him, "I think you . . ."

He didn't finish the sentence; Graubris had marched out with Lord Shoule close on his heel, and Shoule had closed the door behind them.

Graubris had expected to find most of the Imperial Council in the antechamber, but the room was empty; startled, he stopped dead.

The room was not only uninhabited, it was unusually dark—no candles or lamps burned, and the window provided little light. Coals glimmered orange in the fireplace, but there was no other illumination.

"Where is everybody?" Graubris muttered. His eyes felt hot and edged with moisture, and he blinked; he was the Emperor now, he couldn't waste time weeping, not even for his mother. There were rebels to be stopped, and traitors to be exposed and executed.

"I don't know, Majesty," Shoule said. "They should *be* here. . . ."

"Shut up," Graubris said. He heard voices somewhere ahead, and he headed toward them. Behind him he heard the bedroom door open, but he paid no attention. He was almost at the corridor door when Zolous called, "Grau! Wait!"

"Why?" he demanded, turning. He ignored Lord Shoule.

"Don't you think the three of us should present a united front to the Council?" Zolous asked.

"Why?" Graubris repeated. "You say your farewells to Mother, and come along when you're ready—I don't think your presence is needed immediately."

"Grau, have you looked out a window lately?"

The bedchamber's windows had been thoroughly hidden by thick velvet drapes. Graubris threw a quick glance at the antechamber window and said, "Yes." Then he turned and marched out, Shoule just a step behind.

Zolous hesitated, then shrugged and returned to the bedchamber. As his brother had said, he and Darisei had farewells to make.

Graubris burst into the parlor without warning and found a dozen or so men and women clustered by the great curving windows, all of them seemingly talking loudly at once. He recognized them immediately—this was most of the Imperial Council, gathered here, debating something as usual.

"My mother is dead," he announced without preamble. He had intended to say something more formal, more dignified, but the words burst out.

A dozen shocked faces turned toward him, and the conversation died away.

"My condolences, Your Highness," Prince Granzer said after a few seconds of silence. "We all loved her as our Empress, and I as my wife's mother, but to you she was more than that, and your loss that much greater."

Graubris frowned. Granzer had addressed him as "Highness" rather than "Majesty." Perhaps technically that was acceptable, since he had not yet been crowned, but it seemed to lack the proper deference. *Shoule* had called him "Majesty."

"If you wish to pay your last respects, I . . . *we* will allow it," Graubris said.

Granzer hesitated, and the others exchanged uneasy glances.

"Your Highness, I fear we may have more urgent matters to attend to just now," Granzer said.

"And what could possibly be more urgent?" Graubris demanded. "Are the rebels at the city gates?"

"Not yet," Lord Graush replied.

"Haven't you looked at the sky?" Lady Luzla asked.

"Or at the streets?" Lord Dabos added.

Graubris stared at them, baffled.

"I have been where I belonged," he said. "At my mother's side."

"If I may, Your Highness," Lord Sulibai said with a sweep of one very full maroon silk sleeve, "I would suggest you take a look." He stepped aside, opening a path to the window.

Puzzled, Graubris stepped forward and peered out at the night, Shoule at his shoulder.

Odd, he had thought it was almost dawn, but the sky was still very dark indeed. He could see no moons—perhaps a heavy overcast. . . .

But the stars were clear and bright.

They had said to look at the sky, and he looked, and saw, but did not understand what he saw. This was beyond him just now, after the long vigil at his mother's deathbed; he shook his head.

The streets, then—he looked down at the plaza and the streets beyond.

There were mobs in the streets, a mob in the plaza—he could see the paleness of upturned faces as hundreds of citizens stared up at the skies, and at the tower in which he stood.

Why were so many people out before the sun was up?

"What's going on?" he asked. "Why are so many people out at this hour?"

"It's half an hour past dawn, Your Highness," Lady Mirashan said quietly.

Graubris's head jerked up, and he stared eastward.

There was no light on the horizon.

"Nonsense," he said.

"I'm afraid not," Granzer said.

"Then where's the sun?" Graubris demanded, pointing at the glass.

"That's what we'd like to know," Graush replied.

"That's what *they* would like to know," added Sulibai, pointing at the crowd in the plaza below.

"Your Majesty," Shoule suggested, "Surely the gods themselves are mourning your mother's death. . . ."

"The crowds might believe that," Dabos said. "If you announce it properly."

"But you don't?" Graubris said, turning to face Dabos.

"No, Your Highness, I'm afraid I don't. No reports survive of any such phenomena at the death of any previous monarch. Rather, I believe this to be black magic, performed to aid the rebels in their march toward Seidabar."

Graubris turned quickly to Shoule.

"It could be, Your Majesty," Shoule said. "But surely we need not worry; we have our walls, and our army. If the people hear their new Emperor speak, if you reassure them, I'm sure you can rally them to the city's defense. . . ."

"More likely panic them completely," Graush interrupted.

Graubris whirled to face Graush, and Shoule barked, "Show the Emperor the proper respect, my lord!"

"That's another thing," Granzer said. "There remains the question of just who is to be Emperor."

"*What?*" Graubris stared at his brother-in-law in disbelief. "My mother named *me* her heir!"

"But ancient law, Your Highness, gives the *Council* the power to name the heir," Lord Passeil said. "We are to bow to the gods' will, but in the present case they have failed to make their will plain, and we are forced to rely on our own capabilities. And in that regard . . . ."

"Some of you disagree," Graubris said. He glared at Granzer. "Some of you want my sister to become Empress."

Passeil threw Granzer a quick glance. "No," he said. "Your brother."

As if on cue, Prince Zolous and Princess Darisei stepped into the room.

"My brother?" Graubris turned to stare at Zolous. "Zol, you knew about this?"

"Just an hour ago," Zolous replied. "I tried to talk to you just now, but you wouldn't wait."

"This is treason!" Shoule proclaimed loudly. "Treason, I tell you! Beretris named *Graubris* her heir!"

"Shut up, Shoule," Graubris said. He looked around at the Councillors. "And just who supports whom, my lords and ladies?"

Granzer shrugged and said, "We can make that plain enough." He crossed the room to stand by Zolous's left hand, while Darisei stood by his right.

"Dari," Graubris said, "shouldn't you choose your own spot? Surely you have your supporters here!"

Darisei shook her head. "This is no time to be foolish or selfish, Grau. . . ."

"I insist!" Graubris said, cutting her off.

Darisei sighed, and stepped over to one side.

"Now, my lords and ladies," Graubris said, "if you would all be so kind as to accompany the candidate of your choice, perhaps we can settle this matter once and for all! I trust, dear brother and brother-in-law, that you will abide by the majority's decision?"

"Of course," Granzer said. Zolous nodded.

Gradually, the others began to move.

Shoule crowded up close by Graubris's side. Granzer stayed where he was, but watched his wife's face.

Passeil crossed the room to join Zolous and Granzer; Niniam and Graush came close behind. After a brief hesitation, Sulibai, Dabos, and Luzla followed.

Vamia started toward Darisei, then paused, looking over the two groups. With a shrug, she joined the party by the door, gathered around Zolous.

Shoule, Orbalir, Apiris, Mirashan, and Dalbisha stayed clustered around Graubris. He looked around and realized that his group was the smaller.

"This isn't everyone," he said. "Who's missing?"

"Lady Zurni is on her estates," Sulibai said. "Lord Gornir is at sea, on his way to Greya to supervise the restoration of order in the east."

"Kadan," Shoule said. "Where's Kadan?"

"Lord Kadan is commanding our army on the eastern plain, at my order," Granzer said.

"The army?" Graubris said. "The army's in Agabdal."

"I'm afraid not," Passeil said. "Lord Kadan departed yesterday morning."

"*What?*" Graubris turned to stare out the window. "Then who will defend Seidabar?"

"I hope," Granzer said dryly, "that no defense of the city will be necessary. That was rather the point of raising an army in the first place, Your Highness."

Graubris looked at Shoule, who said, "We must evacuate the city, Your Majesty. The enemy approaches."

"I don't think so," Zolous said, stepping forward. "We can't give up Seidabar—to do so would be to give up the Empire, Grau."

"Oh, and you're not ready to do that, now that you think you have it?" Graubris snapped. "Well, you can rot here, Zol—the Domdur *Emperor* is the heart of the Domdur Empire, not a bunch of stone and iron, and I intend to be that Emperor, and to survive the worst this Olnamian wizard can do to us!"

"Should we not first be sure the wizard has not *already* been defeated?" Zolous asked. "We haven't had any word for a few days now." He turned and looked at his little band of supporters. "Lady Luzla, could you see that the Imperial College sends a messenger immediately? I realize that the darkness will slow them, but surely they can manage *something!*"

"At once, Majesty," Luzla said, with a bow. She turned and hurried out.

Graubris stared after her. She had called *Zolous* "Majesty." These upstarts were serious about this!

"Majesty," Shoule whispered, "this wizard has *put out the sun!* Can you really think that anything we could do will stop him? We must flee the city at once! Perhaps when he finds your mother dead, he will be satisfied with killing your brother, and you can return from exile in triumph once the gods have restored balance to the world."

"You're right," Graubris said aloud. He announced, "I am leaving this place, and I strongly advise you all to abandon this treasonous attempt to elevate my brother, and to accompany me. I hereby declare the Imperial Council dissolved!"

Even his supporters stared at him then.

"You . . . you're *dissolving* the Council?" Dalbisha asked.

Graubris did not bother arguing; he pushed Granzer and Zolous aside and stamped out of the parlor toward the stairs, his entourage trailing after him—four Councillors. Dalbisha stayed where she was, standing in front of the windows, leaning heavily on her cane.

The others watched Graubris go in silence. Then Darisei asked, "Now what?"

"Now we see about preparing the city's defenses," Zolous said. "I hope we won't need them, but Lord Kadan cannot have gotten very far in a single day. If this unnatural darkness does indeed mean that the wizard and his nightwalkers are on the move, then it's possible the army might be driven back, or bypassed, and we must be ready for that possibility."

"What about Mother?"

Zolous hesitated, then looked sadly at his sister. "I'm afraid we don't have time to do anything with her now. The living must take priority over the dead. But when this is over, Dari, I promise she'll have the finest funeral in history."

"If there's anyone left to hold it," Darisei muttered—but the others, already discussing strategy, did not hear her.

CHAPTER 60

The nightwalker did not even turn around. Malledd knew it must have heard him, yet it gave no sign; it marched on, seeming almost as lifeless as the corpse it should have been.

This particular walking corpse wore tattered, faded rags that had once been a sumptuous green and gold Matuan funerary robe; though he could see nothing in the moonless night except a vague outline, Malledd had glimpsed the colors briefly when the nightwalker passed a lighted farmhouse window some ways back. Its flesh was dried and shrunken, stretched tight over the bones beneath; it had obviously been dead for a long time. Its left arm had been cut to pieces, and its left leg was deeply gouged in back, ruining the knee and causing a bad limp.

That probably explained why it was the very last of all the thousands of nightwalkers marching westward on the Gogror Highway—but Malledd didn't much care about that. One of them had to be last.

He swung his sword as hard as he could and took the nightwalker's head off with a single blow.

The corpse dropped like a marionette with its strings cut; the head rolled off to one side and stopped facedown, shriveled nose in the dirt.

Malledd wasted no time admiring his handiwork or cleaning up after himself; instead he took three long, fast steps and swung the sword back the other way, decapitating a second undead monster. He almost stumbled over the second corpse as he attacked a third.

Still, none of them resisted; all that still had heads simply kept marching briskly westward.

And, he asked himself bitterly, why shouldn't they? They were already dead and didn't mind dying again; their loathsome spirits weren't destroyed, merely freed into the night air, to fly on ahead and be collected anew in the black end of the wizard's staff. And his efforts seemed so futile against such a horde; he had taken out three nightwalkers. . . .

Out of several thousand. He didn't know the exact number, but it was definitely thousands. They filled the highway completely for as far ahead as he could see by starlight, so far that he could no longer detect any hint of the red glow from Rebiri Nazakri's magical crystals.

But he would have to do what he could; every nightwalker he removed here was one fewer who would threaten the defenders of Seidabar, whoever those defenders might be.

He ran after the nightwalkers, sword raised for another blow.

No ordinary man could have sustained such an effort for more than an hour or two, at most—and that was without considering how long it had been since Malledd had eaten, slept, or rested. He carried a waterskin and had paused in a deserted village to refill it, so thirst was no problem, but hunger was beginning to eat away at him, and as he struggled onward, hacking off head after head, even he, gifted as he was, began to feel his muscles aching with the strain, his head swimming with fatigue.

He kept at it, though.

He lost count quickly, but as time passed he knew he had cut off dozens, scores, even hundreds of heads, leaving a gruesome trail along the highway, through empty villages and past abandoned inns. Malledd, in a delirium of mounting exhaustion and sleep deprivation, wondered what the returning local inhabitants would think of these morbid trophies when the sun finally rose again. Would they understand what they found?

Would they return at all? He saw no signs of life anywhere, save the endless shadowy column of marching nightwalkers. Anyone who had still lived along the Gogror Highway must have fled—if not because of the interminable darkness, then when the wizard and the nightwalkers arrived. Malledd's own companions had all dropped away long before.

At one point, without knowing why, he glanced eastward and saw a dim circle hanging in the sky, a golden brown ember like one of the dullest moons at full—but it was no moon Malledd recognized, and he knew that it shouldn't be full when all the other moons were dark.

Then he realized what he saw—this was the sun, or at least the cooling remnant of the sun. It still rose, though Ba'el had put out its fire.

Malledd shuddered, and for the first time he wondered whether Vedal would be able to rekindle the sun when Ba'el's power passed away. Would it ever burn brightly again, lighting all the world, restoring color to the land and sky?

He had to assume that it would. Anything else would mean yielding to despair and weariness, and that, at the very least, would mean allowing the wizard and the nightwalkers to destroy Seidabar, slaughter the Empress, and plunge the world into centuries of chaos and death.

And that was the *best* possible outcome if the sun was not quickly restored, as it assumed the world would *survive* this long night!

He had to trust in the gods, he told himself—the *other* gods, not Ba'el or those he led.

He turned his attention westward again and saw that he had let the nightwalkers gain a dozen yards on him; with a croak of rage he charged forward and returned to his chopping.

And still the nightwalkers marched on, making no attempt to deter him, to stop the carnage.

To do so, they would have had to slow their march toward Seidabar.

People of Seidabar!" Graubris bellowed from the balcony. "The Empress, my mother, is dead!" He leaned over the railing, looking down at the people below. Behind him Lord Shoule smiled broadly.

A shocked hush fell over the crowd in the plaza.

"The skies themselves mourn her passing!" Graubris shouted.

A new murmur arose.

"There are traitors among us, who have chosen this, the Empire's darkest hour, to strike," Graubris continued. "Members of the Imperial Council have betrayed us all to the Olnamian wizard, Rebiri Nazakri! Even now, he and his nightwalkers are approaching the city."

The murmur grew louder.

"I, your new Emperor, will see you safe—but we must give up this place, and flee to Rishna Gabidéll until a way can be found to destroy the Olnamians!"

Several stories up Zolous leaned out the tower window, listening.

"Shouldn't we stop him?" he asked.

"Evacuating most of the civilians from Seidabar is not necessarily a bad idea, Your Majesty," Sulibai pointed out. "If the enemy *is* coming, they would be of little help in the event of a siege, and that many more mouths to feed."

"He's calling himself Emperor, though. . . ."

Granzer said quietly, "And who out there knows which of you he is? If you'll forgive me for mentioning it, Your Majesty, the resemblance between your brother and yourself is quite striking, and that balcony quite dark. There will be time to straighten it all out later; to say anything now would merely cause further unnecessary confusion. Let him leave the city; if we rule Seidabar, we rule the Empire."

"But can we hold Seidabar? Do we know whether the rebels are coming?" Zolous asked, turning to face the others.

Just then light blazed upward from somewhere across the plaza; Zolous whirled in time to see three glowing figures soaring into the sky and swooping eastward, like immense golden fireflies.

"Lady Luzla's messengers," Graush said. "Good for her!"

"At least now we should have word soon as to just what's happening," Granzer agreed.

I know it's still dark," Lord Kadan roared. "I don't care. We march. Day or night, the men have had plenty of time to rest. This darkness may be the gods' doing, or it may be the wizard's, or it may be something else entirely, and the cause doesn't matter—we came to fight the Nazakri, and we'll do it, and the Nazakri is east of here. We march!"

"The men are frightened," Colonel Tsigisha protested.

"If they're scared now, what are they going to do when we fight the night-walkers?" Kadan demanded. "We . . ." He paused as someone burst uninvited into the headquarters tent. The man wore the white robe of a priest.

"What is it?" Kadan asked.

The priest struggled to catch his breath, then gasped out, "Nightwalkers. Coming."

"What?" Several voices spoke at once.

The priest held up a hand for silence as he gulped air and composed himself. Then he said, "We have a message from the temple in Drievabor. Rebiri Nazakri has crossed the Grebiguata. General Balinus is dead; all the vanguard's magician priests are dead; all the New Magicians are powerless. Lord Duzon sent a messenger to Drievabor to send this warning—the nightwalkers are marching toward Seidabar. Thousands of them."

"By what route?" Kadan demanded.

The priest shook his head. "I don't know," he said. "The crossing was made fifteen or twenty miles north of Drievabor, over an improvised bridge."

"We need to block their path," Kadan said. "If we form a sentry line north to south, covering perhaps thirty miles . . ."

He was interrupted again, by another intruder.

This time it was three men who entered—one in black and gold, and two in the red and gold of Imperial uniforms.

They were not the uniforms of ordinary soldiers, though, but the more ornate dress of the Imperial Guard, while Kadan recognized the black and gold as the livery of Lord Shoule's staff.

"What do you want here?" he said angrily.

"Lord Kadan of Amildri?" the man in black said. "I have a warrant for your arrest, signed by his Imperial Majesty Graubris IV, on charges of high treason." He signaled to the two guards, who stepped forward to stand one on either side of Kadan. "Will you come peacefully?"

For a moment a stunned silence fell over everyone in the tent; then chaos erupted.

"The Empress is dead?"

"Kadan a traitor?"

"What's going on?"

"Is this true?"

Colonel Tsigisha managed to shout loudly enough to be heard over the others. "You, messenger! What of the army?"

The crowd quieted abruptly as they waited for the reply.

The man in Shoule's livery shrugged. "I have no orders about that," he said. "I am to remove Lord Kadan from command; after that, you're not my responsibility."

Tsigisha and the other staff officers looked at one another.

"These men have no authority here," Kadan bellowed. "I swore an oath to the Empire and the Empress, not to Lord Shoule's errand boy. . . ."

One of the guards slapped Kadan across the mouth.

"The Emperor Graubris has named Lord Shoule President of the Imperial Council," he said. He grabbed Kadan's arm. "Come on, you," he growled.

The guards dragged Kadan from the tent.

The generals and colonels milled about indecisively; finally Tsigisha said, "Adikan, you're second in command—what do we do now?"

General Adikan frowned uneasily. "I suppose we await the Emperor's orders," he said.

"But the nightwalkers are coming!" the priest protested.

Adikan shrugged. "If they come we will fight them, of course," he said. "But until we know what the Emperor wants of us, we will remain right here."

"A wise decision, I'm sure," Shoule's messenger said. He saluted. "May the gods favor you all!"

Then he bowed and left the tent.

CHAPTER 61

The sentry squinted into the darkness, trying to make out just what he had seen moving, out there on the far side of the wheat field. "Who's there?" he called, drawing his sword.

Prince Bagar stopped dead at the sentry's challenge.

"It's just me," he called back.

"Who?" the sentry repeated, stepping forward, pushing aside the wheat.

Bagar hesitated. He was a prince, the grandson of the Empress—but he was also a deserter, alone and wearing badly worn clothes, with no one to attest to his identity, and no knowledge of how he would be received were it known. He hadn't expected to find sentries or soldiers here; he had been traveling cross-country, instead of following the Gogror Highway, specifically to avoid them. Desertion was a serious crime.

"My name's Bagar," he said. Giving his own name, without the title, seemed safe enough. After all, Bagar was not a particularly unusual name.

"Step forward where I can see you," the sentry ordered.

Bagar obeyed, walking forward with his empty hands raised.

"What are you doing here?" the sentry demanded when he could see Bagar clearly.

"I'm on my way to Seidabar, to stay with relatives," Bagar replied. "It's not safe in Drievabor—the nightwalkers are too close!"

"Ha! I can believe *that*," the sentry answered. "So you're from Drievabor? But what are you doing out here, instead of on the road?"

"I got lost in the dark," Bagar improvised hastily. He gestured at the sky. "I couldn't see *anything*!"

"Oh," the sentry said. He pointed off to his right, bringing his left arm across his chest to do it without lowering his sword. "The road's that way. About two miles."

"Thank you," Bagar said. He hesitated. He had been avoiding the highway for a hundred miles, but he couldn't think of any good reason he could give this sentry for continuing to do so.

And maybe there really wasn't any reason to go on avoiding it. This fellow seemed to be taking his story at face value, and even now that he was close enough for his face to be visible in the torchlight the soldier didn't seem to have recognized him. Bagar turned and looked to the south, toward the road.

A red glow caught his eye, off to the left—something much redder than any flame. He stared.

There was definitely a red glow there, and it seemed to be moving westward along the highway, coming closer.

"What's *that*?" he asked, pointing.

Just then the distant wail of a horn reached them—someone to the south was sounding the alarm.

"Oh, gods," the sentry said. He looked south, then back at Bagar, then west at the tents and fires behind him. "You stay there!" he ordered; then he turned and ran for the tents.

Bagar watched him go, then stared southward.

Men were pouring from tents and gathering around campfires to the west, and to the south that eerie red light was moving steadily along the highway.

And now, belatedly, Bagar recognized it. He had seen that glow before, but he had never expected to see it here, a hundred miles from the Grebiguata.

That was the glow of Rebiri Nazakri's staff. The wizard had crossed the river and was marching toward Seidabar.

Bagar shuddered.

He had tried, back there at the river. He had fought for several triads, beheaded his share of nightwalkers, but he had known almost at once, once the fighting began, that he was no champion, no great warrior. He had been terrified every time he went into battle; all he had been able to think of, when the foe came charging at him, was staying alive. Every fight had been a constant struggle not just against the enemy, but against his own fears; he had fought as hard to keep from running away as he had fought to remove heads.

And it had all seemed so futile. He had seen the endless rows of nightwalkers watching from the eastern bank, had seen the black essence that spilled free and flew away unscathed, back to the wizard's staff, whenever a nightwalker went down. He had seen the soldiers around him die, one by one, or grow steadily more exhausted as they fought on, night after night, with no hope of victory in sight.

And finally, one day, he hadn't been able to fight anymore. It hadn't been anything specific; he had just known he couldn't continue, and he had packed up some of his belongings and had headed west.

But now the Olnamians and the nightwalkers had come after him. There was no safety here. There was no safety *anywhere* until those things were all destroyed.

He had had a break from the battle, had had time to rest, but now it was time to do his duty to his grandmother, his family, and the Empire once again. He was no divine champion, but he was still Domdur.

He unslung the pack from his shoulder and pulled out his sword; then he lifted the pack again and began trudging southward to meet the foe.

As he walked he saw the red-garbed companies of soldiers forming up between the rows of tents to his right, their tunics bright in the light of the camp-fires. He heard orders being shouted.

This was the Imperial Army, ready at last to meet the rebels in battle. The reinforcements that had never reached the vanguard had existed, after all; they had simply been delayed.

Now, at last, he would have sufficient numbers on his side; that horde of walking corpses could be wiped out, sent back to the graveyards where they belonged.

He walked past the southernmost row of tents just as the first company of soldiers began to march south, paralleling his own path.

And then a messenger came running out to the company's captain, shouting for him to wait.

Bagar stopped, curious, to see why the soldiers were delaying.

The messenger was gasping something to the captain; Bagar was too far away to make out the words. Bagar hesitated, then turned and headed west, toward the soldiers.

The captain and the messenger were arguing now. Bagar picked up his pace, but the dispute ended before he could hear what it was about.

The captain shouted a command, and the entire company wheeled about, each man turning on his heel with a precision no regiment in the half-trained vanguard could ever have matched. Then they began marching north, back to camp.

Bagar broke into a run.

"Captain!" he called.

The captain paused.

"Who are *you*?" he demanded as Bagar came running up.

"I'm ... I'm a deserter from the vanguard, Captain," Bagar said. "I lost my nerve, but I'm ready to fight again—and you're turning back! What's happening?"

"A deserter?"

"That's not important—that messenger, Captain, what did he tell you?"

The captain snorted. "We have new orders. We're to let the wizard and his troops go right on past. They've set up some sort of trap for them in Seidabar."

Bagar blinked. "What kind of trap?"

"They haven't told us that. It's a secret, it seems."

"Who sent the orders? Lord Kadan?"

"Lord Kadan's been arrested for treason," the captain told him. "These orders came from the President of the Imperial Council."

Bagar's jaw dropped. Kadan, a traitor?

But that would explain why the reinforcements had never come, wouldn't it?

And if Uncle Granzer had given the orders ... Bagar had great faith in his uncle, but he couldn't imagine what sort of trap could be waiting in Seidabar if the Imperial Army was out here on the plain.

"You're sure they're genuine?" Bagar asked.

"You've got your nerve, don't you?" the captain asked angrily in reply. "You admit you're a deserter, but you're questioning my authority?"

"Not *yours*, Captain," Bagar said quickly. "But the enemy's a wizard—are you sure that the orders came from Seidabar, and not from the Olnamians?"

The captain stared at him. "Did they try anything like that out east?" he asked. Bagar hesitated.

If he told the truth, then the captain would go on back to camp, maybe have him arrested and chained. If he lied, he might be ruining some scheme his uncle had devised.

"I heard rumors," he said.

The captain stared at him thoughtfully, chewing on his lower lip. Then he turned and stared at the red glow on the highway, already even with the camp's southeastern corner.

"The orders came through the magicians," he said at last. "The *old* magicians. If the wizard can interfere with *them*, then he can defy the gods themselves, can't he?"

"Or at least he can fool some priests," Bagar said. "It's hardly the same thing. I've tricked a priest or two in my day."

"Confound it," the captain said. He looked north, to where his men had reached the camp and formed up in a line, waiting for further orders. Then he shook his head.

"I have my orders," he said. Then he turned back to Bagar and said, "But if *you* want to fight them, I won't stop you, and if any of my men happen to desert and join you . . . well, desertion's to be expected, when the world's gone mad and the sun's gone dark."

Bagar nodded understanding, and ran past the captain, his sword in his hand, into the camp.

"Listen!" he bellowed. "I'm Prince Bagar, the Empress's grandson! I'm not the champion, but if you want a chance to fight the nightwalkers, I'm ready to lead you into battle! Your captain says he won't stop anyone who wants to fight—who's with me?"

Men turned, startled, to look at him, but no one answered.

"The priests say the Council has a trap set, and doesn't want us to fight," Bagar shouted, "but we *came* here to fight, didn't we? Are we going to let them take away our only chance? You left your homes and families, spent the winter freezing your asses in Agabdal—now you're going to go home without ever drawing your swords? Come on, and show them what you can do! Tell your women the truth when you say that you fought the nightwalkers!"

The soldiers looked at one another.

"Who's with me?" Bagar called.

Half a dozen hands went up.

"Come on, then," Bagar said. "And the rest of you, spread the word—if anyone wants to fight the nightwalkers, here's your chance!"

Then he turned and charged southward, toward the highway, his sword held high and half a dozen soldiers at his back.

Ten minutes later the handful of warriors crashed shouting into the line of nightwalkers that marched along the highway. The undead were walking swiftly, focused on their goal of reaching Seidabar, and paid no attention as the soldiers began laying about themselves with their swords.

"Go for the necks!" Bagar shouted. "The only way they *stay* dead is if you cut off their heads!"

His men roared wordlessly in reply, and nightwalkers began to fall.

They didn't resist; Bagar realized, as he lopped the head off his third, that the nightwalkers weren't fighting back.

They had struck at the line of nightwalkers at the nearest point, an open stretch of road; the wizard was already well past, half a mile to the west. Now, however, the motion of that red glow paused.

Rebiri Nazakri had heard the shouting, and turned to see what was happening. He was too distant to make out the details in the dark, but he could see violent motion, could see the neat rows of campfires to the north, and could guess what was taking place.

"Kill them," he said. "Kill them quickly, then move on. To Seidabar!"

The order passed along the line wordlessly, almost instantly, by some means known only to the nightwalkers, and abruptly the foes who had been walking quietly to slaughter a moment before raised their weapons and began to fight.

Bagar and his men were caught off guard by the sudden change; two of them went down before they knew what hit them. The rest gathered into a tight knot, their backs to one another, and hacked and slashed desperately.

One tried to run; a nightwalker pursued him and split his skull.

The rest fought bravely, but they were outnumbered, thousands of nightwalkers against four of them.

And then three.

And finally, none.

And the nightwalkers turned westward and marched on, as if nothing had happened to disturb their relentless progress.

And in the camp, guards were posted to make sure that no other "deserters" interfered with the Council's plans; soldiers with drawn swords lined the southern perimeter, keeping their comrades away from the marching nightwalkers.

Ten miles to the west Bishau looked up at Lord Shoule and said, "Your orders have been obeyed, my lord."

Shoule smiled and sheathed his dagger. "Good," he said. Then he stepped out of the magician's room and saluted the waiting Prince Graubris.

"The worst of news, Your Majesty," he said. "The Imperial Army has been destroyed by the Olnamian's magic; we must flee at once!"

"Destroyed?" Graubris asked, horrified.

"So the magicians say; perhaps they misjudge the situation. Still, I think there can be no more question—we must flee to Rishna Gabidëll at once!"

"As you say, Lord Shoule," Graubris agreed as they hurried down the torchlit stone passage. "As you say."

CHAPTER 62

The brown disc of the sun crawled up the vault of heaven, vanishing betimes behind gathering clouds, and then sank westward, where it finally dropped beneath the horizon, and the first day of Ba'el's Triad was past.

Malledd hewed at neck after neck, removed head after head, staggering unheeding over the corpses he left lying in the dust—and still the horde stretched on before him, the reduction in its numbers barely perceptible.

His arms ached as they had never ached before; though the unnaturally extended night had turned unseasonably cool and would presumably be much colder before it ended, sweat plastered his hair to his scalp and soaked his beard into strings. His legs were so weary that his feet grew numb, and he knew his toes were being jammed and stubbed constantly; when full sensation returned, if it ever did, he knew he would be in agony, a mass of bruises and sprains from the knees down.

His boots, so recently new, disintegrated as he trudged onward. When he reached down to peel away the ruined soles his hand came away wet, and he knew he was bleeding—the nails from the heels had been driven up into his feet and he hadn't even felt it.

Not long after that something snapped under the strain when he needed two two-handed blows to hack through an armored collar and lop off yet another head, and he knew he had broken his left thumb.

He hoped that Lord Kadan, or someone, was rallying the defenders of Seidabar; he would be in no shape to undertake such a task himself.

Still, he slogged on.

The air grew colder and clammier around him. The sun seemed even dimmer when it rose again; Malledd could barely see it through the gathering mists, a shadow against the night sky.

By the time it was low in the west Malledd could see the red glow of the wizard's staff far ahead of him, a spark in the distance. He had cut his way through hundreds of nightwalkers now, perhaps thousands, strewing bodies for much more than a hundred miles.

Somewhere off to his right he saw hundreds of lights—campfires and torches, from the look of them, evenly spaced over a vast area. They seemed to stretch on to the north forever, beginning no more than a mile from the highway. He was too tired to think clearly, but he thought at least those meant that he was not the last living human beneath the Hundred Moons—someone was tending those flames.

Perhaps they were refugees, camped there.

Perhaps that was the Imperial Army, come at last—but then why weren't they fighting beside him? Why was the line of nightwalkers ahead of him still so long?

There were corpses along the roadside, he realized, wearing Imperial uniforms—in the darkness the red and gold appeared black and gray, but the tunics and helmets were still unmistakable. They still had their heads, and their blood had flowed and pooled beneath them—they had been human, not nightwalkers. *Some* of the army had fought, anyway—but only a handful, while the rest must still be gathered around those fires.

Why?

It didn't matter; he was too tired to think about it. He trudged onward, overtaking and beheading the undead, as the sun's ember sank and vanished.

The western horizon was largely invisible once the dead sun had set, but at one point Malledd, peering ahead, realized that he could make out subtle differences in the blackness that he recognized as shapes he had seen before—the palace tower, and the dome of the Great Temple, still far, far away, but growing steadily nearer.

He could not see the third sunrise; the sun had darkened too much to be so much as glimpsed through the thickening fog and the heavy overcast. Three days without sunlight to warm the earth or burn off mist had left the air cold and thick with moisture.

Malledd had lost all sense of time and distance and numbers; his arms were too numb to ache anymore. He needed both hands to hold his sword, and cutting through a nightwalker's neck might take four or five blows. Every breath burned his throat and hurt deep in his chest. He moved forward in half-controlled staggers and lunges. For hours he had focused all his attention on the next nightwalker he meant to destroy—and when that one was gone he shifted his gaze to the next, on and on and on, in trancelike repetition. He judged his progress by the slow nearing of the red glow ahead.

Finally, he tripped over the leg of a sprawled headless corpse, stumbled, and fell.

The temptation to simply lie there in the dirt was overwhelming, an urge as fierce and strong as any he had ever felt, as powerful as the love he had felt for Anva or for each of their three babies—but no more powerful, and as the comparison came to him he found himself imagining Anva and the children at their home in Grozerodz, and an army of nightwalkers sweeping down upon the village. He pictured his own home as plundered and deserted as the farmhouses around the warring camps, Grozerodz as empty as Drievabor.

He couldn't allow that. He forced himself up on his hands and tried to drag his knees forward, under him.

As he did, he saw something, something wrong.

He blinked, puzzled, and forced himself to turn his head slowly back and try to spot whatever it was that had troubled him.

He was on a street, he realized—the highway had reached another town. And something high and dark loomed up on his left.

He forced himself up on his knees and turned to stare upward. It took a long moment before he recognized what he was staring at.

It was the fortress wall. They were already in the eastern suburbs of Seidabar, and the high black walls of the fortress towered over them, almost invisible against the black of night.

And the city was dark.

Oh, a few lights shone dimly here and there, but there were no watch fires on the walls, nor signal fires on the towers. No light shone from the arrow slits or other openings in the fortification, and the glow that showed over the parapet was dim and uneven, not the steady blaze of the city's thousands of torches and lanterns.

"What happened?" he tried to say, but his throat was too dry to force out words, and only a dry rasp emerged.

He found reserves of strength he couldn't believe he still had, and forced himself up onto his bloody, battered feet.

He could guess what had happened. The people of Seidabar had panicked and fled. If his message telling them to stand fast had been received, it had been ignored—or perhaps the warning that the Nazakri and his undead army were on the way had triggered the panic.

But Baranmel had told him that Seidabar must not fall.

If no one else was here to defend the city gates, then he would have to do it himself.

After all, he was the divine champion, touched by the gods before he ever emerged from the womb, Ba'el's clawmark drawn across his face. This was his duty.

He had to stop Rebiri Nazakri.

The remaining nightwalkers were unimportant by comparison; the Olnamian wizard was their leader, their guide, their master.

Malledd had to get between the wizard and the city gates, and stop him.

Of course, the Outer City had no walls; if the Olnamian decided to destroy that, Malledd could hardly stop him. Somehow, though, he didn't believe that would be a problem. The Nazakri wanted revenge against the Domdur Empire, and that meant the Empress, the Imperial Palace, the Inner City. He wouldn't bother with anything less, Malledd was sure.

The Nazakri would almost certainly go on into the Great Plaza and turn onto the ramp there; if Malledd cut through the back streets he might be able to get up onto the ramp from the side before the wizard had gotten very far up the slope.

Somehow, even after three days of travel and slaughter without food or rest, Malledd broke into a run.

They passed the army by," the priest gasped. "Lord Shoule had sent orders to let them pass; he went to the Great Temple with Prince Graubris and the Archpriest, and the magicians there didn't know any better than to obey. And with Lord Kadan gone, no one in the camp dared question those orders until it was too late."

"They're in the Outer City now," a New Magician added. "They'll reach the Great Plaza at any moment now."

"But our defenses aren't ready," Lady Vamia said unhappily. "Prince Graubris took most of the Imperial Guard with him when he left, and we'd already stripped the walls for the vanguard and the camps."

"We should have sent word to the temple sooner," Lord Graush growled. "We should have realized that that was why Shoule wanted Apiris on his side."

"Yes, we should have," Prince Granzer agreed, "but we didn't, and it's too late to do anything about it now."

Zolous waved the matter away as irrelevant. "Send whoever we have to close the gates," he ordered. "We may be unable to stop the enemy, but we needn't make it easy for him. Close the gates and man whatever defenses we can—call for volunteers if you see anyone left in the Inner City. We stand here; if the Imperial Palace falls, then we'll fall with it. We can straighten out who gets credit or blame later, if there *is* any 'later.' "

The others hurried to give the necessary orders.

As they trotted down a corridor side by side, Lord Passeil remarked to Prince Granzer, "I do believe you made the right choice for the throne, Your Highness."

CHAPTER 63

Rebiri Nazakri stood in the Great Plaza and waited while his remaining army formed up around him.

His human companions were long gone, of course; none of them had been equipped for the long march westward from the Grebiguata, and none of them had crossed that crude bridge with him. Even his son, Aldassi, had stayed behind; the two of them would meet again somewhere, somehow, once Seidabar had been burned, its great dome and soaring towers and high black walls thrown down.

But his spirit companions, his nightwalkers, his dark children of the depths of the earth, were still with him. More than half had been butchered on the road, far more, most of their essence collected in his staff for later reuse, and the black crystal throbbed uncomfortably with the overcrowded presence of so much power; three thousand more still wore human form, and were now gathering about him.

And before them, on the ramp to the southeast, were the fabled gates of Seidabar, lit bloody red in the glow of his staff.

Three thousand remaining, the rest butchered along the way—and almost all of those by that one determined man.

If he *was* a man; Rebiri was unsure of the nature of the being that had pursued him from the east.

Nazakri had not dared expend the time and energy necessary to defend the nightwalkers and slay the harrying foe because he knew that both time and energy were limited; the darkness that protected him and left his opponents powerless would not last forever, nor did he have the means at hand to collect more of the magical forces he wielded. He had needed to maintain a healthy reserve for his final goal—Seidabar, which towered above him, black against the night. Turning the nightwalkers against a few ordinary soldiers was one thing; disposing of whatever force it was that pursued them was another, and he had feared that to do so would cost too much.

The fire-magic remaining in the red crystal would still be enough to blast those gates apart, and the undead horde would storm into the citadel. Rebiri smiled in anticipation.

Three thousand would be enough.

He had used much of the red fire simply to sustain himself on the journey westward; he could not use the black for such a purpose without risking losing control of his own body to the earth spirits. Still, enough remained to blast through the gates, he was sure.

He took a step toward the ramp, and another, and set his foot on it—and a ragged shape suddenly appeared before him, vaulting up from one side onto the ramp. This mysterious figure wore the tattered remnants of an Imperial uniform and carried a drawn sword.

"So the city's defenders have not *all* fled in terror," the Olnami said, smiling. He lifted his staff, then paused.

Not the fire; he needed that for the gates and the city within the gates. He needed that to bring down the tower where the foul Beretris dwelt, and to shatter the dome of the temple that had been dedicated to the gods who had favored the Domdur over the Olnami.

But the blackness, the dark spirits . . .

He had intended to unleash it all upon the city. The unalloyed blackness did not destroy directly, did not smash, but a person touched by it was touched by sudden terror, by fear and hatred, by sudden irrational rage or momentary blindness. Rebiri had used that to good purpose back in Matua; on the plains he had relied instead on the nightwalkers, creatures that resulted from allowing the darkness to possess a soulless body.

So many nightwalkers had been destroyed on the way west that the crystal's structure was straining. If he were to unleash just a small part of that darkness, relieve the pressure on the crystal, this poor fool who dared to block the way would surely be reduced to helplessness. The nightwalkers could then butcher him at their leisure.

Smiling, Rebiri pointed the black crystal and let the energy flow.

The sudden shift in stress was too much for the already dangerously strained structure; the crystal shattered spectacularly, and rather than a small portion, *all* the tangible darkness billowed forth in a great wave, sweeping up the ramp.

It washed over Malledd, and he shivered.

Coldness dug a thousand tiny, sharp fingers into him; horrific images played out before him in fractions of a second. For an instant he knew that his children were dead, that Anva had betrayed him and slaughtered them so that she could run away with another man, that she had secretly schemed to send him here, to this slow ghastly death facing this all-powerful wizard. He knew that Vadeviya was sitting comfortably at an inn somewhere, laughing uproariously at how easily he had convinced that poor fool of a blacksmith to play the part of the divine champion. He knew that Lord Duzon was a traitor planning to usurp the throne, using Malledd in his intrigues against the Empress. All the world was darkness and doom, greed and hatred and treachery, and only he, poor innocent trusting idiot that he was, had ever believed otherwise. Even the gods themselves . . .

The image of Baranmel at Berai's wedding came to him, and the blackness in his soul suddenly recoiled. The cold faded; his blood warmed anew. His vision cleared, and he found himself looking at the red-lit face of a tired, bitter old man in a heavy black hood.

Anva and his children were fine, safe at home, loving him and worrying about him; Vadeviya and Lord Duzon were doing their best to serve the gods and the Empire. All his doubts, all the lies, had been black magic.

His grip on his sword had loosened, his knees had sagged; now he straightened up, closed his fingers tight around the hilt, and raised the blade to guard. He took a step forward, ignored the broken shards of crystal that cut his bloody feet afresh.

"Go away," he croaked. "Go away, and we'll let you live."

Rebiri Nazakri stared at him in astonishment.

That overwhelming flood of darkness should have reduced this soldier to utter insanity, or even killed him from sheer despair, and then swept on past him into the city beyond; instead he had overcome it somehow, taking it all in and leaving nothing. The wizard had never before seen anyone who could resist the darkness save himself; he had gained a limited immunity from years of constant exposure to its presence.

This man, though—this great hulking Domdur who stood a head taller than any of the nightwalkers, even without considering the ramp's slope—had brushed the darkness off.

Was he another black magician, another wizard as powerful as the Nazakri himself?

No, that could not be; he carried a sword, not a staff, and had no New Magic crystal anywhere. The only other force that resisted the darkness was sunlight, the light of the gods. . . .

And comprehension burst upon Rebiri Nazakri. He smiled.

"Ah," he said. "You must be Malledd, son of Hmar. I was told of your existence."

Ba'el had never said that *all* the gods had forsaken the Domdur, after all; this poor fool clearly still served those gods who yet favored Ba'el's foes.

"And you are Rebiri Nazakri," Malledd said, trying hard to force the words out cleanly. "Go home to Olnamia; we wish you and your people no harm."

Nazakri could barely make out what the "divine champion" was mumbling, and it didn't really matter in any case. This was the heir to Ruamel of the Domdur, as he was himself heir to Basari Nazakri. This confrontation here before the gates of Seidabar was a mere continuation of the battle that had ended— no, merely paused!—three hundred twenty years before, when Ruamel had captured Basari and forced him to swear that hateful oath.

There could be no other conclusion to this meeting but death. This time there would be no compromise—no capture, no surrender, no attempts at peace-making or conciliation.

He turned to the waiting nightwalkers and called, "Kill him!"

He stood unmoving as the nightwalkers surged past him, their weapons raised.

Malledd met them with his sword swinging back and forth like a scythe; he was not so much attempting to sever necks this time as simply to ward his attackers off.

The horde pressed in on him, forcing him back, step by step up the ramp. He was poised on one edge, so that they could not come at him from all sides, but that also meant that they could try to force him back over, down into the Outer City and away from the gates.

He refused to yield even an inch to the side, but he retreated slowly and steadily upward. Blades nicked and slashed at him, opening cuts and tearing away what remained of his tunic; trickles of blood ran down his legs and droplets sprayed from his desperately swinging arms.

The battle was not entirely one-sided, though; while Malledd stayed resolutely on the ramp, many of the nightwalkers were not so surefooted and were sent tumbling down the sheer sides into the streets below—some of them in pieces. Heads flew off whenever Malledd saw openings, and the bodies that fell were then kicked over the edge by their still-fighting companions. Limbs and less-recognizable body parts were also scattered along the slope and over the side.

Malledd lost all sense of time as he fought; his entire life seemed an endless agony of swinging his sword against a wall of stabbing weapons and dead, grinning faces as he inched backward toward the gates.

He was more than halfway up from the plaza to the gates when the light began to change.

It was almost imperceptible at first. Even when it began to register on Malledd that he could see his enemies more clearly, he attributed it at first to the faint glow from beyond the fortress walls.

But then a pair of larger-than-usual nightwalkers crumbled sideways, as the first's head rolled free and his dead weight was suddenly thrust against another, casting them both over the edge of the ramp and giving Malledd a quick glance at the open sky to the west before more of the undead closed in.

A moon had shone in that patch of sky—*shone*, a soft coppery glow, more than three-fourths full.

Malledd smiled, and fought on with renewed strength and renewed hope.

The sun was relit. Midnight had passed. Ba'el's Triad was over, and Vedal's begun.

The sun was still below the eastern horizon, perhaps still hours away, but its fires were lit, and daylight was coming, and the nightwalkers were still not through the gates.

The sky was still black, the city dark, when Malledd stepped back and felt himself press against hard dry metal. He had reached the gates.

And still the nightwalkers came at him, swords and axes and clubs swinging and stabbing.

He fought on and on, and still the nightwalkers came, their numbers still enough to cover the ramp from side to side and for much of its length.

Behind them, glimpsed over their heads every so often, he could see Rebiri Nazakri, standing on the ramp, waiting impatiently for Malledd's death. The wizard glanced angrily up at the sky every so often, up at the shining moons.

And then the attacks seemed to slow.

Malledd looked out at the western sky and saw deep, deep blue, instead of black.

Dawn was breaking. The nightwalkers were slowing as the first traces of sunlight reached them; when the sun cleared the horizon they would all fall, helpless and inert.

"No!" the Nazakri shrieked. "No, no, no!" He screamed curses in Olnami; Malledd could not understand a word.

And then the wizard swung his staff so that the smoky red crystal that still adorned one end pointed directly at Malledd—and at the gate he stood against.

"I can still do it, Champion," he called. "I have no need of them to smash the gates and destroy your holy places! I yet have enough magic of my own!"

And then flame burst from the crystal, a great gout of angry red flame that swept through the remaining nightwalkers, blasting flesh from blackened bone, bursting over Malledd, blinding him and burning him alive.

Agony swept through him, and the outside world vanished; he felt his skin and hair shriveling and tearing away as tiny flakes of ash, felt his flesh drying and cracking and blackening. His sight flared and died, plunging him into utter darkness awash in pain. His legs could no longer support him, and he crumpled to his knees, then fell backward as the gate behind him was reduced to smoke and cinders.

His hand still gripped his sword—the burning flesh of his fingers seemed welded to the wire-wrapped hilt.

His ears were filled with roaring. He knew the fire had passed over him, but he still seemed to hear it. He knew he was still alive because of the roar, and the pain—surely the dead did not feel such agony!

He couldn't understand *how* he still lived, though. He should be dead. He knew he should be dead. He undoubtedly *would* be dead soon—and he welcomed the thought, since it would mean an end to the horrible, unbearable pain. He just wanted it to be over.

But it wasn't. He still lived, though his flesh was black and sere.

This was undoubtedly more of the gods' gifts, he thought bitterly.

Then the roaring faded, and to his astonishment a faint glimmer of light penetrated the darkness—he had been sure both his eyes and ears were gone, yet somehow he could once again see and hear, at least slightly.

He could hear the wizard's voice cursing, as if at a great distance, and footsteps, the crunching of sandals on ash and cinder, drawing nearer. He could see the indigo sky above, and hanging almost directly overhead a great red halfmoon—Ba'el's moon, mocking him.

The Olnami was undoubtedly coming to finish him off before marching on into the Inner City, to wreak what havoc he could before his magic gave out and the Imperial forces could strike him down.

If the Empress still lingered in the city, the Nazakri might yet slay her. He might yet bring down the temple dome.

But Malledd could do no more. He still lived, still held his sword, but all he knew was pain, and the image of Ba'el above, and the sound of approaching footsteps.

He tried to think of something else, but the only thing he could force through the pain was the thought that Anva was still waiting for him, and might never know how he died, how much he had struggled.

If he could just strike one more blow, raise his sword one more time . . . He focused all his will into his right arm, trying to force the ruined, exhausted muscles to move, the burned flesh to obey him.

Black cloth rippled into his motionless field of view, and then the wizard's face appeared, peering down at him, blocking the sight of Ba'el.

"Dead at last, Malledd, son of Hmar?" the Olnami said, in Domdur. "Good! May demons eat your soul!" Then he pulled up the front of his robe and began to step forward, over the blackened remains of his enemy, through the shattered gate and into the citadel of Seidabar.

And Malledd managed one final effort. The sword swung upright, and thrust upward, catching the old man beneath the breastbone.

The blade, weakened by magical flame and days of constant abuse, snapped off, and Malledd's arm fell back to the ground clutching the hilt.

Malledd saw Rebiri Nazakri fall back, mortally wounded; he saw a thin line of blood spray down the broken stump of his sword. He saw Ba'el's moon again revealed.

And then he thought he saw a single ray of sunlight reach out from the east and strike the moon, and the red glow burst into flame, and the moon shattered, and for Malledd the world went dark again and he sank down into blackness.

CHAPTER 64

The ramp was covered with bodies; Lord Duzon's stolen horse shied away from stepping on them, and he dismounted.

He had ridden as quickly as he could, sleeping in snatches in the saddle; when his own horse had collapsed beneath him he had been lucky enough to find another in the stable of an abandoned inn, and he had taken it without worrying about ownership.

The highway had been littered with headless corpses, an endless line of them—Malledd's doing, Duzon knew. The smith was clearly more than human, truly a divine warrior, to have vanquished so many so quickly.

And now Duzon found himself confronted with more of Malledd's handiwork; the ramp to the inner city was carpeted with rotting gore.

He looked up and saw the broken gate. One valve was still closed, but the other had been smashed somehow, leaving a tangle of broken, burned metal.

From here he could see no other damage, though. He had seen the temple dome still intact and gleaming as he approached Seidabar, and the palace tower still upright.

He had to know what had happened. Had Rebiri Nazakri decided to take the city for himself, rather than destroy it? Was he in there somewhere?

Duzon began picking his way up the ramp, avoiding as much of the carnage as possible, placing his feet around or beside or between the heads and bodies.

The ghastly wreckage thinned after a few yards; many of the corpses had rolled or slid down to the bottom. He was able to pick up his pace.

As he neared the top he saw that several of the bodies ahead were burned rather than beheaded—or in some cases *as well* as beheaded, he corrected himself. Many other bodies were intact, neither burned nor decapitated—those, he realized, might be nightwalkers overcome by the sunlight. They would need to be dealt with.

At the end of the burned area, in a clear space right at the broken gate itself, was a mound covered in black cloth, a mound Duzon couldn't identify. Cautiously, he crept up to the mound and prodded it with his sword.

Nothing moved.

He poked the tip of his sword under one edge and lifted the fabric, then flung it back to reveal what it covered.

Another corpse—no, two, he realized, one sprawled across another, and both still wearing their heads. The one on the bottom was a charred ruin; the one on top, the one whose flowing cloak had covered them both . . .

Was it even a corpse? Perhaps this was someone alive. He knelt and rolled the body off to one side, off the burned and blackened corpse.

When he saw the old man's face, and the staff still clutched in one dead hand, Duzon sucked in his breath.

This was the wizard himself. This was Rebiri Nazakri—and he was indisputably dead, his features dark and swollen, his belly coated thickly in blood. A broken corner of sword blade protruded just below his ribs.

Just to be sure, though, Duzon used his own sword to lop off the wizard's head. He kicked the staff free of the wizard's dead hand and looked at it.

One crystal was shattered; the other looked lifeless and empty, like so much ornately worked glass. Duzon crushed it beneath his boot and ground the largest shards to powder.

Then he turned his attention to the other body, the burned one.

The broken stump of a sword lay by its open right hand, and Duzon frowned; was that Malledd's weapon? He picked it up and studied it, but the sword had no very distinctive markings. The *size* of this body was right. . . .

"Duzon?"

Startled, Duzon leaped to his feet, sword ready, and found Lord Graush staring out at him through the ruined gate. Graush held an ax awkwardly in his right hand.

"It *is* you!" Graush exclaimed.

"Yes," Duzon said. He was too tired, too overwhelmed by events, to manage anything more eloquent.

Graush stepped forward, down the ramp, through the blasted gate. He looked around slowly and carefully, then asked, "What happened here? Who are all these people?"

Duzon could hardly say what had happened, since he didn't know himself, but he prodded the cloaked, freshly beheaded corpse with the toe of his boot.

"This," he said, "was Rebiri Nazakri, hereditary warlord of the Olnamians and master of the blackest magic."

"He's dead?" Graush came and looked down at the corpse. "Interesting; how did you ever manage to strike so exactly in the center?"

Duzon started to protest; he realized he was still holding the broken sword, and he dropped it to the pavement. "I didn't . . ."

"The gods guided your hand, beyond question," Graush said. "I beg your pardon, my lord, for ever doubting that you were in fact the chosen champion of the Domdur."

"No, I cut off his head, but I didn't kill him . . ." Duzon insisted.

Graush interrupted him again. "No doubt the gods themselves struck him down, for daring to strike at the sacred city itself." He looked around. "And if that's the wizard, who are all these others? I see few of our own uniforms."

ALPENA COUNTY LIBRARY
211 N First St.
Alpena, Mich. 49707

"Nightwalkers," Duzon replied. "All of them, uniforms or not—all but this one." He pointed at Malledd's scorched remains. "We need to behead them all before nightfall."

"I'll see that it's done, my lord." He sketched a bow.

"Don't *call* me that!" Duzon protested. "Don't bow. You outrank me. You never called me that before."

"And for that I apologize," Graush said.

Duzon stared at him for a moment, then gave it up. There would be plenty of time to explain it all later, to tell everyone that he had never been the divine champion, that Malledd had been the one selected by the gods, the hero who slew the foe at the very gates of the city.

Right now, though, he was so tired his bones ached and his knees felt ready to buckle, and there were still nightwalkers to be dealt with, things that had to be done.

"Those of us who remained are gathered in the palace," Graush said, "where we could defend the Empress's body to the last—that is, the Councillors and guardsmen who stayed; there are priests in the temple, and undoubtedly a few ordinary people scattered about."

Duzon nodded. "We must cut the heads off these nightwalkers," he said, refusing to be distracted.

"I'll send men to attend to it immediately," Graush agreed. "Might I suggest, my lord, that you rest? You've come a long way very quickly, judging by the message the priests received three nights ago . . . or one *long* night, perhaps I should say. You've come a long way and you've fought long and hard—you must be tired."

"I'm ready to drop," Duzon admitted. "But I can't, not yet—you must see that these bodies are dealt with! Not one head can remain attached!" Then his gaze fell on Malledd. He pointed. "Except that one. He is . . . he was the *true* champion. Have his body taken to the temple."

The gods had attended Malledd's birth; they might want a part in his burial.

Graush looked down at the burned body and grimaced. "I'll see to it, my lord," he said. "Now, come and rest." He took Duzon's arm and led him into the citadel.

Malledd floated in emptiness, the pain vanished. He drifted for a timeless time, seeing nothing, hearing nothing, just enjoying the sensation of painlessness.

Then a light appeared before him, and a voice spoke—a voice he could not describe nor remember once it had spoken, but a voice whose words burned themselves into his mind.

The voice, he knew, of a god.

"You have done well, Malledd," the voice said.

"Am I dead?" Malledd asked. "Are you done with me now?"

"You are not dead. We will not permit you to die until you have lived your full term beneath the Hundred Moons; that is a part of the service to which you were bound before your birth. Perseverance, strength, stamina, and the gift of healing—those are the qualities that came with your birthmark, in payment for your service."

"But champions have died!" Malledd protested. "Some died in battle. . . ."

"Never until *we* were ready," the voice told him. "Each champion's span of years was determined in advance, and nothing was ever permitted to alter that decision. Ba'el sought to violate that covenant, as he violated so many others, but he failed, and has been punished for his defiance and treachery. You will live the years we chose for you."

"Who *are* you?" Malledd asked.

"Your name for me is Samardas. I speak to you on behalf of all the gods in council—all save Ba'el, who has been cast down from the heavens for his crimes and declared no longer one of us."

Malledd could think of no response to that astonishing assertion except, "Am I dreaming?"

"You are experiencing an oracular vision."

"I *am* dreaming," Malledd exclaimed. "I should have known it; the gods no longer speak to mortals, save for Baranmel's appearances."

"No," the voice said. "That limitation has passed. Ba'el spoke to Rebiri Nazakri of the Olnami, in defiance of our agreements, and the agreements have been cast aside with he who broke them. The oracles will speak anew."

"Am I to be an oracle, then? Is that why you're speaking to me?"

"If you wish to be an oracle, your wish will be granted. If you choose otherwise, then you shall not become an oracle. We are indebted to you, Malledd; you destroyed Ba'el's mortal instrument when we could not yet intervene, and you thereby preserved Seidabar and the Domdur Empire. We pay our debts. You shall have what you wish of us."

"I don't want anything," Malledd said. "I don't even know if I believe any of this is happening. Maybe I'm imagining all this while I'm dying."

"You are not dying," the voice insisted. "You will live many years yet. This conversation is your opportunity to choose *how* you will live them."

"With Anva," Malledd said. "That's all I ever wanted—my home and my family and my friends. Let Lord Duzon be the champion—he *wants* the job! Just send me home to Grozerodz!"

"You are the champion," the voice said. "Even the gods cannot change that."

"But no one has to *know* it," Malledd said.

"As you wish," the voice replied.

And then the light was gone, and the voice was silent, and Malledd floated again in the cool, painless void for a very long time.

Listen, my lord," Lord Graush said, leaning forward across the little table in the antechamber. "People are still scared. The Empress is dead, and the succession isn't properly settled yet—Graubris has set himself up in Rishna Gabidéll with Lord Shoule, claiming himself to be the Emperor. We've laid siege to the city and demanded their surrender, and Zolous did a fine job in organizing the siege, but he refuses to order an assault or allow himself to be crowned until the gods have made their will known directly and explicitly. He insists that until we know for sure who is to rule, Granzer's in charge, as President of the Imperial Council." Graush sat back.

"That's all very well," he continued, "it's quite proper and will look good later, but people want an *Emperor*, not a President. I'm sure the oracles will issue a pronouncement eventually and put an end to the matter—they've already told us enough to know that Shoule's head belongs on a spike, and I've no doubt at all we'll have it on one soon enough. As yet they haven't named the new Emperor, though. And nobody's sure whether to really trust them yet, after they were silent so long—that's why Shoule's still alive." He sighed and slumped back.

"It's hard to believe anyone wouldn't trust the *gods*," Duzon murmured.

Graush nodded. "It almost seems as if the whole world has been going mad," he said. "Seidabar itself was attacked and only saved at the last minute; the *sun* was put out for a triad! Ba'el's moon is *gone*, blasted from the sky by mystical fire. The Imperial Council, even the imperial *family*, has been split by treason." He shook himself. "We *need* a champion, my lord, someone we can rally around, someone we can thank for our deliverance, someone we can show off and applaud. We need a *live* champion, not a corpse burned to a crisp."

He leaned forward again and pointed. "We need *you*, Duzon. Half the returning troops are already swearing that you're the chosen one, that you saved them all when Balinus was killed, that you worked miracles to defeat the Olnamian."

Lord Duzon looked helplessly at Vadeviya, seated by the window.

The priest shrugged. "The oracles haven't said anything about it yet; I doubt they will. Malledd certainly wouldn't have minded; he never wanted it known that he was the chosen."

"But the oracles . . ." Duzon protested. "Won't they tell the truth eventually?"

Vadeviya shook his head. "I don't think so," he said. "They've already given instructions about Malledd—we're to send his body home to his wife, just as it is. They never mentioned who he was; they simply called him Malledd, son of Hmar."

"But what if someone *asks* who the champion is?"

"The gods have always been able to keep quiet when it suited them."

Duzon could hardly argue with that. He glanced out the window, then rose, ready to face the Imperial Council.

The pain was back.

Malledd was unsure just how the transition had occurred; he had no memory of anything between the timeless floating in a void and his current existence, though he was sure time had passed between the two states.

He hurt all over; his entire body was burned and raw. He couldn't see anything, as his eyes were closed and crusted over, and he was in no hurry to open them.

He could feel movement, though. He was lying on something hard, something that wavered and vibrated. Every few seconds something would jar him, and the constant pain would suddenly spike up into pure agony.

He could hear, too. A dull wooden creaking was the most common sound, but the jars were sometimes accompanied by thumps or splashes, and occasionally followed by a man's voice cursing quietly. He could smell cool air, damp wood, and the faint scent of manure.

He lay like that for several minutes, wishing the sound and movement would stop, wishing the pain would stop, then finally decided that if he opened his eyes and tried to move he might be able to do something about it.

Reluctantly, straining at the effort, he opened his eyes a crack.

Daylight flooded in, and he quickly closed them again.

Slowly, carefully, he opened them again and stared straight up at the glorious intense blue of a cloudless sky after a summer rain.

The world jolted again, and he glimpsed hard straight edges to either side of that magnificent expanse of sky.

The possibility that he had just seen the sides of a coffin occurred to him. While he didn't want to move yet, he didn't want to be buried alive, either; he forced himself to turn his head to one side.

Sure enough, a wooden plank stood just inches away, but if this was his coffin someone had reused materials—the wood was dark and soft with moisture, patterned with old stains and new. He could see now that he was lying on dull brown woolens spread over more planking.

The creaking continued, and at last he recognized it—the creak of a cart moving at a comfortable walking speed.

He was lying in a cart, an old, weather-beaten cart, being taken somewhere—but where, and why?

Well, there was one way to find out. He could ask the driver. He opened his mouth and tried to speak.

No sound emerged, just a dry gasp of air, and he realized that a part of the pain he felt was thirst, intense, burning thirst. He struggled to lift himself, to speak, and finally managed to force out a rasp that was meant to be the word "Water!"

Exhausted by the effort of speech, he fell back on the woolens and stared up at the blue, blue heavens—and the creaking stopped.

Malledd heard thumping and muttering, the sound of heavy boots on planking, and then a shadow appeared in his field of vision, a dark form blocking out part of the sky that he belatedly identified as a man's face.

"Those eyes weren't open before," the man muttered.

Malledd blinked, and opened his mouth, trying to speak.

The man's own jaw dropped in astonishment, and he fell backward, out of Malledd's view. Then he quickly scrambled back up.

"You're alive!" the man shouted. "By Vevanis, you're alive!"

Malledd croaked dully.

"All the gods, you're *thirsty*, aren't you?" The man hurriedly turned away, and Malledd heard the clattering of metal on wood. "Wait, I've got beer—you'd probably have water, wouldn't you? I'm sorry, I don't have any here, not unless you want the rainwater . . . well, of course you do, though it's not much."

Then the man was back, and a cool, wet cloth was being lowered to Malledd's lips. He closed his mouth on it and sucked feebly.

The pain abated, ever so slightly. Then he closed his eyes and fell asleep.

When he awoke he was still lying in the cart, still in agony, still horribly thirsty—but he felt better than he had before.

Now two men and a woman were leaning over him. The woman was holding a cup to his lips, and he tasted water; he drank greedily, lifting his head to get more of the precious fluid. Hands slid under him to support his head.

Moments later he was sitting up, friendly hands steadying him as he looked around.

He was sitting in an old wooden cart in a small paved yard, surrounded by buildings he didn't recognize.

"Where am I?" he asked.

"Nuzedy," one of the men answered—the cart's driver, he realized, the one who had first discovered he was still alive. "At Igibur's caravanserai."

Malledd blinked—which hurt; his eyelids hurt. *Everything* hurt.

But it hurt less than it had.

"Why?" he asked.

The cart driver looked helplessly at the other two, then back at Malledd. "The priests hired me to take you to the village of Grozerodz, somewhere southwest of Biekedau on the Yildau road, and deliver you to Anva the smith's wife," he explained. "For burial, I thought. They said the gods had ordered it, through an oracle. And I was almost to Nuzedy when you . . . when I found out you were alive. So I brought you here and summoned a physician and a priest." He gestured at the others.

Malledd looked, and noticed for the first time that the other man wore a priest's robe.

The woman smiled at him. "Pashima must like you," she said. "You *should* have been dead; you're healing faster and better than anyone I've ever seen."

Pashima, goddess of health and healing, had undoubtedly been one of the gods who approved of him. He had always healed quickly. He remembered his dream, when he had spoken to Samardas; the voice had said that he had the gift of healing. Had that been a true vision, then?

"Yes, I think she likes me," Malledd murmured, through lips that were already less cracked and painful than they had been a moment before.

"She must," the driver said. "You weren't even breathing, I'd swear to it!"

"Well, he's breathing *now*," the physician said briskly, "and he's probably in considerable pain. I have some salves that might help. . . ." She turned and lifted up a heavy pack, and began rummaging through it.

"An oracle," Malledd said, looking at the driver. "There are oracles?"

The driver turned to the priest, who said, "Oh, yes—you hadn't heard? No, I suppose you were . . . well, if not dead, the next thing to it. Since the Long Night ended, the oracles have been active again—*very* active. The gods have chosen Zolous as Emperor and commanded the people of Rishna Gabidéll to put Prince Graubris and Lord Shoule to death, they've settled any number of lesser matters—it's as if they're making up for lost time. This is an age of wonders, my friend—Ba'el's moon has been struck from the sky, the gods are speaking to us again, and now *you* have risen from the dead!"

"I wasn't dead," Malledd said. "Not quite. The gods wouldn't allow it."

The priest and the driver glanced at each other as the physician lifted a handful of foul-smelling white goo and began smearing it on Malledd's chest.

It stung for an instant, somehow intensifying a pain Malledd would have thought could not be noticeably worse, and then a soothing chill spread across his chest, and the pain faded to a dull ache. He tensed at that first contact, drawing in his breath, then relaxed and exhaled as the cool relief sank in.

"Good," the physician said as she scooped up more of the salve. "That shows you can still feel. Sometimes burns will numb the flesh permanently." She slathered on more of the stinking stuff.

As she worked, Malledd realized for the first time that he was naked; his clothes had been burned away by the Olnami wizard's magical blast. He would have to borrow something to wear.

"Since you're alive," the driver said, "I'm not sure my original instructions still hold. Should I carry you on to this Grozerodz place, or take you back to Seidabar?"

That required no thought at all.

"Grozerodz," he said. "And Anva."

EPILOGUE

Malledd thought he might have been able to stand on his own feet to walk into the house, but the others all insisted that was absurd, so he allowed himself to be carried. Anva didn't help with the lifting, but she was there at his side, weeping hysterically and calling his name, as he was slowly hauled to the bedroom and lowered gently into their bed.

Neyil and Poria stood by, staring wide-eyed at their father's return. Arshui was in his aunt Vorda's arms, clearly unsure what the excitement was about or who this strange man was; he was too young to remember Malledd's departure.

Once he was safely deposited, Malledd smiled and thanked everyone—it seemed half the village had seen his return and helped out. The bedroom was far too crowded for comfort.

"Tell us about it!" someone called.

"You were there, weren't you? Did you see Lord Duzon slay the wizard?"

"Did you fight?"

"Did you help put Lord Shoule's head on the spike? Or the traitor Prince's?"

Malledd raised a hand for silence. It took a moment for the excited babble to subside, but at last he was able to speak without straining to be heard.

"I went to Seidabar," he said. "I fought at the Grebiguata River, alongside Onnell and Bousian and Delazin and the others—and Lord Duzon. And I returned to Seidabar with Lord Duzon and fought there, as well; that was where I was burned by the wizard's magic. Lord Shoule and Prince Graubris weren't yet dead when I began my journey home, so no, I didn't put any heads on spikes. And the rest can wait. I'll be here for many years yet; don't make me use up all my stories at once!"

That evoked appreciative laughter.

"All right, that's enough," Anva announced. "Everybody out—let him rest! Let him heal!" She began herding the others toward the door.

Ten minutes later the room was empty save for Anva and Malledd; even the children had been shooed away. Anva settled heavily onto the bed and leaned over to stare at Malledd's face.

His skin was still red and puckered from the burns, and he knew he looked hideous, but she gazed at him lovingly, as if he was the most beautiful thing she had ever seen.

"I thought you were dead," she said. "Onnell came and told us you had died in the fighting at Seidabar."

"I almost did," Malledd replied. "I was left for dead, and taken for dead."

"You shouldn't have been there in the first place! You're a smith, Malledd, not a soldier!"

He smiled weakly.

"I can't imagine how we could all believe for so long that you were the divine champion!" Anva said, a bit wildly. "It was so obviously nonsense that the gods would choose a smith's son in a little village like this rather than someone like Lord Duzon."

For a moment Malledd was tempted to speak, to tell her the truth, to explain that he *was* the champion—after all, now he had earned the title, as he had not before.

But he said nothing. No good would come of it to speak; it was enough that *he* knew. Instead he just smiled again.

"Onnell and Delazin and Bousian have told us so much about Lord Duzon," Anva said, tugging his pillow into a better position. "He sounds wonderful."

"He's a good man," Malledd agreed. "He deserves to be recognized as the champion."

"And he *should* have been all along! Those priests coming here and telling lies—how *could* they? Why didn't they tell the truth? They almost . . ." Her voice broke. "They almost got you killed!"

"Well, it's all right now," Malledd said, reaching up to touch his wife's cheek. "I'm home." He remembered his vision, when Samardas had told him he would live many years yet.

"And I'll be here a long, long time," he said.